To Stan… My Always and Forever

a tragic wreck

T.K. Leigh

A TRAGIC WRECK

Published by Tracy Kellam, 25852 McBean Parkway # 612, Santa Clarita, CA 91355

Edited by Kim Young, Kim's Editing Services

Cover Design: Cat Head Biscuit, Inc., Santa Clarita, CA

Front Cover Image Copyright Sweet November Studio 2014

Used under license from Shutterstock.com

Back Cover Image Copyright BlueOrange Studio 2014

Used under license from Shutterstock.com

ISBN: 0989740633
ISBN-13: 978-0-9897406-3-0

CHAPTER ONE

MOVING ON

As SARAH OLIVIA ADLER sat on the front deck of the beach cottage she had been hiding in for the past few weeks, the glow of the setting sun behind her casting beautiful shadows over the ocean, she thought about all the decisions she made that led her to that point in her life. *This would be a perfect oyster throwing deck*, she thought to herself, fighting back the tears that threatened to fall at the memory of eating oysters with Alexander. She sighed as she grabbed her wine glass and retreated back inside.

As far as rentals went, she had found a pretty good one. The two-story ocean front cottage on the north end of Amelia Island had an old-school beach house vibe to it that made her feel safe. She loved listening to the hardwood floors creak as she walked through her refuge on the coast. The salty air blew in through the large windows that adorned each wall. There was an open and airy quality to her new home that she relished. It was peaceful. No one there knew her name, and she liked it that way.

Olivia had been avoiding all sorts of technology since she arrived in Florida, not wanting to deal with the reality of what she had done. She got scared and she ran. Again. Her shrink was right. At some point, her friends would give up on her, sick of her always leaving and running.

They'd be better off without me in their lives, she thought.

October gave way to November and the weather began to cool off a bit. Olivia spent her days reading on the beach,

1

trying to avoid all romance novels. She kept to herself, content to be a recluse.

She ran a lot. It helped to clear her mind of everything to do with Alexander Burnham. She ate dinner on her deck most nights, watching the waves roll in. She dreaded nighttime. The nightmares always found her. Often, she woke up screaming, clutching her heart, and then began to cry when she realized that Alexander was no longer there to soothe her sobs. His arms were no longer there to calm her breathing. And every night she continued to see his face in her dreams, uttering those five little words that had changed everything... *It will destroy me, too.*

Olivia loved the mornings as the sun rose over the Atlantic, the sky a soft orange. If a storm was coming in, the street by her house would be lined with cars of surfers hoping to catch a few waves before the rain hit.

"Good morning," a voice called to her one day, catching her eye as she sat on her deck enjoying her morning coffee. He untied a surfboard from his Wrangler and made his way to the beach.

Olivia took in his appearance, watching as his tall, lean body walked away from her. Her heart stopped a little when he turned around and smiled, his teeth bright against his tan skin and sandy hair. *No, Libby. Never again*, she reminded herself before getting up from the deck and retreating inside.

Her heart beat madly, all from a simple smile. Maybe a distraction was exactly what she needed to forget about Alexander. But, the problem was, she just couldn't forget about him. He was permanently ingrained in her mind and heart. She wasn't sure she would ever get over him. She wasn't sure she wanted to.

~~~~~~~~~~

"Come on, Alex. You need to get out of this funk," Tyler said to his brother as they sat at a dimly lit bar on Boylston Street in Boston. "You need to get your mind off of..."

"STOP!" Alexander roared. "Do *not* say that name. I can't

bear to even hear it." He slung back his shot glass and signaled the bartender for another one. His eyes were fuzzy and he wasn't sure another shot was such a smart idea, but he didn't care. He needed to numb the pain he felt. He lost her. How could he miss the signs? She had become so aloof that weekend in Newport, but he ignored it and she left. He had searched for any sign of where she might be, but couldn't find her. Not yet, anyway.

It was as if she simply vanished. He didn't know what happened that day back in October. He wasn't thinking. He was so torn about the fact Olivia was gone that he failed to act. By the time he had finally come around and was able to function again, hours had passed. It was all his fault.

"Okay. Okay. I won't say the name, but you can't go on like this. You know that, right?" Tyler was worried about him. He had never seen him so upset before. Olivia had been gone for almost a month, and he was still angry and hurt over everything that had happened.

"Whatever," Alexander replied, downing yet another shot as he attempted to stand up. "I gotta take a leak." He stumbled away from the bar and in the direction of the restrooms.

"If it isn't Alexander Burnham," a soft, sultry voice called out.

Alexander turned a little too fast and had trouble steadying himself. His vision blurry, he squinted, trying to make out who had called his name. She took a step forward and he took in her brilliant auburn hair, long legs, killer rack, and deep brown eyes. Eyes almost as deep and brown as...

"Chelsea Wellington," Alexander slurred, propping himself up against the wall. "It's been a while."

Chelsea smirked, throwing her wavy hair over her shoulder as she sauntered across the dark hallway to stand near him, taking in his tall, muscular frame. "It sure has. I've missed you, Alex," she exhaled, keeping her gaze trained on his green eyes. "I heard you were dating someone, though. I couldn't believe my ears at first..."

"Well, you heard wrong!" he barked.

Chelsea grinned, crossing her arms over her too tight black

3

dress. "I was hoping the gossip mills were wrong. I mean, Alexander Burnham and girlfriend in the same sentence? There's something wrong with that statement, if you ask me."

Alexander stared off into the distance. There was nothing wrong with him having a girlfriend. He missed his girlfriend more than life itself, but she left and the gap in his heart was threatening to kill him. He needed a distraction.

His eyes narrowed in on Chelsea's chest. "Wanna get out of here?" he asked, his eyebrows raised.

"I thought you'd never ask."

He led her through the bar and past Tyler who simply gaped, wide-mouthed. He couldn't believe Alexander was actually resorting back to his old ways.

Martin pulled up outside of the bar and ran around to open the car door for Alexander. "Sir," he said in greeting, eyeing his boss suspiciously.

"Take us back to my place," Alexander demanded.

Martin exhaled loudly as he closed the door to the SUV and ran around to get behind the wheel. Out of all the women he used to bring home, Martin couldn't believe Alexander chose to get back together with Chelsea Wellington. *At least it's not Adele*, he thought to himself as he maneuvered the Escalade through the busy Boston streets.

When Martin pulled up in front of Alexander's building, Chelsea waited for Alexander to run around and open the car door for her. *Olivia would have just opened it herself*, he thought. He took a deep breath, half-heartedly regretting his decision to invite Chelsea over but, at the same time, feeling that he needed to move past Olivia. This was the only way he knew how. She wanted him to move on. That's what he was doing.

"I just love the view from your place, Alex," Chelsea said as they entered his penthouse. She kicked off her heels and made her way towards the staircase, turning back to look at Alexander. He stood at the door, a dumbfounded look on his face, the normally confident man nowhere to be found. "Are you coming or not? I don't have all night."

He contemplated what to do. Yes, he did invite Chelsea over for the sole purpose of fucking her until Olivia never again

4

entered his mind. But now that she was here, could he really follow through? Just a few months ago, he wouldn't even be having second thoughts. He'd bring her upstairs and bury himself inside of her. Now, after Olivia and everything they had been through, it felt wrong.

Chelsea slinked towards him. "Stop thinking," she whispered, brushing her ruby red lips against his neck, gently nibbling on his earlobe as she ran her fingers through his dark, unruly hair. "This is just sex, Alex. Nothing more. Come on. I know what you need. You need to forget about her. I can help you." She pressed her body against his. Alexander wondered how she could tell he was thinking about a girl.

It all felt so different. There was no spark. Hell, he was even having a little trouble getting an erection. That never happened with Olivia. He was always ready to go when she was around...and even when she wasn't.

Chelsea grabbed Alexander's belt, pulling him toward her, quickly unbuckling it before unzipping his pants. Her small brown eyes met his as she reached into his boxers and helped spring him free. "There's my boy," she smiled.

He exhaled loudly, desperate to feel something other than the excruciating loss that he had been feeling the past few weeks. "Just make me forget, Chelsea. Please," he pleaded with her.

"Okay, Alex." She pressed her lips to his.

He grabbed the back of her neck, deepening the kiss. Slamming her against the wall, he tore her panties from her body and got lost inside of her. The whole time, he was thinking about his Olivia and what she was doing at that exact moment, wondering whether he should have looked harder. Thinking about whether or not Kiera was right. Would she ever come back? Maybe Olivia needed to know that he would fight for her, no matter what. But he didn't fight for her. He just let her walk away from him. Now it was November and the trail had gone cold. Olivia disappeared without a trace. Even with all the resources he had at his disposal, there was nothing. Not one clue.

He thrust even harder into Chelsea, needing to find some

sort of release. Release from the hold Olivia still had over him. Would he ever be rid of that? He didn't see how. Olivia always had a hold over him. Everything he had done throughout his life had been for her. Growing up, he just knew that she wasn't dead. She couldn't be. His lack of serious relationships was due to that, always holding out hope of finding her. And once he found her, he didn't want to let go. And she left him.

"That's it, Alex. Let go!" Chelsea screamed as Alexander bit into her neck, pulling out as he came in his hand. He just couldn't bring himself to come inside of Chelsea. The last person he came inside of was Olivia and he wanted to keep it that way.

He turned and walked briskly down the hallway to the bathroom to clean himself up, leaving Chelsea alone in the living room. Looking in the mirror, he saw a shell of his former self. Maybe it would have been better if he had never found Olivia. Maybe he should move on like she said. Maybe he should just forget all about her. He *needed* to forget her.

He splashed some water on his face, enjoying the coolness of the liquid, before walking back down the hallway into his living room.

"Feel better now, Mr. Burnham?" Chelsea asked coyly as she sat on his sofa.

"Yes, I do. Thank you." He strode over to the couch and took a seat next to her. The air was thick in the room, Alexander not really wanting to initiate conversation.

Chelsea sighed loudly. "So, want to talk about it?"

Alexander looked over at her. "No. Not really. I'd rather just forget about everything that went on these past few months and pretend none of it ever happened."

She grinned. "Would you like my help doing that?"

His eyes met her small brown ones. How could he possibly forget about Olivia's big brown eyes? He would always see them in his dreams. He knew that. But maybe, with time, he could forget. "Yes, I would, Miss Wellington." His eyes became hooded as he pushed her down on the couch, grabbing both her arms and pinning them above her head.

"Oh, Mr. Burnham, I love it when you tie me up," Chelsea

whispered.

"Stop talking. Don't say a word until I tell you to," he growled. He just couldn't listen to her voice. Every time she spoke, all he felt was betrayal. And he didn't want to feel that. He didn't want to feel anything.

Alexander ripped off his tie and wrapped it around Chelsea's hands, binding them together, before pulling out a condom and sinking back into her.

CHAPTER TWO

SOMETHING

OLIVIA DIDN'T EVEN KNOW his name but, every morning, she looked forward to seeing surfer boy park his Jeep in front of her house and untie his surfboard before hitting some waves with his friends. He would smile at her and she would feel heat coursing through her body. It wasn't the same as what she felt when Alexander smiled at her, but at least she felt *something*. And *something* was better than the nothingness and pain she had been feeling since she ran.

The mid-November sun shined through the thick clouds one morning as she sat on her beloved deck and drank her coffee. Olivia actually started to look forward to seeing him. She was surprised that he surfed every day, even when the waves were fairly non-existent. Regardless, like clockwork, his Jeep pulled up in front of her house just as the sun rose every morning.

One of Olivia's favorite things about her new home was the location. It was so peaceful being able to wake up and watch the sun climb up the horizon over the crashing waves. There was something about the sunlight reflecting on the ocean that made everything seem okay. Not good, but okay. And Olivia was content with just okay. Nothing would ever be extraordinary. Only Alexander was extraordinary, so she settled for okay.

Just as the sun rose on that November morning, the Jeep pulled up. And, as usual, surfer boy untied his surfboard and smiled. Nothing ever changed. A smile. A drink of coffee. A sigh. That's what her mornings were composed of.

"My life is pathetic if my only excitement is some guy whose name I don't even know," she mumbled as she read a book on her e-reader, drinking her coffee.

"Cameron. My name's Cameron Bowen, but most people call me Cam."

Olivia jumped, looking for the source of the voice. Surfer boy stood to the right of Olivia's deck in his wetsuit, carrying a surfboard. She hadn't noticed him walk up to her deck, desperate to finally make an introduction.

Cam turned the corner and stood by the steps leading to Olivia's deck, watching as the gorgeous, tall brunette quickly bolted off the lounge chair, turning to her front door, and frantically trying to open it. "You see, usually when someone gives you their name, they may want you to return the favor. At least where I'm from they do."

Olivia listened to his accent, noticing a hint of a southern drawl. "And where is it you're from, Cam?" she inquired, turning around and crossing her arms.

"All over really. But, truth be told, born and raised in South Carolina." His eyes sparkled and Olivia couldn't help but respond to him.

"Me, too. But I haven't lived there in well over a decade."

"That's a pity." His lips turned up into a small but attractive smile that made Olivia want to melt. "I bet you used to sound too cute for words with a little southern drawl." He beamed, showing Olivia a perfect set of teeth.

God, he's really handsome. This was bad. This was very, very bad. She was trying to get over Alexander. It still pained her to think about what she had done, leaving him. She couldn't string someone else along, knowing full well she could never give that person her entire heart. She gave her heart to Alexander and he still held it, although he probably didn't realize it.

Cam took a few steps closer, still on the sandy road by her deck. He was rather attractive and had a good body underneath his wetsuit. Olivia had noticed how handsome he was several weeks ago, but up close, he was even more so. His silver eyes beamed as he smiled, staring up at her. The ocean breeze gusted, blowing his wild sandy hair in front of his eyes. But she was off men. And, no matter how hard she tried, she couldn't get Alexander out of her thoughts.

"So, are you going to tell me your name, or do I have to try to guess it?" He cautiously stepped up the stairs of her deck, making sure he wasn't intruding.

She uncrossed her arms and took a few steps toward him, holding her hand out. "My name's Olivia. People call me Libby, though."

Taking Olivia's hand in his own, Cam felt her soft skin. There was something so tragic about the woman standing in front of him. He couldn't put his finger on it, but she just seemed so alone. He had been watching her every day since mid-October when she appeared out of nowhere, renting old man Robinson's beach cottage. He figured she would only be there for a week, but every day, without fail, she sat outside, drinking her coffee and staring out at the ocean as if it held the answers to all her questions.

The first week, she barely smiled. As she drank her coffee, he noticed tears streaming down her face. Something made her sad. The waves were killer that week because of a big storm brewing off the coast. The second week, the waves died down a bit and, after checking the report, he thought about blowing off surfing in the morning. But something about the sad girl who sat on her deck and drank coffee made him put on his wetsuit and go. And even when the waves were more or less non-existent, every day he drove down to Ocean Avenue in the Fernandina Beach section of Amelia Island and smiled at the girl with the sad brown eyes.

"Libby. It's wonderful to finally put a name to the face."

Olivia took in the man she had grown accustomed to seeing. His silver eyes had a depth and a kindness to them that she had never seen before. She felt as if she could spill her entire life out to him and he wouldn't judge her. His smile was infectious and, before Olivia knew it, she smiled back. She couldn't remember the last time she smiled. It felt good.

"Do you surf?" Cam asked.

"I've tried it a few times. I lived in Hawaii for a bit and I didn't want to stick out as a haole so I learned to surf." She looked over the horizon at the dozen or so bodies bobbing up and down, waiting to ride a wave into shore.

"What's a haole?" he asked.

"It's a Hawaiian term for mainlanders." She took a long sip of her coffee, wondering whether she should offer him a mug.

"Ah, I see." He smiled a genuine smile at the quiet woman. "Want to catch a few waves?" he asked, gesturing toward the water.

"I don't have a board. Or a wetsuit."

"Just grab a bathing suit. The waves are pretty calm today so you'll be fine without one."

Olivia hesitated, thinking about it.

"Come on. I see you sitting here every morning, drinking your coffee, and you just look so sad. Please. Let me at least show you some fun."

She looked at him, shocked that he noticed how empty she was in just those few seconds each day. "Okay," she said after a moment of deep thought. "Give me ten minutes. I need to shower."

"Great. I'll go try to catch a wave or two. I'll see you out there." He ran toward the water, holding his board.

It was a relatively warm morning for mid-November, but Olivia knew the water would be freezing. She had been there several weeks and still hadn't put a foot in the ocean. Even if she didn't get on a surfboard, at least she would finally feel the saltwater against her skin.

She took a quick shower, making sure to shave fairly well. Pulling her long, wavy hair back, she threw on the two-piece swimsuit that she used when training for triathlons. She grabbed a towel, then walked between the sand dunes down to where the water met the shore.

Cam ran up to her when he saw her walking down the beach. "Hey. You made it."

"You sound surprised," she mumbled dryly.

"Well, a little. I thought you would blow me off, maybe go for a run and then just sit in your house the rest of the day."

His statement caught Olivia off-guard. "How do you seem

to know so much about me?"

"You caught my eye. I have a thing for beautiful women." He winked, grabbing her hand and pulling her toward the water's edge.

"Holy crap, that's freezing!" Olivia squealed when her foot hit the cold ocean, stopping dead in her tracks as Cam pulled away.

"Come on. Stop being a baby!" he shouted back. He was already up to his knees in the water.

She took a deep breath before running into the ocean, knowing that once she was fully submerged, she would feel better.

"Here. Grab onto the other end of the board," Cam said when she finally caught up to him.

"Thanks." They swam out to just beyond where the waves crested.

"Hey! Cam-Bam!" a guy on a surfboard yelled.

"Come here. I want you to meet the guys," Cam said to Olivia.

"Hey! Who's this?" one of them asked.

"Everyone, this is Olivia. Olivia, this is Chris, Benny, and Jason." Cam gestured to the three men bobbing on their surfboards.

Olivia waved with little enthusiasm. "Hi."

"Are you going to try surfing today?" Chris asked, trying to spark up a conversation with her.

"Yeah. Might as well." She shrugged. "I've surfed before so I'm not totally useless."

"Why don't you catch the first one? I'll hang back here on one of the guys' boards," Cam said as he swam over to Benny's board and hung on to it. He grinned while he watched Olivia swim away with the board.

"She's hot, man," Jason said, nudging toward Cam in the water. "Is she the one you've been talking about?"

"Yeah. That's her. I'm glad I worked up the nerve to finally talk to her."

"You're such a pussy," Benny laughed. "For a guy pushing thirty-five, you have no balls when it comes to talking to

12

women."

"Suck it, man!" Cam joked back. "There's just something kind of sad about her. I couldn't help it." He returned his eyes to Olivia as she climbed on the board, throwing her legs on either side, getting ready to catch a wave.

After a few minutes, she saw a wave coming in that was ideal for her. She positioned her hands and quickly hoisted her legs onto the board, balancing perfectly as she rode into the shore.

Along the coast, a few people were milling about collecting shells. As the sandy beach got closer, she started to space out and thought she saw Alexander. She saw him everywhere lately. Her heart began to race and she panicked, losing her balance. The board slipped out from underneath her and she toppled off, hitting her head as she sank below the water.

"Shit!" Cam exclaimed when he saw Olivia sink beneath the surface. He swam quickly toward where she went under, desperately searching for her. He was worried that, in the few minutes it took him to get to her, she hadn't resurfaced. He dove into the water, his eyes stinging from the salt. A few feet away, he saw her, her eyes closed, bubbles coming out of her mouth.

He reached her and grabbed her around the waist, kicking toward the surface. "Come on, Libby. Stay with me." He pulled her toward the shore and laid her on her back. The rest of the guys finally joined him.

"I think she hit her head pretty hard." Cam leaned his ear down over her nose and couldn't hear any breathing, but she still had a pulse. He started rescue breathing, frantic for her to cough up the water that appeared to be stuck in her lungs. After a few long moments, Olivia gasped, coughing. Cam helped roll her onto her side, getting the water out of her mouth.

"You scared me there, sweetheart," he said softly, gazing down at the woman lying on the sand.

Olivia looked around, trying to get her bearings. She went surfing. She tried to make a new friend and now she looked like an idiot. She stood up, but her legs were weak, causing her to lose her balance. Cam caught her. "Hey. Take it easy," he said softly. "You bumped your head pretty good. Let's get you back inside your house. You should probably go lie down."

Cam led Olivia up the beach to her house, helping her to the couch. Once she was settled, he walked through her living room and into the kitchen, searching the freezer for some ice. He put some in a plastic bag and brought it to her.

"Here," he said, leaning down and placing the ice pack on her forehead. "You should probably keep this on your head. There's a little bit of swelling." He brushed a piece of hair out of Olivia's eyes.

"Thanks."

"Anytime." He looked around the house, noticing how minimalist everything looked. It was as if she had just rolled into town with a suitcase. There was nothing personal, aside from a guitar case leaning up against a wicker chair. He walked over and sat down. "Do you play?" he asked, gesturing to the case.

Olivia took the ice off her forehead and sat up, facing Cam. "Yeah. A little, I guess. In a former life. I really haven't played lately, though. Since I got here. The guitar's just been sitting there, collecting dust."

Cam looked into her eyes. She seemed so empty.

Out of the corner of his eye, he saw a large, orange long-haired cat walk down the stairs and into the living room. The cat stalked to Olivia, jumped on her lap, and curled up in a ball. "This is Nepenthe," she explained.

"Ah," Cam breathed. "The ancient elixir of depression."

Olivia turned her head. "How did you know that? Not a lot of people know what 'nepenthe' is."

"I have a brain full of useless information." Cam laughed. There was an awkward silence. He was attracted to the woman sitting across from him, snuggling up with her cat, but she seemed so distant and uninterested in anything. He didn't know much about her, but he wanted to learn more.

"Can I take you to dinner tonight? There's this great place right on the water on the other side of the island."

Olivia looked around. "I don't know. I don't think that's such a good idea."

14

"Come on. It'll be fun. I promise. Just as friends. No pressure. I just want to get to know you, be your friend."

Olivia had been avoiding all social situations for the past several weeks. Certain things set her off, triggering a panic attack. Looking out her large front windows at the ocean, she hoped for some guidance about what to do. She was getting to like her new home. If she got involved with Cam, she would just leave him, too. That's what she did. She ran. Always. That was all she knew.

"Hey, Libby. The answer isn't there in the ocean."

She looked back at Cam, a smile still on his face, but also something else. She couldn't quite put her finger on it, but it was almost like a look of compassion.

"I just want to get to know you. That's all. I want to spend some time with you."

"But why?" Olivia asked, her brows furrowed.

"What? Why wouldn't I?"

"I could give you a thousand reasons," she mumbled under her breath.

"As friends. That's all, Libby. Come to dinner with me. Let me be your friend."

Olivia sighed, petting Nepenthe. "I don't need any friends. I'm perfectly happy in my little oasis here on the beach."

"Oh, come on. Don't make me beg."

Olivia's heart stopped. Alexander's husky voice flashed through her memory... *I like it when you beg.*

Her lip started to tremble and she quickly jumped off the couch, walking toward the stairs and away from Cam, desperately trying not to fall apart in front of him. She had finally gotten through an entire week without breaking down and crying when she thought about Alexander, but that memory was too much. She couldn't take it. Her heart was in pieces and she knew it was all her fault, but it still didn't make it hurt any less.

Knowing that he had somehow upset her, Cam caught up to her and grabbed her arm. He didn't want to leave on such a sour note. "Libby, please. Whatever I said, I'm sorry."

She turned to face him, tears running down her face.

15

"I just want to make you smile. Please. Just come to dinner with me. I promise I'll help you forget about whatever it is that has you so upset."

She looked up at Cam, surprised at his height. He was even taller than Alexander, which was a feat at six-foot-five. Maybe he was right. Maybe what Olivia needed was someone to help her forget. She couldn't possibly go on living her life as she had been. Every day was a struggle to get through. She felt something when she looked at him. It wasn't sparks and shivers and tremors like it was when she looked at Alexander, but something was far better than nothing.

Cam pleaded with her with his eyes, desperate to find out more about this mysterious woman who had come to the island and captured his attention so quickly.

"Okay. I'll go out with you."

A smile spread across Cam's face, and Olivia couldn't help but giggle a little at the look of excitement. "Great!" he exclaimed. "I'll pick you up at seven." He left before Olivia could protest.

She fell back onto the couch. For the first time in weeks, she actually had something to look forward to that evening. She was unsure how to feel about that. Would she just find herself in the same situation as she did with Alexander? No. Impossible. She refused to let it get that far. She couldn't. It nearly tore her apart when she had to leave Alexander, and she vowed to never do that again...even if it meant spending the rest of her life alone.

"Damn it, Nepenthe. What have I gotten myself into?" Her cat stood up and stretched before settling back down on Olivia's stomach.

CHAPTER THREE

HOT TRAIL

OLIVIA SCOURED HER CLOSET looking for something to wear that evening. She refused to call it a date. It was just two friends getting to know each other. Olivia was done dating. She should never have gotten close to Alexander. It ended horribly. Life was better before. It was uncomplicated. She could fuck anyone she wanted and never get attached. That was what she needed in order to get her life back on track. Maybe Cam would help her with that.

But after she had gotten a taste of what a real relationship was like, could she even think about going back to her old ways? She loved the butterflies she felt fluttering in her stomach when she thought about that special someone. She loved the cute things Alexander did for her, like sending her text messages just to say he was thinking about her. Sending flowers to her office just because. Is that feeling truly worth it when you know it will end in heartbreak? She wasn't sure.

Olivia fell onto her bed, wishing she still had all her clothes. She left Boston in such a hurry that she barely had much in terms of acceptable dinner attire. Most days she roamed around her house in a pair of gym shorts and a tank top. Other than that and running clothes, she didn't have much need for anything else.

She glanced at the clock. It was just a little past noon. She had more than enough time to go to the mall and get back in time for dinner. She quickly threw on a pair of shorts and tank top, and jumped in her car, heading toward Jacksonville.

Within an hour, she finally pulled off the interstate and into a crowded mall parking lot.

Shit, she thought. Christmas shopping. She had completely lost track of the days and it was a few weeks before Thanksgiving. People were clearly getting their shopping done early. Instead of trying to find a parking spot, she made a bee-line for the valet and threw the attendant the keys to her Audi before running into the mall in search of a store that could have something for her to wear. As she navigated through the swarms of people pushing and shoving their way through the shopping center, she thought about how much she missed Boston and the convenience of living around the corner from a street lined with designer boutiques. She hated shopping malls.

After finally finding a store with clothing that was her style, she scoured the racks, grabbing more clothes than she could ever wear, but she didn't care. The girls at the store were more than helpful, seeing a huge sale in their future. She would deal with what to wear when she got home.

Olivia reached into her purse, opening her wallet to pay with some of the cash that she had grabbed while she was fleeing Boston. She had been using that money to get by on, not wanting anyone to be able to trace her. She suddenly realized that she left the house without grabbing any more cash from the safe. All she had on her was a few small bills and that wouldn't cover what she was buying.

Exhaling loudly, she handed the saleswoman her credit card, visibly cringing when she swiped it. *Great*, she thought. *Now there's a fucking paper trail.*

~~~~~~~~~~

Alexander groaned when he heard a loud banging on the door to his penthouse. He must have passed out on the couch again. He had gone to MacFadden's the night before and proceeded to get incredibly wasted. His brother left, not wanting to put up with his drunk ass.

He sat up on the couch and took in his disheveled surroundings, clothes thrown everywhere, hoping he hadn't done anything in his inebriated state that he would regret.

"What the fuck is that?" a female voice called out from the staircase.

"Shit," Alexander cursed under his breath. "So much for not doing anything stupid." He rubbed his eyes and made his way over to the door, not turning to look at the tall redhead standing at the foot of the stairs. "Don't worry about it," he grumbled, his voice raspy. "Go back upstairs, Chelsea."

"Fine," she said, walking back up the stairs. "Are you actually ever going to make it to bed? It's practically three in the afternoon and you were no use to me last night, Alex."

"I'll be right there," he groaned, rolling his eyes as he opened the door, surprised to see Martin standing in the foyer.

"Sorry to disturb you, sir." He walked into the penthouse and proceeded to the kitchen, grabbing several aspirin and a bottle of water before handing them to Alexander.

"What the fuck, Martin? You think I need a babysitter? I can take care of myself. Plus, why didn't you just use your code to get in?"

"I wanted to make sure I wasn't interrupting anything, sir. I tried calling, but you never answered."

Alexander put the aspirin in his mouth, then drank the water. After nearly finishing the entire bottle, he turned to Martin. "Well, please, by all means, tell me what the fuck you're doing here."

Martin took a deep breath. "Do you remember the conversation we had a month ago when…"

"DO NOT SAY HER FUCKING NAME!" Alexander yelled, his eyes wide with fury.

Martin took a step back, tired of dealing with his rather unstable boss. He didn't know whether or not he should actually inform him what he had come there to tell him.

"Okay…well, you asked me to run her credit cards and keep tracking them to see if they were used at all. For the longest time, the trail has been cold…"

Alexander eyed him suspiciously, his heart rate picking up as Martin continued to talk.

"There's been a hit," he said, pausing as he gauged

Alexander's reaction to the news. "Her credit card was used a few hours ago at a mall in Jacksonville, Florida."

Alexander's eyes went wide.

"And then, just thirty minutes ago, it was used at a liquor store in Amelia Island, Florida."

Alexander swallowed hard. "Martin," he said softly. "Can you…"

"Prepare the jet? Already on it, sir. It's on standby for you as soon as you're ready." He turned to leave.

"Martin?" Alexander said, his mind racing, knowing that if he could find her, anyone could.

"Yes, sir?" he replied, turning back to face him.

"I'm sorry I snapped at you before. I know my behavior lately has been a little off."

"No need to apologize, sir. I just hope it all works out. I'll be downstairs waiting."

Alexander ran up the stairs to the bedroom, his heart beating frantically at the idea that he may finally know where his Olivia was.

"It's about fucking time, Alex," Chelsea said as he stormed into the master bedroom. She sat on the large bed, watching some crappy gossip show on the giant television. *Olivia never watched TV like this*, Alexander thought to himself. *She always preferred to read.* Just thinking about her made his heart break a little bit more, if that was even possible.

"Don't you have something better to do with your time than watch that rubbish?" he sneered, opening the closet and grabbing a suitcase. He began throwing clothes into it.

"It's not rubbish. We're on it from Thursday night at the charity dinner. By the way, it's a good thing I convinced you to take me because, if I didn't, you know that Adele would have sunk her claws into you again."

He rolled his eyes. "Don't remind me."

"So, going somewhere?" he heard her ask quietly.

Alexander turned and saw Chelsea standing in the doorway to his closet, her arms crossed. He regretted calling her to come over the previous night, but he was desperate to feel something other than the dull pain that had accompanied so many of his nights recently.

"Yeah. Work thing," he said quickly before turning back around to resume packing for his mission to find and bring Olivia back home.

Chelsea rolled her eyes and walked over to him, pulling him to her. "Come on, Alex. What is it going to take for you to forget about *her*?" she asked, running her tongue down his neck. He groaned, his erection that couldn't be found the night before finally making itself known. "There's my boy," she whispered, grinding against him. She slowly removed her silk kimono robe.

"Chelsea," Alexander whispered. "I can't."

She threw her robe to the ground and stood in front of him, totally exposed. "Can't or won't?" Pressing her lips against his, she ran her hands through his hair. "I know you want to, Alex. I can feel it." She brushed his lips with her tongue, begging for permission to enter.

Alexander didn't know what to do. Yes, he absolutely wanted to fuck Chelsea at that moment just so he could feel *something*. But he also wanted to get on that plane to try to find Olivia... *His* Olivia.

"Please, Mr. Burnham. Don't make me beg," Chelsea said coyly.

Alexander's eyes went wide. "What did you say?" His lower lip began to tremble, recalling some rather pleasant memories of Olivia saying the same thing.

Chelsea nuzzled up to his neck. "You heard me."

He exhaled loudly. "I need to go, Chelsea." He pushed her away, walking to the bathroom to grab a few things that he would need.

"Fine. Go. Whatever," she hissed. "Did you ever stop to think that maybe I wanted something more from you than just an occasional fuck?"

Stopping dead in his tracks, he turned to face her. "What are you talking about, Chelsea? We have a good thing going here."

She laughed. "Yeah. Sure. Absolutely. Except the part where you scream out her name and not mine when you're coming. But, you're right. We have a *great* thing going," she replied sarcastically, grabbing her clothes that had been discarded on the floor the night before.

"I'm sorry. I didn't know," he responded quietly, shocked that he had actually been doing that.

"Didn't know what? Didn't know that you were calling her name, or that I actually care about you?" she snapped before lowering her voice. "Why are you pushing me away for a girl who ran from you? She left no trace. And now that you have an idea about where she may be, you're just going to leave and track her down?" She frantically pulled on her jeans and sweater, searching under the bed for her shoes.

"How do you even know?"

"Oh, come on, Alex. Give me some credit. I snooped in on your conversation with Martin." She grabbed her purse and began heading out of the bedroom.

"Chelsea, please. Stop. I just never knew how you felt about our relationship."

"Relationship?" she fumed, spinning around to face him. "This isn't a relationship, Alex! You're so fucking obtuse sometimes, you know that?"

Alexander shrugged his shoulders. "I'm a guy. It's how we roll." He turned his lips up in a small smile, hoping she wouldn't leave angry. "If you don't come right out and say something, we're left in the dark."

Chelsea stood there, looking at Alexander's face. After several long moments, she broke out in a smile.

"Does this mean you forgive me?" he asked.

She nodded slowly, taking a step toward him, brushing his wayward hair out of his eyes. "Yes. But I know you have to go. I get it. I just hope that you get the closure you're so desperate for. When you do, I'll be here waiting for you." She placed a gentle kiss on his mouth, lingering for several long seconds, hoping that it wasn't the last time she'd taste those lips. Then she turned and left.

CHAPTER FOUR

ALL I KNOW

AFTER FINALLY GETTING BACK to the beach, Olivia grabbed her obscene amount of shopping bags out of the back seat of the car, as well as the liquor she stopped to pick up, and got to work organizing all her new purchases while she drank a glass of bourbon. *This is good*, she thought. She hopelessly needed to feel like she had a new home. She hadn't felt that yet. She loved living at the beach, but it wasn't home. Maybe meeting some people would make it so, and then she could finally stop seeing Alexander in her dreams every night.

She settled on a form-fitting black dress that hit right above her knees. It was a little big around her waist so she put on an orange belt and accented the rest of the outfit with a long orange beaded necklace and matching earrings. After taming her wavy hair with a hint of gel, she was ready.

At exactly seven, Olivia heard a gentle knock on the door. She slipped on her heeled sandals, taking a deep breath before pulling back the door. Her heart began to race. Cam cleaned up good.

"Good evening, beautiful," he said, smiling and handing her a dozen yellow roses. "I hope you don't mind that I brought you flowers."

Olivia smiled, taking in his appearance. The dark gray shirt brought out the silver in his eyes. His jeans hung from his hips in a way so that Olivia could tell he worked out. "No. Thank you for the flowers. That was very thoughtful of you." She turned to go put the bouquet in some water as Cam waited in the doorway, not wanting to go into her house before she invited him in.

"Ready to go?" she asked, turning around and walking toward the door. She smiled, knowing she just caught him checking out her ass.

"Uh, yes. Let's get out of here." He held out his arm for her and she took it, secretly enjoying the feel of his warm body so close to her own.

He opened the car door for Olivia and she quickly realized the evening was becoming more than just dinner, and she was relatively okay with that. It was a nice change of pace to not have a chauffeur cart her around. It was refreshing and freeing, even.

Cam pulled out of the driveway and onto Ocean Avenue, heading toward the downtown area. Olivia smiled as the crisp November air blew through her hair.

"I hope you don't mind that I kept the top down," Cam said, shifting into third gear.

"Not at all. I thought you had a Wrangler. How many cars to you have?"

"I do have a Wrangler. But that's my surfing car and it's covered with sand so I figured I'd take the Lexus tonight."

"Nice. Reminds me of that movie *Three Kings*," Olivia said as she watched the rugged beach transition into a tree-lined boulevard.

"Oh, yeah? How so?"

"One of the lines in the movie is 'Lexus doesn't make a convertible'. Of course, that movie was made in 1999 or something so I think, at that time, Lexus *didn't* make a convertible."

He shifted into fourth. "Well, they do now."

Olivia laughed politely. "Obviously."

A few minutes later, Cam drove his car through the downtown Fernandina Beach area, easily finding a parking spot on the street. It was the off-season, but there were still a few tourists milling about, checking out the quaint beach shops and grabbing dinner.

"Wait right there," he said as he turned off the ignition. He swiftly got out of the car and ran around to Olivia's side, opening the door and bowing in an exaggerated fashion. "M'lady."

Olivia couldn't help but laugh. There was something so refreshing about Cam's personality. He was fun. There was no drama. With Alexander, it was intense from the beginning and never let up. But there wasn't that spark with Cam. There was *something*, but it was nothing compared to what she felt when she was in Alexander's presence.

"You're a goofball," she smiled.

"That I am." He grabbed her hand, pulling her down the sidewalk toward the water. "Is this okay?" he asked, referring to his hand clasped around hers.

She glanced over at him, a hopeful look in his eyes. "Yes. It's fine."

He beamed, his smile reaching his eyes. He had dimples. *God, he's hot*, she thought to herself.

"Good. I like touching you," he said quietly, gently rubbing her knuckles.

Olivia didn't know whether she should respond to that. She wasn't sure she wanted to. What would she even say? Tell him that she relished his touch more than anything she could remember in recent history, but that she was ninety-nine shades of crazy at that moment, her thoughts consumed by one man she never should have let in? Her craziness was too much for Alexander, and it would surely be too much for Cam.

"You don't talk much, do you?" he asked as they crossed a set of railroad tracks, walking across Front Street toward a restaurant on the water.

She shrugged. "I don't know. I guess I do, as long as I have something to say."

"So you have nothing to say?" Cam asked, grinning.

"I don't know."

"Well, surely there must be something going through that brain of yours right now. You have this look on your face and I want to die, it's so fucking cute." He stopped walking at the edge of the water.

Olivia's heart began beating rapidly as he turned to face her with a hopeful look on his face, clutching both her hands in his.

"I don't know what it is about you, Libby, but I'm drawn to you. I noticed you way back in October. I even remember the date... October seventeenth. It was a Wednesday. You looked so fucking sad, and it killed me. I wanted to find out what made you so incredibly sad, and I swore I would do whatever I could to fix it."

Olivia turned her head, gazing out at all the shrimp boats docked for the evening, trying to tame the butterflies that slowly fluttered in her stomach.

"Come on, Libby. Let me in," he quietly pleaded.

A tear fell down Olivia's cheek as she continued staring at the blackness on the water. "You don't even know me, Cam," she whispered.

He sighed before grabbing her chin, pulling her face toward his so they were mere inches apart. Olivia could feel the heat coming off his body. "All I know is that you love the smell of the ocean." He smiled thinking about how beautiful she looked when he pulled up in front of her house each day. "Every morning, you sit outside, drink your coffee, and close your eyes when a gentle breeze rolls in, inhaling deeply as if the salty ocean air will fix everything."

Olivia stared into his eyes, not saying anything, her breathing becoming heavy.

"All I know is that you used to take your coffee with cream, but lately you've been drinking it black."

She felt shivers as Cam brushed his hand across her forehead where her scar was.

"All I know is that last week you couldn't decide what color to paint your toenails so, instead of making that decision, you painted one foot green and the other foot orange."

She looked down at her feet and smiled.

"And all I know is that I desperately want to get to know even more about you." He gently cupped her cheek, staring into her deep brown eyes. "So please, Libby. I'll take whatever you can give me. Just let me know you."

Another tear escaped from her eye. "But what if I'm too broken for that, Cam?"

He pulled her to his chest and she reveled in the warmth emanating from his body. "Then let me fix you," he whispered.

Her heart raced as she looked into his eyes, wondering why she wanted him to kiss her so badly. Was it because she liked him, or did she just want to forget about Alexander?

Cam leaned down slowly, his hand moving to the small of her back. She licked her lips and his mouth hovered near hers. She met his lips, brushing against them softly before deepening the kiss. Cam groaned, pulling her further into him, their kiss soft but full. He was gentle, letting Olivia remain in control. It was nothing like kissing Alexander. It wasn't passionate and forceful. It was tender, the intensity present during Alexander's kisses was lacking.

Olivia pulled back, staring into Cam's eyes, wishing she could feel that spark.

"Your lips are so soft, Libby," he whispered, brushing his thumb against her lower lip as she stared into his eyes with a blank look on her face. She still seemed so empty. She simply stood there, looking sad. "Come on. Let's go eat. Okay?"

Olivia nodded, remaining silent.

"Good," he said, kissing the top of her head softly, inhaling the vanilla scent of her hair.

He clutched onto her hand and led her toward the restaurant. It was a relatively large place, circular in shape with panoramic views of the ocean. Of course, with it being evening, all that was visible were the lights on the shrimp boats.

"The view must be spectacular during sunset," Olivia remarked as the hostess walked them to their table.

"It is. It's tough this time of year with the sun setting so early, but if you're agreeable to it, I'd love to come back and share that with you." Cam winked, making Olivia blush.

"I'd like that," she replied, thinking she would do anything to try to forget about Alexander. Maybe Cam was her answer.

Once they were seated and a bottle of wine was on its way, she began to relax a little bit.

"You look better," Cam commented. "I'm sorry about

27

before." He eyed Olivia, gauging her reaction.

"What are you sorry about?" she asked, her eyebrows raised.

"I don't know what came over me," he explained, grabbing her hands in his. "You just looked so sad, and I really wanted to kiss you." He smiled gently, remembering the feeling of her lips on his, hoping he would get to feel that again. "I just thought maybe it would make you smile," he said sheepishly.

"I'm sorry, Cam. I'm still dealing with a few things, I guess." She dropped her hands in her lap and gazed across the dark horizon, wondering what Mo and Kiera were doing at that moment. Wondering if they even cared that she left. Again.

"Do you want to talk about it?" Cam knew there was something that made her end up on a relatively unknown island in Florida. She was running from something. That much he was certain of. Then there was the sadness that seemed to consume her whole being. It was as if her entire world had been ripped from underneath her and she wanted a brand new start.

Olivia's face was blank as she turned her eyes back to him. The emptiness in them was all-consuming. "I'm not ready for that yet, might never be," she replied dryly.

Cam grabbed her hand across the table once more. "It's okay, Libby. If and when you ever want to talk about it, I'm here." He gently brushed his thumb across her knuckles. "You need someone to listen. You can't shut everyone out."

She eyed him suspiciously. "Who says I'm shutting people out?"

Cam exhaled loudly, withdrawing his hand. "I don't know." He ran his fingers through his hair, reminding her of Alexander. "It seems like you are. I don't know anything about your past, but I'm certain that's what you're running from. Whatever it is, it's not worth closing up and shutting off. Just know that if you ever want to talk about it, I'm here for you. I'll always be here for you." His eyes met Olivia's. She noticed the hint of a spark.

Olivia was torn. There was something about Cam that she was drawn to. He seemed so patient and understanding with all of her drama, but how long could that really last? Alexander

28

had admitted that all of her pain and drama would destroy him. The same would be true for Cam, and she would end up in the same position again.

Their server finally returned with their bottle of pinot noir, bringing Olivia back from her thoughts. "I'm glad you ordered a pinot. It's my favorite," she remarked. "I mean, don't get me wrong, I love pretty much any wine, but there's something about a pinot."

Cam smiled, taking a sip of his wine and swirling it in his mouth, savoring the smoky flavor. "I'm right there with you. I hope you like it." He raised his glass. "To new friends."

Olivia mirrored his movements. "New friends," she smiled, clinking glasses with him.

"So what made you move to Florida?" she asked several minutes later after the server dropped off their crab cake appetizer.

"It just kind of happened. I don't know if it was any one thing. I always loved growing up in the south and, let's face it, there's nothing like good ol' southern cooking."

Olivia smiled, remembering her childhood in Charleston, particularly her summers on Folly Beach where the smell of Low Country Boils permeated the neighborhood practically every weekend.

"I wanted to find somewhere I could see myself settling down. I'm not a fan of huge cities. Then I found this quaint little island, and I was sold."

"Did you go to school around here?"

"No. California, actually. UCLA."

Olivia took a sip of her wine. "I lived in Cali for a bit."

"Really? Where at?"

"All over, really. Spent some time in Brentwood and then needed a change of pace from all the L.A. craziness so I ended up living in a cabin in the woods in Big Sur. No cable, no internet. It was wonderful. It was actually when I was living out there that I got more into running. I always loved running, but out in Cali, there were so many races that I couldn't help but take advantage of it."

Cam eyed her. "Races? What do you mean?"

"Oh, like marathons."

"You run marathons?"

"Yup. Actually, I qualified for Boston a few…" She stopped short, the memory of leaving Alexander just after running the Newport Marathon still fresh in her mind.

Cam could sense her growing unease with the subject. He grabbed her hand again.

Olivia looked down at his strong hand clutching onto hers. His touch didn't send shivers up her spine like Alexander's did, but she felt a little something. They weren't huge fireworks. Maybe they were sparklers.

"Hey, Libby. Relax. It's okay. You don't have to talk about anything with me that you don't want to. I'm not going to pry. Whatever you want to tell me, I'm happy with. Okay?"

She sat there, staring into his silver eyes, wishing they were green. "Okay. Thank you." She took another sip of her wine, desperate for the liquid to work its magic.

"I'll never hurt you, Olivia. I promise you that," he said quietly, barely above a whisper.

She sighed. "That's a pretty big promise. I don't think anyone can ever keep that promise."

"You can at least let me try to keep it. Don't shut me out like you want to. I'm okay if you just want to be friends. I just want to know you. If the only way I can get you is by being friends, then I'm happy." He gave her an encouraging smile just as their entrees arrived.

"I don't know if I'm ready…"

"I get it. I do. So let's just hang out. No pressure. Okay?"

Olivia smiled. "Okay." She grabbed her fork and dug into her ahi tuna salad, eyeing Cam's shrimp and grits. "You're going to have to run, like, ten miles tomorrow to work that meal off," she joked.

"Sounds like a plan. Want to come with me?"

"I don't know. Think you can keep up?"

"Is that a challenge?"

"Damn straight it is."

Cam chuckled as he took another bite of his cheesy grits, exaggerating how delicious the rich dish was.

Olivia was happy to finally feel some sort of normalcy in her life since fleeing Boston. It was good. It was what she needed to finally move on. As she took a bite of the crème brûlée that she and Cam decided to share for dessert, she wondered if Alexander had moved on, as well.

CHAPTER FIVE

EMPTY

ALEXANDER'S JET TOUCHED DOWN at Jacksonville Airport a little after eight that evening. Within an hour, Martin pulled up in front of the Ritz Carlton on Amelia Island. As Alexander sat in his Gulfstream heading south earlier that day, he debated where he should start looking for Olivia. The liquor store was the key. He figured she was probably living on Amelia Island somewhere and not in Jacksonville. Also, doing a bit of research, he found out that shopping on the island was limited mostly to beach-style boutiques. Knowing Olivia as he did, she needed some sort of fashionable store similar to that which she had become accustomed to shopping at in Boston. It made sense that she would find a mall to shop at so he was putting all his money on her living on Amelia Island. He prayed that he was right.

"What's the plan, sir?" Martin asked as he began setting up various computers in the large suite.

Alexander sighed. "I'm not sure, yet. She's got to be somewhere on this island. Maybe we both should get some sleep so we can wake up refreshed."

Martin finished booting up all the gear and turned to Alexander, who was sitting on the sofa and drinking an amber liquid. "Yes, sir. I'll see you in the morning then."

"Thank you, Martin."

When he heard the door to his suite close, he walked from the couch out onto one of the large balconies overlooking the beach and the Atlantic Ocean. Had he made a mistake jumping on the plane and coming down to Florida to find Olivia? Maybe Kiera was right. Maybe she didn't want to be found.

He downed his drink and decided to go for a stroll out on the beach. Quickly changing out of his suit and into a pair of jeans and a polo shirt, he left the suite, wandering out of the back of the hotel toward the beach.

He walked down to where the waves invaded the shoreline wondering if, at that moment, Olivia was looking out over the same exact waves. If she was there, she had picked a perfect location. The island was small and seemed relatively secluded from what he had found out. It was almost Thanksgiving and there were a few tourists walking about, but it was still uncrowded, unlike so many other Florida beaches.

As he strolled north along the coastline, he thought about everything that had happened over the past several months. He had been so happy with Olivia, but something spooked her and she fled town. It all went to shit in Newport. He should never have let her go run that damn marathon. She started to remember things and it scared her. That Saturday in Newport, she changed. When he stopped to let Olivia run up to Harris House, it was as if the fun, carefree girl he had become so accustomed to during their short relationship had left herself on the side of the road. After that, she was quiet and reserved. He tried to regain control of the situation and he thought he had it. Apparently, he was wrong.

Alexander lost track of time as he continued walking along the beach. Large hotels and condos transitioned into smaller beach houses. The north end of the island was markedly different from the south end. He wondered whether Olivia lived out on the beach somewhere. Or whether she was really here at all.

As he walked past a noisy bar, his cell phone rang. "Hey, Carol," he said, answering the call.

"Jesus H. Christ, Alex. What the fuck is going on?"

Alexander laughed. "Oh, not much. Took the jet and I'm in Florida. Just another day at the office."

"You're shitting me, right?"

He sighed, looking out over the sand dunes. "Nope. I'm in Amelia Island, Florida. I've got a good feeling about this place, Carol."

"What are you doing there? Did you find out something? This must be about Olivia if you're there. And if you were able to figure it out…"

"I KNOW! All right? I get it. If I can find her, so can *they*. That's why I need to find her and take her back home with me so I can keep her safe." His mind began to race. What was he talking about? Could he really keep her safe? Was that what this was all about?

"Alex," Carol said, lowering her voice. "What if she doesn't want to come back? What if she sees you and she takes off again. You can't really think you can keep this up much longer. There are people back home who need you, who love you. I ran into Chelsea just a little while ago and, well, maybe she's the type of girl you need to be with. Someone stable from a good family. How much longer can you put up with the drama?"

"For as long as I need to, Carol. It's Olivia we're talking about here. I love that fucking girl, and I will do everything and anything I can to get her back."

"Anything?" Carol asked.

"Yes! Of course!" Alexander shouted, staring at the crashing waves. "Except…"

"Except telling her who she is," Carol said quietly, finishing her brother's sentence.

"Carol, I want to. But I want her to come back to me because she wants to, not because she thinks I hold the answers to her past. I need to fix this on my own terms. We belong together. And when two people belong together, *nothing*…not time, not distance, not a misunderstanding…*nothing* can keep them apart. I will get her back. It may not be tomorrow or next week or next month or even next year. But I know, deep down, that she will come back. And that's good enough for me. But for now, I want to beg and grovel and, really, just see her. Make sure she's okay, or as okay as she can be, considering the shit life she's been handed. I need to do this because I refuse to always wonder 'what if'. Maybe I'll get some closure out of this and I can finally move on. Or maybe, just maybe, she'll tell me how much she's missed me. I've got to find out. Then I'll come home."

Carol sighed on the other end of the phone. "Okay. You do what you have to do, but I swear that if I have to put up with Mom at Thanksgiving and tell her all about what you're doing in Florida, I will murder you in your sleep and leave no physical evidence whatsoever."

Alexander laughed as he rounded the corner to his hotel's entrance. "Okay. I got it, sis. You have a great night and we'll talk soon, I promise. Love you."

"Love you too, baby brother. And just so you know, I'm totally rooting for you and Olivia."

"So am I, sis. So am I."

~~~~~~~~~

The following morning, Alexander was up at dawn as he took in the beautiful sunrise over the ocean. He grabbed a cup of coffee and, as he sat on the balcony enjoying the gentle breeze, he reminisced about all the mornings he shared coffee in bed with Olivia. *This is paradise*, he thought.

Several stories below his suite, people started to wander about on the beach. Tourists and locals seemed to be out getting their morning exercise. His thoughts returned to Olivia, wondering if she was out for a run. He grabbed his laptop and decided to continue doing a bit of research on the island to see if he could figure out where she lived.

Until the previous day, none of her credit cards had been used since she left Boston in October. The day she fled, there was a hefty cash withdrawal from one of her bank accounts. That was the last activity he could find. She clearly didn't want to leave a paper trail. So why now? Alexander was thrilled that there finally was a clue as to where she was. Now he could at least try to find her. He secretly wished he had Carol go with him. He couldn't think clearly when it came to Olivia, and he needed someone to remain level-headed.

His cell phone rang, breaking him out of his thoughts. "Good morning, Alex," Chelsea crooned.

"Hi." He was a little nervous speaking with her after her revelation to him the day before. He never thought that she was interested in a relationship with him. He didn't have to worry about her only wanting to be with him for his money. She also came from money, but he thought all she was interested in was the occasional hook-up. Granted, recently, it had become more than just an occasional thing.

"I just wanted to call and say that I was thinking about you…"

"Chelsea…" Alexander interrupted.

"Alex, please," she said, her voice strong. "Let me finish. I have no problem telling you my feelings. If you don't return them, I'm okay with that. I was just thinking about you and I want you to be able to do whatever you feel you need to do. Just know that, no matter what your decision is, I will always be here for you. I won't run. I will never push you away. The thing is, over the past several years, I've come to care for you during our occasional encounters. I should have said something sooner, but I didn't want you to think I was some clingy girl who went from just wanting a once-in-a-while hook-up to suddenly wanting more."

The line was quiet for several long moments while Alexander processed her words, thinking that maybe he could start to feel something for Chelsea. He didn't feel the fireworks like he did with Olivia, but there was *something* there. "So, you do want something more?" he finally asked, breaking the awkward silence.

Chelsea exhaled loudly. "I do. And I know that, right now, you're not ready to make that decision. But know that when you come back, I'll be here. And if, at that point, you're ready for something more, then I am, too. Until then, know that I'm thinking about you and missing your touch. Good-bye, Alex."

"Good-bye, Chelsea," he whispered softly, placing his cell phone on the lounge table next to him, thinking about Chelsea. And Olivia.

As he grabbed his laptop and powered it up, he heard the

familiar sound of a woman's laugh. *God, I love that sound,* he thought as his body came alive with electricity. It had been over a month since he had felt that sensation. Looking out over the horizon, his heart raced as he searched for the source of that laughter. He heard that sound in his dreams every night. Only one person had a laugh that beautiful. He was certain his Olivia was near. Grabbing his coffee, he walked over to the edge of his balcony, taking in several people running on the beach.

That's when his heart almost stopped.

There she was, running up the shoreline toward his hotel. He stilled, watching as she placed one leg in front of the other in rapid succession, her hips moving in perfect rhythm. She made running look so easy.

His brain tried to tell his body to move, to run out of his suite and onto the beach. But he remained completely frozen, shock etched across his strong face. He stared as Olivia stopped running, looking in the direction that she had just come from. He could almost feel her smile as she stood gazing up the beach, laughing at something. Alexander followed her eyes to see a relatively tall man running toward her, obviously having trouble keeping up. He kept watching as she took a deep breath, the smile gone from her face. She slowly turned and looked out over the ocean.

And that's when Alexander saw it. The sadness. The hurt. The loss. He knew that look all too well.

Because it was the same way he felt.

~~~~~~~~~~

Olivia looked toward the shore, waiting for Cam. As she watched a few small children run out from the back of the Ritz and into the ocean, their parents trying to catch up, she felt that familiar tingling sensation. Her eyes began searching the beach as if certain that *he* was there. But how could that be? She hadn't told anyone where she was, and she had made it quite clear that it was time to move on. But there was an electricity in the air that Olivia hadn't felt since the day she left

Boston.

She scanned the beach, half expecting to see Alexander running up to her. She secretly *wanted* to see him, to run into his arms, have him swing her around and declare his undying love to her. But that only happened in the movies, not real life. And her life was as real as it got.

She looked out over the ocean waves, and the sadness took over. Her smile disappeared and that's when she felt it…the emptiness. She thought she had felt empty before, but this was a new kind of emptiness. She realized how big of a mistake she made when she left Alexander, and she began to regret that decision. But there was no way he would take her back, knowing that the risk of her doing the same thing all over again was so high.

No. Olivia had made her decision and she would have to live with it. Those five little words still played over and over in her head… *It will destroy me, too.*

Hearing a child scream in excitement, she turned. People strolled along the white sand beach behind her. Tourists sat on their balconies of the Ritz, most likely enjoying their morning coffee. She wanted to cry when she thought about all those mornings she drank her coffee in bed with Alexander.

Her heart dropped when she noticed someone on the top floor of the Ritz, standing on a wrap-around balcony, staring down at her. It was too far away for her to make out who it was, but the stature was eerily familiar. Or maybe she just so desperately wanted Alexander to come searching for her, even though she had told him to move on.

"Jesus, you're fast, Libby," Cam said, finally catching up to her as she stared at the top floor of the swanky hotel, not responding, a blank look on her face. He wrapped his arm around her waist and gently kissed the top of her forehead. "You okay?" he asked, noticing her lack of reaction to him.

"Yeah. I'm fine." She squinted, still looking at the man standing on the balcony, knowing there was something so familiar about whomever it was. She closed her eyes, trying to clear her head. She felt as if she was losing her mind. She needed to forget about Alexander. She saw him everywhere and it needed to stop.

Turning to Cam, she placed a gentle kiss on his lips, making him smile. "Ready to go back?"

"No," he laughed. "But I guess I don't have a choice, do I?"

"Not really!" she shouted as she took off running, glancing back over her shoulder at the balcony on the top floor of the Ritz, unable to shake the feeling that Alexander was nearby.

CHAPTER SIX

OKAY

THAT BASTARD! ALEXANDER THOUGHT as he watched the tall sandy-haired guy kiss Olivia's forehead near her scar. It made him furious to think that someone else was touching her. His face flashed red with anger as he watched Olivia kiss him on the lips. *Those are my fucking lips!*

He wanted to cry. He wanted to scream. But mostly, he wanted to kiss her, to feel those soft lips again. He was losing control of everything.

As she started to run away, Alexander saw her look back, her eyes trained on his balcony. She was a long distance away but, in his heart, he knew that she felt the same electricity and turned to find the source. He was certain of it. Pacing back and forth, he needed to figure out what his next step should be. He was lost. She was within his reach. He could have shouted her name. Screamed it. Made her recognize him. Just seeing her made him feel as if he was breaking all over again, if that was even possible.

He faintly heard the door to his suite open and close. "Martin!" Alexander shouted, still shaken up over his first Olivia sighting.

"Yes, sir?" Martin appeared on the balcony as Alexander stood locked in place, watching Olivia run away, now just a tiny speck.

Alexander's heart raced, thinking about how close she was to him. He very easily could have run out of his suite and caught up with her, but he had no idea what to say. No. Before he approached her, he needed more information.

"She's here, Martin. I just saw her running on the beach. I don't know what to do, but she ran north. She must live out there somewhere." His eyes frantically searched Martin's, desperate that he had a way of finding her. Alexander couldn't think at that moment. He normally had an answer to everything, but he was so rattled after seeing Olivia that he was frantic, his mind racing over a thousand different scenarios.

"I'll look into public records and see if there have been any transfers of real estate or anything else in the last month," Martin responded calmly.

Alexander sighed, his brain function finally returning. "I highly doubt she would have done that. She didn't want to be found. That defeats the purpose. No. I think our best bet is just to explore this little island. It's not that big. It's maybe three miles wide and ten miles long so let's not rush this. Let's not scare her off. I don't want her to realize I'm here and then run again."

"Yes, sir. I'll look into rentals and do some public record checks anyway, see if I come across anything." Martin disappeared into the suite, leaving Alexander alone with his thoughts, the sun now shining brightly over the Atlantic Ocean.

~~~~~~~~~~

Olivia saw her beach house appear as she rounded the corner and began sprinting, glancing back to see Cam far behind her. She still couldn't shake the feeling that Alexander was on the island. But how? And why? Would he really track her credit card? Of course he would. She knew that.

Quickly retreating into her house, she grabbed two glasses, filled them with chocolate milk, and brought them outside, sitting down on her front steps. A few minutes later, Cam ran up, panting.

"Fuck, Libby. You're an animal." He exhaled loudly. "Remind me to never take you up on another challenge. Jesus…"

"It's not as easy as it looks, is it?" she smirked.

"Whoever said it looked easy?"

Olivia shrugged, handing Cam a glass of chocolate milk. He eyed it suspiciously. "It's chocolate milk," she explained. "It will help your muscles recover. Trust me."

"Okay," he said cautiously, taking a sip of his drink. "I take it back. That's actually really good after a run."

"Told you," she replied, bringing her own glass to her lips as Cam watched, sitting down on the front steps next to her.

Olivia looked out over the sand dunes, wondering why she had a feeling that Alexander was on the island. She had seen him everywhere but, this time, there was an electricity in the air, as if he had found her.

"I can tell the wheels are turning in that head of yours. You have that look."

Olivia whipped her head back toward Cam. "What look?" she asked, furrowing her eyebrows.

"You know. *That look*. The one that, last night, I said was so fucking cute that I wanted to die. That's your 'thinking' look, and it's adorable. But I wonder what's going through that head of yours. I know you're not thinking about me, and that's okay." He grasped Olivia's chin, bringing her face toward his. "But I really wish you *would* think about me, and forget about whatever or whoever did all this to you."

"Did what?" Olivia asked softly, her breathing increasing along with her heart rate.

"This," he responded quietly. "I know there's a spirited, energetic, and passionate young woman in there somewhere, desperately screaming to get out. And I'm going to do everything I can to bring that person back."

"Oh, Cam," she exhaled, looking to the sky for her answer as she watched the seagulls swoop into the ocean, searching for their next meal. "I wish it was that easy. I think that girl stayed in Boston."

"AHA!" he exclaimed. "Boston." A huge grin crept across his face.

"What?" Olivia looked at him skeptically.

"Nothing. I'm just hungry for information about you, but

I'm not going to press you. At least now I know where you came from, beautiful." He winked.

"Yeah. Boston…"

"Do you miss it?" he asked.

Olivia thought about it. Did she miss Boston? Or was it something more? She shrugged as a truck pulled up along Ocean Avenue, a bunch of surfers getting out to catch some morning waves. Cam nodded a greeting. Of course he knew them.

"You don't have to talk about it if you don't want to, Libby," he said, turning his attention back to her.

"No. It's okay. I mean, it's hard to say if I miss it or not. When I got in my car with the few possessions I chose to bring, a strange feeling overtook me. I wasn't just leaving my friends, but I was also leaving behind the girl that I was at that time in my life. Leaving Boston was so much more than saying good-bye to the city that I had grown to love over the last ten years or so of my life. It was also saying good-bye to the person the city turned me into." A tear escaped as she thought about the girl she was back then.

When Olivia first moved to Boston right after she finished high school, she was shy and scared, her only outlet being music. She still remembered the day she met Kiera like it was yesterday. She had just gotten back from a run around the Charles River late one evening and there were quite a few people hanging outside the small three-story apartment building in the Allston section of the city.

Olivia lowered her head, trying to avoid eye contact as she made her way up the steps. "Hey!" she heard as she unlocked the front door to the building. "You're the girl that just moved in, aren't you? The new tenant in 1B?"

She turned around to see a petite girl with soft red hair, tons of freckles, and fiery green eyes. She looked far more sophisticated than Olivia. She guessed the girl had to be in her mid-twenties. Her smile was contagious and Olivia knew immediately that she could trust her. There was something about her that was so open and honest and she felt, for lack of a better word, comfortable.

"Yes. That's me. I'm Libby," she said, extending her hand to the

redhead.

"Libby! So happy to finally meet you." She wrapped her arms around Olivia, obviously not caring that she was drenched in sweat from a long run around the river during the humid August heat. "I'm Kiera!" she exclaimed after releasing her.

"Hi, Kiera. Nice to meet you." Olivia retreated into the building, heading toward her apartment.

"Hey, Libby!" Kiera shouted, running down the short hallway to Olivia's left rear apartment. "I'm having people over tonight, as you can tell. You should come, too. My boss sent a shit ton of liquor over, and I need someone to help drink it!"

"I don't know," Olivia responded, facing Kiera, noticing the hordes of people in the apartment across the hall.

"Oh, come on. Go shower, then come over. It'll be fun. Plus, if your butt isn't out of your apartment within an hour, I know where you live. I will come drag you out."

Olivia rolled her eyes, turning to go into her apartment. "Okay. I'll see you in a little bit then."

"Goody!" Kiera said, jumping up and down as she rushed back out front to where a few people were smoking. "You know that shit will kill you dead!" she scolded her friends. Olivia laughed at her new acquaintance.

That night, she and Kiera had become friends. Over the next month, they had become inseparable. She even got Olivia a job at the bar on Boylston Street where she worked. It was Kiera who broke her out of her shell to begin with, but it was Alexander who opened her heart again.

"Hey, Libby. Come back to me, sweetheart."

Olivia snapped out of her memory when she heard Cam's voice. She looked up to see him standing in front of her.

"There's my girl," he said, grabbing her hand and pulling her up. "Listen, I need to get back home. Can I call you later?"

Olivia looked down at her feet.

He noticed her apprehension. "What is it?"

"You're going to laugh," she said, meeting his eyes.

"Try me."

Olivia shrugged. "I don't have a phone. I left Boston and didn't want anyone to be able to find me so my phone is still sitting in the kitchen of my old house, along with the rest of my possessions."

Cam stared, curious as to what happened in Boston to make her want to leave everything behind. "Okay. Well...can I see you later? We'll go up to the Ritz. They have a great bar. We can talk or just do absolutely nothing."

She thought about it. Over the last several minutes as they sat on the steps to her deck, she hadn't thought about Alexander as much as she expected she would. Maybe Cam was just what she needed to forget about him. Turning and kissing him gently on the lips, she smiled. "I'd like that."

He beamed at her as he picked her up, playfully swinging her around. "Good because I'd be in a terrible mood if you turned me down." He kissed her neck and placed her feet back on the sandy road. "Even after a long run, you still smell divine." He jumped into his Jeep and started the engine, rolling down the window. "I'll see you later, gorgeous." He blew her a kiss and drove away, leaving Olivia feeling surprisingly content. For the first time in over a month, she felt okay. Not happy, but okay. And, for now, that was, well...okay.

But she still wondered why she felt that Alexander was on the island.

Chapter Seven

Found

ALEXANDER DECIDED THAT THE best thing to do was to spend some time exploring the island and try to get a feel for the place Olivia now called home. At least until he knew where she lived.

After breakfast, he grabbed a rented Mercedes convertible and drove out of the hotel complex, passing by a golf course on his way toward the western part of the small island. He soon found himself driving in the downtown Fernandina Beach district. Large Victorian homes dotted the area, giving way to a marina that housed several shrimping boats.

He parked under an old moss tree and decided to get out to do a bit of exploring. As he strolled down the tree-lined street, he knew why Olivia came there to escape. It really was cute and quaint. The downtown district was just six short blocks. It almost reminded him of his boyhood home in Mystic.

And Olivia's childhood home.

In the back of his mind, he wondered whether that had something to do with her decision to come there.

There were tourist shops lining the boulevard, as well as some beach boutique stores. And, of course, the one building that had a line out the door – an ice cream parlor. After walking around for a few hours, he made his way down one of the side streets and found a Mexican restaurant, thinking that maybe few shots of tequila, some beer, and a little food would help him with the next step of his mission...finding Olivia.

Martin had a bunch of feelers out around the island, asking

about a girl who had arrived in mid-October. On an island this small, he was confident someone knew her. It would only be a matter of time before Alexander found her. When he did, he was unsure of what to do, especially after seeing her running on the beach that morning. His face flashed red with anger when he remembered seeing some guy kiss her gently on the forehead. It made him raging mad to think that someone else was near her, touching her, enjoying her essence.

But, then again, he hadn't remained faithful, either. Did he really expect that she wouldn't meet someone else, as well? Maybe it wouldn't hurt so much if he knew she hadn't moved on. That was what hurt the most.

After ordering a shot of tequila and a beer, his cell phone rang. "Martin. What is it?"

"Are you ready for this?" Martin asked.

Alexander exhaled. "Shoot. I can handle it."

"Okay, sir," he said, then paused. "I have an address."

Alexander's heart began to race, knowing that he possibly could be seeing Olivia that day.

"It's a cottage in Fernandina Beach on Ocean Avenue on the north end of the island. She's been renting it for the past few weeks. Paid for six months up front. Owner is a Terry Robinson. Lives a mile or so inland from where the beach cottage is. He took cash in exchange for no paperwork being filed regarding the rental. You're right that she had no intention of being found, sir."

Alexander signaled the bartender for another shot after downing the one in front of him. "How did you find this out?" He was floored at Martin's efficiency. He made a mental note to give him a raise and a bonus.

"When the search through property records turned up nothing, I started contacting beach rentals, mostly ones that were booked solid. I found one online that was booked through April with no availability whatsoever. Not even one day. So I made a phone call. Mr. Robinson was rather helpful. But I'm not sure you're ready for that conversation yet, sir. With all due respect," he said, not wanting to get into Mr. Robinson's description of the empty woman who rolled up out of nowhere to rent his beach cottage.

Alexander downed his second shot of tequila. "You're probably right about that. I'm having trouble processing the fact that we've actually found her. And I don't need you to remind me that if we can find her, so can anyone else."

"Yes, sir," Martin replied. "So, how would you like me to proceed?"

Alexander thought for a moment. He wasn't sure. He desperately wanted to see Olivia. To hold her in his arms. To convince her that she didn't need to run, that he would never leave her. But then he recalled his sister's words from the night before. What if she got scared and ran again? No. He needed to have a plan. He couldn't risk her fleeing. Not when he was so close.

"Give me some time to process this. I'll go over there soon." He hung up and signaled the bartender to pour him another shot.

CHAPTER EIGHT

NEW LEAF

"EVENING, BEAUTIFUL," CAM SAID sweetly as Olivia opened the door. He nearly took her breath away with his smile and overall good looks. Stepping toward her, he kissed her softly on the cheek, lingering just a few seconds longer, shifting the kiss from friendly to affectionate.

Olivia closed her eyes, savoring the feeling of Cam's lips on her skin as she inhaled his delicious scent. It wasn't the same as Alexander's, but she reminded herself to stop comparing everything about Cam to Alexander. Cam was a breath of fresh air. He was easy-going and affectionate. He had a sense of humor. And, most of all, he didn't pressure her into talking about anything that she didn't want to.

He pulled back, beaming at her as he stood on her front deck, the ocean air blowing through his wayward sandy hair. His white linen shirt rippled as the wind picked up. "Ready to go?" he asked, extending his arm out to her.

"Yes. Thank you," she responded, grabbing her clutch and slipping on her beige pumps.

"You look amazing, as always," Cam said softly, gazing at her red halter dress. His eyes shifted to her chest and he hoped she didn't notice.

Olivia blushed, taking his arm, and he led her out to his Lexus. A few short minutes later, they pulled up to the Ritz Carlton. "Where are we going?" she asked as they walked through the impressive lobby.

"Just a bar I really like. They have this fantastic five-diamond restaurant here, and the bar is killer. A nice change of pace from the normal 'beachy' southern bars that dot the rest of this little island," he replied, leading her into a classy dimly lit lounge.

Olivia looked around, noticing the place appeared to be relatively busy for a hotel bar. "It seems quite popular," she remarked.

"It is. It's a little gem on this island. So, table or bar?"

Olivia thought about that. Normally, she would opt for a few stools at the bar, but something about that evening made her want a little bit more privacy. She wanted to get to know Cam. She wanted to begin to open up to him. It was the only way she could start moving past Alexander. "Let's sit at a table."

Cam beamed his brilliant white smile as he led her past a piano player, placing his hand on the small of her back and walking her to a secluded table with tea candles lit. He held out the chair for her, and Olivia's brain rewound several months to that first night with Alexander. How he walked her from the elevator to her office in order to retrieve her things. How his simple touch sent fireworks through her entire body. And how, when Cam repeated the same gesture, her nerves didn't stand on end.

Within a matter of moments, a server came over to take their drink order and returned rather quickly. *Points for quick service*, Olivia thought. She took a rather large gulp of her Manhattan as her eyes met Cam's. The way he looked at her, Olivia felt a little something stirring in her body. He seemed genuinely happy to just be with her, to spend time with her. He had said that he didn't care where their relationship led. There were no expectations, which made Olivia feel comfortable with him when, normally, she wouldn't want to open up to anyone.

"My parents died in a car accident when I was six," she said out of nowhere, breaking the deafening silence.

Cam placed his beer on the table, shocked at Olivia's sudden decision to share information about her past. "I'm sorry, Libby. That's awful."

She shrugged. "Yeah. I still dream about the crash nearly

every night. I don't really remember my parents all that much. After they died, I was shipped off to a private boarding school in Charleston. I stayed there until I went away to college. I had an uncle who was my guardian, but we weren't really all that close so I pretty much had to raise myself."

"Hmmm," Cam said, thinking about her story. "I get it now."

"What? What do you get?" Olivia asked, raising her voice slightly.

"Just why you seem so closed off. You didn't have a parental figure in your life after your parents died. That could have stunted your emotional growth. It's common. You see it all the time, especially after such a tragedy."

"Wait a minute," she snapped, holding out her hand. "How do you know all that shit?"

"I'm a psychiatrist when I'm not chasing a certain beautiful woman around the island, trying to get her to talk to me." He winked. "But, please don't hold that against me, Libby. I beg you," he pleaded with her, seeing her demeanor change from one of calmness to one of anger. "I didn't want to scare you off. I knew you were going through something and I was so worried that if I told you what I do for a living, you would bolt. I just couldn't stand the thought of that."

Olivia pushed her chair back, contemplating doing what she always did. She wanted to run as far away as she could.

"Don't run, Libby. Please. I couldn't bear the thought of you running again because of me. I want to give you some stability in your life." He ran his hand through his hair, reminding her of Alexander yet again. "Yesterday, when you finally agreed to come to dinner with me, I couldn't relax the rest of the day. I was so fucking excited to be able to spend some time with you."

He reached across the table, grabbing both her hands, lowering his voice to just above a whisper. "When you opened the door, my heart fucking stopped, Libby. You are the most beautiful woman I have ever seen, and I have a feeling you always will be. I like you. A lot. You're the first thing I think about every morning. You have been since I first set eyes on you. I fall asleep with a smile on my face every night because, with nightfall, I'm that much closer to seeing you again the following morning. And I'm both scared and confused as to why and how I feel this way about a woman I barely fucking know. But, please, let me get to know you. Let me in. That's all I ask."

Olivia sat there, her heart racing as she listened to Cam's heartfelt plea. She knew she couldn't keep running her entire life, but that's all she had known up until that point. When things became too complicated or scary, she ran. She was tempted to run again, but the more she thought about it, the more she knew it wasn't going to solve anything. She would end up in a new town or city where she would inevitably meet someone else, and she'd find herself in the same position all over again. No. For once, she wasn't going to run.

She took a deep breath and turned her eyes up to look at Cam. "Okay. I'll stay."

"Good," Cam said, smiling. "Are you okay, though? And not with what I just told you. I'm worried about you, Libby," he remarked, sincerity etched across his face. "Are you okay? I mean, really okay?"

Olivia looked out the window, her chin quivering as she gazed at the moonlit beach, honeymooning couples holding hands and strolling along the white sand paths.

"Hey, Libby," Cam said, bringing her attention back to him. "It's okay to admit that you're not okay, but you need to at least realize that something is making you sad or upset or angry. Too many people walk around saying that everything's fine when, in all reality, things aren't fine. Sometimes we're bruised, beaten, shattered, or destroyed. I just hope you're not, but if you are, let me be the one to fix you. I'm not talking to you as someone who happens to be a therapist. I'm talking to you as someone who is so incredibly attracted to you that it hurts sometimes."

A tear fell down Olivia's cheek. "I'm not okay, Cam, but I want to be. Hopefully the more time that goes by, the more okay I'll be." She stood up. "I'm just going to go powder my nose. I'll be right back."

Cam eyed her suspiciously. "You're not running, are you?"

Olivia took a deep breath. "No, Cam. For the first time in my life, I'm not going to run. I can't run from things that scare me for the rest of my life so I may as well turn over a new leaf."

Standing up, he snaked his arm around her waist and pulled her close to his body. "Is this okay?" he asked quietly, a bit of huskiness in his voice.

Olivia gazed into his eyes and, unable to find her own voice, simply nodded.

He leaned down and planted a gentle kiss on her lips. "Is this okay?" he asked, his lips still pressed lightly against hers.

She nodded again and could feel his mouth turn into a huge smile.

"Good because I can't seem to get enough of your lips." He pressed another gentle kiss on them before sending her on her way to the ladies' room.

When she returned, their evening continued on a much lighter note, both sharing stories from their childhood.

"So, where in South Carolina did you grow up?" Olivia asked after they ordered their third round of drinks. The liquor helped her open up a bit, and Cam seemed to enjoy learning about her.

"Myrtle Beach, actually. And the answer is no, I absolutely do not golf," he joked.

"That's too bad," she responded, placing her martini glass on the table. "I was just thinking how hot you'd look in some plaid pants." She giggled.

It took Cam's breath away. "That's quickly becoming one of my favorite sounds."

Suddenly, it felt as if the floor fell out from under her. It was the second time in two days that Cam said something that reminded her of Alexander. She rewound back to that day she bumped into him running through Boston Common. He had told her the same thing.

"Libby, where did you go?" Cam asked, interrupting her memories. He looked at Olivia, her face paler than he had ever seen it before. He was concerned about the girl who sat in front of him. There was something, or someone, that she was

53

running from, and certain words seemed to be triggers of very painful memories.

"You know what, Cam?" Olivia said before draining her glass. He quickly signaled the server to bring her another. "It's not the bad memories that hurt," she quivered. "It's the good ones that cause the most pain. Those are the memories that stay with you, making you smile. Then you realize that the source of those memories is gone and you'll never have that feeling again." She took a deep breath, her voice barely a whisper. "And that is what is most painful."

Cam grabbed Olivia's hand, gently brushing her knuckles. "Lucky guess, but we're not talking about your parents here, are we? It's something, or some*one*, that you ran from up in Boston, isn't it?"

She opened her mouth, unsure of whether she could speak the words about what happened between her and Alexander.

He held his hand up to stop her. "I told you. I'm not going to pressure you to talk about anything you don't want to. Let's stop talking about all this heavy stuff and just enjoy each other's company. I'm so sorry for whatever I said that would cause you any pain. That's the last thing I want to do."

The server dropped off another Manhattan and Olivia began to feel rather tipsy. She felt that familiar tingle and electricity, wondering whether it was simply the effects of the liquor. Whatever the reason, she didn't care. Her body shuddered as Cam picked up her hand, softly kissing her knuckles. She was feeling something.

CHAPTER NINE

FIVE LITTLE WORDS

THAT FUCKING BASTARD! ALEXANDER thought as he sat at the far corner of the bar, his eyes trained on the table near the windows. He couldn't believe that she was at his hotel, at the bar where he was drinking. What were the chances? And there *he* was, comforting her when she got upset and kissing her perfect fucking skin. It was taking all of his self-control to not walk over there and cause a scene.

No. Now was not the right time. He had been drunk nearly all day, and he was certain that nothing he could say to her at that moment would be swoon-worthy. And that's what he needed.

He signaled the bartender to pour him another scotch as he sat there staring at Olivia. *His Olivia.* He was concerned about her drinking, but that was like the pot calling the kettle black. But four Manhattans? Really?

He couldn't understand why he kept freezing up when she was nearby...on the beach earlier, now at the bar. He was unable to tell his legs to put one in front of the other and walk over there. Maybe his brain was trying to tell him something.

He watched as the guy sitting across from her caressed her skin, signaling their server for the check. Then she giggled and Alexander lost it. How could someone else be making her happy? That was *his* fucking job! Throwing several bills on the bar, he downed his scotch and walked out. He didn't know where he was going, but he knew he needed to get away from there.

~~~~~~~~~~

"Ready to go, beautiful?" Cam asked, extending his arm and helping Olivia up from her chair. She wavered slightly, the multiple strong drinks affecting her balance. "Easy there, Libby. You drank a bit tonight."

Olivia smiled. "I definitely did," she slurred, clutching onto Cam's arm. "I'm shmammered." She wished she hadn't ordered so many Manhattans. Cam was smart, ordering only beer. She should have stuck to beer because she was fairly drunk right now. And when she was drunk, she made awful decisions.

"Shmammered? What's that?" he asked, smiling at her.

"Kind of like a combination of smashed and hammered," she giggled as Cam led her out to the lobby, snaking his arm around her waist to help steady her. His body felt so warm against hers. She enjoyed the closeness that she was beginning to feel with him.

"Shit!" she exclaimed just as they reached the front doors to the hotel. "I left my clutch in there."

"I'll go get it," Cam said quickly.

"No. I'll get it. I need to use the ladies' room anyway."

"Are you sure you'll be okay?" he asked, raising his eyebrows.

She smiled as she placed her hand on his chest. "I love that you worry about me," she whispered against his neck.

Her breath smelled sweet, a combination of the alcohol and just her. She planted a quick kiss on Cam's neck before turning around to head back into the bar. "I'll be right back. Promise."

Cam chuckled as he watched her walk away, her hips swaying in such a way that made his entire being harden. "Okay, gorgeous. But if you're not back in five minutes, I'll send out a search party."

Olivia turned her head around and winked as she walked back into the bar, searching for her clutch.

~~~~~~~~~~

After leaving the restaurant bar and roaming around for a while, Alexander walked into the lobby bar. He was less than impressed with their scotch selection, but he desperately wanted another drink, needing to forget about seeing Olivia with another man. It drove him crazy to even think about it.

He decided that one more scotch was in order so he returned to the restaurant bar he had just left, still feeling the unbearable pain. He wanted something to numb it all. Placing his order with the bartender, he glanced over at the empty table where Olivia had been sitting. Out of the corner of his eye, he saw a small purple clutch lying on the floor under the chair.

He took a deep breath before walking over there with the purpose of turning it over to the bartender so that no one stole anything out of it. After bending down to grab the small wristlet, his heart stopped as he stared into those big brown eyes again.

Olivia wavered a bit, obviously drunk from all the liquor he had watched her consume that evening. He noticed a small tear escape her eye and her chin quivered. The atmosphere immediately changed from one of hurt to one of hope. He could see it in her eyes. There was still hope for him.

He held out the clutch. "You left this. I didn't want anyone to steal it," he said quietly.

Olivia didn't know what to think. That morning, she had a feeling that Alexander was on the island. And now there he was, standing in front of her, handing her clutch to her. Knots began to form in the pit of her stomach. Leaving him was so easy when she didn't have to look into those green eyes. She took the coward's way out, writing him a letter saying good-bye. But now that she was face-to-face with him, could she really tell him that she didn't want to be with him?

Slowly, she reached her hand out to grab the clutch, Alexander's fingers softly brushing hers. Inhaling quickly, she dropped her eyes to his fingers delicately caressing her hand. It was such a simple gesture, but the fireworks erupting within her body sent shivers throughout.

"You still feel that?" Alexander asked sadly, noticing her

57

reaction.

Olivia looked into his eyes again, opening her mouth, willing her brain to say something. Anything. But she couldn't. A lump formed in her throat and she knew that she made a mistake leaving Alexander and Boston. Then his words echoed in her head. *"You always try to stay strong, ignoring the past, but you can't keep it all inside, love. It will destroy you. It will destroy me, too."*

It was selfish of her to string Alexander along, knowing full well that the baggage she carried was too much for him to deal with. That's how this all began. Those five little words... *It will destroy me, too*. Olivia knew they were true. And what she did no longer seemed selfish. It was *selfless*. She was saving Alexander from the inevitable pain of her path of destruction.

"I...I can't do this, Alexander. I have to go," she cried, turning abruptly and running out of the bar, leaving him alone.

"Olivia, love," he called after her, trying to catch up. He saw her bolt out the front door of the hotel into a silver Lexus convertible. "Damn it!" he shouted as the car drove off, but not before she turned her head around, meeting his eyes one last time.

Reaching into his pocket, he grabbed his cell phone, punching a button. "Martin," he growled, his speech slurred. "Go over there and keep watch for me. Alert me if there's any movement." He hung up before retreating back to the restaurant. He downed the scotch on the bar and retired to his suite for the evening. Tomorrow was another day, and he wouldn't start drinking at noon.

CHAPTER TEN

FEEL AGAIN

"ARE YOU SURE YOU'RE okay, Libby?" Cam asked as he drove down the tree-lined streets on the south end of the island. "You look like you've seen a ghost or something." Taking in her appearance, he wondered if maybe she had gotten sick in the ladies' room. Her eyes were red and her face was pale. The playful Olivia was nowhere to be found. He grabbed her hand after shifting into fourth. "Come on, Libby. Don't shut me out. We were making so much progress."

Olivia tilted her head toward him. "I'm sorry," she replied dryly. She was desperate to get the evening out of her head. It had started out so nice. Earlier, she actually felt something she hadn't in so very long…hope. Hope that she could survive life after Alexander, and then *he* had to go and show up at her little oasis.

After a silent car ride that felt as if it had lasted hours instead of mere minutes, Cam pulled up outside of Olivia's beach cottage. She didn't even wait for him to open the door for her. She bolted out of the car, anxious to forget the whole night.

"Libby, wait. Please," Cam begged, catching up to her as she fumbled with her keys, frantically trying to unlock her front door with shaky hands. "Please," he repeated, grabbing the keys out of her trembling fingers. "Let me fix this." He trailed his hand down her arm, trying to calm her down.

Olivia turned around and met his eyes as he unlocked the door. "There. All better," he said quietly, gently pushing the door open.

"Would you like to come in?" she asked, her voice soft. She wanted to forget about seeing Alexander, and she needed Cam to do that.

Running his hand through his hair, a look of hesitation spread across his face.

"Please, Cam. I just don't want to be alone right now," she begged, her eyes brimming with tears.

All of Cam's resolve to do the right thing melted at that moment. "Okay. I won't leave you, Libby." He followed her into the quaint house. Olivia needed him, and it felt good to be needed.

"Would you like a coffee?" she asked as she made her way through the open living room into the airy kitchen, placing her clutch on the island and throwing off her heels.

"If it's not any trouble," Cam replied, following her into the kitchen and sitting on a barstool.

"No trouble at all. How do you take it?"

"Black." He winked.

Olivia smiled, remembering how Cam had noticed the little things about her, like how she began drinking her coffee black. She felt it matched her mood lately.

After preparing two cups of coffee in her one-cup brewer, she handed one to Cam and led him over to a large white couch in her living room. It was a small space, but the high ceilings made the room seem much larger and open.

"This is a great view you have," Cam remarked, looking out the enormous front windows at the ocean.

"I'm quite fond of it myself," Olivia replied, sitting on the couch, facing the large windows. "Who needs TV when you have this view? And, of course, the hot guys that come here to surf aren't bad to look at either." She winked, nudging Cam with her elbow. *This is good*, she thought. She was letting him in. Even if it didn't work out, she knew it was a pain that she could deal with.

Cam's heart raced when he heard her words. She looked at him, her lips turned up gently in the corners as if inviting him to respond. "Well, I've known a few surfers who blow off work in the morning just to come and try to get a certain girl to notice them."

"Slacker," Olivia joked, sipping her coffee.

"Definitely," he responded, placing his mug on the coffee table in front of him. "Give me that," he said, grabbing her mug and setting it beside his.

Olivia turned to face him, her body instantly becoming warm as his eyes bore down into her. She knew it wasn't fair to him, but she needed to feel close to someone. Desperation took over as she took his face in her hands and placed her lips on his, the kiss gentle at first before exploding into a passionate exchange.

His tongue entered her mouth as they feverishly explored each other's bodies, Olivia pushing Cam down on the couch and straddling him. She broke her lips away from his, trailing kisses down his neck and collarbone, nibbling on his earlobe as she felt his erection grow between her legs.

"Fuck," he exhaled. "God, your lips are soft, Libby," he breathed as she continued torturing him with her mouth, gently kissing his chest through his shirt. She wanted to feel *something*. She tried to feel the electricity that she felt when she was with Alexander. As she traced her tongue against his neck, savoring the taste of his salty skin, her body refused to ignite on fire.

She sat back, grinding her hips against Cam's midsection, reaching for the buttons on his linen shirt, hoping to feel even the hint of a spark. At the very least, she wanted to forget about seeing Alexander. But, if that was true, why did she wish Cam's blazing silver eyes were green when she looked into them? She closed her own eyes, not wanting to look at Cam as she continued torturing him with her body, moving on top of him in a way that made his entire body flame with desire. She slowly began to unbutton his shirt, lowering her lips to his chest, tracing circles with her tongue.

"Libby," Cam said. "You don't have to…"

Olivia held a finger over his mouth, hushing him. "I know," she said, her breathing ragged. "I want this, Cam. I need this. Help me feel again, please." She continued circling his midsection, finally beginning to feel a familiar throbbing between her legs.

She knew she was just using Cam, but she didn't care. She needed to feel again. She didn't care if there were no sparks or fireworks. She was tired of feeling so numb and empty.

Returning her lips to his, Olivia finished unbuttoning his shirt, leaning down to nibble on his earlobe. Savoring the feeling of his muscular body beneath her own, she trailed kisses from his neck down his chest, toying with his little trail of hair, eager to see where it led.

Groaning, Cam flipped Olivia onto her back, his tongue continuing its exploration of her mouth as his hand roamed up and down her long legs. With each journey up, he went a little further north, drawing her dress even higher, finally feeling her ass.

She moaned, deepening the kiss before pulling back and dragging Cam's lower lip between her teeth, nibbling gently. She wrapped her legs around his waist, wanting to feel him inside of her.

"Easy, Libby, or I'm not going to last long," he exhaled into her neck. "I want this to last."

"Please, Cam. I need to feel you..." Olivia pleaded with him.

"And I want you to feel me," he whispered into her mouth, pressing his lips to hers. "I want you to feel so fucking complete when I'm moving inside you that you forget about whatever it is that's got you scared."

Olivia's heart swelled at Cam's gentle words and touch, the heat emanating from his body making her desperate for him to keep touching her.

"Do you want that?" he asked, pulling back and looking down at her as she lay panting on the couch.

"Yes, Cam," she said breathlessly. She wanted that more than anything. She wanted him. She needed him. He was the only one who could make her forget about *him*.

He grabbed the bottom of her dress, looking into her eyes as if asking permission. She bit her bottom lip and nodded. Within seconds, she lay on the couch wearing only a red lace strapless bra and matching panties. She felt Cam harden even more between her legs.

"Fuck, Libby." He lowered his head to her chest, tracing his tongue across the top of her breasts. Olivia squirmed under his mouth, the heat sending shivers through her body. His fingers gently slid underneath her bra, lowering it and exposing her nipples. The cool air and her desire for him made them harden. He ran his tongue over one nipple, tugging lightly with his teeth.

Olivia let out a soft moan, enjoying the feeling of ecstasy from such a simple gesture.

"You like that, Libby?" Cam asked, tracing her other nipple.

She nodded, her breathing picking up pace as she moved her hips, desperate for some sort of release.

Cam pulled back and looked at Olivia, a sexy smile across his face. "Patience, gorgeous. Let me help you feel again." He reached down and slipped a finger in her panties, finding her clit and gently rubbing it. "Do you feel that?" he asked softly, feathering his lips across her neck.

"Yes," she responded quietly, throwing her head back and reveling in the sensation of his touch on the most intimate part of her body.

"Good," he replied before lowering himself down her body and grabbing her panties by the hips, sliding them down her long legs. "I want to taste you, Libby," he said in a husky voice. He slowly trailed kisses down her stomach, watching her chest rise and fall in a quick rhythm. "Do you want that?" he asked as he circled her bellybutton with his tongue, his finger slowly entering and withdrawing from inside her.

"Yes, Cam. God, yes," Olivia breathed softly. She didn't know how much more she could take. The anticipation was killing her. She was desperate to feel something other than the numbness that had taken over her entire being since fleeing Boston. For the first time in over a month, she was feeling something. And it felt amazing.

He continued trailing kisses down her stomach, pausing before pressing his tongue against her clit, slowly lapping up her juices as he continued pleasuring her with his finger. "I love the way you taste, Libby," Cam commented before returning his tongue to the spot that made her feel for a change. "You feel that?"

"Yes, Cam. I feel it." She closed her eyes, desperate to block out the rest of the world and only concentrate on the amazing sensation of Cam's mouth between her legs.

"Good." He began sucking ever so gently as he inserted another finger inside her. She felt like she was on the brink of exploding, the incredibly full feeling of his tongue on her and fingers inside her about to send her over the edge into a million tiny pieces. It wasn't as intense a feeling as she felt with Alexander but, at that moment in time, she was finally feeling.

She moaned out as Cam continued his gentle movement, softly licking her. "Faster, Cam. Please."

He looked up and met her eyes as his tongue moved at a quicker pace over her clit, picking up speed with his fingers. "You like that, Libby?" he asked before returning his mouth to her sex, slipping another finger inside of her.

All of a sudden, it became too much for her to handle. Her body began to tighten around Cam's fingers. She was torn at that moment. She wanted her release, but she didn't want to *not* feel anymore.

He felt her clench around him. She was almost there. He knew it. She was feeling it and that's all he wanted. "Come on, Libby. Feel it." He thrust his fingers even faster inside her, sucking on her clit.

She screamed out in pleasure as she came apart underneath his tongue, the waves of gratification overtaking her entire core, her vision blurry from the intense sensation. When the last of the aftershocks subsided, she reached down and grabbed Cam's face, bringing it to hers. She kissed him deeply, tasting her juices on his lips.

"Cam," she said quietly. "I need you inside me." She pressed her lips on his, running her hands down his back, savoring the feeling of his muscles through his shirt.

He groaned before reaching into his pocket and pulling out a foil packet. He quickly lowered his pants and removed his shirt, his eyes locked on Olivia's. "Are you sure, Libby?" he asked when he returned to the couch, staring down at her beautiful naked body.

She nodded fervently, reaching up for his arm and pulling his body down on top of hers. "I need it, Cam. Please."

He leaned back and quickly tore open the condom packet, sliding it on. Propping himself on one arm and positioning himself at Olivia's opening, he leaned down and kissed her gently. "I've been waiting for this since I first set eyes on you, Libby," he breathed against her lips as he slowly slid into her, filling her with his arousal. He didn't fill her like Alexander did, but it was still an incredible sensation.

"You okay?" Cam asked as he steadily moved back and forth inside of her, stretching her to match his size.

Olivia nodded her head. "Yes, Cam. Don't stop," she begged as he picked up his pace. She began thrusting with him, meeting the tempo he set, desperate to find her release again, but she had a feeling it wasn't going to happen. The electricity wasn't there. Not like it was with Alexander.

"You feel that, Libby?" he grunted as his pace quickened.

"Yes, Cam. Yes," she exclaimed loudly.

"God, you feel amazing," he said against her neck, gently tracing lines up to her earlobe. "Libby, what are you doing to me?" He looked down at the woman lying naked below him, moving with his rhythm.

His words flooded Olivia with guilt. *What am I doing to him?* she thought. She knew she was using him. It was clear Cam had real feelings for her. Maybe she could have feelings for him, too. She gazed into his eyes, hoping to feel something for him. But it never came. Not wanting to stare into his eyes, she pulled his face to hers and kissed him, running her hands up and down his chiseled back.

His tempo increased and he grunted against her neck. Olivia knew he was close. She could feel it in the way he thrust into her. She dug her nails into his back, setting him off.

"Oh, Libby!" he quivered, his body shaking on top of her as he shuddered, finding his release and pumping into her a few last times. He collapsed on top of her, totally spent, as she gently caressed his sweat-drenched hair, both their breathing still ragged.

After lying there for several long moments, Cam slowly got up, withdrawing from her. He removed the condom and pulled on his boxer shorts, sitting back down next to her. She leaned up and gave him a gentle kiss on the lips. "Thank you, Cam."

"What are you thanking me for?" he asked, running his hand up and down her arm, savoring the soft flesh.

"For making me feel again. I needed that."

Cam smiled. "Well, anytime you need to feel, I'm more than happy to help. Damn, Libby," he exhaled, running his hands through his hair. "That was fucking intense."

Olivia smiled, his compliment sending sparks through her body. Not fireworks, but it was still better than nothing.

"I hate to do this, but I should probably get back to my place. I do need to work tomorrow." He stood up, grabbing his shirt and pants.

Olivia grabbed her underwear and put them on. "Wait, Cam. Stay. Please. I don't know if I can bear being alone tonight."

Cam's heart sank as he stared into her big brown eyes. The sadness was overwhelming. He sighed, wondering what made her seem so broken. "Okay. Anything for you, beautiful." He winked and grabbed her hand. "Bedroom is upstairs, I assume?" Olivia nodded and followed him up the stairs.

That night, for the first time in over a month, she fell asleep with a man's arms around her and it felt good.

Until those haunting green eyes invaded her dreams again.

CHAPTER ELEVEN

HUMANITY

"JESUS, LIBBY, WAKE UP!" Cam shouted, shaking her.

Her eyes flung open, taking in her surroundings. It was warm, and there was something else in her bed. Cam. *He's still here*, she thought.

"Fuck, Libby. What's going on with you?" he asked, flipping her around so she faced him. Olivia searched his silver eyes that were awash with concern and compassion. Reaching out, he wiped her tear-stained eyes with his thumb, gently brushing his lips against her forehead. "You're worrying me," he whispered.

Olivia bolted from the bed, grabbed a t-shirt, and threw it on. "I'm fine, Cam," she spat out viciously. "I don't want you to worry about me. I don't want anyone worrying about me. Just let it go, okay?"

She scurried down the stairs, trying to forget her dream. The boy with the green eyes continued haunting her dreams, and he kept morphing into Alexander.

"Libby, wait!" Cam cried, running down the stairs and into the kitchen. He watched as Olivia opened a semi-full bottle of whiskey and drank straight from it. "What are you doing?"

She took a breath before throwing the bottle back, drinking more. "What does it look like?! This is the only thing that takes those fucking dreams away, Cam!" she cried out, her hands shaking. "How the fuck would you feel if, every night, you watch your parents die?! EVERY! FUCKING! NIGHT!" Her cries became more and more desperate with each breath.

"And then you see the person who saved you and you don't know who the fuck it is, but you know that you should! I don't know how much longer I can do this," she moaned, sinking down to the kitchen floor, clutching the bottle in her hand as if her life depended on it.

Cam lowered himself to the ground and sat next to her. He leaned against the cabinets and watched with sympathy as she threw back the bottle once more, taking another long drag. He said quietly, "You know, there are pills that you can try if you don't want those dreams anymore."

She shook her head vehemently, her sobs heavy. "No. I'm not going to use chemicals. My doctor already gave me valium, which I refuse to take, to help with the panic attacks."

He raised his eyebrows. "So, then, what's the deal with that whiskey bottle you're holding?"

"Fuck you," she spat out, glaring at him.

Cam sighed, placing his arm around her shoulders, trying to comfort her. "Sorry, Libby. I just hate to see you upset. Tell me what I can do and I'll do it."

Olivia took another swig of the bottle. "Nothing, Cam. There is nothing you can do. There is nothing anyone can do. This is my fucking life. I destroy people so you should stay far away from me because I'll just destroy you, too." She stood up and threw the now empty whiskey bottle into the garbage before walking over to the window, staring out into the dark ocean. She noticed a black SUV parked a few hundred yards down the sandy road. Her heart fell as she stumbled over to the couch, falling flat on her stomach. She was emotionally drained. She wanted to shut it all off. Why did *he* have to come to her island and find her?

"Easy, Libby." Cam scurried off the kitchen floor and into the living room, kneeling down next to the couch.

"I'm broken, Cam," Olivia slurred, turning her head to look at him. "I'm broken and he keeps popping up. I can't make it fucking stop."

He pulled back slightly. "What are you talking about, Libby? Who are you running from? Did somebody hurt you?" The worry in his voice mirrored the unsettled look now etched across his face. He had dealt with many victims of domestic violence in the past. He wondered if that was what made Olivia leave her home and come here, trying to escape an abusive relationship.

Olivia sighed. "Nobody hurt me," she murmured. "Although I probably deserve it. I'm the one who did the hurting. I ruin things, Cam. I ruin everything. I *ruined* everything."

He brushed away the brown tendrils of hair that had fallen into her eyes, caressing the scar on her forehead. He wondered where that had come from. "I don't know what you're talking about right now, Libby, but I want to know. I want to help you."

Olivia eyed him suspiciously.

He chuckled. "Not as a therapist. As a friend."

Wiping her eyes, she turned her head and looked into Cam's eyes, wishing they were green. "I could really use a friend right now. I hate feeling so alone."

"I promise you. I'll never let you feel alone again. Okay, Libby? You can trust me."

Fuck! Those words. Olivia howled, her sobs overtaking her entire body.

Cam had no idea what he said that could have possibly set her off like that. "Come on, Libby. Calm down. It's all okay," he reassured her, rubbing her back.

Olivia shook her head back and forth, closing her eyes. "No. I don't think it will be," she spat out through her tears. "Maybe it would be better if I couldn't feel anything, Cam. I just don't want to feel anymore."

He continued soothing her sobs, wrapping his arms around her small frame. "You don't mean that," he said, kissing the top of her head. "I know sometimes our feelings can be a little overwhelming, but that's what makes us human. You don't want to shut that off, Libby. Now, let's get you back to bed so you can try to forget all about whatever's upsetting you, even if for just a minute."

Cam helped her off the couch and brought her back to the bedroom, pulling her to his body, gently comforting the last of the tears away. He sighed as he heard her breathing become even, indicating that she had finally found sleep.

Over the course of the night, he held her tightly, comforting her screams and cries when she woke up. He was terrified for her having to deal with those dreams nearly every night. He wondered if what she told him was true. Could simply reliving the night of her parents' deaths really be causing all this pain? Or was it something else? Was it some*one* else? As he listened to her breathing, he heard her start mumbling the name Alexander over and over again.

Cam knew he had his answer.

CHAPTER TWELVE

BROKEN

THE FOLLOWING MORNING, ALEXANDER woke up early, nursing a hangover, and checked in with Martin. He was somewhat evasive when responding to Alexander's questions so he decided it was time to see for himself where Olivia lived. He grabbed the Mercedes and set out for a short drive to the north side of the island. The sun had begun to rise through some rather ominous-looking clouds over the horizon, and he wondered whether Olivia was up and feeling as miserable as he was.

He watched large condo towers turn into smaller stilt houses as he made his way north. Turning onto Ocean Avenue, he drove a few short blocks before finding the house that he was searching for. He nodded to Martin, indicating that it was okay for him to go. Looking over the two-story beach cottage, he saw Olivia's Audi parked in the driveway, but there was another car, too. It was the Lexus from the night before.

Alexander pulled on the side of the sandy road between Olivia's house and the sand dunes, punching the steering wheel, anger overwhelming his entire being. How could she move on so quickly? He became sick at the thought of someone else kissing her, touching her, making her feel good. *He* wanted to do that. It was his job. But, no. She pushed him away and now here he was, ready to beg for her to come back.

Putting his car in park, he watched as surfers rode some large waves into the shore, the sun trying to peek out behind black storm clouds lighting the entire beach in an orange hue that made Alexander want to see red. He felt as if his entire world had been ripped apart. His heart ached thinking about another man lying in the same bed as Olivia…not caring that *he* hadn't remained faithful.

He heard a door open and close. The only other sounds were the ocean waves and the distant rumble of thunder. Watching a tall, lean man walk out of Olivia's house, he had to control his desire to walk up and punch him for no reason other than that he was fucking the love of his life. At least, that's what Alexander assumed.

He observed Olivia's overnight guest appear to be somewhat disheveled as he made his way from her front deck to his Lexus. It was readily apparent that he was upset about something. Then Alexander noticed the front door open and Olivia ran out.

"Cam, wait!" she shouted. "I'm sorry. I just…I just don't do this thing very well."

The fucker's name is Cam, Alexander said to himself as he crouched down in his rental car, listening to their conversation, thankful that he was close enough to overhear it above the crashing waves and wind.

"Don't do what, Libby?" Alexander heard Cam cry out. *Her name is Olivia, fucker!* It took all of his willpower to not run up to her at that moment and sweep her into his arms. She looked miserable.

"Because there is something going on with you, and I don't know what the fuck to think!" Cam exclaimed and Alexander could hear the exasperation in his voice. He had sounded that way with Olivia on countless occasions himself. "Didn't you enjoy last night?"

Red! Red! Red! All Alexander could see was red. The thought of someone else being inside of her made him wild with anger. Alexander looked at her, noticing a touch of hesitation as she gently caressed Cam's cheek.

Sighing deeply, she responded. "Of course I did. I just needed to feel something again, Cam. But I don't know how to do the relationship thing very well. So, please, let's just start over, okay? I'm sorry if I sounded so cold before. I was wrong.

Please."

"Damn it, Libby! All I did was ask if I could see you tonight and you flipped out, asking why I would ever want to spend time with you! Why are you doing this? You're pushing me away. Don't do that. Please. Just..." Cam dropped his voice to an almost whisper. "Just let me in. I beg you." He brought his thumb up to Olivia's cheek, wiping a tear that had begun to fall.

"I don't think I can. I already gave my heart away once and, the thing is, I never really got it back. Not all of it, anyway. I'm broken and I don't think I'll ever really be able to let you in. Not all the way."

Cam pulled Olivia into his arms, gently kissing the top of her head, trying to soothe her sobs. "I've said it before and I'll say it again. I'll take whatever it is you can give me. If you can't give me all your heart, you don't have to. Just give me something. I just want to be able to spend more time with you. Okay?"

Olivia pulled out of his embrace and looked into his gentle silver eyes moist with emotion. She slowly nodded. "I guess I don't understand why you want to spend time with me so badly, knowing that I can't give you what you probably want."

He leaned down and kissed her forehead. "I don't care about that, Libby. Maybe today you can't give me what I want. And maybe not next week or even next month. But maybe, just maybe, you'll wake up one day and finally see what's right in front of you." He brushed her lips with his, kissing her gently. "And knowing that you may open your heart to me eventually is good enough for me. You deserve to be with someone who makes you happy, someone who won't hurt you." Clutching her hands in his, he took a deep breath. "I don't know what it is about you, Libby, but I can't stay away from you. Please. Don't push me away."

She searched his eyes for the answer she needed.

"Don't say anything right now. I'm going to go to work. Let's forget about tonight. Take some time to yourself, and I'll see you tomorrow morning like old times. Surfing. Then you can tell me what you think you want. Okay?"

Alexander watched with bated breath as Olivia pulled her bottom lip into her teeth, contemplating Cam's words. *Tell him to fuck off!*

"Okay. I can do that." Olivia looked down at her feet, something that made Alexander's heart race. She always did that. Then she looked out at the horizon before settling her eyes on the Mercedes parked where the SUV was the night before.

"Are you okay, Libby?" Cam asked after seeing her intake a quick breath as if something caught her off-guard. He turned his head to follow Olivia's gaze and noticed a nice red Mercedes convertible sitting on the road, the driver clearly interested in looking at the storm bringing crashing waves to the shore.

"Yes. I'm fine," she responded. Cam looked at her with a questioning look as she straightened her back, keeping herself turned in the direction of the Mercedes.

"Okay, beautiful." He grabbed Olivia's hand and planted delicate kisses on her knuckles. "I'll be thinking about you all day."

She blushed, returning his gaze.

"Until tomorrow, angel," he said, his voice husky as he pulled Olivia into a tight embrace, kissing her deeply on the mouth.

She half-heartedly returned the kiss and Alexander could feel her lack of enthusiasm. *Good*, he thought to himself.

Cam pulled out of the kiss, noticing Olivia's hesitation. Sighing, he walked down the front steps of her deck and retreated into his car.

Olivia stood frozen in place, watching the ocean waves, unsure of what to do next, knowing Alexander had seen their entire exchange.

Once the Lexus pulled down the road, Alexander jumped out of his Mercedes. Olivia immediately turned to head back into her house, desperately wanting to forget that he was even there. She needed to forget about him, which was becoming difficult since he had shown up on her little island.

"Olivia, love!" Alexander shouted, leaping up the stairs and onto her front deck, grabbing her arm. Shivers ran up and down her spine from the contact. He spun her around, making her face him. "Please. I beg you. I just want to talk," he said quietly, his eyes pleading with her as thunder sounded in the distance.

Crossing her arms, she gazed into his deep green eyes that held so much pain. She knew she had caused that pain, but she couldn't be with him. Those five little words still replayed in her memory each and every day. They haunted her dreams at night. *It will destroy me, too.*

"Please, Olivia. I don't know who I am without you…" Alexander said quietly, taking a step closer and lightly caressing her bare arm. He leaned down. "I know you can still feel it," he whispered, his breath hot against her neck. "I feel it, too. Don't deny your body…or your heart." A large rain drop fell on the deck followed by several more.

His words broke Olivia apart. "No, Alexander. I'm not doing this. I told you why I left. I'll only hurt you. So, please, forget about me. I beg you." She whipped around quickly, frantically seeking the comfort of the four walls of her beach house.

"Just answer me one question, Olivia," Alexander said loudly over the rain that had begun to drench them both. His tone gave her pause. She slowly turned around to face him.

Taking a step toward her, he gently brushed her damp hair back, caressing the scar on her forehead. "Does he make you come the way I do?" he asked, his voice husky with desire for the woman standing in front of him.

Olivia's head shot up.

"Does he know how to make your body react with just a simple touch?" He ran his fingers down her arm, making her entire body want to melt into his. "Does he drive you wild when he's inside you?" Placing his hand on the small of her back, he pulled her against him. Lightening coursed through her soul from feeling Alexander's body flush with hers again. He leaned down, his lips feathering soft kisses along her neck. "Is he strong enough to be with you? Does he make you feel whole?"

Olivia scrambled to get out of his embrace, needing to distance herself from him. She looked down at her feet, not wanting to look into the same green eyes that found her in her dreams each and every night.

"Olivia, look at me."

She raised her head quickly, her body betraying her by so eagerly obeying Alexander's demand.

"Do you really want to live life without me in it?!" he cried out.

Olivia's chin trembled as she thought about what life without Alexander had been like. She hated every second of it, but she couldn't be with him. It would only end badly for all involved. "I can't, Alexander," she quivered. "I wish I could, but I just can't."

"Why, Olivia? Please. Tell me why and I'll leave you alone. Why him and not me?"

She stared into his eyes as they fought back tears. "You want to know why?" she spat out. "Because I'll never love him. I can walk away from Cam anytime because I don't feel anything for him. And I just don't want to feel, Alexander. I'm done feeling. It hurts too much. My entire life, everyone I've ever cared about has been ripped from my world. You said it yourself. I'll just destroy you, too. So, please, go home. Find someone else and forget that I ever walked into your life that night back in August. Please. I beg you. I'll never be able to get over my past." Olivia brought her hand up to wipe at the tears that were flowing down her cheeks.

"That's not your decision to make, love."

She melted at his term of endearment. Alexander placed his hand on the small of her back again, pulling her body toward his. She gasped at his erection pressed against her stomach. "I want you to feel, Olivia," he whispered. "I want to you to feel me. Don't deny your body what it needs." He leaned down, planting gentle kisses on her neck. "I've missed the smell and feel of your skin, love."

She stilled, not wanting to get pulled back into his web. "Do. Not. Call. Me. That." She pushed against him, ridding herself of his embrace and heading toward her front door.

"Please, Olivia…" Alexander begged.

"I've kept my end of the bargain, Alex," she hissed, spinning around, her eyes blazing. "I told you why him. So leave." She lowered her voice. "Please, Alex. You need to forget about me." He was so close and Olivia could feel her resolve starting to melt. She secretly wanted to jump on him, kiss him deeply, and feel him inside of her. But she couldn't do that. She needed to forget about him. The attraction scared her to death and she knew that she would only end up shattered in the end. She knew she couldn't deal with that pain.

He pulled back, looking at her. "Tell me you don't want me in your life and I'll go. I want to hear you say the words, Olivia. Tell me you don't care about me. That you've moved on. That you're happy. Say the words, and I'll leave right now and forget all about you." A tear fell down his cheek as a lump formed in his throat from the thought of losing his Olivia once more. "Say the words, love, and you'll never have to see my face again."

Olivia stood staring at him while rain pummeled the coast, causing her to shake from the dampness and cold air. "I'm happy, okay?!" she shouted. "I'm so fucking happy without you in my life!" She spun around, trying to get away from him. Olivia had no idea what had come over her. She didn't mean those words, but she said them anyway.

As a last desperate act, Alexander grabbed her, pulled her body into his, and crushed his mouth against hers. His hands roamed her body. She tried to push him away, but his strength was too much. The feeling of his tongue exploring her mouth and his hands caressing her body sent tremors through her entire being. She melted into the kiss as he dipped his hand into her shorts. "You can't possibly tell me you don't feel this, Olivia," he growled, inserting two fingers inside her. "Your body betrays your words. I don't believe a fucking word you say." He covered her mouth with his before she could even protest.

He forced her against the door, reaching for the handle with his spare hand as he continued his relentless assault against her.

T.K. Leigh

She didn't know what to think. She needed Alexander out of her life, but her body was on fire from his mouth pressed against hers, his tongue and fingers invading her. She couldn't help but to kiss him back, running her fingers through his hair and pressing her body against his even more. No matter how hard she tried, she couldn't get close enough to him.

Alexander dragged her inside, pushing her up against the wall as he closed the door.

"Alex," she whimpered.

"Tell me you don't want this, Olivia. I need to hear you say the fucking words." He continued thrusting his fingers inside of her. He lowered her shorts before quickly unbuttoning his own, sliding them down. He positioned himself at her wet entrance, panting from the proximity. "Tell me, Olivia," he growled, waiting for her to respond. "Say you don't want me."

Olivia couldn't form any thoughts, the feeling of his arousal on her clit overwhelming. Staring into his intense green eyes, her mouth refused to form the words that weren't true.

"God damn it, Olivia." He slammed into her, causing her to throw her head back in ecstasy. "Tell me Cam makes you feel like this when he's fucking you. Tell me he drives you crazy like I do." He continued thrusting into her, savoring the feeling of being inside her. It felt right. It felt like home.

"Lift me up, Alex," Olivia breathed out. "I need to feel you closer," she begged.

Alexander did as she asked and lifted her up, steadying her as she wrapped her long legs around his waist.

"Is that better?"

"God, yes," she responded. "Faster, Alex. I need to feel you." She began thrusting against him, savoring the closeness that she had been missing ever since she ran. He matched her tempo. Something about Alexander being back inside her made everything seem alright again. She was climbing higher and higher toward her peak, and she could see the edge in sight. But, unlike so many other times, she didn't know if Alexander would always be there to catch her. She didn't know if she wanted him to catch her anymore.

Olivia's breathing became heavy and Alexander felt a

78

familiar clenching around him. He continued driving into her, wanting to come with her. As she screamed out his name, he let go. "Tell me every time that Cam fucks you he makes you come like that!" He thrust one last time, emptying himself inside of her as she convulsed around him. He kept her pinned to the wall for several long moments as he tried to regulate his breathing.

After she finally came down from her earth-shattering orgasm, Olivia opened her eyes and stared into Alexander's haunting green ones...the same green eyes that she kept seeing in her dreams. Those eyes that told her she would only destroy him, too.

She desperately needed to clear her head. *What the fuck just happened?* She couldn't let Alexander back in. She pushed against him, ridding herself of his grasp, tears flowing. With shaky hands, the aftershocks of her orgasm still ravaging her body, she raised her shorts and stormed upstairs, embarrassed about what had just happened.

"Olivia!" Alexander shouted, his chest heaving as he raised his shorts. "Answer me! Does Cam make you feel as good as I do? Do not run away from me!"

She turned around, bolting back downstairs, and slapped his face hard. "You want a fucking answer?!" she roared. "YES! He makes me come better than that every fucking time! His dick fills me up like I've never been filled before! Now get the fuck out of my house!" Tears streamed down her face as she fell to the ground, unable to muster the strength to stand anymore. "Please," she whimpered. "Leave me alone."

Alexander looked down, knowing that it was his fault the girl in front of him appeared so broken. He thought about telling her everything, but he just couldn't. He couldn't form the words that she probably needed to hear. So, instead, he remained silent as he took in her shaking form.

"Please. Move on. I beg you. Forget you ever met me. I need you to do that," she pleaded quietly. "I can't survive if you don't."

"Olivia," Alexander whispered, his voice soft. "Is that really what you want?"

She looked up at him, the hurt in her eyes overwhelming. "Yes," she answered, lying through her teeth.

Alexander's heart sank, not really believing her but deciding to respect her wishes. He had no fight left in him. "Okay. I'll go then." He took a few steps toward the front door and opened it. "I'll be sure to have your credit card reported as stolen so that no one else can track you."

He turned and walked out of her house, hearing loud crying wails as he made his way down the front steps and into his rain-soaked car, angry at himself for causing her such pain. He thought about going back, but knew it would only make matters worse.

He grabbed his cell phone and dialed a number. "Martin, Burnham here. Prepare the jet. We're leaving immediately." He threw his phone on the seat, not caring about the torrential downpour covering him with water as he drove through the streets of Amelia Island for the last time.

CHAPTER THIRTEEN

A STEP IN THE RIGHT DIRECTION

OLIVIA STAYED CURLED UP on the hardwood floor of her beach house for most of the day, bawling her eyes out, certain that her loud wails overpowered the steady rain that pounded the shore that cold, dismal Monday in November. Her entire body hurt from lying on the hard floor, but it was a pain she welcomed with open arms. It helped dull the ache in her chest. She could still feel his hands on her, she could still smell his scent covering her body, and she could still feel the overwhelming sensation of pure ecstasy from him being inside her.

Screaming, she shot up, desperate to wash every trace of Alexander off her. She gazed out the large windows to see that night had fallen. Out on the horizon, lightening streaked through the sky, highlighting palm trees swaying steadily back and forth in the strong winds. The weather fit her mood perfectly. Dismal.

Running up the stairs to her bedroom, she nearly tripped over Nepenthe as she stripped out of her clothes, eager to burn them. They still smelled like *him*, too. She turned on her shower to the highest setting possible and, over the next twenty minutes, tried to scorch Alexander off her body, scrubbing frantically at every inch of herself.

After finishing her shower, she quickly got dressed, tossing her clothes into the garbage. She crawled into bed, wanting to forget the day. Sleep avoided her most of the night, Alexander's green eyes appearing every time she closed hers.

As she watched the sun begin to rise on the horizon, she screamed, desperate to find some relief from the pain that she felt. Then she remembered that Cam would be there to go surfing soon. A sudden feeling of relief washed over her. That was her answer. *Cam.* He could take the pain away, just like he had done the past few days.

She jumped out of bed and ran downstairs to make a cup of coffee, hoping that Cam hadn't already been there. Grabbing her now filled coffee mug, she ran to the front door, searching for his Jeep. She breathed a sigh of relief when it wasn't parked out front. As she sat down, taking in the waves that the storm from the previous day had left in its wake, she heard the familiar rumble of his Wrangler driving along the sandy road.

She smiled weakly, thankful there was someone in her life that could help her forget Alexander, even if for just a little while.

"Morning, beautiful," Cam called out, hopping out of his Jeep and walking the short distance toward where Olivia sat on her deck. He took in her disheveled appearance. Something looked off. Her eyes were swollen and puffy, and it looked like she hadn't slept. "You okay?" he asked, a concerned look on his face.

"Yeah, I'm fine. Just didn't sleep last night."

"Anything I can do to help?" he asked.

She wanted to tell him all about Alexander unexpectedly showing up, but she just couldn't. She wanted to tell him that she fell apart when Alexander pressed his body against her, making her feel things that she had pushed away those last few months, but the words never came. Instead, she simply smiled. "No. I'll get over it."

He leaned down and gave her a quick kiss on the forehead. "I'm going to go catch some waves. See you in a little bit?"

Olivia nodded as she watched him run away toward the shoreline, wondering if she could really replace Alexander with Cam. She had to. It wasn't an option. She made it quite clear to Alexander that she felt nothing for him. It wasn't the truth, but it had to be done.

"Penny for your thoughts?" a voice said several minutes

later.

She turned and smiled at Cam. "What are you doing back so soon?" she asked, taking in his naked chest as he stood in front of her with his wetsuit unzipped and hanging off his hips, that delicious little V showing. Her heart raced as she thought of Sunday night and his rather talented tongue. For a brief moment, she forgot all about Alexander and the heartache she felt from pushing him away. Again.

"I missed you. Why surf when I can spend time with a beautiful woman?"

Olivia blushed as Cam sat down in the wicker chair next to her, staring her deep in the eyes. "Have you given any thought to what we talked about yesterday, doll face?"

She exhaled loudly, placing her coffee mug on the small lounge table in front of her. In fact, she hadn't really given much thought at all to what she wanted with Cam. She knew that, once she slept with him, things would change. But she wasn't sure she wanted that. Maybe all she really wanted was someone to make her feel something other than the dull pain.

"Come on, Libby. Talk to me. You've got that look again, and it's taking all my willpower to not take you into that house and bury myself inside you." His voice was husky and sexy. Olivia thought about how much she would really enjoy that. She desperately wanted to erase all traces of Alexander from her life and she needed Cam to help her. "But I'm not going to do that," he admitted, bringing Olivia back from her thoughts.

"Why?" she asked, the hurt apparent across her face.

"Because, Libby. You use sex as a coping mechanism. You use it so you don't have to deal with your real emotions. And, as fucking great as it was, I can't, in good conscience, sleep with you again, knowing that it's only stunting your emotional development."

Olivia stood up quickly. "You know what? Fuck you. You don't know anything about me, *Dr. Cameron*," she hissed snidely. "So take your psychobabble bullshit somewhere else, okay?" She stormed across the deck toward her front door, the pain of pushing Alexander away threatening to return. She needed Cam to dull that pain and now he was telling her he didn't want that role. He saw right through what she was doing and she hated him for it.

"Jesus Christ, Olivia. Calm down!" he exclaimed, shooting up and grabbing her arm before she could retreat into the house, locking away the world and all its problems as she wallowed in her own misery. "I like you, Libby. A lot. And I want to help you feel again. And, holy shit, do I ever want to feel your body spasm as I make you come. But I think we rushed into things. I genuinely care about you. I want to sleep with you for the right reasons and not the wrong reasons." He took a step closer, brushing a wayward curl behind her ear. "I'm scared to lose you," he said quietly.

Olivia stood there, staring at her feet, the warmth from Cam's body sending tiny shivers up and down her spine at his sweet words. "I'm not yours to lose, Cam." A tear fell down her cheek. God, she was sick of only feeling pain. When would it all end?

"Olivia, please. I want you to be mine, but I also know you have problems that you need to start addressing. I couldn't live with myself if I don't at least recognize that. It's going to take all my willpower to not sleep with you right now. I want to help you…as a friend who really wants to get into your pants again." He winked. "We need for you to find a more healthy coping mechanism than sex. That would be a step in the right direction. Please, Olivia. For me." He grabbed her hand, caressing her knuckles. "And for you."

"I need to make a phone call," she said dryly.

"But you don't have a phone. Who are you calling?"

"You're the doctor who told me I need to find a healthy coping mechanism. I'm following your fucking advice," she explained.

Cam raised his eyebrows at her, looking for further explanation.

"Are men really that obtuse? Music. I need a piano."

A smile spread across his face.

~~~~~~~~~~

After landing back in Boston, Alexander went about his normal routine. Get up. Shower. Walk the dog. Eat. Work. Go home. The last vestige of his military training: When it all goes to shit, remember the routine. So that's what he did. He resumed his routine, trying to block Olivia from his memory.

He had his answer. He tried to make her want him, to need him, but she didn't. It was time to move on. As he poured himself a scotch to dull the pain, the door buzzer sounded.

"Chelsea," Alexander said breathlessly as the door slid open.

"Alex. I heard you were back in town," she said quietly, looking around the penthouse for any indication as to whether he had a guest or not.

"You heard right," he responded, running his fingers through his hair. "I'm sorry. I meant to ca…"

"It's okay, Alex," she interrupted. "I was just wondering if you've thought about what I said on the phone…"

"I have," he said nervously.

Chelsea raised her eyebrows, wanting an answer.

Taking a deep breath, he closed the distance between them, pulling her body against his. "I'm sorry I was such a fool, Chelsea," he breathed against her neck. "I should never have ignored what was right in front of me. I want to make it up to you. I want to do this right."

Chelsea searched his eyes. "So, you want…"

"Yes, Chelsea. I want something more, too. Let me take you to dinner. A real date."

A smile crept across her face. "I'd like that, Alex," she responded.

He placed a kiss on her forehead before grabbing her hand and leaving the apartment, eager to forget that he ever found his Olivia all those months ago.

~~~~~~~~~~

It felt like Christmas came early later that week when a large truck pulled up outside of Olivia's cottage. Within ten minutes, a piano sat in the spare bedroom downstairs, waiting to be played. Olivia wondered why she hadn't thought about buying a piano before.

Earlier that week, Cam drove her to a piano showroom in Jacksonville where she purchased a Kawai console piano. Thankfully, on that shopping trip, Olivia remembered her stash of cash from home. Cam raised an eyebrow when she pulled out stacks of hundred dollar bills to pay the six thousand plus sum for the piano.

"I told you. I don't want to be found. No paper trail."

"It's not that. It's just...I don't know. You don't work, yet you just pull out six grand in cash like it's nothing. I mean, I do well for myself, but what did you do? Rob a bank or something?" he asked semi-jokingly.

Olivia shrugged. "Mom was loaded. She left me with more money than I can even fathom spending in a lifetime. It's not all it's cracked up to be. I'd give up the money in a second if it meant my mom would still be alive."

As she sat in front of her piano, recalling Cam's reaction earlier that week, a warmth spread through her core. After her admission, he pulled her body into his, kissing her full on the mouth right in the middle of the piano showroom. "God, Libby. You get more and more attractive every minute I spend with you."

She wished she had the same enthusiasm for him as he appeared to have for her. To her, Cam was just someone who could dull the pain. Nothing more.

Just as Olivia placed her fingers delicately on the cool ivory that breezy Thursday morning, she heard a gentle knock on the door. She smiled weakly when she saw Cam standing on her deck wearing his wetsuit. "Morning, beautiful," he crooned, a sparkle in his intense silver eyes. "Everything okay?"

Olivia shrugged, turning away, leaving the door open for him to follow her. "As okay as it'll ever be, I suppose."

Cam stopped, wishing he could get her to come out of the shell she seemed to be in. "Don't do that, Libby."

She turned around from the coffee maker, thrusting a cup of coffee into his hands. "Do what?" she spat.

He narrowed his eyes at her. "You know what," he said

quietly, taking a long drink from his mug. "You're doing it again. You're trying to push me away."

Olivia sighed. "Please, Cam. I just want to be alone right now. I want to sit at my piano and play until my fingers bleed. You said yourself that I needed a healthy coping mechanism. So unless you want to sprawl me out on my bed and fuck me, I suggest you leave me be."

Setting his coffee mug on the kitchen island, he placed his hand on the small of Olivia's back, pulling her body toward his and gently pushing his erection between her legs. "Has anyone ever told you how exasperating you can be sometimes?" he whispered in a sultry voice, the warmth of his breath hot against her skin. "And, for the record, I'd love to fuck you, but I refuse to be your enabler."

Olivia's body was aflame with desire, her mind consumed by the thought of Cam being inside her to dull the heartache. She pushed her body even further into his, wrapping her arms around his neck and running her fingers through his hair. "Cam," she exhaled breathlessly. "Either fuck me or let me get back to playing my piano." She dragged her tongue against his neck, causing the hair follicles on his body to stand on end.

"Damn, Libby." He stepped back, needing his distance from her before he did the one thing that would hurt her. "I'll let you get back to your music."

Olivia frowned. "What's it going to take to get you to crack?"

"A lot more than just a pretty smile, although yours is spectacular." He winked before walking out the front door toward the shoreline.

Returning her attention to the piano, she poured her heart and soul into the ivory keys, willing it to dull the pain. After playing all morning, the heartache was still there, all the songs reminding her of Alexander. She wished she could just erase him from her mind. And her heart.

~~~~~~~~~~

Over the next several weeks, Olivia remained glued to her

piano, seeking comfort among the white and black keys. Comfort that never came. She thought about Alexander, wondering whether he had moved on. She hoped he had. As much as the thought of his lips touching someone else made her want to scream, she needed him to move on.

Cam's visits were the only thing she looked forward to, although she would never admit it. She remained distant and aloof, still trying to get him to break down and sleep with her to take away the ever-present pain. He remained strong, but Olivia could tell it was only a matter of time before he cracked.

"Happy Thanksgiving," he said one morning as he walked into Olivia's kitchen after she opened the door for him.

"It's Thanksgiving?" she asked, a confused look on her face. "I guess I completely lost track of time." She shrugged, returning to the guest bedroom and the only friend she felt she had in the world. Her piano.

"Yes, it's Thanksgiving, and I'm not going to let you spend the holiday alone," he said, following her into the guest room and closing the cover on the piano. "Come out with me tonight. It's 'Open Mic' night and I think you could really benefit from playing in public again."

Olivia eyed him suspiciously.

"Come on, Libby. Just the other day, you said how much you missed performing in front of an audience. This is the perfect opportunity. Even if you don't want to get up on stage, at least come out with me and the guys tonight. It'll be fun. I promise."

Olivia searched his eyes. "I don't know. I'm not so sure it's a good idea."

"Libby, you need to get over whatever it is that's keeping you down. Staying locked up and playing piano all day is not the way to do that. You're closing up again. Please. Come back to me."

Exhaling loudly, she took a sip of her coffee as her eyes remained glued to Cam's. "Fine," she said, caving in to his request. "But I'm not getting up on stage."

"You don't have to," Cam said quickly, putting his empty mug in the dishwasher. "Gotta run, gorgeous." He kissed her cheek sweetly. "Pick you up at eight." He planted a more affectionate kiss on her neck, leaving her body wanting some form of release as she watched him walk out the door.

CHAPTER FOURTEEN

GONE

THAT EVENING, CAM WAS at her house a few minutes before eight. "You're on time," Olivia said, opening the door. "You're always on time."

"I hate being late," he replied, holding his hand out for her. She grabbed it and he led her down to his car.

He glanced over at Olivia as she sat there, her eyes void of any emotion. The spark was gone. He raised her hand to his lips, kissing it gently, reminding her of all the times that Alexander used to do the same thing. She still couldn't get him out of her head, no matter how hard she tried. "You look beautiful tonight, Libby."

She returned a half-hearted smile, sick of how empty she felt. Nothing worked. Every time she closed her eyes, she saw Alexander's green eyes and felt his hands all over her body. She felt lifeless without his touch, her heart aching at the thought of never feeling his hands on her again. She wanted to stop feeling that pain.

They headed west toward the downtown area and pulled in front of a local bar. Olivia scowled when they walked up to the old building. From the outside, it appeared rather rundown.

"I know it doesn't look like much, but the drinks are strong and the music is good. I promise." Pressing his hand to the small of her back, he opened the door and steered her toward a table. She recognized three of the guys from surfing a few weeks earlier.

"Hey, Olivia! How's your head?" Benny asked as Cam held

a chair out for her.

"Better, thanks," she said, smiling. "Please, call me Libby."

"This is my girlfriend, Elsie," Benny said. Olivia smiled across the table at a tall woman in her twenties with raven black hair and bright red lipstick.

"Are you going to play anything tonight?" Elsie asked Olivia cheerily.

"I hadn't thought about it," she replied. She was happy to get out of her house and meet some new people. If this was to be her new home, maybe setting down new roots would help her forget about her old ones. But she didn't know if she could get on that stage and pour her heart out through music. The pain was still too raw.

"Libby used to go to 'Open Mic' night every week up north before she came here," Cam said.

Olivia shot daggers in his direction.

"She even used to sing in a band."

"That settles it then," Chris said excitedly. "You've got to get up there."

"Go put your name on the list," Jason chimed in.

She looked around the table, noticing how different all the guys looked out of their wetsuits. They all had that typical surfer look…sandy hair, tan skin, and a sparkle in their eyes.

"If you don't do it, I will," Cam said. Olivia stared back, ready to kill him. "It will make you feel better, I promise," he whispered before signaling a server. "What would you like to drink, sweetheart?"

The term of endearment sent shivers up her spine. She was eager to feel something for Cam again. Hell, maybe if she got up there and performed, he would finally cave and give her what she needed.

She smiled at him. "Well, if I'm getting up on that stage, I need something strong. Sapphire and tonic, easy on the tonic."

"That's my girl," he replied as Olivia got out of her chair, walked up to the small table next to the stage, and wrote down her name on the sign-up sheet. There were only about five people in front of her so it wouldn't be too long before it was her turn. She just hoped she had enough time to down a few drinks. A little liquid courage never hurt anyone.

Olivia returned to the table, thankful that her drink had arrived. "I ordered you a double, just in case," Cam said, bringing his drink to his mouth. Olivia's heart rate picked up a bit as she watched him lick his lips after tasting his whiskey.

"Thanks. I'm going to need it." She looked around the bar, noting that it was starting to fill up. No one had begun to perform yet so she assumed Open Mic didn't start until nine. She looked at the large stage, lit with just a few key lights casting low ambient light on the various guitars. There was a full-sized keyboard set into the shell of a baby grand piano, as well as a drum kit. As the bar filled up and the atmosphere buzzed with excitement, she actually started to look forward to performing.

After twenty minutes or so, an M.C. jumped onstage, warming up the crowd before announcing the first performer. Butterflies fluttered in Olivia's stomach. Cam looked over at her, dropped his hand underneath the table and, finding Olivia's, clutched it. "You'll do great," he said quietly, his breath warm on her neck. She held onto his hand, desperately wanting to feel something. Anything. But the spark that was there just a few minutes earlier was gone again.

After a few more performances, the M.C. walked back to the microphone stand. "Looks like we have a new one this week." Everyone cheered enthusiastically. Olivia assumed the bar got a lot of repeat performances. "Miss Olivia Adler."

"Good luck, Libby," Cam whispered in her ear and Olivia felt a sliver of a tingle. Nothing like she felt when Alexander would whisper in her ear, but at least she felt something other than the dull pain. Maybe Cam was right. She needed to get back on stage and perform to help her rid herself of the hold Alexander still had over her. She desperately wanted to be free of him. As she walked up to the stage, she knew exactly what song she needed to sing.

Sitting down at the keyboard, she adjusted the microphone to her level. She played a short little chord, checking the feeling of the keys. "Thanks. This is *Gravity* by Sara Bareilles. Hope you enjoy it."

She took a few breaths and began playing the opening lines, the melody slow and haunting. Cam sat on the edge of his seat watching her performance, her sweet voice cutting through the room, unable to mask her obvious pain.

As she sang, Olivia thought about the hold Alexander still possessed over her, causing her heart to ache from the loneliness of life without him. But it was a necessary self-imposed loneliness. It was almost Christmas and she had no one left with whom to celebrate the holidays. She pushed everyone away again, refusing to let anyone in. She hopelessly wished that her entire life was just a bad dream and that she would wake up in bed with Alexander any day. But she knew that wasn't the case. He found her and begged her to go back to him, and she pushed him away. Again.

Benny elbowed Cam. "She's good, man. Seems a little sad, but she's rocking." Cam simply nodded, staring at Olivia as she sang the first chorus, a hurt expression on her face while she pleaded to be set free. At that moment, Cam knew that something happened to her. Something recent. Maybe something to do with a man named Alexander, the name she murmured over and over again in her sleep that one night. Maybe he was the reason she left Boston and ended up on the little island. Nothing about her said that it was a planned move. Cam knew that she ran from something, but what? He told Olivia time and time again that he wouldn't pry, but how could he really help her get past it if he didn't know what it was?

Olivia continued singing as Cam scanned the room. Everyone was immersed in the performance. She definitely knew how to capture an audience. The emotion of the song was raw and real, and Cam was sure everyone in the audience could feel her pain. *He* could feel her pain. He wanted to take her pain away. He knew that if she begged him, he would crack. He didn't want to, but the pain was unbearable. He could see it now.

As she sang the bridge, Olivia turned her eyes from the audience, staring out into the distance as if singing to someone far away, and Cam knew that she was. That song wasn't meant for anyone in the room. The person the song was aimed at was in Boston. The song reached a fevered pitch and she belted out a desperate plea, the audience cheering wildly for the strength of Olivia's voice ringing through the bar. She moved on to the last chorus, her voice soft once more.

Olivia closed her eyes as she played the final chord, a tear escaping when she thought about the hold that Alexander would probably always have on her. Almost immediately, the crowd erupted in cheers and applause. She opened her eyes and stood up, turning to look at the audience cheering madly for her. She took a slight bow and walked off the stage, heading in the direction of the restroom, needing a moment before returning to the table.

She was standing in front of the bathroom mirror, composing herself, when Elsie walked in.

"Hey. There you are. Cam was getting worried, but I told him you probably just went to the bathroom. You okay?"

Olivia looked down at Elsie. She was absolutely beautiful. There were some girls that made some extra pounds look attractive and she was one of them. She had such a bright personality.

"Yeah. Sorry. I just needed a minute before going back to the table."

"Tough break-up, huh?" Elsie asked, leaning against the wall.

Olivia eyed her suspiciously. "How could you tell?"

She turned toward Olivia. "I'm a girl. We just know these things." She angled her head, looking at Olivia as if she was trying to put a puzzle together. "That's it!" Elsie shouted. "I knew you looked familiar. Duh!"

Olivia stared at her. "What do you mean?" she asked.

"You're the girl who used to date that rich guy up in Boston, right? Or who was rumored to be dating him anyway. Sorry. I'm obsessed with all those gossip magazines and shit. Your picture was in there a few times. Well, at least you look like her. I mean, there were only rumors and what not, but damn… Alexander Burnham. What a hottie! He's the type of guy that you just look at and think, 'Let me take your shirt off… And your pants'." Elsie laughed.

Olivia just stood there, shocked, her eyes wide, unable to formulate any response.

"Oh, whatever," Elsie continued. "Doesn't matter. But you look like her. That girl he was rumored to date. Never knew her name, though. No one did, but I guess he's dating someone else now. I was so distraught when I found that out. I was hoping to nab him next." She winked.

Olivia continued to stare at her reflection in the mirror. What did she mean Alexander was seeing someone else? So soon? It hadn't even been two weeks since he showed up on her doorstep, pleading with her. Was he already seeing someone back then?

"You must be thinking of someone else," Olivia said, finally finding her voice, trying to talk past the lump that had begun to form in her throat. "It wasn't me, whoever that girl was." She walked out of the bathroom, wanting to be alone.

Making her way past the bar, she stole a quick glance at the table where Cam sat speaking animatedly with his friends, then walked out the front door into the brisk Florida night. She looked up and down the street, trying to figure out where she was. Once she had her bearings, she headed east, deciding to walk the roughly three miles back to her cottage.

"Hey. Where's Olivia?" Cam asked when Elsie returned to the table several minutes after Olivia had stormed out of the ladies' room.

"She left the bathroom," Elsie replied, looking around the bar. "I thought she came back here. I hope she's okay."

"What did you say to her?" Cam growled.

"Hey," Benny interrupted, glaring at his friend. "Back off, man. Elsie isn't like that."

Cam took a deep breath. "I know. Sorry. But where'd she go?"

"Well, I mean, we were talking about how stupid men are," she replied, shooting Benny a glaring look as she feverishly typed something into her cell phone. "And then I saw her face in the light and it totally reminded me of that girl that was rumored to be dating that hot rich guy up in Boston. That

Navy SEAL hottie who has, like, a gazillion dollars and his own private security firm." The guys stared at her as she kept her eyes glued to her phone, looking for something. "Whatever. It's a girl thing, I guess. He's like the J.F.K., Jr. of the twenty-first century. He's one of the most eligible bachelors in the country. He's all over those gossip websites."

"Because we read those," Benny joked.

"Anyway," she said, rolling her eyes, keeping them locked on her phone. "I told her she looked like that girl, but she didn't say anything so I said it wasn't her. Then I told her the hottie was dating someone else. Here." She handed Cam the cell phone. "It looks like her so I wasn't totally crazy."

He looked at the photo. It had apparently been taken at a restaurant with a nautical theme. A fairly well-built man sat at the table, smiling at a beautiful woman, a dozen oysters sitting in front of them. The woman had dark hair and dark eyes. She was smiling a beautiful smile that lit up her entire being. "Damn it, Elsie," Cam said, shoving the phone back into her hands and standing up from the table. "It didn't look like her. It *is* her."

He left the bar in a panic, running down the street and jumping in his car. He slowly drove down Atlantic Avenue, desperately looking for Olivia. Unless she found a cab, which was hard to do on the island, she would be walking.

After about five minutes, he finally spotted her. He slowed and pulled up beside her, lowering the window. "Olivia. Get in the car. I'll drive you home."

She didn't even glance at him. "No, thank you. I could use a walk. Clear my head and all. I'll be fine."

Cam pulled the car along the side of the road. He quickly got out and sprinted toward her. "Hey," he said, running in front of her, stopping her in her tracks. "Don't be stupid. Let me give you a ride home. Something could happen to you. It's not safe to walk at night."

Olivia glared at him. "Why do you care?"

He sighed. *This woman is exasperating*, he thought. "Because that's the kind of person I am, Libby. I care about people, and I want to make sure you get home safe. That's all. I made you come out tonight, and you clearly did not enjoy yourself. So just let me drive you home."

Olivia glared at him, not saying a word. Her feet were starting to ache. It wasn't easy walking three miles in heels. "Fine. But the only reason I'm agreeing is because my feet hurt. I don't need you to be my 'white knight', saving me. Got it?"

"Fine. Fine. You're coming with me on your own terms. Got it." Cam winked.

"I really hate you sometimes," Olivia spat out, throwing open the door to the Lexus. Cam simply grinned at her. Something about her fiery spirit drew him in.

A few minutes later, he pulled up in front of Olivia's cottage. He walked her to the front door and stood by her side as she unlocked it. She turned to face him, searching his compassionate silver eyes. "I'm sorry I walked out on you," she said dryly.

He exhaled and looked down. "I know you're going through some stuff." He ran his hand through his hair, closing his eyes and taking a deep breath. "And, well, I just want to say…" His eyes returned to hers, blazing, as he leaned in, his face inches from hers. "I'll help you, Libby," he said, his voice husky. "I'll do whatever you want me to, as long as I never have to hear the pain in your voice that I heard tonight when you sang."

A tear fell down her cheek, unable to hold it in anymore. "Will you make it stop hurting, Cam?" she pleaded. "I don't want to feel anymore." She stared into his eyes, willing herself to feel anything other than the pain. But nothing came. Just the same dull ache and emptiness that she had grown so accustomed to since Alexander showed up here.

He exhaled. "How do you want me to do that? I need you to tell me exactly what you…"

Olivia crushed her lips to his. He moaned as he walked her into the house and, closing the door, pushed her against it, his mouth never leaving hers. He grabbed her ass and lifted her legs, wrapping them around him, savoring the contact. He moved from her mouth down to her neck, both of their breathing heavy. He had remained strong for so long when, over the past few weeks, all he wanted to do was bury himself inside her to help her feel something again.

"Just take it away, Cam," she said breathlessly. "Take away the pain." Her legs found the ground as he grabbed her breasts through her dress and squeezed gently. Olivia threw her head back, moaning in pleasure, thankful to feel something other than emptiness and hurt.

She looked up into Cam's eyes. "Tell me what you want, Libby," he growled, reminding her so much of Alexander. Except he wasn't nearly as forceful.

He felt her body from her neck to her chest, her legs to her ass, and everything in between. Olivia panted. "I want to feel anything other than the pain, Cam. I want to feel something."

"How do you want me to do that?" He crushed his lips to hers, pressing her to his body so she could feel his erection, wanting her to say exactly what she wanted.

Olivia felt as if she was having an out-of-body experience. She felt in total control of what was happening. It was like all those times that she sought comfort from so many other men. With Alexander, she felt as if she had no control. He held it all. But here, Olivia was sure that Cam would do whatever she wanted.

"I want you to fuck me, Cam. Fuck me and take it all away." His eyes met hers as his hand disappeared underneath her dress, feeling the warmth between her legs.

She closed her eyes, moaning with pleasure as he caressed her through her underwear, thankful that he had finally lowered his guard. He slipped a finger inside her panties, toying with her clit. "Fuck. You're so wet, Libby."

She cried out, finally feeling something if only for a minute. Cam pressed his lips to hers as he continued torturing her with his fingers. He growled and ripped Olivia's panties from her body, throwing them to the floor.

He reached into his pocket for a foil packet and tore it open as he unzipped his pants, pulling himself out. Olivia stared at him, the blank expression still on her face. She pulled his mouth to hers, not wanting to look at him. He pushed into her in one quick motion as he lifted her up, wrapping her legs around his body again.

"God, you're so tight," Cam grunted, thrusting into her. He set a punishing pace. Unlike the previous time they had sex, Cam was rough, pulling and biting on Olivia's skin. It was almost as if he knew she needed that.

"Do you feel that, Libby?" he growled. "Am I taking the pain away by fucking you?" He hated what was going on. He almost felt as if he was taking advantage of her situation, but the pain in her voice was so real. So raw. And he would do anything to take it away, even for a brief moment. Plus, it wasn't like he didn't enjoy the feeling of being buried deep inside of her.

Olivia moaned. "Yes. Take it all away," she panted breathlessly.

Cam groaned, biting her neck and pushing her even further against the wall. Olivia was immediately reminded of the day Alexander found her and tried to convince her to take him back. She closed her eyes tighter, wanting to forget that moment.

"Harder," she breathed. Cam pumped into her with even more enthusiasm.

"No. Bite me harder." The pain of his teeth on her neck distracted her from everything else. She needed the pain now, but it was an entirely different kind of pain. A pain she craved to dull all the other hurt she felt.

He bit down even harder, breathing rapidly against her skin.

Olivia screamed out, a mixture of pain and pleasure coursing through her body.

Cam released his hold on her neck. "You like that, Libby? You like it when I hurt you?" Beads of sweat fell from his forehead.

She stared into his eyes, noticing a confused look on his face. "Yes. I need it, Cam. I need you to hurt me."

"Fuck," he growled as he continued thrusting into her, slamming her back against the door with each motion. He lowered his head and sucked on her nipple through her thin dress, biting down. She flinched, gasping in pain, the feeling sending her over the edge. Cam felt her spasm around him and he thrust even faster before grunting as he found his own release, holding her while their breathing slowed.

In the aftermath of sex with Cam, Olivia felt embarrassed. She didn't know what came over her. This time, it was clear she was only using him. She felt guilty for what just occurred. Granted, he didn't seem to mind, but would he expect to see her again now? Olivia wasn't sure she wanted that anymore. She wanted to hide inside the comfort of her beach house and never see another human being for the rest of her miserable existence.

"You should probably go," Olivia said, breaking the silence, lowering her legs to the ground, and adjusting her dress before walking toward the bathroom to clean up.

"Libby, come on. Don't be like this," Cam pleaded with her as he pulled off the condom and threw it into the nearby garbage.

"Don't be like what, Cam?!" she exclaimed. "This is who I am so take it or leave it! I don't really care either way!"

"Damn it, Libby! For crying out loud! You just let me fuck you like that and now you're kicking me out?" He stared at her, dropping his voice. "I thought we were past all this bullshit."

She shrugged her shoulders at him. "Cam, I'm not the girlfriend type. I don't do relationships. I like to fuck and that's it. So if you're looking for someone to fill another role, look elsewhere. You know where the door is." She turned and walked into her bathroom, slamming the door. He took a few steps closer to the bathroom door, feeling guilty for what just happened as he listened to Olivia's sobs emanate from the room.

For the first time, he didn't know what to do. The girl he had grown to care for seemed so empty and broken. Instead of trying to rectify the situation, he turned and left the house, his shoulders slumped forward, wondering what had come over him. He had sworn that he would not enable her to use sex as a coping mechanism, but he completely lost his head when he heard the pain in her voice. Then she kissed him, and it all escalated so quickly.

He drove away from the beach house, hoping to find some clarity in the light of day, but he had a feeling that clarity would never come.

When Olivia finally heard the front door open and close, she left the bathroom and ran up to her bedroom, stripping off her clothes and changing into a pair of gym shorts and tank top. She ruffled through her belongings and finally found what she was looking for...her laptop.

She found the power cable and turned on her MacBook. She knew the answer would destroy her, but she needed to know. She ignored her thousands of unread e-mails, went straight to the Google search page and typed in Alexander's name.

Her search returned several recent news articles, if you could call gossip websites news. She clicked on the first link and let out a small gasp, willing herself not to cry. Alexander was at a formal function, dressed in a tuxedo. On his arm was a very beautiful woman with red hair and small brown eyes. Olivia scrolled down and read the article.

Alexander Burnham was spotted during a charity dinner at the Four Seasons in Boston on Saturday evening, accompanied by his new flame, Chelsea Wellington. Chelsea, the daughter of a wealthy architect, has been seen on Alexander's arm for the past several weeks although, apparently, their relationship goes back almost ten years.

Olivia scrolled down even further and let out a small cry. It was Alexander kissing the red-haired woman. That was supposed to be *her* kiss. She could feel the passion between the two. Why did she push him away when he found her? Why couldn't she take a leap?

"I can't believe he moved on," Olivia whispered. "What did I do?" she cried out to no one in particular, flopping onto her bed, grabbing a pillow and bringing it into her chest, clutching at it as if her life depended on it.

All of her walls came crumbling down as her body convulsed. It was a silent cry. Her eyes became blurry from all the unshed tears that immediately rushed forward. She stared at the laptop still open to that awful website, and wanted to scream. She couldn't breathe. She couldn't talk. She couldn't even make a sound. She finally realized that she pushed away the one person who meant the world to her. She said that she let go of him, but had she really? It wasn't until he had let go of her that she realized Alexander was really gone.

CHAPTER FIFTEEN

THE APPLE OF MY EYE

"ANY WORD, CHERYL?" DONOVAN spat into the phone. He was losing control. He hated losing control.

"I'm sorry, sir. Nothing. The trail has gone cold. I think he's given up on ever finding her. The last trace was a large cash withdrawal the day she left town. After that, nothing other than a stolen credit card that turned up to be a dead end."

"What about that suspicious trip he took back in October? Make any headway on that?"

Cheryl sighed. "I've tried to get flight records, but those are sealed tight. I didn't want to arouse suspicion by asking Martin about the trip."

"Well, stay on it, if you can. Proceed discreetly. The second anything turns up, let me know."

Cheryl exhaled loudly. "I honestly believe he's moved on. He seems happy now. At least, I think he does. Maybe it's for the best, sir."

He banged his fist on his desk. "No, damn it! Those documents are still out there. I know they are! I won't be happy until they are destroyed. Neither will my client and I don't need to remind you what is at risk if we fail to turn those documents over in a timely fashion. Until we find that box, everyone is at risk of being exposed."

"Yes, sir. I understand. I'll remain vigilant in finding the girl. How should we proceed when I do?"

"Let me worry about that." Donovan hung up and ran his fingers through where his hair once was.

~~~~~~~~~~

"Hey, Mo!" Alexander said upon arriving at Johnny D's and seeing Mo sitting at a table alone. He couldn't pull himself away from the bar. Not yet, anyway. Even though Olivia was gone, Mo and Kiera still showed up every Thursday night for Open Mic. Alexander had moved on like Olivia wanted him to, but it was still comforting to see people that had a connection to her.

"Hey, man. Good to see you. How's Chelsea?" Mo asked, taking a sip from his beer.

"She's great. Thanks for asking," he replied, his eyes dropping.

"Hey," Mo said, placing his hand on Alexander's arm. "It's okay to move on. It's what she wanted you to do."

"I know, but she's still on my mind." He looked down, trying to cope with his mixed feelings.

"And she will be, at least for a while," Mo said, remembering how he felt the first time Olivia ran. "But you just wake up in the morning and get through the day and, eventually, it will get easier. Then you'll move on. She'll always be there in the back of your mind but, soon, it won't hurt as much."

Alexander simply nodded. "I guess I'm officially a member of the Olivia Adler Survival Club, aren't I?" he laughed, clearing the air a bit.

"Yeah, and it's quite a club, isn't it?" Kiera said, sitting down at the table.

"Hey, Kiera. Any word?" Alexander asked the short redhead hopefully, wondering if Olivia had contacted her friends for the holidays. He never told them that he had found her, the pain of her rejection still too raw.

"No. Nothing. It's been a few months and nothing." Kiera looked into Alexander's eyes and could see the hurt there. She knew exactly how he felt. She had been there all those years ago, too. She couldn't understand why someone would just leave, not saying anything to anyone. Over the years, she had begun to accept it. The more she learned about Olivia, the more she understood why she ran. It didn't make it right, but she knew why she did it, at least.

"I know it's stupid, but I even made her a tofu turkey for tomorrow. I guess I'm just still hoping she'll show up. No one should be alone on Christmas Eve." Kiera looked away, trying to hide her tears.

Mo wrapped his arms around her petite frame, comforting her.

"We're quite the fun bunch, aren't we?" Alexander said, lightening the mood.

"You doing anything tonight?" Mo asked, trying to change the subject.

When Alexander arrived home after finding Olivia in Florida, he knew he needed to try to get over her. He was still angry. He wasn't coping very well without her in his life. That's when he turned to music, just as Olivia had done all those years ago. He found that it helped to have an outlet for his emotions, instead of keeping them all bottled up.

"Yeah, and I think it'll be the last time. It's time to let go."

Mo simply nodded his head. "You do what you gotta do."

They all turned their heads when the M.C. jumped back on the stage. "Okay, next up, Alex! Get on up here!"

Alexander took a deep breath and made his way to the stage for the last time. He sat down at the piano and adjusted the microphone. "Thanks everyone, and thanks for letting me play a little bit these past few weeks. For those of you who don't know, I went through a pretty nasty break-up a few months ago. It felt as if my entire world was ripped out from underneath me when this girl left. I tried to figure out where it all went wrong, but now I know I need to let her go and move on because finally, there is someone in my life who I think could make me happy. But before I can move on, I just need to do one last song. For me. And for the girl I lost. This is *Eve, the Apple of My Eye* by BellX1."

Alexander placed his hands on the piano and began to play the slow melody. As he sang the words, all he thought about was his Olivia, how he was certain she still cared about him.

.K. Leigh

But when he confronted her in Florida, she turned him away, desperate to protect herself. He didn't care about that. He still loved her with every fiber of his being, and he knew he would probably always love her. But, at the same time, he needed to move on. He hadn't been living those past few months. He'd simply been existing.

He still didn't understand why Olivia ran. Maybe things moved too quickly. She was a girl who was dealt such a shit life. She had never really coped with anything. Over the past several months, he had become angrier with his father over everything that had happened in Olivia's life. He wanted to think that it was all his father's fault. He covered up her very existence, ripping her from the only friends and family that she had. Now, twenty-one years later, she couldn't form any meaningful relationships because of her fear that she'd lose those very people. It was tragic, in a way, how empty she was.

"Do you think he'll ever be over her?" Mo asked, leaning in close to Kiera, listening to Alexander's passionate plea.

She simply shook her head, not wanting to think about the fact that her best friend was gone and she didn't know where she was. Alexander wasn't the only one hurting.

"I just want her to come back home," Kiera cried, Mo placing his arm around her. "This is where she belongs. Not out in the world somewhere, trying to run away from the people who care about her. I just don't understand why she does it."

"Yes, you do," Mo responded, glancing back to the stage.

Alexander sang the chorus, thinking about how empty he felt since Olivia had walked out of his life. A part of him died that day. Then he found her and felt something he hadn't felt since she left...hope. But the look of pain on her face after he tried to convince her to come back with him was so much worse than he imagined. And he did that to her. Now that he was singing the words to the emotional song, he realized that maybe he and Olivia were never heading in the same direction. He had waited most of his life to find the girl that stole his heart all those years ago, but maybe there was a bigger reason that she was taken from him.

He knew it was time to accept what had happened between them. It was time to move on. Why put in any more thought and effort into a bad situation? It will only make it worse. As he neared the end of the song, he thought about all the dreams he had where Olivia appeared on his doorstep, begging him to take her back. But, with Olivia, she could make any relationship sink or swim at the turn of a dime, and he didn't know if he could put himself through that again.

After he played the last few notes, Alexander stepped off the stage to thunderous applause. He walked toward Mo and Kiera's table, almost breaking down upon seeing Kiera's tear-stained eyes. "I need to take off guys," he said, a lump in his throat.

"Well, have a Merry Christmas, Alex," Mo said, shaking his hand.

"Thanks. You, too." He turned to leave the bar and was met by fierce brown eyes standing near the door.

"Who's your Eve, Alex?" Chelsea asked quietly, the hurt in her voice evident after hearing Alexander sing the song, clearly thinking about Olivia and calling her the apple of his eye.

"Chelsea..." he said, taking a step toward her. "How did you..."

"What? Know that you'd be here?" she spat out, her eyes wide with fury. "I followed you here, Alex. You don't tell me anything. You say that you love me, yet you lie about some bullshit meeting. Did you not think I would figure it out when you make up the same excuse every Thursday night?"

Alexander looked down.

"Please, Alex," she begged, her voice soft. "Just answer me. Who's your Eve?"

He shook his head, running his hands through his hair. "I'm sorry, Chelsea," he said, grabbing onto her arms, his eyes blazing into hers. "I really am. I just needed to do that for me. So I can move on. Olivia was my past. You're my future. I know that now. I do." He was surprised at the words coming out of his mouth. He had never given too much thought to his future with Chelsea before, but the more he thought about it, the more sense it made.

A smile crept across his face and he dragged her body flush with his, calming her fears before continuing, "I guess, in a way, she'll always be my Eve. She'll always be the one girl who got away. That's why I had to do that song. To remind myself that she isn't the girl for me. She only brings me down." He pulled back, staring into Chelsea's eyes. "Being with you has made me realize that the entire time I was with her, I was sinking. I'm so sorry you had to see that," he whispered, his voice soft and pleading for forgiveness.

Chelsea wrapped her arms around him, sighing as she took in the warmth of his body. "No. I'm sorry," she said quietly. "I should never have doubted you. I just get nervous sometimes that you're slipping away from me. I know these past few months haven't been easy on you, but you have to know that I'll never leave you. I love you, Alex." She looked into his eyes, desperate for him to see how much she truly cared for him.

He planted a deep kiss on her lips. "I love you, too, Miss Wellington. Now, let's get out of here." He winked, grabbing her hand and leading her out of the bar. He knew he had strong feelings for Chelsea, but was it love? He couldn't be sure. But, at the same time, he didn't want to lose her. He cared about her quite a bit. He was surprised how quickly he fell for her once he realized she wanted something more than just an occasional hook-up. He enjoyed her company, but that feeling of electricity running through his body anytime she touched him was missing. She wasn't Olivia.

Olivia would always be the one he cherished above all others, the apple of his eye, but she pushed him away. Chelsea was the type of girl he could see himself spending the rest of his life with. Even though they had only been dating for a few months, he had known Chelsea for nearly a decade. She was ready for the next step.

And maybe he should be, too.

CHAPTER SIXTEEN

LAST NIGHT

ON NEW YEAR'S DAY, Olivia lay on her couch, her tank top and gym shorts no longer fitting properly. She clutched onto Nepenthe, desperate for him to work his magic and take away her sorrow. For the past few weeks, she had remained a relative recluse in her little beach cottage. Hoping to avoid Cam, she no longer took her coffee on the front porch. Instead, she tortured herself nearly day and night, looking at photos of Alexander on the internet.

New photos poured in on an almost daily basis. Her heart would catch in her throat once in a while when she stumbled across a photo of her and Alexander that had been taken early in their relationship. But she was now just a footnote in his life, reporters never even finding out her name. She didn't want to be in his life. She had to keep reminding herself of that.

As she started to drift off to sleep, she heard a loud banging on the door. Olivia remained on her couch, refusing to get up and answer. The banging continued. After several minutes, she got up, swearing as she swung open the door.

"Hey. There you are," Cam said, a wild look in his eyes. "Are you okay?" he asked, taking in Olivia's disheveled appearance, wondering if she had heard the news. When he received the text from Elsie that afternoon, he quickly jumped in his car, speeding through town to Olivia's house, hoping she had no idea.

As Cam's eyes surveyed her body, Olivia immediately felt self-conscious. In the back of her mind, she tried to remember the last time she showered. Her face felt oily and she was sure the grease in her hair would give the Exxon-Valdez spill a run for its money.

"I'm fine, Cam." She started to close the door.

"Hey. Hold on," he said. "I thought maybe you'd want to go have oysters or something later. We can watch the shrimp boats come in. It'll be fun."

Oysters. Why was it always oysters? "No, thank you." Olivia tried to close the door again, but Cam put his hand on the jam, preventing her from closing it all the way. He regretted leaving things the way he did all those weeks ago. He should have kept a better eye on her but, for some reason, he couldn't bring himself to knock on her door each and every morning. He would drive up, walk up the stairs, and just stand on her deck. Now, looking at how broken she looked, he regretted his decision. She needed a friend and he failed.

"Listen, Libby. I know things have been off for you since the last time we, well, ya' know." He looked at her, hoping she would open up to him. "Do you want to talk about it?"

"No, Cam. I don't want to talk about it. All I've done my entire life is fucking talk about it and, well, I'm all talked out. So, if you don't mind, I'd like to crawl back into my hole and return to my future of being the crazy cat lady."

"Okay. I was just trying to be a friend." Cam took a step back and stared at her, not knowing how to react. "We don't have to talk. I can just keep you company."

"That's what Nepenthe is here for. Have a nice day." She turned around and Cam took in her side view.

"Wait, Olivia," he said, making her stop. "When was the last time you ate anything?" He sounded worried.

Olivia searched her brain. It was probably the same day she showered and she couldn't be sure of what day that was.

"You have no idea, do you?"

She looked down, not wanting to look into Cam's concerned eyes. She didn't need his help. She didn't need anyone's help. She could take care of herself, but she didn't want to. She wanted to turn everything off. That way, it wouldn't hurt anymore.

She retreated into her house, not closing the door. "If you're so worried about me, feel free to come in then."

Cam stepped into the house, taking in his surroundings. All the shades had been drawn and no lights were on. The house was dark and depressing. He walked into the living room toward the front windows. "First things first, vitamin D is important." He opened the shades and sunlight streamed into the living area.

Olivia squinted her eyes, not being accustomed to any light other than the glow from her laptop. Cam walked over to the kitchen and opened the refrigerator, hoping to find something that she could eat. He found a few containers of Greek yogurt and, after checking the expiration date, grabbed a blueberry-flavored one, opening it.

"Here. Eat this," he said, thrusting the container into Olivia's hands as she sat on the couch, eying him with disgust. "I'm not kidding, Libby," he barked. "You're on the verge of being malnourished. You need food."

She rolled her eyes, and shakily began to spoon the creamy substance into her mouth.

"See. You're so weak you can't even raise your spoon."

"I'm eating, okay? So you can leave if all you're going to do is criticize me," Olivia sneered.

"I'm not leaving until I know you're okay." He sat down next to her, his eyes trained on the woman he had grown to care immensely for over the past few months.

Olivia took another spoonful and thought about that. Was she okay?

"Then you'll be stuck here a while because I don't think I'll ever be okay." And that was the truth. She was done hiding from her own feelings. She was in pain. She pushed away the one good thing in her life and, in the crosshairs, lost her two best friends. She had no one. She was all alone. It was exactly what she wanted, but now that she was alone, she felt lonelier than she could handle.

"I'm not going to ask you if you want to talk about it, but just tell me what to do and I'll do it," Cam said, clearly concerned.

111

Olivia raised an eyebrow, remembering their last encounter when he said the same thing.

He laughed. "Well, except that. That didn't work out too well, did it?"

Sighing, she leaned back into the couch. "Can you turn the clocks back a few months? I made the biggest mistake of my life. Why do I always do this?" she cried out. "You saw it. You tried to get close to me so I kicked you out and avoided you for the past God knows how many weeks. And why do I do that?" she laughed. "Because I'm scared I'll get close to someone and then they'll leave me. Does that make sense? I'm scared of being alone so I push everyone away, and the result is the same. I still end up all alone."

Cam stared at her, not knowing how to respond without setting her off. "Is this about Alexander Burnham?" he asked quietly.

Olivia shot up and glared at him, her eyes narrow. "How do you know about him?"

"I'm sorry. I just figured as much. Elsie told me what she talked to you about at the bar that night, and since then, you've been locked in your house. You've barely eaten. It looks like you haven't slept. You haven't been taking care of yourself. I'd guess you're dealing with a broken heart here. It's got all the signs," he said, smiling, trying to lighten the atmosphere in the room.

"I was the one to do the breaking so I have no reason to be upset. It's my own damn fault. I pushed him away, and then he found me and begged me to go back to him. I told him I wanted nothing to do with him, telling him to forget about me. He's moved on, and it's exactly what I wanted. But, if it's what I wanted, why does it hurt so damn much?"

Cam pulled Olivia close, trying to calm her down. "Sometimes, to protect ourselves, we hurt the people who mean the most to us. It doesn't make us a bad person, and it doesn't mean we've moved on. I can guarantee that he hasn't moved on, Olivia. If you were mine, I wouldn't let you go without a fight." He pulled a strand of her hair, tucking it behind her ear.

112

"I didn't let him fight. I left without saying a word. I told him everything in a letter, making sure he wouldn't find it until I was three hours out of town." Tears kept streaming down her face. "And then, when he found me, I made it quite clear I no longer cared about him. I lied through my teeth."

"Well, maybe it's not too late. Maybe it's time to go back to Boston. At least give him a chance to tell you to your face that he's happier without you. I think you need closure."

She pulled back, looking at Cam. "I can't do that. I left town, running like the coward I am. I can't go back and face everyone."

"Can't? Or won't?"

"You sound like my therapist," Olivia laughed.

"I just want to help you. Yes, when I first started noticing you, I wanted nothing more than to get in your pants…"

"And you did," Olivia joked.

Cam held up his hands in surrender. "Hey. I'm just trying to be honest here. You're a beautiful young woman. And that night, after you kicked me out, I realized you were still hung up on some other guy. And that's okay. When you were nowhere to be found the past few weeks, I got worried. I know when people are depressed. All the signs were there. I just wanted to make sure you didn't do something stupid." Also, Elsie's text still hung heavy over his head. He wondered how long he could keep Olivia occupied without her finding out about that news. He knew that he would have to tell her, but he wanted to make sure she was emotionally in a better place before he did so.

She processed everything Cam said. Was it that obvious she was bat-shit crazy? "I need a glass of water," she said, getting up from the couch.

"Libby, let me ask you a question," Cam said as she grabbed a bottle of water and poured it over ice.

"Okay. Shoot. But, first, I just want to make sure you're not expecting me to pay your hourly rate."

Cam laughed. "No. I'm just here as a friend wanting to help out a friend."

"Okay. Go ahead with your question then." She leaned

against the kitchen island.

Cam stood up, walking into the kitchen and sitting on a barstool. "Have you always had problems communicating your feelings? It just seems like you hide them from everyone, and even lie to yourself about them."

Olivia stared, wide-eyed. "You barely know me…"

"Yes, I know," Cam said, interrupting her. "But I know people. So just humor me and answer the question."

"I guess I've always had problems with that. It goes back to the whole 'worried that people would leave' thing. I always worry that once people know how I feel, it would make them run."

"So you run instead, keeping all your feelings locked up inside."

"Yes, Dr. Cameron," Olivia responded sarcastically.

"So how do you communicate your feelings? You can't keep them all locked inside. No one could survive carrying that burden."

Olivia lowered her eyes, looking at the floor, noting how dirty it had gotten.

"Libby," Cam said, bringing her attention back to him. "It's New Year's Day. You've been here for nearly three months, running from your feelings. Just confront those feelings and let the chips fall where they may."

Olivia thought for a minute. She knew he was right. "Fine. I'll do it. But what am I going to say to Kiera and Mo?"

"And they are?"

"My best friends. This is the second time I've run out on them."

"Well, you're going to have to deal with that. Call them. I'm sure they'll be thrilled to hear from you." Cam stood up and walked over to the couch, lying down. "Take a shower. Freshen up. I'll wait here." He grabbed a fitness magazine off her coffee table and started flipping through it.

Olivia eyed him suspiciously. "For what?"

"I'm taking you out to dinner so go get ready."

"I don't need you baby-sitting me, Cam. So either leave and let me get ready in private, or leave and don't come back."

His mind began to race. What if he left and she found out? Could he risk that? Should he just tell her? But maybe she wouldn't return to Boston if she found out, and she needed to go back for her own sake.

"I mean it, Cam. Get the fuck out."

Sighing, he raised himself off the couch and walked over to the front door, opening it. "Fine. I'll be back in an hour and we'll go for oysters."

"No oysters," Olivia said, raising her hand.

"Okay. Okay. No oysters. Promise. See you in a little bit, Libby. We'll celebrate your last night on the beach." He hated that he was leaving her, but knew she would become even more suspicious if he insisted on staying with her while she got ready for dinner. He hoped he made the right decision.

Chapter Seventeen

Overboard

AFTER CAM LEFT, OLIVIA took a shower. It was the first time she had looked in the mirror in days, or possibly weeks. The reflection looking back disgusted her. Her face was sunken, her skin clearly too big for her frame. As she got ready, she threw on a pair of jeans that wouldn't stay up. She felt weak and needed to sit down. She wondered how she would get through dinner if she could barely stand to get ready.

As she collapsed on her bed, she heard a ding on her laptop, signaling her to a new Google search alert. She had set one up several weeks ago for Alexander, realizing that it was far easier to keep track of any new developments that way. As she clicked on the e-mail, she felt her heart shatter into millions of tiny pieces.

With shaky hands and desperately trying to subdue the painful lump in her throat, she navigated to the link contained in the e-mail. The story seemed to be headlining not only various gossip websites, but also more respectable news outlets. Olivia looked at the article, staring at a photo of Alexander standing next to *that* woman. They were clearly out at a formal gathering for New Year's Eve, him in a tuxedo and her in a tight fit silver gown. Beaming, she stood in Alexander's arms with her left hand placed on his chest.

And on the ring finger of her left hand sat an enormous diamond.

Olivia scrolled down and read the news article through her tears.

A Tragic Wreck

One of the country's most eligible bachelors is no longer eligible after proposing to his now fiancée, Chelsea Wellington, at a swanky New Year's Eve Ball last night in New York City. Although they have only been dating for a few months, the couple appears to be rather excited to get on with their future, their eyes focused on a February wedding. Good luck and congratulations.

The pain was back. It never really left, but Olivia had been hopeful earlier when she decided to return to Boston and pour her heart out to Alexander. But now it had returned and the hurt was too much. She needed something to dull the ache. Her heart beat rapidly and she felt a panic attack coming on. Running to the bathroom, she rummaged through her medicine cabinet looking for the bottle that Dr. Greenstein had prescribed to help with her anxiety.

She grabbed it and walked downstairs with her laptop, searching for the bottle of bourbon with her name on it. Popping two valium, she gulped down the liquid, thankful for the warmth spreading through her body. After throwing another couple of valium pills into her mouth and finishing almost half the bottle of alcohol, the pain of seeing Alexander's ring on another woman was finally dulled. The last thing she remembered was staring out at the crashing waves of the ocean before the numbness took over.

~~~~~~~~~

Cam left his house early, anxiously hoping that Olivia hadn't found out the news in the past hour that he'd been gone. He sped through town, recalling the fragile state Olivia was in earlier that day. The longer he sat at each stop light, the more irritated he became. As storm clouds rolled in, a bad feeling formed in his gut.

He pulled up to Olivia's house and leapt up the stairs onto her deck, tapping gently on the door. There was no answer. Then he heard a gentle scratching on the other side of the door, coupled with a loud meow. He stilled, continuing to listen. He heard it again, wondering what Olivia's cat was doing. He knocked again, becoming rather concerned. Several moments passed and all he could hear was Nepenthe's scratching and meows. He tried the door, but it was locked. Walking over to the front window and peering inside, his heart fell. Olivia was sprawled out on the floor, a liquor bottle lying beside her, the contents of a prescription bottle poured out on the coffee table.

"OLIVIA!" he shouted, running back to the front door, desperately trying the lock again. When it wouldn't give, he took a deep breath and kicked the door jam, forcing the door open.

He ran to her, grabbed her in his arms, and carried her to the bathroom, frantically trying to find a pulse. Sticking his hand down her throat, he tried to force her to vomit, hoping that he wasn't too late. Finally, he felt her shudder and gag before she emptied the contents of her stomach into the toilet. Cam breathed a sigh of relief when he saw four blue pills fall out of her mouth, hoping that was all she took.

He rubbed her back while she came around, dry heaving. "Let it go, Libby. Just let it go," he comforted her as she collapsed on the bathroom floor, curling up in a ball.

"It hurts too fucking much, Cam," she wailed out, convulsing on the cold tile.

Fuck. He had never heard pain as intense as the hurt in Olivia's voice. He wouldn't wish that on even his worst enemies. It was excruciating watching her shake, clutching her knees as her body continued to spasm.

"You need help, Libby. You just fucking overdosed. If I didn't find you when I did…" His voice trailed off, not wanting to think about what would have greeted him if he left his house a minute later.

"I'm not suicidal, Cam. I felt a panic attack coming on so I took a few pills."

"How many did you take?"

"Four. I just wanted to be numb for a little bit."

Cam wrapped his arms around Olivia, thankful that she expelled all the pills she took. "You're only supposed to take one, and not with alcohol, Libby. Jesus…" A tear fell down his face, the adrenaline pumping through his body finally subsiding.

The aftershocks of violently ridding her stomach of its contents continued to consume Olivia's body as she shook in Cam's arms. "He's engaged. He's really gone now, and it hurts," she sobbed.

"Come on, Libby. I know there's a fighter in there somewhere. Are you really going to give up? I saw the pictures. If you ask me, that's not a guy who's too sure about anything. He doesn't look happy, and I'm not just saying that to make you feel better. You need to go talk to him, at least. Get closure." He gently rubbed her back, leaning down to kiss her head. "Make him tell you to your face that he's happy with that redheaded bimbo."

Olivia laughed through her tears. "She does look a little bit like a bimbo."

"There's my girl," Cam crooned as he continued rocking her in his arms. "How do you feel?"

"A little light-headed," she responded, her voice raspy.

"Probably because you have no food in your system." He squeezed Olivia tight, relieved that she was coming around. "Here's what we're going to do. I'm going to order a ton of pizza, and we're going to stay in and watch stupid movies all night long. Sound good?"

Olivia looked through her tear-soaked eyes into Cam's vibrant silver ones brimming with hope. She nodded. "Yes."

He leaned down and kissed her forehead before lifting her in his arms and carrying her over to the couch. As he ordered pizza, Olivia grabbed her laptop, finding the photo that sent her over the edge less than an hour ago. Cam eyed her suspiciously as he placed the rather large order with a local pizza house. She gave him a reassuring nod before returning her eyes to the screen in front of her.

Cam was right. There was something very off about Alexander's expression in the photos. And it wasn't just in one photo. It was in *all* of them. He looked like a shell of his former self, as if he was simply going through the motions, desperate to overcome something...to overcome her. At that moment,

Olivia knew that he hadn't moved on. She had to act fast.

"So what are you going to do?" Cam asked, plopping down on the couch next to her after putting on a Blu-Ray of *Old School*.

She shrugged. "What I have to do. I need to see him, beg him to take me back, even after everything I've put him through, and hope that there's part of him that still cares enough to forgive me."

Cam put his arm around Olivia and pulled her close. "Good," he said quietly, trying to hide the lump that had formed in his throat at the thought of her no longer being in his life. It was bittersweet, but he knew Olivia needed to go for her own survival. And as much as Cam wished she would be able to forget about Alexander Burnham, he knew that would never happen. He was still concerned about her, particularly after what had happened that evening, but he knew that once she was back where she belonged, she would get the closure she needed and begin to move on.

That night, Cam savored his time with Olivia, knowing that she would leave the island in the next few days. They sat on her couch most of the night, gorging themselves on pizza, mozzarella sticks, and fried zucchini as they watched movie after movie, laughing. Every time Cam thought how he could get used to doing that with her, he had to remind himself that she needed to leave. His heart ached, but he refused to be the one to keep her in pain and hurting.

As Olivia slept with her head on his lap, he decided it was time to go. He tried to re-adjust her body so he didn't wake her, but had no such luck.

"Where are you going?" she asked drowsily, wiping the sleep from her eyes.

"It's late. I should go home."

"Wait. No. Stay. Please."

Cam looked at her, the hesitation clear on his face.

"It's just, I'm going to miss you when I leave, and I want to spend as much time with you as I can before then."

"When are you planning on heading back?" Cam asked.

"Day after tomorrow, I think. I have to pack so I'll need a

day to do that. Please. Stay with me until I go."

Cam sighed, dropping back down on the couch next to her. "Do you have any idea how impossible it is to say no to you?"

Olivia giggled as she nuzzled into Cam's arms, savoring the warmth and his smell.

"God, I'm going to miss that sound."

CHAPTER EIGHTEEN

BELONG

"SO LOOKS LIKE YOU'RE all set then," Cam said a few days later after he finished loading up Olivia's car with all her things. He closed the trunk and turned to look at the girl that had arrived out of nowhere back in October.

"Yup. Looks that way," Olivia answered sadly. She didn't want to admit it, but she was definitely going to miss Cam. Over the past few months, he had been her rock, the only person who understood her. A tear fell down her cheek, thinking how she would no longer see his smiling face every morning as she enjoyed her coffee. She wished she hadn't avoided him those last few weeks.

"Hey, hey," Cam said, wiping Olivia's tear. "Enough of that. This isn't good-bye, but you can't stay here, Libby. You know that. You need closure so you can get on with your life. And then, if it all goes to hell, I'll be here waiting for you." He wrapped his arms around her. "I'll always wait for you," he whispered, kissing her gently on the top of her head before helping her into the car. As he watched her Audi disappear down Ocean Avenue, a tear fell down his face, hoping that wasn't the last time he would ever see her.

The following evening, Olivia pulled off the Mass Pike and onto Huntington Avenue, heading toward her house, feeling overwhelmed as she drove past Boston Common Park. She missed her home, and that's what Boston was. It was home.

She pulled her car in front of her house and grabbed Nepenthe, wondering how she would feel being back in the place filled with so many memories of Alexander. Her hands shaking, she punched her code into the keyless entry and opened the door before disarming the security system.

She walked into the kitchen and let Nepenthe out of his cat carrier. After helping him settle back into the house, she ran out to her car and finished unpacking her items before driving down the side alley, parking in the back.

Leaving all her things in the living room, she walked up to her master bedroom. Everything was exactly as she had left it. Nothing had changed, but everything was different. Everything reminded her of Alexander. She walked over to the bed that was still covered with the clothes she haphazardly threw around as she was packing to flee town. She flopped down on what had become Alexander's side of the bed and inhaled. Months had passed, but it still smelled like him. She shot up, tears threatening to fall once more. She couldn't stay there.

She ran downstairs and put Nepenthe's bowls out, filling his food and water. "I'm sorry, pal. I just can't stay here, but I'll be back every day to check on you." She picked up her cat and gave him a kiss before he leapt out of her arms, more interested in his food.

She grabbed her suitcase and re-armed her system, leaving her house again. But this time, she wasn't running. She just needed to collect her thoughts. And she couldn't sleep in that bed, not when it smelled so much like Alexander.

She drove around town and soon found herself on her way to Arlington. She didn't know why, but she wanted to see Mo. About twenty minutes later, she parked her car outside Mo's house and sat there for several long moments, staring blankly at the steering wheel before finally gathering enough courage to get out of the car. As she walked up the front steps and rang the doorbell, she thought about how Mo would react when he saw her standing on his doorstep after being gone for so long. A few moments passed and she didn't hear anything stirring. She rang again and finally heard some shuffling.

Mo pulled back the door to his house, curious as to who it could be that late at night. He almost couldn't believe his eyes. Olivia stood at his front door, looking frail, a shell of her former self. He had seen her at her lowest of lows, but this was unlike anything he had ever seen before.

"Livvy?! Oh, my god! Get in here!" he said, pulling her toward him, hugging her tightly.

Olivia tried so hard to stay strong, but she couldn't take it anymore. All her emotions and everything she had felt over the past several months came rushing forward. She sobbed as Mo walked her toward his living room. He gingerly lowered her to the couch and simply held her as she cried. He was so thankful that she was okay. Or as okay as she could be.

After several minutes of just sitting there, Olivia's tears started to wane. Mo kept holding onto her. He didn't want to say anything. He just wanted to hold her, hoping that he wouldn't wake up and it all be a cruel dream. Brushing her hair behind her ear, he placed a gentle kiss on the top of her head.

Olivia looked into his dark eyes. "I'm so sorry, Mo," she exhaled, tears starting to flow down her face again.

"Hey. Don't cry, Livvy. It's okay. Just tell me what's going on and I'll do whatever I can." He had a feeling that after news of Alexander's engagement got out, she might return to Boston. But never did he expect to see her looking as horrible as she did.

"I ruined everything, like I always do. I push people away trying to protect myself, but it never works out, does it?"

"I won't ask if everything's okay because that seems like such a stupid question. I know things aren't. But tell me what I can do right now."

She looked at him and snuggled into his embrace once more. "You're doing it. Thank you." Before Olivia knew it, she had fallen asleep, grateful to be back where she belonged.

~~~~~~~~~~

Alexander's phone had been buzzing all night, but he was enjoying his time out with Chelsea. She had become a breath of fresh air those past few months, and he was actually starting to look forward to their wedding. While he still thought about

Olivia more than he should, Chelsea was a nice distraction.

He walked Chelsea out of his favorite Italian restaurant in the North End, the memory of taking Olivia there after the Red Sox game all those months ago was still strong. But he was eager to replace all those old Olivia memories with new ones. Happier ones. It was the only way he could continue to move on.

Martin pulled up outside of the restaurant. "My place, Miss Wellington?" Alexander asked, taking Chelsea's hand and kissing it gently.

She giggled. Alexander cringed a little. It was a high-pitched squeal type of a giggle. It wasn't Olivia's giggle. "I'd love to, Alex," she said, pushing him aside and getting into the SUV. "But you do know that, at some point, we are going to have to move in together."

Alexander had been putting that off, wanting to enjoy his last few months of being single. Plus, Chelsea wanted him to get rid of Runner and he wasn't ready for that just yet. He loved that dog, although he was another painful memory of Olivia. He started to wonder whether he would ever be able to fully rid his life of her. He didn't think he could even if he wanted to. And he wasn't sure he really wanted to, as much as he knew he should.

As he walked around to the other side of the car, Martin stopped him. "Sir, Carter has been trying to get in touch with you. He wouldn't say what it was about, but you should probably call him."

"Okay, Martin. I will when I get home." He opened the door and climbed in beside Chelsea, grabbing her hand and planting a sensual kiss on it. Her heart fluttered a little, loving the feel of Alexander's lips on her skin.

A few minutes later, Alexander led Chelsea into his large penthouse apartment.

"Jesus Christ, Alex," she scowled as Runner bounded down the stairs. "Will you get rid of that fucking dog already?" She cringed when the dog jumped on Alexander, his tail wagging, obviously happy to see him.

"Why don't you like animals?" he asked.

"They're just so dirty."

"Runner, down." Alexander looked at Chelsea, who appeared horrified. "Give me a minute. I'll put him somewhere. And I need to make one quick phone call. I'll be right back." He turned to Runner. "Come here, boy."

He walked away from Chelsea and the dog followed him down the hallway toward his office. After punching his code into the keypad, Alexander strode over to the desk as Runner walked to his doggie bed in the corner and lay down. Picking up his phone, Alexander called Carter.

"Sir."

"What is so important tonight, Carter?"

"Sir, it's Miss Adler," he replied cautiously. Alexander could almost hear the hesitation in his voice. "You asked me to remotely monitor any entry or exit on her home security system. Well, tonight, there was an entry just after eight in the evening and an exit a few minutes before nine."

Alexander sunk into his chair, his heart dropping to his stomach. Just when everything was starting to go well. Just when he had finally gotten over her, or so he thought. "Has there been any follow-up?" he asked, his voice quiet.

"Yes, sir. No one who had access to her key-codes has been there."

"Okay. Thank you, Carter." He hung up and went back out to the living area. Chelsea was sitting on the couch, batting her eyes.

He sighed and walked up to her. "Chelsea, I'm sorry, but I have some work business I need to attend to this evening. I need to go. Martin will drive you home." He turned abruptly and dashed to the elevator, pressing the call button repeatedly. An elevator car arrived almost immediately.

Within a few moments, he jumped into his Maserati and drove the few miles to Olivia's house. He leapt out of his car and ran up the steps, banging on her front door. It all seemed so familiar. He did the same thing the day she left. Why was he getting roped back into her life when everything seemed to be going so well with Chelsea? He was supposed to be getting married in a few weeks.

There was no answer. He banged again. "Olivia! Are you in there? I just want to make sure you're okay. That's all. Then I'll leave you alone." Nothing. No movement. He checked inside and the house looked dark. He punched the code into her keypad door lock and quickly disarmed the security system, surprised that nearly three months later, he still remembered those numbers.

Walking through the foyer and into the kitchen, he took in his surroundings. A thousand happy memories came rushing back before he noticed her cell phone still lying on the island, the battery long dead. *Has she even been here?*

He turned when he heard a faint sound coming down the stairs. "Nepenthe!" Alexander exclaimed when the cat appeared in the doorway. Olivia was back. And she would be coming back there. She would never leave Nepenthe alone for too long. He sat on the couch and let the cat snuggle next to him for a while, thinking about what Olivia being back in town meant for her own safety. And for him.

He had moved on, but he desperately needed closure. He knew she lied to him all those months ago when he confronted her. He willed himself to remain strong. She had hurt him more than any other person had hurt him in his entire life. If he simply took her back, could he possibly survive when she left him again? He didn't know. And she would, inevitably, leave him again. It was what she did. It was all she knew. Raising himself off the couch, he knew that he would just have to be patient.

CHAPTER NINETEEN

TEAM OLIVIA

THE NEXT MORNING, OLIVIA sat at the table in Mo's kitchen, reunited with her two best friends.

"I swear to god, Libby. If you ever pull a stunt like that again, I will cut a bitch. And that bitch will be you," Kiera said, laughing. "I knew something was up last night when Carter called asking if I had gone to your house for any reason."

"What are you talking about?" Olivia asked, raising her eyebrows in confusion.

"Well, I guess Alexander asked them to monitor your alarm system and let him know if there were any entries or exits. And last night there were."

"Controlling bastard," Olivia muttered.

"That he is." Mo laughed. "So what did you come back here for? It surely wasn't just for me and Kiera." He eyed Olivia, knowing full well the reason that she was back in town but wanting her to open up and not keep it all locked inside for once.

"No. You're right," she sighed. "I mean, you're part of the reason, but after hearing about Alexander's engagement to that Chelsea girl..."

"Uggh," Kiera interrupted. "Don't even get me started on that fake bitch."

"She's not that bad," Mo said.

Kiera glared at him. "Team Olivia all the way!" She threw a donut hole at him.

Olivia laughed. "Please don't turn my life into a stupid love triangle."

Kiera whispered, "Go Team Olivia!"

Olivia couldn't help but smile. "Yeah, well, anyway, after I found out he had been seeing her, I just snapped. I shut myself in my house and barely ate, probably didn't shower, and just closed the world out. Then I found out about the engagement and things got worse. I wanted to stop feeling and I wanted to forget, but this surfer boy I got to know fairly well helped me snap out of it. He pretty much pushed me into my car and made me drive back up here." Olivia left out the part about them screwing and him finding her practically comatose on her living room floor.

"Well, he's officially my new best friend," Kiera said, clutching Olivia's hand. "I'm just so glad you're back."

"So am I." She smiled weakly. "But I won't feel like I'm home until I do one more thing. Maybe I just need some closure. If he's happy with Chelsea, so be it. I get it. But I just need to see Alexander face-to-face and tell him those things I said when he…" Olivia stopped short, wondering how much she should tell her friends about what happened when Alexander found her in Florida.

Kiera stared at her. "When he what, Libby?" she asked calmly.

Olivia took a deep breath. "When he tracked me down in Florida," she responded.

"He WHAT?!" Kiera screeched. "That fucking bastard never said anything to us about that! What the hell happened?"

Shrugging, Olivia raised her coffee mug to her lips, savoring the taste and remembering all those mornings Alexander brought her coffee in bed. "He found me on my little island in Florida and confronted me, begging me to tell him to his face that I wanted nothing to do with him. He said if that was what I really wanted, then he would leave and never bother me again. And, of course, stupid me told him exactly that, even though I didn't mean it. So not only did I push him away once, but I did it twice."

Kiera stared at her, her eyes wide as she processed what Olivia just told her.

"What are you going to do?" Mo asked.

"I don't know yet. I just want to talk to him. Explain everything. And if he still hates me, I guess I'll have to live with that."

"I don't think he hates you, Olivia," he said. "But you hurt him pretty bad."

"Wait a minute. How do you know that?"

Kiera and Mo shared a look. "We got to be pretty close friends these past few months," Mo explained.

Olivia stared at her two best friends, shocked at what they were saying. She immediately felt a twinge of jealousy. Her best friends were hanging out with Alexander on a regular basis. Then she remembered it wasn't her place to be jealous. She pushed him away, like she always did.

"You have to stop running when things get bad. You need to start letting people in, Olivia," Kiera said, interrupting her thoughts.

"I know," Olivia sighed. "And it took my surfer boy psychiatrist friend to help me realize that."

"Ooh… So surfer boy is a shrink? Kinky." Kiera laughed.

Mo shoved her playfully. "Get your mind out of the gutter, babe."

Olivia gave them a look, wondering if they finally hooked up. She made a mental note to talk to Kiera about that later.

"Yes. He's a shrink. I realized that the pain I felt when I found out Alexander was engaged to someone else, even though I told him to move on, was worse than anything I have ever felt in my life. I just wanted to end the pain. I tried to turn it off. To stop from feeling. That way I wouldn't hurt anymore. But it didn't work. Nothing did. And I was the one that caused the pain. Me. Not anyone else. And I think that's what made it hurt even more. If I hadn't been so selfish and thinking only about myself, I could have avoided that hurt. But, instead, I did it to myself so it's my own damn fault if Alexander slams the door in my face. He should, especially after the way I treated him when he found me and begged me to come back

130

to him. But I, at least, want to talk to him."

"When are you going to do it?" Mo asked, ever the practical one.

"I was thinking about just heading over to his office today," Olivia said, her heart racing at the thought of possibly seeing Alexander that day.

"Great," Kiera said excitedly. "Have you thought about what you're going to wear?"

Olivia laughed. "No. I haven't thought about that yet."

Kiera stood up and grabbed her hand. "We'll be back later, Mo. Girl thing." She dragged her out of the house and, within a few minutes, they were on their way back into the city.

"So, what's the deal with you and Mo?" Olivia asked. "I noticed something a little different between you two. Come on. What's the status?"

"Status?" Kiera asked, a look of disgust on her face. "I'm not one for labels. Just, suffice it to say, he's my one-way ticket to pound town, okay?"

Olivia laughed, happy to be back home.

CHAPTER TWENTY

THE HURT

WITHIN A FEW HOURS, Kiera had successfully helped Olivia find a new outfit to wear when she confronted Alexander. Their last stop was a swanky shoe boutique on Newbury Street. Boston was flooded with tourists still milling about in the city after celebrating the New Year. Shops were packed, and there was a chill in the air that Olivia had missed when she lived in Florida. The gray clouds made it feel like the sky would open up at any second and cover the city with a fluffy blanket of snow.

"I don't know, Kiera. I don't think I really need another pair of shoes. Have you seen my closet?"

Kiera stared at her friend, indignant. "Of course I have, and I'm incredibly jealous. However, never underestimate the power of a pair of shoes. Cinderella is living proof that a pair of shoes can change your life."

Olivia wrinkled her nose. "I'm not so sure Cinderella could be classified as 'living proof'. Aren't you in publishing?"

"Yeah. I read that somewhere. Isn't it a great quote?" Kiera laughed.

Olivia ended up buying the shoes because her friend was right. She wanted to face Alexander feeling the best she possibly could, given the circumstances. The shoes were pricey, but she had missed Christmas so she considered them a gift to herself.

The girls got back to Olivia's house and Kiera helped her friend get ready. She put on her tight black sweater dress and accented it with a thin red belt. Then she pulled on the overpriced black leather boots.

"Hot!" Kiera announced when Olivia walked downstairs. "You look fucking smoking!"

"Thanks for the vote of confidence. Want to give me a ride?" Olivia asked, butterflies forming in her stomach.

"Okay. Come on."

A short ten minutes later, Kiera pulled up outside the office building in the Financial District. She turned to her friend. "Nervous?"

"A little," Olivia responded, fidgeting with her coat. "He might not even be here."

"Well, at least you're giving it a shot."

Olivia opened the car door, taking a deep breath, her hands shaking.

"Good luck, Libby. And, no matter what happens, I love you."

She smiled. "Thanks, Care Bear."

Olivia's heart began to beat rapidly as she walked into her old work building. She made her way across the large lobby toward the turnstiles, unsure of whether she would actually be able to follow through with what she had planned.

"Olivia! You're back!" Jerry shouted as she swiped her keycard through the turnstiles.

"Yeah. For now, at least."

"Hey. Are you okay? It looks like you lost a lot of weight. And you didn't have it to lose." He looked at her, the concern apparent on his face.

"I'm fine, Jerry. Don't worry about me," she said dryly.

Olivia hit the call button for the elevator and one arrived almost immediately. She pressed the button for the top floor, sliding the extra key card Alexander had given her months ago into the slot. She gasped when it actually worked. Within a few seconds, the doors opened and she walked out into the reception area in front of Alexander's office.

His secretary jumped up almost immediately. "Oh, Miss Adler. How are you?" She ran over to Olivia, taking her coat and hanging it up in the closet.

"Fine, thank you. I was wondering if Alexander is around and available. I only need a few moments of his time."

"Oh, of course. Mr. Burnham had mentioned you might stop by."

Arrogant bastard, Olivia thought to herself.

"He is in a meeting right now, but has instructed that you are welcome to wait in his office. He should be out within the next ten minutes." She walked over to the large glass door and buzzed Olivia in.

"Thank you." Olivia walked down the long corridor leading to Alexander's office. She heard voices on the opposite side of the hallway coming from the conference room, and stopped dead in her tracks when Alexander's voice echoed through the room. Could she really go through with this? Just hearing his voice again made her heart ache.

Opening the door to his office, thousands of memories came rushing back. The first night she met him. How he gently took care of her after Simon attacked her. The numerous times during their brief courtship that he summoned her upstairs and all the things they would do on his couch.

She walked over to the sitting area and ran her fingers across the back of the large couch. "A lot of great memories on that couch," a voice said, interrupting her thoughts. She spun around, her heart dropping to her stomach. Alexander stood in the doorway, wearing a crisp black suit and a green tie.

"Oh my god, Olivia. Are you okay? Is something wrong?" He rushed toward her, wrapping his arms around her, electricity coursing through her body. "Are you sick or something?" Alexander took in the sight of her. She had lost too much weight. He wondered whether she had eaten at all over the past few months. And he felt partly responsible.

Tears fell from her eyes at the concerned sound in his voice. "Why does everyone ask me that?"

Alexander released his hold on her, stepping back to look at her. "Because you don't look like yourself, Olivia. You look…upset."

"Well, you could say that," she replied, glancing around the room, trying to hide her eyes from him.

"Here. Have a seat." He led her to the love seat across from the couch and helped her sit down before he took his place next to her.

"So, what is it that I can do for you today?" he asked very matter-of-factly. Mr. Businessman was back.

Olivia took a deep breath and straightened her spine, looking for the inner strength to tell him what she had come there to say. "This is kind of hard for me to say so, please, just let me get it all out before you interrupt me."

"Okay." He nodded.

"Here goes nothing." She turned toward him. "Alex, I fucked up. I know that now. I pushed you away because it's what I do. Or did. I got scared because I was getting so close to you. And I knew that, at some point, you wouldn't be able to put up with all my craziness anymore. I thought I would never be able to make you truly happy and that killed me. I cared about you so much that I hated myself for doing that to you. So I figured I would push you away, which was the most difficult thing I ever had to do." She took a deep breath as she stared into his green eyes. "That last morning in Newport..." she said softly.

"On the yacht?" Alexander interrupted, his voice trembling.

"I needed you one more time. I was so addicted to your body, and the thought of never being able to feel you inside of me again broke me apart."

"So that was you saying good-bye then?" he asked, his eyes meeting hers before she looked away.

"It was the only way I knew how," she replied, staring at her fingers.

"Look at me, Olivia."

She obeyed, lifting her water-filled eyes to meet his.

"I knew there was something different that morning, but I never would have guessed that you would be running from me. I had a feeling you were slipping away from me, but I thought we got that spark back after the race. You say you thought I could never be happy with you. That wasn't your decision to make. I was so deliriously happy with you, Olivia," he said quietly, his voice full of hurt. "And I knew you were going

135

through some issues. I was more than willing to be patient with you while you worked through those, but you pushed me away. Twice."

"I know!" she exclaimed, clearly agitated. She took a deep breath. "Just let me finish," she pleaded.

Alexander nodded. "Okay."

"When I first arrived in Florida, every morning I woke up hoping, in the back of my mind, that you would show up on my doorstep, begging for me to come back. And then I met Cam and I thought he would be the perfect person to help dull the pain because I felt nothing for him. And nothing was better than the hurt. When you confronted me…god, Alexander. It took all my willpower to *not* melt into your arms. When you found me, I was secretly thrilled. You're right. My body did betray me. I've never felt as fulfilled or complete as I did with you. You're the only one that gives me an orgasm so intense that I feel my entire world shake, and it scared me all over again. So I lied. I told you what you needed to hear to leave me alone."

Olivia stared into Alexander's intense green eyes, tears beginning to fall down both their faces. "I'm so sorry, Alexander. I took the coward's way out. I pushed you away to prevent myself from being hurt. But, in the end, I was the one who hurt myself. I experienced *inexplicable* pain. And then I saw all those photos of you with another woman and heard about your engagement, and I shut down. I tried to shut everything off. Because that pain, Alex…" her voice trailed off, her chin trembling. She took another steadying breath. "That pain is worse than anything I have ever experienced. Knowing that you're with someone else is tearing me apart." Tears continued to fall down Olivia's face.

Alexander took a deep breath, trying to compose himself. Olivia had come back to him. It was what he always hoped for and wanted. But now that she was here, could he really dive head-first back into her life? "Olivia, do you have any idea how hurt I was when you left? Do you have any idea what the words you said in Florida did to me?"

Olivia nodded her head. "I do now. I realize the pain that I cause other people when I leave. And I swear to you, I'm done running. I'm begging you, Alexander. You need to believe me. I am ready for this, whatever it is."

Alexander stood up, needing to distance himself from her. "I believe you, but I'm not sure I'm ready. You hurt me, Olivia. You let me go, and I had no choice but to do the same. I moved on, just as you asked me to. It was hard but, each day, it became easier to get out of bed and think about you a little less. You never left my thoughts and I don't think you ever will, but I can't put myself through that again."

Olivia stood up and walked toward Alexander. She grabbed his hands in hers, that spark of electricity back.

He stared down at her, wanting to not feel that anymore.

"I understand, Alexander. Just answer me one question and, I promise, I will be out of your life." Looking deep into his eyes, she asked, "Are you happy?"

He broke his gaze from her, looking out the large expansive windows surrounding his office. He thought about the question for a while, Olivia waiting patiently for her answer. His eyes slowly returned to hers. "I am happy. Chelsea's not perfect but, right now, she is what I need, Olivia."

She brought her lips together, closed her eyes, and nodded. Releasing Alexander's hands, she walked toward the door, turning to take one last look at him. She noticed that his shoulders had dropped. "I know this is good-bye then. Before I go, promise me one thing." She paused. "Promise that you'll never forget me."

"Olivia, please," Alexander said, taking a step toward her, his eyes pleading.

She held her hand up, stopping him from getting any closer. "Let me get this out, Alexander. I need to."

He nodded, his heart unsure of whether he could listen to her words without breaking all over again.

"Promise me you'll always remember me. Walking out on you, then coming back here and losing you all over again has been painful enough. But as long as it wasn't for nothing, as long as it meant something, then maybe I can move on like you have." She opened the door and turned around once more, taking one last look at the only man who really saw her and accepted her for who she was.

"I don't think I can go on knowing that I mean nothing to you." Her chin quivered and she stared deep into his eyes. "I think I could have loved you, Alexander." She took a deep breath, holding his gaze. "I just thought you should know that."

He watched Olivia walk out his door and sank down onto the couch, wondering whether he did the right thing.

As she walked down the hallway, she heard Alexander speak one last time. "You'll always be my Eve, love." She was about to turn around, wondering what he meant by that, when she ran right into someone coming through the security door.

"Oh, I'm sorry," Olivia said, raising her head, unable to believe her luck. "Oh, my. You must be Chelsea."

"Yes, that's me. Are you friends with Alex?" Her voice was high-pitched and annoying.

"Yeah. Olivia Adler." She held her hand out.

Chelsea just stared at her. "You're Olivia? Jeez, I thought he had better taste."

"Listen, I've had a rough day. I just got my heart stomped by that man in there. You won, okay? You get to keep him. I hope you appreciate just how wonderful of a human being he is. I mean, *really* appreciate it. He deserves someone like that. He is unlike anyone I've ever met. He deserves to have every happiness so you better make him happy…"

Chelsea simply stared at Olivia as she took a deep breath, her lip trembling. She didn't know why she had been so catty to her. Chelsea could tell that she was hurt and in pain. But if it meant that Alexander turned her away, Chelsea was okay with it because that could have easily been her pain.

Olivia lowered her voice, her chin quivering with emotion. "I wanted to be the one to do that, ya' know? Make him happy. But I didn't realize that soon enough. And now that I have, I guess it's just too late. But it's hard to tell your mind to forget about someone when your heart aches for that person." She walked into the reception area, sobbing uncontrollably, desperately needing to get away from everything that reminded her of Alexander. She pushed the button for the elevator and got in before realizing that she had forgotten her coat. *Fuck it*, she thought. *I don't need it.*

After watching Olivia practically run into the elevator, Chelsea turned to see Alexander standing inside the doorway to his office. He had overheard every word.

He was beginning to think he had made a terrible mistake.

CHAPTER TWENTY-ONE

HELP MYSELF

"CHERYL, PLEASE TELL ME you have some good news," Donovan said calmly into his phone. "It's been nearly three months!"

Cheryl laughed. "Well, I have some for you. I just read Carter's reports from last night. Olivia is back, and here's the kicker... She just left Burnham's office. I was in a briefing with him and stayed a few minutes after to discuss some things with a few of the other agents when I overheard her in the hallway. She stormed out of there pretty quickly."

"Has she left the building?" Donovan asked, standing from his desk, his mind racing.

"Yes, sir. I grabbed some camera feeds and she was seen leaving the building on foot through the front doors, turning right onto State."

He exhaled loudly, thankful that, after several quiet months, he finally had a location on the girl. He didn't care that he had promised Simon that he could finish her off. She had disappeared and now that she was back, he needed to act. "I'm on it. Thank you, Cheryl. Keep me posted."

"Yes, sir."

He hung up and immediately dialed another number. "Grant. It's me. It's go time. She was seen leaving Burnham's building on foot. Get on it," he growled.

"Yes, sir."

~~~~~~~~~~

A gentle knock woke Alexander from his daydreaming. Chelsea was going on and on about some shopping spree she just went on and, of course, various wedding plans. All he could do was think about Olivia and whether he had made the right decision sending her away.

"Come in," he said.

His secretary entered carrying a red belted coat. "Sorry to interrupt you, sir, but Miss Adler left without this. I tried to stop her, but didn't get to her in time. I apologize."

He grabbed the coat from her. "Thank you. I'll make sure it is returned to her." His secretary turned and left. He looked out the windows and noticed that snow was falling from the sky.

"Shit," he muttered.

"What?" Chelsea asked, annoyed at the fact that Alexander had interrupted her story about some bridal boutique she had visited earlier in the day.

"It's snowing and Olivia doesn't have her jacket."

Chelsea exhaled loudly. "Who cares? She's a big girl. She'll be okay. I mean, you don't really need a jacket in a car anyway."

"She wouldn't have driven over here," Alexander said, realizing how much he really did know about Olivia and how little he knew about Chelsea. He knew Olivia was probably walking around the city at that moment. How could he just let her leave? He should have at least made sure she got home okay. He hadn't been thinking clearly and now he feared for her safety.

He looked over at Chelsea as she filed her nails. "I have to go." He ran out the door, leaving her.

"Alex, wait!" Chelsea said loudly.

Alexander ignored her cries and ran down the hallway, thinking how it was the second time in so many days that he walked out on Chelsea. He called Martin quickly, telling him to meet him outside with the SUV immediately. Within a few minutes, he jumped into the car.

"Martin, she's walking around out here without a jacket. I need to find her. Just drive to her house. Maybe we can catch her on the way."

Martin didn't even need to ask who. He knew there was only one person that could cause Alexander to look so rattled. At that moment, he knew that Olivia was back.

~~~~~~~~~~

As she walked through the Boston streets after leaving Alexander's office, snow falling at a steady clip, Olivia didn't know what to do. She needed something to dull the pain. Her mind went to the first thing she could think of...alcohol. She spotted a liquor store and ran into it, grabbing several bottles and paying. Back outside, she continued down Boylston Street, clutching her bag of alcohol as if her life depended on it.

Out of nowhere, a broad-shouldered man stepped in front of her, glaring. "Olivia," he sneered. "I knew you would come back to town."

She gaped at him, wide-mouthed. "Could my luck get any worse today?" She tried to push him aside but he grabbed her, holding her in place. He looked familiar, but Olivia couldn't place him. "Listen, if we used to sleep together, great. But I'm so not interested, okay?"

"Oh, we never slept together, but if you're offering..." A crooked smile crept across his face as his fingers traced down her damp dress.

Her heart started racing as she attempted to step back. "How do you know my name then?"

"We've been looking for you for quite a while, Olivia. Or do you go by Sarah?"

Olivia looked around. The street was bustling with rush hour commuters coming and going. Cars crawled at a sluggish pace along the busy road. No one appeared to notice her predicament so she did the only thing she could think of...she opened her mouth and screamed as loud as she could before pushing the man aside and bolting down the street. Her hands were shaking and numb from the cold as she clutched her brown paper bag.

~~~~~~~~~~

Martin turned the corner onto Boylston Street and the SUV continued to crawl. Alexander scanned the streets, desperate to find Olivia, if only to make sure she wasn't walking in the snow.

"Shit!" he exclaimed, seeing a woman who looked like Olivia running away from a large man. He threw open the car door and ran across the street onto the sidewalk. "Olivia!" he shouted.

She paused briefly, hearing a familiar voice. Turning around, she saw Alexander running after her, clutching her jacket. She shook her head before she continued down the busy street. The strange man gained on her as she desperately ran away from him, wondering why no one thought it was odd that a large man was chasing a woman during a snow storm on one of Boston's busiest streets. Within a few moments, Olivia heard a scuffle behind her. She paused, catching her breath, before she glanced over her shoulder. Alexander was on top of the strange man, punching him repeatedly.

Fearful that he would do some serious damage, she turned around and ran to him. "Alex!" she cried out. "Stop!" She took a deep breath as he raised his eyes to meet hers, his fist in mid-air, ready to strike again. "Please," she begged quietly.

Alexander glared at the man he had pinned to the ground. He looked familiar, but he couldn't remember where he had seen him before. That was never a good sign. The man moaned out in pain. "You go near her again, I'll fucking kill you." Alexander slammed his head into the pavement one last time before standing up, watching as the strange man quickly raised himself off the ground and ran away in the opposite direction.

Alexander walked over to Olivia. "You forgot your jacket," he said softly, handing her the coat in his hand, switching from angry, temperamental, controlling Alexander to sweet, caring, compassionate Alexander.

She stared at him, still clutching her brown bag.

"You shouldn't be out here walking. It's not safe," he said quietly.

Olivia grabbed her jacket out of his hands. "Stop trying to save me, Alex," she hissed. "I don't need your help." She turned and continued down the street.

"Well, then, what do you want from me, Olivia?" he asked loudly, watching her walk away.

She spun around abruptly and searched his eyes. "I don't want you to always feel like you have to come and help me, Alex," she whimpered, her throat beginning to close up again, thinking about the man who was no longer hers. "I just want you to stand by my side while I try to help myself."

Her words caught Alexander off-guard. He had always tried to protect her. He failed to do that at an early age and spent the last several months trying to make up for that.

Her eyes narrowed, staring at him as he remained silent on the busy Boston street. "Do you think you can do that?" She looked at him as snow continued to blanket the sidewalk, desperately wanting him to say that yes, he could do that. That he would stand by her side. That he would forget all about her running out on him. That he would do anything he could to make sure she never did the same thing again.

But, instead, Alexander just stood there and stared, not saying anything.

Several moments passed, the silence deafening. "That's what I thought." Her eyes fell as she turned and continued to walk, shivering from the snow and the last shattered pieces of her heart being stomped on.

Alexander tried to open his mouth to say something, anything. Tell her to wait. Stop. He made a mistake. But nothing came out. He knew he had just let the only woman he would ever truly love walk out of his life, and he did nothing. He watched his entire world fall apart and he didn't do anything to stop it. All of a sudden, he felt more lonely than he had ever felt in all his thirty years.

~~~~~~~~~~

144

Olivia flung open the door to her house, soaked from the snow that continued to fall steadily around the city. She bolted the door, not wanting to see anyone, even some well-meaning friend. She needed some time alone. Stripping off the sexy black boots that, just a few hours ago, made her feel confident and ready to face the world, she walked into the kitchen and poured some Sapphire gin over ice, wishing she could turn the calendar back to October. Taking a gulp, she exhaled loudly, feeling the effects of the alcohol warm her stomach.

She grabbed the bottle and collapsed on the couch. Nepenthe walked over and sat down over the floor heater, warming his body. Olivia was chilled to the bone, but she had no desire to go upstairs and change. The cold helped take her mind off how much pain she felt.

"Why did I ever come back here?" she sobbed to no one at all. "I don't belong here... I don't belong anywhere."

~~~~~~~~~~

"Grant. Did you get her?" Donovan asked, hopeful.

"No, sir. I was in pursuit, but Burnham tackled me to the ground."

"Shit," he spat into the phone. "Did he recognize you?" He sounded worried.

"I don't believe so."

"Fuck. Why is one girl so fucking hard to kill?"

Grant laughed. "I didn't realize we were going to kill her. I just thought we'd abduct her and make her lead us to those documents."

"Well, yes. And then we're going to kill her, Grant. I don't leave any loose ends."

"Then what's the plan?"

"The plan is to lay low. There have been too many fuck-ups. Burnham could have recognized you and, even though he's engaged to that other woman, he'll probably be on high alert over the next several weeks. So we wait. Let Burnham forget that we're after her. Once he lets his guard down, we make our move. When they least expect it."

CHAPTER TWENTY-TWO

THE SURE BET

"HEY, ALEX," TYLER SAID as he pulled up a barstool next to his brother on a Thursday night in early January. "How's everything going?" He signaled the bartender to pour him a beer.

Alexander looked at his brother. "I've been better," he replied, downing a shot of tequila.

"Shit. What happened?" Tyler inquired as he took in his surroundings at the bar in Davis Square. At the far end of the room, a pair of college students sat on stage and performed to a captive audience. He had never been there before and had hoped to convince Alexander to meet him closer to Boston University, but his brother was adamant about going to a place called Johnny D's.

"She's back, Ty," Alexander said, staring down into his pint glass filled with an amber liquid.

"Who is?"

"Olivia." The word fell off his tongue in a way that made him miss her even more.

"Does Chelsea know?"

"Yup. She ran into her outside of my office, after she came to me and begged me to take her back."

"And did you?"

Alexander raised the glass to his mouth and slowly shook his head. "No. I just couldn't do it. All I could remember was how I felt when I left her in Florida after she begged me to leave her alone because it was the only way she could survive. I knew she

146

didn't want that, but she looked so broken. And now I don't know what the fuck to think. I'm supposed to be getting married next month."

Tyler exhaled slowly, thankful that he didn't have the girl problems Alexander seemed to have. He loved his brother and was grateful that, whenever he needed someone to talk to, Alexander would always call him. They were never that close when they were younger, but once Tyler started college, they became closer. Over the years, he watched Alexander go home with woman after woman until Olivia walked into his life. Little did Tyler know at the time that it was Alexander's Olivia from all those years ago, but he did know that Olivia was the best thing to ever happen to his brother. It made him change his ways and open his heart to love…a heart now possessed by Chelsea.

"Are you in love with her?" he asked.

"Of course I am!" Alexander exclaimed. "I wouldn't have gone all the way to Florida if I didn't love her!"

Tyler lowered his voice. "No. Chelsea, man. I was talking about Chelsea. Are you in love with her?" He raised his eyebrows, realizing that he probably already knew the answer.

Alexander paused, thinking about the question.

"Come on, Alex. You put a goddamn ring on her finger. You shouldn't have to even think about it. Just answer the question. Are you in love with Chelsea?"

Alexander sighed. "It's not that easy, Ty."

"It should be. There shouldn't even be a doubt in your fucking mind if you're about to give that girl our last name."

Alexander nodded, knowing that his brother was right. Why did Olivia have to show up and throw herself at him, begging for forgiveness? After the months spent with Olivia, his life finally had some semblance of normalcy. Chelsea offered him security in a relationship, which was something he never felt with Olivia. And he was in control. He needed the control. With Olivia, he had none. With Chelsea, he didn't feel as if his world was about to fall out from beneath him any second.

Alexander shook his head, knowing that he wasn't in love with Chelsea. He knew he probably never would be. There was only one girl he would ever love. A girl that captured his heart years ago, and he never got it back. The apple of his eye. His Eve. His Olivia.

"Tyler! Alex!" a voice called out, bringing Alexander back from his thoughts.

"Hey, Mo! Good to see you." He looked at Mo and Kiera with anxious eyes. "I didn't expect to see you two tonight." He wondered whether Olivia would be there, as well. It was Thursday night after all. Immediately, his heart started to race at the thought of seeing her.

"You know how it is, Alex," Kiera said. "We're never one to break with tradition. It's Thursday, and Thursday night is Open Mic night."

"Have you…?" Alexander raised his eyebrows, not sure if he could finish his question.

Mo shook his head. "No. She won't let us in, and she's not answering our calls. I think she just needs some time to process everything." He led Kiera away from the bar toward their usual table, wondering if they would see Olivia that evening.

A worried look spread across Alexander's face. Was she okay? He prayed that she didn't do anything stupid. "Excuse me for a minute." He walked away with the intention of calling Carter and ordering him to coordinate round-the-clock surveillance outside of Olivia's home. He wasn't thinking clearly earlier in the week when she was being followed. Now, could *they* have figured out she was back in town? What if she was in danger? He needed to at least make sure she was alive.

~~~~~~~~~~

As Olivia exited the Red Line subway station, climbing the stairs to street level, she wondered what had possessed her to go to Open Mic. It had only been three days since Alexander stomped on her heart, leaving it to bleed all over Boylston Street. During those three days as she wallowed on the couch, all she could hear was Alexander's voice calling her name. As much as she tried to forget about him, he had a tighter hold on her than she realized.

On Tuesday, she felt horrible, using all of her willpower to not dull the ache with drugs and alcohol. So she begrudgingly picked up the phone and called Dr. Greenstein, who showed up at her door within an hour, a look of concern etched on her face as she took in Olivia's appearance.

Without saying a word, she embraced Olivia while all the sadness, anger, hurt, and pain spilled out of her eyes. Dr. Greenstein ended up canceling all of her appointments that day, ensuring that Olivia was going to be alright. It was the doctor who encouraged her to resume her normal routine, little by little. And that meant Open Mic. So it was with a heavy heart that Olivia walked the block from the Davis Square subway stop in the snowy Boston streets to Johnny D's on Thursday night.

She didn't know what to expect when she opened the door to the bar. She had been gone for so long but, as she made her way through the familiar bar, nothing seemed different. It was as if everyone's lives had gone on without her there, as if her life wasn't important. And she knew that was true.

"Holy shit, you're here!" Kiera said, jumping up from their usual table, eyeing Mo suspiciously.

"Yeah. I'm here. Might as well try to get back to my old life," Olivia said dryly as a server came to the table to take her drink order.

"You singing tonight?" Mo asked, wondering whether he should tell her that Alexander was sitting at the bar.

"Yup. And if either of you say the 'A' word, I will leave immediately and never speak to you again. Got it?"

Kiera sighed. "Libby, you need to talk about it eventually. You know that, right?"

Olivia took a sip of her much needed gin. "Of course I do. But only when I'm ready. It's just too painful right now," she quivered. "So, please, I beg you both to give me time."

Mo draped his arm around her, kissing her temple gently, wishing he could take away the pain that so clearly consumed his friend's entire being. "Of course, Livvy. We get it."

"He said I would always be his 'Eve', and I have no fucking clue what that means!" Olivia downed the rest of her drink, signaling the server to bring her another one as she got up from her chair, leaving Mo and Kiera alone.

"He what?" Kiera asked under her breath.

"It's that song, K. The one he did right before he asked you-know-who to marry him. Livvy's his Eve. She came crawling back, begging for another shot. He knows that she's still the only one for him. He wants her back, but he's just too scared to admit it. That's what that song's all about. It's about something beautiful arising out of pain."

"Well, then, why the fuck is he torturing her?"

"He's doing the same thing she always did. He's too scared to get hurt again so he's sticking with the sure thing."

Kiera turned around and shot daggers in Alexander's direction, wanting to hurt him for destroying her friend.

~~~~~~~~~~

Alexander signaled the bartender for his check as the M.C. jumped back on stage. Carter said he was held up on another assignment, but would report to Olivia's house as soon as he could to make sure she was alright. But what if she wasn't? Alexander needed to go over there and check on her. He was starting to shake with apprehension about what he had said to her and the way he just let her walk away from him, knowing that there could be a possible threat to her life out roaming the streets of Boston.

"Okay. Next up, an old favorite back from parts unknown."

Alexander's heart stopped. Could it be?

"Ladies and gentlemen, Miss Olivia Adler!"

The crowd roared with applause as Alexander watched Olivia rise from her table on unsteady legs and walk toward the stage, positioning herself behind the piano. It felt like no time had passed at all since that first night back in August when he watched her perform on that very stage. That was less than five months ago. Everything had happened so quickly. But things were very different now.

"Thank you," Olivia murmured into the microphone. "You're all probably wondering where I've been."

The audience clapped in response.

"Well, it's kind of a long story, but the short end of it is that I got spooked, I guess. I got scared, and my gut reaction is to run when that happens. So that's what I did," she explained to the crowd, her voice shaking. "I ran to a beach in Florida, and I pushed away the one person that meant the world to me. Then I came crawling back only to find out that he wants nothing to do with me anymore. Which kind of sucks, but I guess I deserve it."

Olivia took a deep breath as she surveyed her captive audience. "Anyway, as I sat around my house today, I debated what song to do tonight. I didn't even want to come, but my persistent therapist was fairly persuasive in making sure I made an appearance here. This song came on my iPod and I knew it was perfect. This is *What Did I Ever Come Here For* by Brandi Carlile. I hope you all enjoy."

Gingerly placing her fingers on the piano, she played the opening chords of the song before her voice filled the bar. It felt good to be back there, doing what she did best. It was all she knew. It was all she had left. Alexander had taken everything else from her. He took her heart and she now knew that she would never get it back. He continued to hold onto it, even though he was going to marry Chelsea.

As she sang, she thought about her decision to leave Alexander all those months ago and how, at the time, it seemed like her only option. His words still haunted her. *It will destroy me, too.* She still heard him saying that in her dreams. Was her inability to deal with her past still destroying him?

Alexander stared intently at Olivia as she sang about being away, then returning only to have her heart ripped out. She was right. It was the perfect song for the situation because that's exactly what happened. Olivia showed up, desperately wanting him to take her back, but all he did was push her away to protect his own heart. How was that any better than what she had done to him? How was it any different?

"Hey. You okay, bro?" Tyler whispered.

"Yeah. I'm good." Alexander stood up, throwing several bills on the bar.

"Wait. Where are you going?"

"I don't know, Ty. I just can't be here right now. I shouldn't be here. I should be home with Chelsea." He walked toward the front door of the bar.

Tyler leapt up, running to catch up to Alexander as Olivia sang about a worn out soul. "Do you mean that?"

"What?" Alexander looked at Tyler with a questioning expression on his face.

"Do you really think you belong at home with Chelsea? If that's truly what you think you want, I will support you one-hundred-and-ten percent. You know I will."

Alexander glanced over at the stage, his eyes meeting Olivia's. He inhaled sharply at the expression on her face, and their eyes remained locked for several long seconds. Bowing his head slightly, he shook it, unable to look into her sad brown eyes anymore...eyes that always looked large on her face but now looked like they didn't even belong there.

He walked outside, Tyler following close behind.

"Alex, please. Think about it."

"I *have* thought about it, Tyler," he replied, stopping in his tracks to face his brother. "I've thought about it so much over the past few months. And then even more so over the past few days. At first, when I let her walk away from me this past Monday, I kept kicking myself for not screaming out her name and pulling her into my arms, telling her that I forgive her. But I don't know. She's only going to run again. And next time, I don't know if I could possibly survive it. So I need to do this for me. I need to move on and regain control of this situation, and marrying Chelsea is the only way I know that I can." He turned, walking briskly in the direction of his car.

"Goddamnit," Tyler muttered, following his brother and trying to catch up to him. "Don't you think that's a little rash?" he shouted.

Alexander turned around again, stopping in front of a brick building, the chilly Boston air sending shivers down his spine, causing his teeth to chatter.

"Have you thought about how hypocritical you're being?" Tyler asked quietly. "You push her away because you're scared

152

of getting hurt. That's the exact thing she did to you. What makes it okay for you to do it?"

"Don't you think I know that?!" he yelled, running his hands through his hair, glaring at his brother. "And it doesn't make it okay, but I need to do it."

"Call it self-preservation," a sweet voice interrupted.

Alexander and Tyler both turned to see Olivia standing to the side.

Tyler lowered his eyes, unsure of how much of his and Alexander's discussion she had overheard. Alexander couldn't do anything but stare into those big brown eyes. He was drawn to her eyes as much that day as he was the first time he gazed into them.

Noticing a tense situation, Tyler cleared his throat. "Well, I'll just leave you two alone. I'll call you tomorrow, Alex." Tyler turned, leaving Alexander alone with Olivia.

"Olivia, I..."

"Alexander, please." She pulled her jacket tighter around her body, desperately seeking warmth. "Don't say anything. Let's just pretend we never ran into each other. I'm sure that's what you want. That way you can go on with your life. I know I threw your perfect little world into a tailspin the minute I came back to town and I'm sorry. I just thought..." She trailed off, not knowing how to finish her sentence without breaking down.

Alexander took a step toward her, their bodies almost touching. Olivia whimpered at the intense feeling coursing through her from the proximity of his strong muscular body to hers once more. She looked up into his green eyes, wondering if she still had the same effect on him that he had on her. Seeing the desire pooling behind them, she had her answer. She quickly lowered her head, looking down at her boots as she stood on the snowy sidewalk, hopelessly trying to avoid his gaze.

"Look at me," Alexander said.

Olivia shook her head. "No, Alexander!" she cried. "Please. I understand your reasons. Believe me, I do. But I just can't stand to look into your eyes right now. They haunt me enough in my dreams already. Every night for the past four months that's all I've seen. Your eyes. I could draw them from memory. I just can't bear to look at them right now, knowing that you don't..."

Alexander wrapped his arm around Olivia's waist, pulling her body close as electricity coursed through his entire being from the feeling of her delicate frame crushed against his.

"Please..." she whimpered, her head buried in his chest as she inhaled his scent, still avoiding his eyes. "My heart can't take it, Alex. Please. Set me free," her voice pleaded with him, still keeping her eyes turned down.

"You... You can't mean it."

Olivia brought her hand to her cheeks, wiping her tears and trying to hide the pain in her face. "You're getting married to someone else, Alexander. Please. I need you to release this hold you still have on me. I'm trying to stay so strong, and then you pull me back in and I fucking crumble in your embrace. You made your decision. Now I need you to honor it so that I can survive."

Alexander's heart sank as he released her. "What do you mean, Olivia? Survive what?"

She took a deep breath and turned to walk toward the subway station. "Life without you in it."

"Olivia, love."

She stopped in her tracks at the mention of that term of endearment. She heard his voice calling her that in her dreams, only to wake up knowing that his new love was Chelsea.

"Please. You broke me, Olivia," Alexander explained, wanting her to turn around and face him. "You, of all people, must understand."

Olivia nodded slowly. "I understand." Looking over her shoulder, her eyes finally met his. "And I wish you all the happiness in the world," she said, turning her head forward. "But, please, release me."

Alexander took several deliberate steps, standing mere breaths behind her. "I don't think I can."

She sobbed. "That's not fair. You need to. You're getting

married. Why are you marrying her if you won't let me go?"

He placed his hand on her stomach, pulling her back into him as he leaned down and kissed her hair, attempting to soothe her sobs. "Because you already have my heart. You've had it for longer than I think you realize," he explained. "And I don't want it back, but that still doesn't mean I am prepared to leave Chelsea. She cares about me."

"And she's a sure bet," Olivia muttered, finally realizing his reasons for pushing her away.

"Yes. She won't run when things get tough, and I need that control in my life, Olivia. And with you, I am anything but in control. You've got to understand that."

Olivia turned around to face Alexander. "Do you love her, Alex?" She searched his eyes for the answer she already knew.

He rolled his eyes. "Why does everyone ask me that?"

She shrugged. "It's a simple question," she said quietly. "Do you love her? Does she set your body on fire with a simple touch? Does the thought of her bring a smile to your face? Do you miss her when you're at work? When you get a new text message, does your heart race as you run to your phone, desperately hoping that it's her because just the thought of a kind word from her sends butterflies dancing in your stomach?" Olivia took a step closer. She leaned in and whispered in his ear, her breath hot on his neck. "When you get home from a long day of work, do you want nothing more than to just bury yourself inside of her, savoring the closeness of your two bodies?" She stepped back, staring into his eyes. "Alexander, do you love her?" she quivered.

Alexander stood there, speechless at Olivia's words. With each question, he could answer yes...but not about Chelsea. Only Olivia made him feel that way, but he couldn't tell her that. It was too painful to admit. As much as he wanted to scream to the world that he loved Olivia, he didn't. He stayed mute, as he so often did those days.

"You may want to answer that question before you marry her." Olivia turned and made her way down the steps to the subway station, leaving Alexander in the snow, watching her walk away from him yet again.

CHAPTER TWENTY-THREE

A FAVOR

OLIVIA COLLAPSED ON THE couch after finally getting home from Open Mic, not wanting to leave her house ever again. She couldn't go anywhere. The entire city reminded her of Alexander. The Commons. Open Mic. Her work. MacFadden's. Everywhere she turned, there was yet another reminder of what she lost.

Days drifted by and Olivia stayed in the confines of her house, refusing to go into her bedroom, the smell of Alexander on the sheets still ever-present. She spent most of her days on the couch, curled up in a ball. Kiera and Mo had called and texted multiple times, but she wasn't ready to face them just yet. Thankfully, her friends knew enough to give her some space and time. They say that time heals all wounds. Olivia prayed that was true.

As she checked her e-mail each day, a new Google search alert would appear, discussing new details about the Alexander-Chelsea wedding. Photos emerged of the happy couple at a variety of pre-wedding activities. Engagement parties. Bridal showers. An internet poll was already taking bets on when their first child would be born. Over the weeks, tears wouldn't flow anymore. But the dull ache was still there. It had never left.

She would occasionally look out her front window to see a black SUV parked on the street, Carter usually in the driver's seat, his eyes trained on Olivia's home. He would nod at her, a stoic look across his face. At first, Olivia would ignore him.

Then she started to leave the couch to sit in the bay window, drinking her coffee as she stared at him. After a few days, he caught on and would have a coffee with him during that time each day. It made her smile.

In the evenings, Carter left and Martin would sit in the SUV, keeping an eye on things. Olivia wondered why, even after everything, Alexander still felt the need to protect her. Maybe he did still care about her. She recalled her last conversation with Alexander and how he couldn't even tell her that he loved Chelsea.

One day, after several weeks passed, she woke on the couch and trudged over to make a cup of coffee. She was pretty much surviving on just coffee and alcohol. After preparing her drink, she walked over to sit in her bay window, feeling the cold winter air on the window. She spotted the black SUV and raised her cup to her mouth, hoping to meet Carter's eyes.

But the eyes that stared back weren't Carter's. They were those green eyes that she kept seeing in her dreams every night. Her throat let out a silent cry. She sat there, drinking her coffee and staring at Alexander. She willed him to get out of the car and come talk to her, tell her that he made a mistake and that he wasn't going to marry Chelsea. She pleaded with him with her eyes, but he never moved.

He sat there every day that week, not getting out of the car, keeping watch over her house. Her self-imposed prison.

She listened to all the people on the street, bustling about the busy Boston neighborhood, and Olivia sat on her couch. All alone. Exactly how she wanted everything, or so she thought. Her only comforts were the multiple bottles of liquor that she had.

On a snowy day, Olivia stood up from her couch to feed Nepenthe and felt weak, wondering when she ate last. Walking to the cupboard, she found a few snacks to munch on as she looked at the calendar. She didn't know how long she had been moping around her house. Alexander still remained outside in his SUV. He hadn't come crawling back to her, saying he made a terrible mistake. He had said nothing. He just sat and watched her.

Olivia heard a buzzing in her kitchen and walked over to the island. It was her cell. She continued to ignore it, just as she had been doing since she got home after Open Mic night all those days ago. But she finally realized that she couldn't ignore life forever.

"Hey, Kiera," Olivia said, reluctantly answering the phone.

"Jesus H. Christ, Libby! What the fuck is going on?! Your door is dead-bolted, and that's cool, but holy shit!"

"Yeah. Sorry. It's been a rough week, I think," she replied dryly.

"I figured as much. But try several weeks, bitch. I'll be there in twenty minutes. Do not lock me out or I swear to God…"

"I know, I know," Olivia interrupted. "You'll cut a bitch."

"Yes. Yes, I will," Kiera said chirpily before she hung up the phone.

Olivia groaned and unlocked the dead-bolt before dragging herself upstairs to take a shower. She stood underneath the running water, thinking about what went wrong. She knew she was taking a risk pouring her heart out to Alexander. And he did say he was happy, although he didn't sound too convincing. He couldn't even say that he loved Chelsea.

"Olivia? Where are you?" Kiera's voice cut through her thoughts.

"I'm in the shower," she shouted. "Be out soon." She jumped out of the shower and, after being absolutely disgusted looking at her skeletal frame, threw on some yoga pants and a sweatshirt. She brushed out her hair and put it up in a messy bun before heading downstairs to see Kiera.

"Happy birthday!" Kiera and Mo shouted when Olivia walked into the living room. She stopped in her tracks, surprised. It was long past her birthday, but she had missed celebrating it with her friends.

They made up for it, carrying in bags of food. "Sorry. It's all we could manage last minute," Mo said as Olivia grabbed a piece of sushi. She looked at her friends and immediately started crying, feeling overwhelmed by their kindness.

"Thanks, guys." Her friends pulled her close and the three of them stood in the living room, embracing. Sushi was her favorite thing in the world, except for oysters. But Alexander ruined oysters for her.

"I don't know what I'd do if you two weren't in my life." Olivia looked at her two friends.

"Okay," Kiera said, bouncing up and down. "No more crying. From now on, only smiles."

"Don't I wish…" Olivia said, giving her a sideways glance. She grabbed a glass of wine from Kiera and walked over to the large bay window, meeting Alexander's eyes.

He gave her a weak smile, taking in her frail figure as Mo walked up to her and put his arms around her. Alexander thought how he wanted to be able to comfort her now, but it was Mo instead.

A tear fell down his face, wishing he could turn the clock back several weeks, or at least build up enough courage to face the woman he let walk away from him more times than he could count. But he was with Chelsea now, and she tried to make him happy.

"Come on, baby girl," Mo said, leading her away. "Let's get some food in your system." He looked out the window, nodding in Alexander's direction.

Olivia and her friends sat down at her dining room table and dug into the food, eating in relative silence for several moments. When everyone seemed to get their fill, Mo finally spoke. "So tell us. What's going on?"

Olivia glared at him.

"Livvy, I'm not putting up with your shit so just spill it. You need to talk about it and I won't give up until you do."

"Fine," she exhaled. She proceeded to tell them about going to Alexander's office, pouring her heart out to him, bumping into Chelsea in the hallway, running out of the building, and Alexander finding her on Boylston Street to return her jacket. She left out the part about some weird guy chasing her, not wanting to worry her friends. Then she told them all about her exchange with Alexander outside of Johnny D's that same week, when he all but said he wanted to be with her, but had to push her away to protect himself. And that he couldn't admit that he loved Chelsea.

"You should give it one more shot, Livvy," Mo said. "He's definitely not over you. You need to give him a reason to fight for you."

"Mo, he made it quite clear that he wanted nothing to do with me. Apart from him telling me that I'll always be his 'Eve', which I have no fucking clue what that even means, he's shown no indication that he's not going to go through with that goddamn wedding."

Olivia began breathing heavy, noticing her two friends exchange a look. "What? What is it you're not telling me?"

Mo sighed. "You're his Eve. Come here, baby girl. Take a look at this." He grabbed his cell phone out of his pocket and, after searching for a video, handed the phone over to her.

She hit play on the screen, not fully comprehending what she was seeing. She glanced up at her two friends as she watched Alexander sitting at the piano at Johnny D's, starting to play a song she knew quite well. It was actually a band she had turned him on to.

"I don't understand," Olivia said softly.

"Every week for about a month, starting right around Thanksgiving, he would show up at Open Mic and perform," Kiera explained. "This is the song he chose to perform right before proposing to Chelsea."

Olivia's heart sank in her chest. She could see the pain in his face as he sang about someone he loved leaving, making him empty inside. Then about finding that person, only for them to push him away again. "I'm his Eve," she whispered.

"Exactly," Mo said. "The one he'll always put above all others. The one he'll always care about. The one he'll never be able to let go."

Olivia stood up from her chair and walked over to the bay window, staring at Alexander. "I don't know if I can put myself through that again."

"The fight's not over yet," Kiera said. "I mean, he's sitting out there, keeping an eye on things over here. Apparently, he's had round-the-clock surveillance on this place. He still cares about you, Libs. A lot! I don't believe for a second that he's going to go through with that wedding. Hell, he barely spends any time at his place anymore. Just the other night, we ran into him and his dog when he was heading to the office just to get out of the house."

Olivia sat there, thinking. Maybe there was another way.

"Is there anything I can do, Livvy?" Mo asked, seeing the wheels turning in her head.

Olivia turned around and faced her friends. "Well, funny you should ask. Can you think of any way you could convince Alexander to go to MacFadden's next time you guys play? There's a song I'd love to do if you don't mind, Mo. It's a little slower, but I would really appreciate it if you back me up."

"We're playing Friday, as usual."

"Well, good. Wait. What day is it?"

Kiera laughed. "It's Wednesday."

Olivia looked down. "What month is it?" She had completely lost track of time.

"It's February thirteenth, jackass," Mo sneered.

"Jesus. I'm sorry, guys." Olivia straightened up, hoping to find her backbone to actually go through with her plan. "Well, let's do it this Friday then."

Mo stared at Olivia. "Really? You're willing to get up in front of over five hundred people and pour your heart and soul out, all with the hopes that Alexander is actually there and listening?"

She thought for a minute. "Well, yeah. That about sums it up."

"Let's get to work then. I've got a song to learn," Mo said, dragging Olivia upstairs.

"Oooohh. I'll be your pretend audience," Kiera said, leaping up from her chair and following them up the stairs. "Wait a second, guys," she said as Olivia opened the door to the music room. "It's the thirteenth. That means…"

Olivia's heart sank. "That means he's getting married this weekend."

Mo grabbed his cell phone. "Don't worry. I got this." He searched his phone, finally landing on the number he needed before dialing. "Tyler, it's Mo. I need a favor."

CHAPTER TWENTY-FOUR

OUT OF CONTROL

"YOU WANT TO GO to a bar with your brother after the rehearsal dinner tonight? Are you crazy? For crying out loud, we're getting married tomorrow morning, Alex!" Chelsea huffed, glaring at him as he stood in the lobby of Old Trinity Church waiting for their guests to arrive to go over the wedding processional.

"Yes, I do. Just for a little bit. A few of my friends will be there. Mo's band is playing and I want to go and support him. Plus, Tyler feels short-changed that he didn't get to throw me a bachelor party. So, yes, I'm going to the bar. You can feel free to come with some of your friends, if you're that worried about me."

"That is so not how I was expecting to spend my last night as a single woman," Chelsea replied, taking a step closer, running her fingers down his chest. "I was hoping this weekend would be incredibly romantic and not spent at some shitty bar," she whispered in a sultry voice.

"Chelsea. Please, don't. I want to spend some time with my friends before I have to spend the rest of the weekend with you." He stared at her, his eyes fierce. No matter what he wanted to do, she had something to say about it.

She took a deep breath. Going to the bar that night wasn't worth losing Alexander over. At least he had finally invited her out with him and his friends. "Fine. We'll go to your little bar then." Chelsea grabbed Alexander's hand, leading him toward the vestibule to begin their rehearsal.

"Alexander, darling." An older woman stopped him, pulling him into her arms while Chelsea stayed firmly planted at his side. "Wonderful to see you again, Chelsea. I wonder what you ever said to convince my son to marry you."

Alexander chuckled a little at his mother's words and Chelsea's scowl.

"Oh, come, dear. It's just a joke. But I would like a word with my son before we begin, if you don't mind." Colleen Burnham glared at Chelsea, waiting for her to give her some privacy with Alexander. After returning the glare for several long moments, Chelsea finally spun on her heels, seeking out her sister.

"Hi, Ma," Alexander said, kissing her cheek. "How's Miami?"

"Oh, you know. Same old thing. Sun, sand, and sangria." She winked.

"I'm glad you were able to be here this weekend. It means a lot to both of us," Alexander said, smiling at his mother's gentle face. Although she was in her mid-sixties, she still had a youthful appearance about her.

"Well, I needed to be in town anyway to help plan our charity auction next month so I'm killing two birds with one stone, although I'm sensing something's just not right here, Alex." She grabbed her son's hands in hers, staring deep into his eyes. "What's going on? Are you sure you're ready to marry that girl?"

Alexander exhaled loudly. "Why does everyone ask me that?"

Colleen narrowed her gaze on him. Even though he towered over her by a foot, he would always be her baby. "Because we care about you, Alex. And we want to make sure you're not getting into something you can't get out of. Marriage is a big deal. One you should not enter into lightly. Have you signed a pre-nup?"

"MOM!" Alexander exclaimed, aghast.

Colleen shrugged, her demeanor unchanged. "It's a legitimate question. Have you?"

"I don't need one."

"Oh, come on, Alex. I'm sorry, but you better be damn sure you want to spend the rest of your life with that one if you're not going to make her sign a pre-nup. Yes, she comes from some money, but nothing compared to what she's about to marry into."

Glancing over at Chelsea showing off her ring excitedly to people that he didn't even know, Alexander wondered what he was getting into. And why Chelsea wanted to rush into a wedding so badly. "If it will make you happy, I'll have my lawyers draw one up." He turned to walk away.

"Alexander," Colleen said, gently placing her hand on his shoulder. "What will make me happy is you doing what you think is right. Doing what your heart wants. I know all about the other girl you were dating…"

Alexander whirled around, glaring at his mother before shooting daggers at Carol and Tyler over her shoulder. "Ma, I…"

"Just think about what I said, Alex. Follow your heart and not your head, for once."

Alexander stared at his mother and felt an arm wrap around his waist as someone planted a kiss on his neck. No sparks. No electricity. Nothing. Could he really resign himself to feeling nothing for the rest of his life?

"Come on, Alex," Chelsea crooned. "We're ready to begin."

Alexander blankly followed Chelsea down the long aisle leading to the altar of the historic church. He always loved the architecture of Old Trinity Church. He wasn't raised in a religious household and normally would never have considered having a religious wedding, but something about that church called to him. With the sun seeping through the large stained-glass windows, it always reminded him that there was something bigger at play in his life. Call it God. Call it fate. Call it whatever you want. He was a strong believer in some higher power, no matter what you called it. But now, as he made his way down the aisle to take his place for the wedding rehearsal, he wondered if he had been ignoring that higher power those past several months.

Alexander blanked out as the minister walked everyone

through the ceremony. It was an excruciatingly long process and Alexander wanted nothing more than to get out of there. Even with the sun setting over the city, illuminating the entire church and making it seem more open, he felt the walls crushing him. His heart raced and he struggled to breathe.

"Dude, you okay?" Tyler whispered as he listened to the minister talk about love being patient.

Alexander swallowed hard. "Fine. I'm fine."

"Bullshit," Tyler said a little too loud. Everyone glared at him.

Alexander chuckled a little before trying to compose himself.

"Sorry. Just trying to clear up an irritation in my throat," Tyler laughed.

After the minister was content that everyone knew what they were to do the following day, he dismissed the wedding party. Martin drove Alexander and Chelsea the few blocks to the rehearsal dinner at Atlantic Fish, an awkward silence filling the car. Alexander thought back to the last time he had been there. He couldn't believe Chelsea chose that restaurant, of all places, to have the rehearsal dinner. That was where he had taken Olivia on their first official date.

"What's going on with you?" Chelsea asked, breaking the silence.

"What do you mean?" he replied nervously.

"Do you think I'm stupid, Alex? Because I'm not. The past several weeks, you've been distant. And I don't know what it is. You told me that you were over Olivia and ready to start our life together but, lately, I don't know. I know you've been going over there, sitting watch outside her house."

Martin pulled up outside the restaurant, discreetly getting out of the car to give the two occupants a little privacy. Alexander stared out the passenger window, spotting the table he sat at with Olivia all those months ago.

"Please, Alex. We're getting married tomorrow. I just... I just want to make sure you actually want this. Or will Olivia always be your 'what if?'" A tear fell down Chelsea's face. "Will she always be your Eve? I don't want to always come second to her."

Alexander slowly shook his head and looked at her, staring deep into her brown eyes. "Chelsea, I love you. And tomorrow, I'm going to marry you. You're what I need, not Olivia." He brushed his lips against Chelsea's, encouraging them apart with his tongue, exploring her mouth as he had done so many times over the past several months.

Chelsea groaned and tugged on Alexander's hair, bringing her body closer to his. As he kissed her, all he could think about was Olivia. That made him want to kiss Chelsea even more, desperately trying to erase Olivia from his thoughts. He needed to.

Reaching for the buttons on Chelsea's coat, he quickly rid her of her outermost layer, planting kisses along her neckline.

"Alex, wait," she breathed out. "Our guests."

"Let them wait," he growled.

"What if someone sees?"

Alexander raised an eyebrow. "When has that ever bothered you before?"

Chelsea grinned. "You're right." She pulled his face back to hers, finding his lips as he quickly raised her dress to her waist. She moaned out in pleasure as he entered her. He didn't know why he was fucking her in the SUV, but he needed to regain control of everything, and that was the only way he knew how.

CHAPTER TWENTY-FIVE

A CHANCE

"LIBBY! OH, MY GOD! It is you!" Melanie exclaimed when she saw her old friend walk into the upstairs bar of MacFadden's with Kiera and Mo. "How are you?" She wrapped her arms around Olivia and squeezed, not wanting let go. "I've missed you so fucking much." She pulled back and took in her appearance. "We all have."

Bridget nodded, hugging her friend. "We're glad you're back, Libby."

"Thanks, girls," Olivia responded, taking in her friends. "I missed you guys, too. I'm sorry I haven't called or anything, but things have been rough." She watched as Bridget and Melanie passed a meaningful look.

"So are you back with the band then?" Melanie asked, taking a sip of her drink and breaking the tension.

"No. Well, kind of. I'm doing one song tonight."

Bridget's eyes lit up. "Really?"

Olivia nodded as she took a long drag of the drink Kiera handed her. "Yeah. I still can't believe he's getting..." her voice trailed off, unable to even say the words.

Bridget wrapped her arms around her, trying to comfort her. "Hey. I'd be surprised if he actually goes through with it. I mean, after you left, he was down at the wellness center, pestering poor Mel every day, asking if you had contacted anyone there. Hell, we finally figured out you were back that second week of January when he stopped coming down."

Olivia stared at Melanie and Bridget. "Even in November

and December?"

Melanie nodded. "Yeah. Even the week after his engagement hit the papers, he still came in, every day, asking if anyone had heard from you. I was secretly thankful that you hadn't reached out to anyone there because I didn't know what I would tell him. He looked so sad, even after he put a ring on that bitch's finger."

"Mel!" Olivia said, playfully smacking the lively blonde.

"No. She's right," Kiera interrupted. "She's a bitch."

"Go, Team Olivia!" Bridget said, pumping her fist in the air.

"Oh, god. Not you, too!" Olivia laughed. It felt good to finally smile and joke around with her friends.

"We'll always be on your side. You know that, right?" Bridget said, a warm look in her dark eyes. "We'll always be here for you when you need us. We won't ever leave you, Libby."

Olivia raised her glass to her lips, trying to fight back the tears that threatened to fall.

"So, are you ready for this?" Mo asked, walking up to the group of girls.

"As ready as I'm going to be," Olivia answered. "Are you sure he'll be here?" she asked him.

Melanie and Bridget surveyed Olivia, a questioning look on their faces.

"Yeah. Tyler convinced him to come, but we don't want him to see you before it's time so just hang out in back of the stage. Kiera will keep a look out. When he gets here, we'll bring you up."

"Okay." Olivia took a deep breath.

"We better get going then," Mo said, wrapping his arm around Olivia's waist and leading her away from her friends and toward the stage. "When Kiera gives me the go ahead, we're going to re-arrange the setup a little so the piano is center stage. We want you to be the focus. Okay, baby girl?"

"Thanks, Mo." She gave him a quick peck on the cheek before disappearing behind the curtain, waiting for her call.

The band did some final sound checks as the large room began filling up. At around ten, Mo stepped up to the microphone and faced a packed bar. "Happy Valentine's Day, everyone. Of course, a day late. Thanks for spending your night here with us!" The band kicked off, playing some Rolling Stones, the crowd dancing along.

At that moment, Tyler and Alexander walked up the stairs to the second floor, Chelsea just a few steps behind with her sister. "I don't know why you like this bar so much!" she shouted so Alexander could hear her over the music.

He turned around, waiting for them to catch up, glowering at her. "I'm here to support my friend, Chelsea. That's all."

As they reached the back of the bar, Tyler turned to Alexander and the girls. "What would you all like to drink?"

"Whatever Alex is having is fine by me," Chelsea replied, her sister nodding in agreement.

"Okay. Wait here. We'll be right back," Alexander said, leaving the girls standing toward the back of the large room as he made his way over to the bar with his brother.

"Alex! You're here! We weren't expecting to see you tonight!" Kiera said, walking over to him, wrapping her arms around him. "Good to see you, too, Tyler," she said with an appreciative nod. "Happy Valentine's Day!" She winked.

"You, too."

"Nice to see you, Mr. Burnham," Melanie said, grinning. She had a feeling she knew what was going on.

"You, as well, Melanie. Bridget." He nodded toward the girls before looking back into Kiera's green eyes. Several moments passed without anyone saying anything, Kiera thrilled that Tyler was able to convince him to come to the bar that night.

All of a sudden, Alexander gasped. "Wait. Carter said Olivia was over at your house. Is everything okay?"

"Of course, but you know Olivia. She's moody." Kiera saw Alexander's face drop. "She's okay, Alex. She just needs to get through this. She'll come out fine on the other side. She always does. But I just needed to get out of the house for a little bit. Grab Chelsea and come meet us back here." She changed the conversation so that Alexander didn't become suspicious and leave. Kiera had Tyler on her side anyway.

"Okay. I'll be right back." Alexander turned to leave.

"I'm Tyler, by the way," he said, extending his hand to Melanie.

She giggled, shaking his hand. "I'm Melanie, but everyone just calls me Mel."

"It's wonderful to meet you, Mel," he beamed. Melanie blushed at the mini version of Alexander standing in front of her.

"Do you think this will work?" Tyler asked Kiera, breaking the silence.

She shrugged as she reached into her purse. "I sure hope so."

"What is going on?" Bridget asked.

Kiera winked. "You'll see. Patience." She found her cell phone and texted Olivia.

A few minutes later, just as the final note of the band's last song rang through the bar, Mo looked at the audience, finding Kiera standing with Melanie and Bridget. A grin crossed his face when he noticed Alexander, Tyler, Chelsea, and someone he didn't recognize standing directly behind them. Kiera gave Mo a brief nod.

"Quick set change, guys," Mo said into the microphone as his band quickly moved the grand piano center stage, readjusting their positions on stage to make room for it.

"Great. Thanks. Here's one we've never done before."

That was her cue. Taking a deep breath, Olivia stepped onto the stage while the crowd cheered. When she was set behind the piano, Mo spoke again. "Miss Olivia Adler everyone."

The crowd erupted in loud applause and cheers. Several people began chanting, "Libby! Libby! Libby!"

Olivia smiled. "Thank you. Mo, thanks for letting me perform tonight."

Alexander gaped at her. What was she doing? Now that he saw her up close and not through a dirty window, he couldn't believe his eyes. She had lost even more weight, her eyes looked cold and empty. The spark was gone. It looked as if her soul had been sucked out of her body. All that sat up at the piano was an empty shell, and he knew it was all his fault.

"I'm here tonight to sing a song from the bottom of my heart." Olivia looked over the audience and saw Alexander standing near Kiera. Chelsea was clearly unhappy. "You see, there's this guy and, pardon my French, I royally fucked up. I pushed him away, and he's getting married tomorrow." The audience gasped and a smile spread across Olivia's face. "The funny thing is, he made me so fucking happy."

A voice shouted from the audience, "I'll make you happy, Libby!"

Alexander glared in the direction of the voice, surprised by his reaction.

Olivia looked toward the rather drunk man. "Thanks, I appreciate that. But here's the thing." Her eyes roamed the audience, speaking to them as if it was a big group therapy session because, at that moment, that's what she needed. "I've gone my entire life pushing everyone away, scared that if I got too close to someone they would leave me. And I did it again. I ran from this wonderful person fearful that, in the end, he wouldn't be able to deal with all my craziness and would eventually leave me. I tried to protect myself from getting hurt." A tear escaped from Olivia's eye. "But the pain I have been through these past several months is so much more than anything I have ever experienced." She scanned the audience and locked eyes with Alexander. "And when I realized how big of a mistake it was, I came groveling back, only to realize he moved on. Like I asked him to."

The audience was silent, listening intently to every word. Olivia returned her eyes to the rest of the crowd. "He was someone I hated to leave in the morning. I couldn't get enough of him while we were together. He accepted me for who I was, never wanting to change a thing about me." She returned her gaze to Alexander, her eyes pleading with him, her chin quivering. "Alexander, you were someone I think I could have fallen madly in love with." She took a deep breath, needing the inner courage to get through what she was about to do. "I know it's over. I do. I never gave our relationship a chance. But I'm hoping you will now, for both of our sakes. Life is too short to waste on a mediocre relationship, don't you think?"

Olivia looked down, placing her hands on the piano keys. "This is *Ashes and Wine* by A Fine Frenzy."

Alexander listened to the opening chords of the song, mesmerized by the woman on the stage, a deep sadness enveloping his body.

"Come on, Alex," Chelsea said, her heart racing. She had been worried about losing Alexander since Olivia returned to town. She felt everything was spiraling out of control. "Let's get out of here." She turned to face her sister. "She's clearly lost her mind," she said loudly so Alexander could hear.

"Chelsea. Enough," he growled.

Tyler smiled, wrapping his arm around Melanie's small waist and leaning over toward Kiera. "I think it's working."

Alexander returned his attention to the woman on stage. The pain in Olivia's voice was so real that he could physically feel it. He couldn't believe that she was up on stage, pouring her heart out in front of hundreds of people. Granted, she had done the same at Open Mic nights in the past, but that was to a crowd of maybe fifty people. At MacFadden's, there were easily five hundred people, if not more, listening to her beg for one last chance. It was unlike anything she would ever do. Her fear of rejection and abandonment controlled her. And there she was, facing her fears head on.

Olivia sang the chorus, her voice sweet and quiet, holding back unbidden tears as she pleaded for a second chance. She wanted Alexander to feel her pain, to hurt as she hurt. Regret coursed through her body as she remembered how she pushed him away over and over again. She wanted one last chance so she begged, hopelessly wanting him to change his mind or, at least, not marry Chelsea.

Alexander looked at Chelsea, her eyes shimmering with tears as she sent him a pleading look. He knew that he had done exactly what Olivia did. He pushed her away, ignoring the best thing that had ever happened to him, scared that she would run again, leaving him hurting and in pain. Up until that moment, he was content with his decision to keep his heart at arm's length, desperately needing the control he felt from that. As he stared back and forth between the two women that knew him better than anyone else, he was torn.

Olivia watched Alexander stare into Chelsea's eyes but couldn't figure out if the connection between him and Chelsea was still there or not. As she finished the first chorus, her heart sank when Alexander leaned down and kissed Chelsea. Olivia's eyes immediately snapped back to the piano, thankful to have the familiarity of the white and black keys laid out in front of her.

As she continued singing, her voice became stronger, remembering all those mornings waking up next to Alexander, sharing coffee and kisses. A tear escaped her eye, falling down her cheek. She shook her head, reminding herself that those were no longer her lips to kiss. He was very nearly a married man and once the song was over, she would stop fighting for him. She had been fighting for him since she arrived in Boston. She was mentally and physically exhausted. There was no fight left. There was nothing left.

Olivia's eyes roamed the audience, locking on Alexander's wet eyes once more. She sang the last chorus to him as if he was the only person in the entire audience because, to Olivia, he was the only one that mattered at that moment. But she couldn't continue on if he wanted nothing to do with her. As the final chord rang through the bar, she resolved that she would walk away from him if that really was what he wanted.

"Olivia Adler, ladies and gentlemen!" Mo shouted, leering in Alexander's direction as Olivia finished the song to enthusiastic applause. Tears fell down Alexander's cheeks as he kept his arms tightly wrapped around Chelsea, desperate to feel something for her. He watched as Olivia quickly jumped off the stage, making a bee-line to the bar. She hovered for a moment, waiting for Alexander to say something. But it never happened. He simply gazed at her and slowly bowed his head, shaking it.

Olivia felt all the wind rush out of her body. It was over. She lost him. He was going to leave that bar and marry Chelsea the following morning.

"Come on, Libby. Let's get you out of here." Kiera grabbed

Olivia's arm and dragged her away.

Alexander watched as Kiera led Olivia out of the bar, wondering if he would ever see her again. Wondering if he made the right decision, wondering if wasn't too late to change his mind.

"Come on, Alex. Let's go home," Chelsea crooned in his ear. "We have a big day tomorrow."

~~~~~~~~~~

A man stood in the corner of a bar in downtown Boston, looking at a sad, beautiful woman being led away, clearly too heartbroken to even stand. Nathan Roberts knew it was risky to come to Boston after all these years, but he needed to.

When Thomas Burnham died, he thought all hopes of ever finding her again were gone. But one clue led to another, which led to another, and he eventually found out that she had returned to Boston. He heard that she had been singing with a band on Friday nights at a bar in the Financial District, and he wanted to see it for himself.

When the lead singer of the band announced a guest performer that night whose name was Olivia, his heart skipped a beat. He wondered why she still went by Olivia and not her real first name…Sarah. Or, at least, her real first name on paper.

He hid himself in the back of the audience, his eyes glued to the woman sitting behind the baby grand piano. The face. The eyes. The lips. They belonged to her mother.

Then she sang, and he knew. He found Olivia. After all these years of looking, his search was finally at an end. She was there, her voice full of pain.

And then he saw who she was singing to. *It couldn't be,* he thought to himself. But she had said his name.

Alexander.

What did Olivia know?

CHAPTER TWENTY-SIX

WRECKED

OLIVIA WOKE UP THE following morning, still wearing her dress from the night before. The rising sun peeked through the blinds, and she looked outside, hoping to see green eyes staring back at her from a parked SUV. But there was nothing. No car parked out front. Nothing. The street was empty, just like she felt inside. Empty.

Always a glutton for punishment, she walked over to her TV and flipped on the news, knowing there would be coverage of the wedding since it appeared to be the event of the year in Boston.

She was right.

Olivia watched as teams of reporters stood in front of Old Trinity Church in Copley Square, naming off various dignitaries from numerous countries in attendance. She felt her stomach churning at the thought of Alexander saying those vows to Chelsea, placing that ring on her finger, and the minister declaring them husband and wife until death do they part.

Bolting off the couch, she ran for the bathroom and emptied the contents of her stomach into the toilet, dry heaving because she barely ate anything the previous day. At that moment, she knew she needed to leave Boston. Everything reminded her of Alexander. Knowing that he would be married within the next few hours broke her even more than she was before.

Raising herself off the bathroom floor, she ran up to her bedroom and began throwing some of her belongings into her suitcases. She had paid for the beach house until mid-April. That's where she would go. She knew she was running, but this time, she was running from someone who wanted nothing to do with her. Someone that made her very presence painful in that city of so many amazing memories.

As she packed, she heard a loud knock on the front door. Not expecting company, she ignored it, wanting to get out of Boston as soon as possible.

"What the fuck do you think you're doing?!" Olivia heard a few minutes later. She turned her head to see Mo and Kiera standing in the doorway, their arms crossed and eyes wide.

"I'm packing. That's what the fuck I'm doing!" she cried out. "I need to get out of here!" She ran around to the other side of the bed, grabbing another suitcase, and began taking more clothes off hangers and stuffing them into the bag. "Shouldn't you two be on your way? You'll be late for the wedding of the fucking year." Olivia's breathing picked up. She clutched her chest, falling to the ground, collapsing under the absolute heartache she felt at that moment.

Mo rushed to her, enveloping her in his arms as he cradled her, rocking her back and forth. "Come on, baby girl. Let it out. Let it all out. It's okay." He kissed her head as sobs wracked through her entire body.

"I can't stay here, Mo. Please, just let me go. I'll be in Florida. I still have that beach cottage. I just can't be in this city, not when every street, every building, every park bench reminds me of everything I lost." Olivia's eyes searched Mo's. "Please," she whispered, her voice full of pain. "Let me go."

Kiera walked over and sat down on the floor, wrapping her arms around her friend, her own heart breaking from how hurt she looked. She had seen Olivia at her absolute worst. The wreck sitting in front of her was far more tragic than anything she had seen in all her years of knowing her.

"If you really think that's what you need to do, we'll support you, Libby."

Mo's eyes flashed toward Kiera, shock etched across his gentle face.

"Thank you," Olivia replied weakly.

"We couldn't go to the wedding, Libby. It just didn't seem right. Nothing about it seems right. Plus, we were your friends first. You need us more than he does today." Kiera clutched Olivia's hand.

She nodded, her breathing stabilizing. "I'm going to miss you both, but I have to go. You can come and visit anytime you want."

Mo nudged her. "I'm going to hold you to that."

Olivia smiled as she wiped the tears from her eyes, trying to compose herself.

"Are you sure you'll be okay to drive?" Kiera asked, her face full of concern.

"Yeah. I'll be fine. It will help take my mind off things. Give me time to think."

"Well, let's get you on your way then. It's a long drive." Mo winked as he grabbed a few of her suitcases, bringing them out to her car. An hour later, Olivia maneuvered her way through the Boston city streets for the last time.

~~~~~~~~~~~

After begrudgingly waving good-bye to their friend, Kiera and Mo made their way to Kiera's house by the community gardens to forget about the past few months. They were sad to see Olivia leave but understood why she had to go. The pain in her face was worse than either one had seen before.

They spent most of the day curled up on the couch, watching snow fall outside and reminiscing about all the good times they shared with Olivia. As the beer ran out, Kiera decided it was time to kick the party into second gear, not caring that it was nearly three in the morning. She poured several shots, both Kiera and Mo needing the liquor after all the drama of the past several weeks.

"To Olivia," Kiera slurred, raising her shot glass, tears starting to form beneath her eyelids.

"To Olivia," Mo responded, slinging his shot back in unison with Kiera. "Remember that crazy piercing phase she went through, what, her junior year of college?" he asked after the burn of the liquor subsided.

Kiera laughed, wiping her nose with her sleeve. "Yeah. I went with her to get her tongue pierced. I dragged her to a party that night and she did a few keg stands with a brand new stud in her tongue. It was all swollen and shit. God, it was a riot. She was so much fun."

"The two of you together behind the bar at Scotch. Jesus. I think security had to work overtime those nights to make sure no one laid any hands on either of you. I can't even tell you how many times I saw them kicking someone out."

Kiera sighed. "Yeah. That happened a lot, didn't it?"

"Sure did. But, man, she wouldn't put up with shit from anyone. She used to be so quiet when she first started working there. And then this whole other girl came out of nowhere. Once she got behind that bar, she had this spunk. Remember the time she grabbed that guy in the nuts and twisted so hard I swear the entire bar heard them pop?"

Kiera laughed hard at the memory, tears that streamed down her cheeks now tears of joy instead of sorrow. "Yeah. We had some good times."

"Yup." Mo raised another shot glass and Kiera followed suit. Just as they swallowed the liquid, a loud knock sounded. Kiera looked at the front door, wondering who could possibly be pounding on her door at that late hour, or early hour, depending on how you look at it.

"Expecting anyone?" Mo asked, his eyebrows raised.

"No. Not really." She got up from the table and stumbled over to the front door, pulling it open.

"What the fuck?" Kiera exclaimed in complete shock when Alexander pushed through, wearing a formal tuxedo. His bow tie was all disheveled and it looked like he had been running. Or drinking. Or both.

"Where is she?" he asked frantically.

"Who?" Kiera asked.

"Cut the crap, Kiera," Alexander growled. "You know damn well who."

"Oh, you mean the girl whose heart you stomped on last night and now it's all bled dry on the dirty, nasty floor of a bar?

Is that who we're talking about here?" she spat out, unintimidated by Alexander's size as he stood hovering over her petite frame.

"Damn it! Where is she?!" Alexander roared.

"Ya' know what, Alex? I like you. I do. But you're toxic to her. She poured her heart out to you, and all you did was spurn her, not even giving her the time of day. You did exactly what she did! And you continued to hold what she did to you against her! Leave her alone! You're married now. You need to let her go so that she can move on with her life. She's better off without you in it!"

Kiera returned to the table and poured another line of shots.

Alexander followed, stalking into the kitchen and nodding a greeting to Mo.

"Kiera, please. I need to know where she is." He turned to Mo. "Please, Mo. I'm begging you."

Mo shook his head. "I'm with Kiera on this one. You need to leave her alone. You should have seen how she..." Mo trailed off, the memory of one of his best fiends looking so broken and emotionally beaten permanently ingrained in his memory. He would do everything within his power to make sure that never happened to Olivia again.

"How she what?" Alexander asked quietly.

"How she looked!" Kiera exclaimed, spinning around to face him yet again, her green eyes on fire. "You've ruined that fucking girl. I love her like a sister and I've seen her go through a lot of shit, but what I walked in on earlier this morning, the hurt and unbearable pain taking control of her entire body, was more than I could bear to see. So she left, Alex." She took a deep breath, trying to control her Irish temper. "Please. Go home to your wife." Kiera downed another shot and turned back around, desperately wanting to put some space between her and the man that broke her best friend into millions of tiny pieces. The man that crushed her soul. The man the killed her spirit.

Alexander grabbed Kiera's arm, spinning her back around to face him. Raising his left hand, he growled, "Do you see a fucking ring on this finger?!"

Kiera gasped, not speaking for a moment while her brain processed what he had just said. "What do you mean, Alex?" she asked quietly.

"What do you think I mean, Kiera?" he replied, lowering his voice and releasing his grasp on her arm. "I couldn't do it. I just couldn't go through with it."

"Why do you want to know where Livvy is?" Mo asked, wanting to protect his friend. "I'm not so sure it's a good idea, telling you that."

"Please, Mo. I'm begging you. I know I've been such a prick these past few weeks. I should have stopped all this foolishness the second she walked back into my life, but I didn't. I pushed her away because I was scared of getting hurt again and losing control. I knew that it was the same thing Olivia did so why was it okay for me to do it and not her? Earlier, as I was watching Chelsea walk down the aisle, all I could hear in my head was my mother's voice, saying to follow my heart and not my head. And when Chelsea's father pushed back her veil, all I could think about was how I wished it was Olivia standing next to me. And then the minister started going on and on about Adam and Eve, the first woman and man…"

Kiera gasped.

"I think it surprised Chelsea, too. She looked at me and just knew that I was about to walk out. It was almost like it was a sign. Olivia is my Eve, and she always will be. So please, you need to tell me where she is. I'm begging you both."

Kiera looked up at Alexander, and could see how upset and sincere he looked. "She's back in Florida," she whispered.

Alexander's eyes lit up and he kissed Kiera on the cheek. "Thank you. Thank you. Thank you."

He ran from the room.

"Go get her, Alex!" Mo shouted. "But if you hurt her again, I swear I have ties to the mob!"

Alexander laughed as he leapt out the front door into the snow storm, speeding to his waterfront penthouse, hoping that the airport had a runway clear.

CHAPTER TWENTY-SEVEN

SOLACE

AT MIDDAY ON SUNDAY, Olivia pulled her car into the sandy driveway of her little beach cottage. The air was thick with an early season humidity as she hauled her luggage from the trunk into the house, making sure Nepenthe was comfortable with food and water before unpacking her belongings.

Everything looked just as she had left it, including her piano. It was still there. Nothing had changed, but everything was different. Alexander was now married. It was over. She lost him. Trying to subdue the lump that had formed in her throat at the thought of Alexander and Chelsea spending the rest of their lives together, she raided the cabinets, hoping that she had left some liquor behind. No such luck.

Grabbing her purse, not caring that she looked like hell from driving for the past twenty hours with barely any breaks, she headed out her front door, slamming into a tall, hard body wearing a wetsuit from his hips down.

"Jesus!" she exclaimed before looking up. "Cam." She inhaled sharply when her gaze met his intense silver eyes. "What are you doing here?" she whimpered, unable to avert her eyes from his naked chest and sculpted body, thinking that it was sinful for a psychiatrist to look that good. *Damn it, Libby! Get your head out of the gutter!*

"I guess I can ask the same of you," he said, interrupting her thoughts. "But I know the answer." He lowered his eyes, brushing a wayward curl out of her face. "Are you okay?"

She searched Cam's gentle face, his kindness overwhelming

her. After everything she had been through the past several months, after everything she had put Cam through, she was surprised to see him standing on her deck, still worried about whether she was okay.

All of her emotions rushed forward under the gentle stare of Cam's eyes. She fell to the ground, wailing through her tears. She was anything but okay.

"Hey, Libby," he said, lowering himself and pulling her into his arms. She exhaled through the sobs, savoring the comfort of his embrace. She needed him at that moment.

"I'm not going to say that it will be alright because I'm sure you don't want to hear that right now."

"I couldn't stay there, Cam. I just cracked," she cried. "I had to leave that city. Everywhere I turned there was another reminder of how I ruined everything. I couldn't bear it anymore."

Cam soothed her tears as he held on to her fragile body, worried about how much weight she had lost. "Libby, when was the last time you ate anything?" he asked after several long minutes.

She wiped her face, the tears finally subsiding. "I can't remember. Maybe Friday?"

"Jesus, Libby. It's fucking Sunday afternoon. We're going to get some food right now," he growled, standing up and pulling her with him toward the Wrangler that she had failed to notice was parked in front of her house.

"Cam, please. I just want some liquor to dull the pain. That's all. I'm too much of a wreck to be out in public."

He sighed. "Fine. Then I'll take you to my place and cook for you. No argument. If I have to kidnap you, I fucking will, Libby."

Her eyes grew wide as she listened to his voice full of anger and passion. It reminded her of Alexander. Her Alexander, except he wasn't hers anymore and he never would be again.

"I'm sorry," Cam said quietly, getting his emotions under control. "You need to eat, Libby. Please. Come with me. We'll open a bottle of pinot." He winked.

"Fine, but I need to shower."

"You can shower at my place while I'm cooking. If you think I'm going to let you out of my sight right now, you're crazy."

She went inside and packed a small bag of things that she would need to shower at Cam's. When she emerged, he snaked his arm around her too small waist and led her down her deck to his Wrangler.

She stepped up into the Jeep and closed the door, admiring the view of the beach. It was her solace from the pain. It was exactly what she needed to get through this rough patch in her life. And maybe Cam was what she needed. Maybe she had been looking at things all wrong. Maybe all the troubles she had with Alexander were meant to lead her to Cam.

"Hey, Libby?" Cam said, pulling Olivia out of her thoughts as he drove away from the beach.

"Yes?" She glanced across the car at him, admiring his wayward sandy hair blowing in the wind.

"I'm glad you're back."

Olivia reached over and grabbed his hand as he shifted into fourth. "Me, too."

~~~~~~~~~~

A few minutes later, Cam pulled up in front of an old Victorian-style home just a few blocks from the downtown area of Fernandina Beach. The wrap-around deck boasted several lounge chairs as well as a porch swing, complete with nautical themed pillows. Olivia made a mental note to use that swing sooner rather than later. It looked so peaceful.

Cam led her up the steps and into his house, giving her a tour of the lower level.

"Did you decorate this?" Olivia asked, astonished at the décor throughout the bottom floor. To the right of the entryway sat a large living room, the walls painted a light shade of yellow with a rather comfortable-looking sofa and love seat against the walls. Natural light shined through the entire house. Cam nodded as he led Olivia past a staircase and down a narrow hallway leading to a gourmet kitchen, the large windows overlooking a rather nicely manicured backyard complete with in-ground pool and hot tub.

"Swing set?" Olivia asked, raising her eyebrows at Cam, eyeing the large wooden play set in his backyard.

"I have nieces and nephews who like to come visit. Don't worry. No kids, or at least none that I know of," he replied, lightening the mood, happy to put a smile on her face.

She looked at the crystal clear water in the pool, wishing she had packed her bathing suit. *Oh well. Maybe next time*, she thought. She surprised herself, thinking about a next time at Cam's. It felt refreshing, as if maybe she would survive life after Alexander.

"Come, Libby. I'll show you the rest of the house." He led the way upstairs where there were two guest bedrooms complete with bathrooms, and an even larger master bedroom. Everything was decorated in light yellows, greens, and blues. The house definitely belonged in a beach community, that much was clear.

After Cam left her, Olivia ran the water in the master bathroom, hopping in the shower and savoring the feeling of the warm water on her skin. Her eyes began to droop slightly, the long drive finally catching up with her. For the past few hours, she had been running on pure adrenaline. Now that she had reached her destination, the lack of sleep over the past several days came rushing forward. She just needed to get through the shower and lunch, and then she could collapse.

"Feel better?" Cam asked when Olivia walked into the kitchen, the smell of garlic making her stomach growl.

"Yes. Slightly exhausted, but I'll be okay." She grabbed the glass of wine Cam held out to her.

"Do you like salmon?" He raised his glass to his lips and swirled the wine around in his mouth.

Olivia stared at his gorgeous face as he savored the taste of the wine, the liquid dancing across his tongue. *Stop it, Olivia!* she screamed in her head. She couldn't help it, though. It had been far too long since she had sex and, for lack of a better word, she was horny. And Cam was hot.

"Libby?" he asked, smirking as he watched her stare at him

with heat in her eyes. "Everything okay?"

"Yes," she replied, still openly gawking at the little tufts of hair that were visible beneath his V-neck t-shirt, wondering when he had changed out of his wetsuit.

"So, do you?"

Her eyes met his. "Do I what?" she asked breathlessly.

He took a step closer, their bodies almost touching. Olivia could feel the electricity coming off his body. "Like salmon?" he asked, his voice husky.

"Yes," she whispered.

"Good."

Desire flooded through her body as she continued to gaze into Cam's eyes. But he looked troubled.

Slowly shaking his head, he turned away. "Sorry, Libby, I just…"

Olivia looked away, embarrassed. "No. It's okay. You have nothing to apologize for," she spat out, downing her glass of wine, needing to feel the burn of the liquid, her face turning a shade of red similar to that of the wine.

"Libby, don't be like this. Please. I just…"

"What, Cam? Spit it out already."

Taking a deep breath, he gazed at her. "I was fucking heartbroken when you left back in January, but I know I sent you away. It was for your own good. You had to do it, but there was this part of me that didn't want you to go, that wanted to keep you for myself. And now that you're back, I just don't know how to act around you. I love you, Olivia. I know you don't feel the same way. I don't want to be your rebound. I want something so much more from you, but I know you're not ready for that. So until you are, please, let's just be friends. It hurts too much otherwise."

Olivia opened her mouth to respond, unsure of what to say. *Cam loves me?* She was shocked.

"Please. Don't say anything. Let's just go back to how things were five minutes ago. Wine?" He winked.

Olivia nodded, still reeling from his admission. "Yes, please."

After enjoying a filling lunch of salmon with mango salsa,

exhaustion caught up with her as she lay on the sofa, Cam rubbing her feet. On the TV, *The Dude* kept shouting that he wasn't Mr. Lebowksi as Olivia slipped into unconsciousness. Cam gingerly raised himself off the couch, not wanting to wake her up, watching her chest rise and fall in an even pattern. He grabbed a blanket and draped it over her shrunken frame. Placing a gentle kiss on her temple, he whispered, "Sleep well, angel. I love you."

His heart stopped when Olivia shifted. "I love you, too, Alex."

Cam shook his head, knowing deep down that Olivia would never get over Alexander enough to pursue any sort of relationship with him, even though his heart yearned for it.

Olivia slept all day and into the night. Cam thought about waking her up so she could eat dinner, but she looked so tired. She had barely stirred all afternoon as she rested on his couch. And, for once, she didn't wake up screaming every few hours because of the nightmares. No, he'd let her sleep.

When the clock struck midnight and she still hadn't awoken, Cam gingerly wrapped her in his arms and carried her upstairs to his bedroom, laying her down gently before crawling in next to her. He knew it wasn't the smartest idea, but he desperately wanted to feel her body in his arms. He wrapped himself around her and fell asleep dreaming about what life would be like if Olivia had never met Alexander.

CHAPTER TWENTY-EIGHT

SECOND CHANCES

THE FOLLOWING MORNING, CAM woke up as the sun shined brightly through his bedroom windows. Looking over at Olivia, he smiled as she continued to sleep. He quietly slipped out of the bed, seeing that it was practically noon. He wondered if Olivia was ever going to wake up. Then he thought about her cat. He wasn't sure how long Olivia would sleep, and he wanted to make sure Nepenthe didn't starve as she rested in his bed. He secretly loved the sound of that. He found her keys and headed over to her house so he could check on her cat.

Pulling up in front of Olivia's house, he was surprised to see a rental car parked in her driveway. Grabbing her house keys, he walked up to the front door.

"Hey, buddy. Can I help you with something?" Cam bellowed to a figure slumped over, sitting on her deck and leaning against the railing. The figure jumped, startled, and raised his head to look at Cam. *Shit, it's him.*

Pushing past him, Cam walked to the front door, not wanting to look into the face of someone who had damaged Olivia past repair.

"Hey! What are you doing here?!" Alexander roared, following Cam into Olivia's house, Nepenthe stalking the front door, hissing at both men.

"What am *I* doing here?!" Cam shouted. "I'm taking care of my fucking friend! That's what I'm doing. What the fuck are *you* doing here? Shouldn't you be off on your honeymoon with your *wife*?!"

Alexander shuddered at the term.

Cam lowered his voice. "Please. You need to leave her alone. She doesn't need someone like you in her life." He walked toward Nepenthe's food bowls and began filling them up, freshening his water before throwing some cat nip on the ground for him to roll around in.

"You barely know that fucking girl," Alexander growled. "Who are you to tell me who she needs in her life? What is this? You want her for yourself?"

Cam exhaled, not wanting to tell Alexander what he thought he needed to hear, wondering if Olivia had told anyone about what happened the night she found out that Alexander had gotten engaged.

Lowering his voice, he turned to face Alexander. "Listen, when Olivia first got here, she was so sad. I knew she was depressed. All the signs were there. Then we started to spend some time together, and I got to know her."

Alexander's temper flared just thinking about someone else being able to spend time with his Olivia.

"She started to come out of her shell. Then she found out you were dating that girl and she broke down again. And I was stupid enough to give her space. I knew it was the last thing I should have been doing, but I fucked up. I pissed her off and then let her stew. Weeks later, my friend texted me, letting me know about your engagement, and I rushed over here. Olivia didn't seem to know about it just yet, which was good. So I left her with the promise of coming back in an hour to take her to dinner. When I got here..." Cam trailed off, remembering the scene he saw when he kicked in the door.

"When you got here, what?" Alexander inquired, his voice shaky, unsure of whether he wanted to hear what Cam was about to tell him. He followed Cam's eyes to Olivia's front door, noticing the repaired door jam.

"When I got here, I knocked and no one answered." Cam gulped, remembering the sinking he felt in his chest that night. "So I knocked again, but there was still no answer. Then I heard a scratching."

"Nepenthe…" Alexander breathed, looking down at the cat.

"I knew something was wrong so I looked into the window…and she was lying on the floor over there, a pill bottle spilled out on the coffee table and an empty liquor bottle next to her. She was unconscious. She had taken four valium and drank far too much liquor…"

"Fuck…"

"If I arrived any later, I wouldn't have been able to get those pills up. But I did. And then I pushed her out the door, thinking that if your love for her was as strong as it seems hers is for you, then maybe you'd forget about all this bullshit and take her back. It killed me to do it, but I knew she needed the closure at least. But now, I don't know. She's just so empty, as if she's just going through the motions, waiting…"

Alexander sat down on the couch, trying to process everything Cam had told him. Olivia hadn't mentioned any of that to him. "How is she? I mean now? Is she okay?"

"She's pretty banged up, mentally and emotionally. But she'll smile again one day. She's stronger than this."

"Why didn't she tell me?" he asked, staring at the floor, unable to truly comprehend what he had done to Olivia.

"Would you have listened if she did? Please, you need to let her heal, and the only way she can is with you out of her life. I can't bear the thought of walking in on her and seeing her like that again. Please. You need to leave. Go back to your wife. It will be too painful for her to see you now that you're married."

"I didn't do it," Alexander said quietly.

"Do what?" Cam asked.

"Get married," he replied, still processing everything Cam had just told him. "I left her at the altar. Literally. We were about to say our vows and I left."

Cam chuckled. "Seriously?"

Alexander simply nodded.

"Come on. Want a drink?" Cam asked, gesturing Alexander out of the house toward his Wrangler.

"I could definitely use one after the week I've had," Alexander said, standing up and following Cam out the door.

~~~~~~~~~~

Olivia woke up, unsure of where she was. Sun seeped in through large windows, illuminating pastel blue walls with beige trim. Inhaling deeply, she knew she was in Cam's bed. It smelled like him.

"Morning, beautiful," Cam crooned, sitting on the foot of the bed and staring at Olivia's resting body. "Sleep well?"

Olivia stretched. "Yeah," she croaked. "I'm sorry I fell asleep on you yesterday. I was exhausted."

He grinned. "That was Sunday. It's Tuesday."

She shot up. "It is? Fuck! Nepenthe! He needs to be fed." She jumped out of bed, scrambling to pack her things and get back home.

"Relax, Libby. I found your keys and made sure he had food." He smiled, watching her frantically run around the room wearing just a pair of boy shorts and tank top.

She stopped abruptly, turning to look at him. "You did?"

"Yeah. I didn't want to wake you up. It looked like you needed sleep. Of course, every few hours or so you'd wake up and stumble into the bathroom, then stumble back to bed. I didn't know if you were ever going to wake up. I tried to get you to eat, but you could barely open your eyes." Olivia's stomach grumbled loud enough for Cam to hear. "Get ready. I'll take you out for breakfast and then back to your place, okay?"

"I'm sorry, Cam. I've made you miss work. I'm the worst friend."

He shrugged. "Don't worry about it, Libby. You needed me. I'd be a worse friend if I ditched you for my job." He walked out of the room to let Olivia get ready in private, grabbing his cell phone and sending a quick text message to his new friend.

A few hours later, after a nice relaxing breakfast, Cam pulled up in front of Olivia's cottage. Grabbing her bag, he ran around to the passenger side of the Jeep, helping her out and handing her bag to her.

"Thank you. For everything." She planted a kiss on his

cheek before walking across the sandy road abutting the coastline toward her house, her eyes settling on a figure standing on the deck. Her chin quivered and she spun around, heading back toward the Jeep.

"Libby," Cam said, glaring down at her.

"No. Take me back to your place. I can't…"

Cam clutched her hands in his. "Libby, look at me." She slowly raised her gaze, meeting his kind eyes, the sun reflecting in them and making them sparkle. "Just listen to what he has to say."

Olivia visibly shook. "I don't think I can. I'm not…"

"Yes, you are, Libby. You're stronger than you think you are. I'd never make you do something if I didn't think you could handle it. You can do this. Go. He flew all this way to see you. At first, I wanted to kill him for how he hurt you, but then we talked yesterday over a few drinks and he explained everything to me. Just talk to him. And then, if you want, you can drive back over to my place, okay?"

She took a deep breath and nodded as Cam brushed that same errant curl behind her ear. "Good girl." He planted a kiss on her forehead and watched as she walked toward her house. At that moment, he knew he would probably never see her again.

Olivia slowly crossed the narrow beach road back to her front deck, her heart beating loudly in her chest. Walking up the steps to her deck, her eyes met Alexander's, his green eyes empty, the usual vibrancy gone.

"Hi," she said sheepishly as she made her way to the front door, noticing the mark from when Cam had to kick it in. She shuddered at the memory, hoping that she would be strong enough to survive the impending conversation.

"Can I come in?" Alexander asked softly, approaching Olivia from behind.

Her body overheated from the proximity of him. A tear fell down her cheek as she thought how unfair life was.

"Shouldn't you be with your wife, Alex?" she asked, turning around after unlocking the door.

"Please, Olivia. Let me in. I just want to talk to you. If you don't like what I have to say, I promise I'll never show up on your doorstep again. Please. Give me five minutes."

Olivia exhaled, opening the door and walking through the living room, Alexander following.

He surveyed her house and noticed a piano in the guest room. "Here, come with me," he said, grabbing her hands. He led her toward the piano and sat down at the bench, patting the seat next to him.

Sighing, she sat down beside him, their arms and shoulders touching, making her entire body tremble. Not with excitement. Not with fear. It was something far more devastating. She trembled with the excruciating pain of complete heartache and loss.

"Play it again, Olivia," he whispered into her ear, his breath hot on her neck.

Olivia shook her head, unsure what he was talking about.

"The song you played the other night. I beg you. Play it again."

Her eyes flung open, wide with curiosity and fear. She didn't know if she could torture herself like that again.

"Please, Olivia."

Inhaling deeply, she placed her shaky hands on the piano, playing the opening chords of the very song that she sang just a few nights beforehand in her last attempt to win Alexander back, pouring her entire soul into the notes and lyrics. Memories of that night came flooding back as she sang, her eyes boring holes into Alexander's, tears flowing down both of their faces.

Sobs wracked through her body as she sang the chorus, begging for another chance...a chance that she never got.

Alexander stared into her eyes as she struggled to get through the words. He knew he messed up. He was such a fool to think he could forget her. He never forgot about her during those twenty-plus years he thought she was dead. His heart belonged to her and he needed her in his life. Her soft plea nearly tore him apart.

He grabbed Olivia's hands in his, cutting the song short. "Smile, love. It's the second best thing you can do with those beautiful lips of yours."

Before Olivia knew what was happening, Alexander crushed his lips to hers, pulling her body against his own.

For a brief moment, they were the only two people in the universe that mattered. They poured all the emotions that they felt over the past several months into that kiss. It was desperate and passionate and, no matter how much they devoured each other's mouths, it wasn't nearly as deep as they wanted or needed.

After several long, intense moments, Alexander pulled back, gasping for air. "I never had a chance with you, Olivia," he whispered against her neck. "It's you. It's only ever been you."

"What about Chelsea?" she asked, confused about what happened.

Brushing a tear from her eye, Alexander cupped her cheek in his hand. "I couldn't do it. I was such an idiot to keep pushing you away. You're the only woman for me. No one else has ever compared to you. Please, Olivia. Forgive me for being such an ignorant ass. I'll do anything. Name it and it's yours. Just, please, don't make me go through life without you in it. I need you. I…"

Olivia pressed her lips to his, not letting him finish his thought. Alexander groaned, running his hands all over her frail body as he told her with his mouth just what she meant to him.

He pulled back, catching his breath. "Bedroom?"

"Upstairs," she responded, panting.

Alexander scooped her in his arms and carried her up the short flight of stairs and into her bedroom. Placing her gently on the bed, he slowly shrugged out of his jacket, followed by his t-shirt and jeans as Olivia watched, her eyes intense. Lowering himself back down on the bed, he hovered over her body and planted soft kisses on her neck, savoring the sweet smell of her vanilla body wash and a scent that could only be categorized as Olivia's natural essence.

She moaned as Alexander trailed his mouth down her collarbone, fumbling to remove her shirt. As he lifted it over her head, he looked down at her body.

"Olivia," he said in an almost horrified voice as he took in the sight of her ribs poking through. A tear fell down as he returned his mouth to hers. "I'm so sorry I did this to you. I'll make it up to you. Just tell me what to do to make it right."

Sobs shook her body from the closeness of Alexander to her again. She couldn't remember ever being so happy in her entire life. "Please, Alex. I want to feel again. Let me feel you."

He groaned, nipping Olivia's neck as he slowly slid her shorts down, tossing them to the side before taking off his own boxer briefs. Running his hands up and down her body, he positioned himself between her legs.

"Please, Alex. Make me feel again," she sobbed out, the closeness of his erection to her apex was overwhelming. Slowly, he entered her, filling her.

"Do you feel that?" Alexander asked sweetly as he lowered his body on top of her, leaning on his elbows, worried that he would crush her.

"Yes, Alex," Olivia cried out. "I feel it. Don't stop." Running her hands up and down his back, she gasped at the absolutely complete feeling she had as Alexander slowly moved in and out of her.

"Don't ever leave me again, love," he grunted. "There's no one else for me. Only you. You're my Eve. Always and forever."

Olivia sobbed at his sweet words, wrapping her legs around his waist, not wanting any space between their bodies. His motions were slow and deliberate, and for the first time that she could remember, that's what she wanted and needed.

"God, I missed you, Olivia," he said, his eyes searing holes into hers. She reached up and grabbed his head, forcing his lips against hers. She thrust her tongue inside his mouth as she continued moving her hips with the tempo that he set.

"Alex," she whimpered into his mouth as her body climbed higher and higher.

"Yes, love," he exhaled.

Olivia's body was on fire. She had never felt so much pleasure from Alexander before. There was something so different about having sex with him at that moment. For the first time, it was so much more than sex, and it didn't scare her anymore because Alexander was someone worth facing her fears for.

She closed her eyes, fighting against her impending orgasm, not wanting to finish so quickly. She was feeling, and she wanted to keep feeling. She never wanted to turn it off again.

"Open your eyes, Olivia," he demanded.

She smiled, following his command. She relished the dominating side of Alexander.

He leaned down and feathered kisses against her neck. "I want to see your eyes when I make you come," he said, reminding Olivia of the very first orgasm she ever had at his hands. The happy memory was all too much and she exploded around him, her orgasm shaking her entire body, surprising her.

"Olivia," Alexander moaned out as she continued convulsing underneath him. A big smile spread across his face. He loved watching her as she shuddered from an orgasm that only he could give her. Maintaining a steady rhythm, he released into her seconds later, savoring the feel of her body so close to his once again. This was right. This was home.

Chapter Twenty-Nine

Home

"PENNY FOR YOUR THOUGHTS," Alexander said a week later as they flew north in his Gulfstream. They had spent the last week locked in a suite at the Ritz, neither one wanting to leave the other's side for too long. Over that week, they made up for lost time. Alexander was happy to keep Olivia in Florida a little bit longer. He was worried about taking her back to Boston. There were still unanswered questions and unknown threats to her safety, but they couldn't stay in Florida forever.

"I just feel bad that I didn't get to thank Cam for..." She stopped short, wondering how much Alexander knew about what had gone on.

He reached across the seat and clutched Olivia's hand. "It's probably best this way." There was a loud silence in the air. "He told me everything," Alexander said quietly.

Olivia looked up. "You mean..." She trailed off.

He nodded his head slowly, a tear falling down his cheek. "I could have lost you. That will never happen again, Olivia. I will always look out for you. You don't ever have to worry about me leaving you because it will not happen. I swear to you."

She looked into his eyes. "I'm sorry. I wasn't thinking. I just wanted to numb everything, turn it all off because it hurt too much. I didn't want to feel anymore, and it was the only way I knew how."

Alexander wrapped his arms around her, bringing her body close to his. "Don't ever do that again," he said forcefully,

196

gently nipping on her neck. "I want you to feel. I want you to feel me every fucking day."

She moaned from his words and his tongue drawing circles against her warm skin.

"I can't get enough of you, Olivia," he said before bringing his lips to hers, forcing his tongue into her mouth. She pressed her body against his, but no matter how close she was to him, it wasn't close enough. Running her fingers through his hair, she deepened the kiss, not caring that Alexander's flight attendant could walk in at any moment.

He pulled out of the kiss, panting. "Jesus, Olivia. You drive me fucking wild." He stood up, pulling her up with him, and walked toward the back of his plane, opening a door.

Her jaw dropped, shocked to see a bedroom. She glanced at Alexander. "Is there a reason you have a bedroom on your plane, Mr. Burnham?" she asked sweetly, grabbing his tie and dragging him flush with her body.

"No reason," he replied nonchalantly. "But I'm pretty fucking glad I have it now." He pressed his lips against hers, picking her up and wrapping her long legs around his midsection, pressing her back against the door. "But I'm not so sure I want to fuck you in that bed. I want you here, and I want it rough. Do you want that?" he asked forcefully.

Olivia moaned, loving the feeling of Alexander's erection between her legs again. She didn't think she would ever tire of feeling his body so close to hers.

"Tell me you want that, Olivia. Tell me right now that you want me to fuck you against the wall." He continued thrusting against her, nuzzling her neck, nibbling on her earlobe. "Say it," he ordered.

"Yes, Alexander," she responded finally. "I want you to fuck me against this wall."

A smile spread across his face as he looked down at her, panting. "I love it when you say shit like that. Do you have any idea what a turn on that is?"

She lowered her legs to the floor and glanced down at his pants. "I have a pretty good idea, Mr. Burnham," she replied coyly.

He glared at her, her heart racing from the intense stare he was giving her. "Are you trying to be funny, Olivia?"

She swallowed hard, thinking how every time she was with him, she never knew which version of him would be present in the bedroom. And she loved it. "No, Mr. Burnham," she replied quietly.

"Good. Now, take off your dress, Olivia. We'll be starting our initial descent soon, and I want you good and fucked when you walk off this plane."

Olivia felt moisture pool between her legs at his words, a grin spreading across her face as she quickly removed her dress, bending down to unzip the same knee-length black boots she wore that snowy day back in January when she confronted Alexander in his office. The boots that she hoped would change everything.

"Oh no, Miss Adler. The boots stay on," he said.

Olivia straightened up, keeping her boots in place. Alexander swiftly removed his clothes and stood back to admire Olivia in her pink lace bra with matching panties and, of course, the boots.

"Fuck, Olivia…"

She grinned as she lowered her eyes to his erection, noticing it grow even harder under her intense stare.

He rushed to her, wrapping his arms around her and kissing her passionately. She pressed her body against his, thrusting against his erection, savoring the closeness of him. At that moment, she knew she would never run again.

He swiftly lowered her panties down her legs and over her boots. Lifting her up, he rubbed his arousal against her swollen clit. "You're always so wet, aren't you?" he asked with a smirk on his face.

"Yes," she exhaled, her heart racing as Alexander continued teasing her with his erection. She was ready to come from that contact alone.

"I'm the only one who can make you wet like this, Olivia," he growled. "I've barely even fucking touched you and you're ready to come, aren't you?"

Olivia stared at him. *How does he know that?* she thought.

"I know your body better than you think I do," he whispered against her neck, entering her. Olivia moaned as he picked up his pace. She moved against him, wanting him to just crawl inside of her and never leave.

She closed her eyes, savoring the feeling of Alexander's body pressed against hers as he thrust into her, slamming her repeatedly against the wall. Her breathing became erratic as she thought how no one had ever satisfied her the way Alexander always did. She was never left wanting. "Faster, Alex," she begged.

"You want it faster?" He leaned down, his voice husky in her ear. "You like it like this, don't you? You like it hard…and fast…" He picked up the pace, pushing further and further into Olivia. "God, I love fucking you, Olivia."

She moaned, throwing her head back.

"Do you love it when I fuck you like this?" He drove harder and harder into her, wanting to savor the feeling of her around his erection but knowing that he was about to explode. Olivia opened her eyes, looking at Alexander's blazing green ones, his forehead dripping with sweat as he continued moving inside of her.

"Just fucking say it, Olivia, or I'll pull out before you can come. I know it's true. I know you like it hard and fast, and that I'm the only one who can make you feel like this." He pressed his mouth against hers, kissing her with such passion.

Olivia's body convulsed around his, her vision becoming fuzzy from the waves of pleasure overtaking her entire being. She screamed out Alexander's name as her body trembled against his. "Yes, Alexander," she said, finally finding her voice. "You're the only one…"

A smile crept across his face as he continued pumping into her. "Damn straight I am. And you're the only one for me, love," he said before moaning out her name, finding his own release, relishing in the feeling of her body still shaking around his. When the last of his tremors ceased, he pulled back, staring down at Olivia. "Don't ever leave me again," he said, his voice pleading with her. "I don't ever want to be the person I was without you in my life. Okay? Please. Promise me. Promise you won't run again."

Olivia reached up and grabbed Alexander by the neck, bringing his face to hers. Brushing her lips against his, she said, "Never again." She felt his lips turn up into a smile.

"Good. Now get dressed. We'll be landing soon."

She smiled, secretly relishing in the bossy side of him. She had missed that. And the gentle side. And the dominating side. And the angry side. And the passionate side. And every side in between.

"Where are my panties?" Olivia asked, searching the bedroom for where Alexander had thrown them during their intense moment.

"You're not getting them back, and don't you dare go clean up, either. I want my come dripping down your leg, reminding you that I'm the only one allowed to do that." He turned abruptly and walked to the main cabin, leaving Olivia completely speechless. And happy.

She made her way to the main cabin and sat down next to Alexander, taking the glass of bourbon he held out for her.

"Now, there's one thing that we need to discuss before we land."

Mr. Businessman was back. She rolled her eyes, secretly thrilled to see that side of Alexander again. "Okay. What is it?"

"As you probably recall, we had a conversation about a very serious threat to your safety back in October. That threat is still out there so, until I know you're no longer in any danger, I want to assign a protection detail for you. Mainly Carter and a few other agents."

"Alex, please. I was fine in Boston. I was there for over a month without an incident…" She trailed off, remembering the strange man that Alexander attacked on the snowy street back in January.

Alexander raised his eyebrows at her as she recalled exactly why she had felt safe those weeks she was in Boston. She remembered seeing an SUV parked outside her house nearly every day after the attack. He had been protecting her, even though they weren't together. As the plane made its final approach into Logan, she realized that Alexander never stopped caring for her. And it warmed her heart.

"Welcome home, love," Alexander said, kissing her temple as they stepped off his plane and onto the tarmac.

Olivia inhaled the crisp February air, thankful to be back with Alexander in the city that she had grown to love over the past decade. Everything was as it should be.

CHAPTER THIRTY

SELFLESS

"CHERYL, WHAT'S THE PLAN today?" Donovan shouted into the phone.

"Do you really think it's a good idea that you do this, boss? I mean, what if you're made?"

"I don't care. So far, nothing has been going right. We've waited long enough. It's March, for crying out loud! When you want something done, you do it yourself. Now that she's back in town, we need to make some fucking headway. Enough time has passed that Burnham won't be on high alert anymore. So, are we good to go this afternoon?"

Cheryl exhaled loudly into the phone. "Yes, sir. I've been able to ensure that she will be alone after her morning appointment. She'll be heading back to her place around noon."

"Perfect. Thank you, Cheryl. You're a gem."

~~~~~~~~~~

"Olivia? Where did you go?" Dr. Greenstein slowly brought her patient back to earth. Olivia sat staring out at the Boston cityscape, her thoughts revolving around one person again. Alexander. It seemed that all she had been doing lately was thinking about him. The past month had been the happiest in her life. She finally had started to let Alexander in.

Olivia turned her gaze from the office window as snowflakes began to fall in the mid-March sky. "Sorry, doctor. I'm here."

"I want to go back to something we had started talking about this past Tuesday before you stormed out of here." She eyed Olivia, waiting to see her reaction.

"I did not storm out of here. I graciously left after I said you were full of shit and had no idea what you were talking about." Olivia crossed her arms in front of her chest, avoiding the doctor's eyes.

"Do you really feel that way?" Holding her pen and paper as if ready to write down whatever crazy thing was about to fall out of her mouth next, Dr. Greenstein looked at her.

"No, I don't. I know I say that a lot."

"Usually when you know I'm right about something. Olivia, you need to start facing these fears that you have. I know we've been working on this for the better part of a decade now but, at some point, I need you to start reaching out of your comfort zone."

Olivia looked at the doctor, not responding. Her therapist was right. She just didn't want to admit it, especially to her. She knew Dr. Greenstein just wanted to help her but, sometimes, ignorance was bliss.

"Now, what is it that scares you most about Alexander?"

Olivia exhaled loudly, leaning back against the couch, not really wanting to talk about any of that, but she knew she had to. "I don't know. That I'm falling in love with him. That he's going to be taken from me just like everyone else in my life. And, well, I don't know. I still feel like he's holding something back from me."

"Do you think he may be holding something back because he never knows the next time that you'll want to run away? He wants to share things with you and get close to you. He wants to know you. He wants to show you how much he cares about you. If you keep pushing him away, one of these times may be the last time and he might just walk away for good, like he almost did last time."

Olivia turned her head, not wanting to hear the words coming out of her mouth, the memory of Alexander almost marrying another woman still painful. The doctor got up from her chair and sat next to Olivia on the couch. "If you keep pushing people away, you will end up alone. That's not much of a life, if you ask me. Just remember how you felt all those months when you left Alexander. Don't forget that pain, Olivia. Carry that with you as a constant reminder so you don't do that again."

Tears started to form in Olivia's eyes. She fought to contain them as the doctor handed her the tissue box. "I don't want to talk about this anymore." She tried to inch away from Dr. Greenstein.

"Okay. What do you want to talk about?" She got up from the couch and returned to her chair.

"Alexander asked me to the annual charity auction this weekend."

"And how do you feel about that?"

"I don't know. I haven't given him my answer yet." The doctor started to scratch away at her notepad. "What are you writing?"

"It's nothing important, but if you want to know...here." She handed Olivia the notepad. The only things written down were her name, the date, and charity auction. "Happy now?"

"Yes, thank you." Olivia smiled, handing the paper back. "But if you need to write that I'm a crazy bitch, feel free to do so because I already know that I am." She laughed, hoping to break the tension that slowly filled the room.

"I don't like the word 'crazy'. Why do we go through this every time? Stop deflecting. You know that's not healthy. Now, getting back to the charity auction. Let's work through this. I think this is a big step, but one you should take. What are you worried about?"

"Well, I'm worried that it'll be more than I can handle, ya' know? I'm worried about not fitting into his world. His mom will be there and I'm worried about meeting her."

"And is he close to his family?"

"I think so. I mean, he speaks well of everyone, but I don't think he's ever forgiven his dad. When Alexander was in high school, his dad was never around. He was always working. And every summer, he would go away the entire three months, missing Alexander's birthday, to work some protection detail.

Apparently, they got into a pretty big fight the night before Alexander left for SEAL training. That was the last time he had seen or really spoken to his father before he died several years later."

"Do you think he's still mad at his father, or is he mad at himself?"

"I'm not sure. Why don't you ask him?" Olivia was getting snarky. That always happened the longer the session went.

"I'm not interested in his opinion. I'm interested in yours."

"Well, I think it might be a little of both."

"How did his father die?" she asked, her interest piqued.

"He was on a protection detail. High security. He was protecting the identity of someone. Alexander is unclear of many of the details but, somehow, someone found out that Alexander's dad was protecting this person's identity and location. These people tried to get the information out of him, he refused and, after torturing him for days, they killed him. Alexander said his body was worse than anything he had ever seen, even in Afghanistan when he was deployed with the SEALs. And it's like his father knew something was going to happen because he wrote Alexander a letter days before his abduction and death. He still hasn't opened it."

"Hmmm." The doctor appeared deep in thought. "What do you think is in the letter?"

"I don't know, but it sits in the top drawer of his desk in his office at home. He says he looks at the envelope every day and thinks about opening it, but doesn't."

"It sounds like you both tend to ignore things so you don't have to confront them. If you really want this relationship to work, I need you to start to confront some of your fears. Maybe this will help him, as well."

"I'll try. I really will."

"And you'll start by agreeing to go to the charity auction." She winked at Olivia.

"Dr. Greenstein, your twelve o'clock is here," Olivia heard Kathy, the receptionist, say over the office intercom. That was usually her nice way of saying that the hour was up. "Well, I guess that's my cue." Olivia got up from the couch and grabbed her purse.

"I'll see you Tuesday, right?" Dr. Greenstein got up from her chair and started walking to the door.

"Yes. I'll be here."

"Okay. I want to pick up where we left off." She opened the door. "And I want you to work on being selfless. Stop this self-preservation bullshit and start thinking about what losing you would do to other people, instead of the other way around." With that, the doctor closed the door to her office, leaving Olivia totally speechless. She had never really been so blunt with her before.

CHAPTER THIRTY-ONE

FOLLOWING

OLIVIA LEFT THE DOCTOR'S office, surprised that Agent Thompson, her escort, wasn't sitting in the reception area waiting for her. Instead of milling about, hoping that he would eventually return, she decided to walk back to her house. She didn't live far so it wasn't that big a deal.

As she walked out of the Prudential Center onto Boylston Street, she noticed that the snow had begun to fall at a more rapid pace, starting to blanket the city in a coat of white. Olivia inhaled deeply as she looked up at the gray sky, loving the smell of the city during a snowfall.

On her way home, she started to think about what Dr. Greenstein had said. She remembered the pain that she felt those few months when she pushed Alexander and everyone else away. It was the worst thing she had ever experienced in her life, and maybe remembering that pain once in a while would help her.

Olivia reached her house but, instead of turning to go in, she kept walking. It didn't bother her that there was already about an inch of snow on the ground. She knew Alexander would be furious if he found out she was roaming the streets of Boston without her assigned cavalry, but she didn't care. She needed to think.

As she walked down Commonwealth Avenue toward Boston Common, she thought about everything. About her parents. About her Uncle Charles. About meeting Kiera for the first time and her dragging Olivia out, helping her get a fake ID.

About the first time she met Mo and started to sing with the band. About the feeling of total contentment she still felt every time she got on stage. But mostly, Olivia thought about Alexander.

She thought about how perfect it felt every time he held her in his arms. She thought about the feel of his lips on her mouth. She thought about all the sweet things he whispered to her when she fell asleep next to him. He would comfort her when she woke screaming and covered in sweat from yet another nightmare. He always made sure she was safe, calling several times a day to ensure everything was okay. He would send her flowers for no reason at all. He would show up at her office with lunch on days that he knew she barely had time to breathe. He would come to listen to the band perform at MacFadden's. He even came to their practices when he could, as well as nights that she performed at Open Mic.

Olivia immediately sank onto the first stoop that she came across. She realized how much Alexander truly did care for her. She had been trying to ignore it for the past month, but the feelings were all too obvious. Dr. Greenstein was right. *Fuck.* She hated when that happened. Maybe it was finally time to let love in.

As she sat there thinking about whether she could fully open her heart to Alexander, Olivia felt chills run up and down her entire body. She quickly snapped out of her daze when the familiar feeling of someone watching and following her swept through her entire being. Looking down the street the way she had come, she saw just two sets of prints in the snow on an ordinarily busy street. Olivia thought it was odd that there was no one else around. Looking closer, she noticed one set of footprints disappear down a side alley just two houses from where she sat in front of a brownstone several blocks north of her Commonwealth Avenue home. *Maybe I'm losing my mind*, she thought. *Who could possibly be following me?* She got chills again so, raising herself off the stoop, she continued down the street in the same direction that she had been heading, a little more conscious of her surroundings, but still not wanting to return home.

Olivia started to head toward the theater district, not really having a destination in mind. As she walked and thought more and more about Alexander, she decided that she wanted to see him. She set out for his penthouse on Atlantic Avenue, knowing that he had flown back earlier that morning from a training exercise.

She continued to walk the two miles there, taking mostly side streets and shortcuts. The snow came down faster and faster, but she didn't care. Then she felt the chills again. She glanced over her shoulder to see if anyone was following her, observing a man wearing all black trailing a few lengths behind. The snow obscured his face, making it difficult to see any details, but something about him reminded her of that night months ago at 28 Degrees with Kiera.

Olivia quickly turned down another side street, taking a detour, as she looked over her shoulder again, her heart beating frantically. The mystery man followed, maintaining a discreet distance behind her. She took another turn and he followed. She started to get nervous and began walking faster. The man followed suit. Olivia became conscious of the fact that he was clearly following her. She always thought Alexander was just being paranoid where her safety was concerned but now she realized that maybe it wasn't paranoia. She grabbed her cell phone and called Alexander. His voicemail picked up. *Where the fuck is he?*

"Hi. It's me," Olivia spoke into her phone, her voice shaking. "I'm heading to your place. I think there's someone following me." She hung up and, with nervous hands, attempted to put the cell phone back in her purse but dropped it in a snowdrift. As she stopped to bend down and pick it off the ground, the man pursuing her sped up. Fight or flight kicked in and she started to run, leaving her phone in the snow. Her mind raced about who that man could be and what he could possibly want from her. She finally turned on Atlantic and was about a half-mile from Alexander's building, glancing behind her to see the strange man running after her. Nerves wracked her entire body. *Why the hell is this guy after me?*

Olivia sprinted toward Alexander's building, turning around

every so often to see the strange man following closely behind. He began to gain ground when Olivia's legs became sore from the boots she wore. She started to panic, desperately hoping she would be able to outrun whoever was behind her. The snow fell at a rapid pace, and there wasn't anyone on the streets of Boston except for a lone individual across the street, sitting on a bench. Olivia had forgotten about the Nor'easter that was predicted to bring over a foot of snow during the day.

She finally reached Alexander's building and fumbled for the door just as it was opening. She slammed right into Alexander's muscular chest, frantically grabbing onto him as if her entire life depended on it because, at that moment, it did.

"Hey, hey. Slow down." He put his arms around her. "Are you okay? I got your message. I was on the other line. What is going on?" he asked, scanning the streets with a concerned look on his face.

Olivia's entire body shook from a combination of the cold, her wet clothes, and pure adrenaline. "I thought I was crazy. I left my shrink appointment and wanted to go for a walk. Then I realized that I've really been a selfish bitch and my relationship with you scares me to death, and then someone started following me all the way from Comm. Ave. to the North End, and then I called you, but I dropped my cell phone in the snow bank and when I bent to pick it up, he started to rush toward me so I left it in the snow and ran into you." Olivia took a deep breath.

"Where the fuck was your escort, Olivia?!" he yelled as he led her toward the elevator and punched the code for the penthouse, taking out his anger and frustration on the keypad. "What the fuck were you thinking?! I told you to never go anywhere without someone! Did you think I was joking?!" Alexander was furious.

Olivia stared at him and immediately broke down crying. "I know! I'm sorry, Alex! Okay?!" she screamed out. "You've made your fucking point!" She glared at him as tears fell down her face, willing him to say something.

His face softened immediately when he saw the frightened look on her face. "It's okay. You're safe now." He held her close, lowering his voice. "Jesus, you're shivering. Your clothes are soaked through. How long were you out in that weather?"

"I don't know." She shrugged. "A few hours."

Alexander's face flamed red in complete frustration.

~~~~~~~~~~

Nathan Roberts had finally found her. He hadn't seen the girl for over twenty-one years, and he had spent the last several years looking for her. Thomas Burnham kept everything hidden and covered up. So much so that when he died, he had no way of finding her. It had been years since that day all those years ago when his entire world fell apart around him.

It wasn't too hard to find out where she lived. However, he was rather thankful that, at the moment, she had round-the-clock security detail. She seemed to spend quite a bit of time at Alexander Burnham's house. He thought that if anyone would make sure Olivia was safe, it was Alexander. He reminded him so much of his father.

He sat in his rental car outside of Olivia's house, waiting for her to come home from her appointment. He had been watching her the past several weeks and had become quite familiar with her schedule. It was Thursday so she was at her therapist appointment. Nathan wondered whether his actions may have been the cause of her need for therapy.

At half-past noon, he saw Olivia walking down the street. He thought it was odd, considering that she had left with her security detail. How did she lose him? He recalled the first several years of his protection all those years ago. It was nearly impossible for him to go anywhere without someone at his side.

He watched as Olivia kept walking past her house. *Where is she going?* He started his car and sped through the snow in the opposite direction that Olivia was walking, desperate to get onto the other side of Commonwealth Avenue to hopefully find her. *Damn Boston and its one-way streets!* he thought. He drove through the city, eager to find her. She was all alone, walking through the snow with no one looking out for her. It had taken him years to finally set eyes on her again. He felt the need to know where she was at all times.

He searched for what seemed like an eternity, hoping to find her. He drove to her office building and never saw her. Then he drove to Alexander's apartment building, desperate for some clue. He parked in a nearby garage and ran onto Atlantic Avenue, keeping watch from a bench across the street.

Finally, he saw Olivia approaching. She was running, constantly glancing over her shoulder behind her. Nathan turned his head to see what she was looking at and, presumably, running from. He couldn't make out much, but it was a man dressed all in black, wearing a back beanie.

He jumped off the bench and made his way across the street just as Alexander came running through the lobby of his building. The man in black saw Alexander and immediately turned down a side street. Nathan followed the man in black, catching up to him with ease.

"Oops. I'm sorry," Nathan said, bumping into his shoulder as he walked past. He turned to get a better look at him. The man in black stared at him, as if trying to place him. Nathan knew who it was. He walked briskly away in the direction of the parking garage, hoping that he hadn't been made. Apparently, Mark Kiddish - or, as he was now going by, Donovan O'Laughlin - had started doing his own dirty work. He couldn't know that Nathan was in town. Not yet, anyway.

CHAPTER THIRTY-TWO

COMING TOGETHER

THE ELEVATOR DOORS OPENED into Alexander's foyer. Martin immediately appeared. "Sir, I have Marshall and Kerrigan on this. Nothing has turned up yet. I have no idea what happened to Thompson."

"Thank you. Please alert me the minute you have more information. Do we have any street camera feeds yet?"

"Not just yet, but the tech team is working on it." Martin turned to face Olivia. "Miss Adler, do you remember where you dropped your cell phone?"

Olivia tried to remember exactly where it was, but it was all kind of a blur. "I think it was around Congress and Milk."

"Jesus!" Alexander exclaimed, running his hands through his hair in exasperation as he paced the large living room, trying to compose his thoughts. After several long moments, he stopped in front of Olivia, glaring at her. "What the fuck were you doing over there?"

Martin excused himself, leaving them alone.

"I was trying to be evasive." She shrugged. "I thought if I kept going down side streets, I would eventually lose the guy," she replied meekly.

"What the fuck, Olivia?! Rule number one... When you're being followed, large pockets of people are your friends!" Alexander raised his voice, unable to control his anger any further.

"I know!" she shouted at him, pushing him away and stomping further into his living room. "I don't need a lecture right now, Alexander." Olivia sat down on his couch. "Just, please, let it go. I feel foolish enough bursting in here like this." She shivered.

"Come here." Alexander's face softened as he walked toward her and pulled her into his arms. She immediately started to sob uncontrollably. She had no idea why she was crying. Maybe because she was so cold. Maybe because she was so scared. Maybe because she realized that she was starting to depend on Alexander. She had lived most of her life depending on no one but herself. If she was being followed a few months ago, she would have dealt with it on her own. Now, her first instinct was to call him.

She nuzzled into him as he sat holding her, gently stroking her hair and soothing her. Something about being in his arms had an amazing calming effect on her. She took a few peaceful breaths and pulled her head out of his chest, looking up into his eyes. He leaned down and wiped the tears from her face. He kissed her nose softly. "Feel better now that's out of your system?"

Olivia nodded. She did feel better. She hadn't had a big cry like that in a while. It felt good to get it out.

"Good. Now let's get you warmed up," he said, winking at her.

"What did you have in mind, Mr. Burnham?" Olivia asked sweetly, feigning innocence.

"You'll see," he replied, picking her up and carrying her upstairs. He opened the door to the master bedroom and strode into the bathroom, placing Olivia on the ground and starting the water in the tub.

"We need to get you out of these wet clothes," he said in a deep voice. Suddenly, the atmosphere between them changed from one of fear to one of desire.

"Yes," Olivia said, her eyes intense. Alexander started to unbutton her winter coat, slipping her arms out and throwing the coat, scarf, hat, and gloves on the ground.

"Sit down," he commanded, pointing to the cushioned stool underneath the dual vanity.

She immediately obeyed, loving how demanding Alexander

was being. He slowly unzipped each of her knee-length boots, his eyes remaining intently focused on her. Her heart raced at the fierce look in his eyes as he gingerly slid each boot down her leg and off her foot.

"Stand back up, Olivia," he ordered, Olivia obeying him rather quickly. "Turn around."

She followed his command. Turning around, she stared into the large wall-sized mirror above the vanity. She gazed into Alexander's eyes in the glass as he slowly lifted her sweater over her head. Her white lace bra was practically transparent from being so wet.

Olivia felt Alexander's arousal grow as he stood behind her, caressing her stomach, planting deep kisses on the back of her neck. The warmth of his breath on her skin sent chills down her spine. She felt moisture pool between her legs, her body throbbing with anticipation.

Alexander reached around and unbuttoned her jeans, sliding them down her legs and helping her step out of them. He unhooked her bra, lowering it down her arms until it fell to the floor. After slipping her panties off, he stood back, admiring the beautiful woman in the mirror.

Olivia watched as he held onto her panties, bringing them up to his nose. She gasped.

"I love the way you smell, Olivia," he said, his voice cutting through the stark bathroom. "I can never get enough of your scent." He pulled her naked body against his and she felt his arousal against her back. "When you're not with me, I can't fucking focus. All I can think about is you and that delicious pussy of yours." His hands roamed her body and she closed her eyes, relishing in the feeling of his large hands covering every inch of her body. "Do you think about me when I'm gone, Olivia?" he asked, bringing her back to the present.

"Yes," she replied. It was the truth. Alexander occupied her thoughts all day and all night. Not one minute went by that he didn't cross her mind.

"Do you touch yourself when I'm gone?" he asked, his hand sliding down her stomach, hovering over her clit, barely touching her. She squirmed, the closeness of his hand to the part of her body that she wanted him to touch unbearable.

"Alex... Please..." she begged. She needed to feel him.

"Tell me you think of me when you touch yourself," he whispered against her neck. "I know you do. I think of you when I touch myself."

"Yes. I do, Alexander. You're always on my mind. When you're gone, I think of you inside me when I touch myself. Now, please. Touch me."

Alexander growled, spinning Olivia around to face him, crushing his mouth to hers. She ran her hands up and down his back before grabbing the waist of his pants, pulling him closer to her. She made quick work of unfastening his belt and unbuttoning his jeans, her mouth never leaving his.

She felt Alexander's mouth curve into a smile. "Something I can help you with, Miss Adler?"

"Damn it, Alex. I'm dying here. You were gone all fucking week. I want you right now," she said, pulling him back to her, grinding her hips against him.

"Oh no, Olivia. Not yet. Turn back around."

She did as she was told and faced the mirror again, watching as Alexander stripped out of the rest of his clothes.

"Bend over and hold onto the edge of the vanity," he ordered.

She leaned over, hoping he would get on with it already. Alexander bent down and planted rough kisses all along her shoulder blades, biting her neck. Olivia gasped in surprise before arching her neck, giving Alexander better access.

"Harder," she whispered. Olivia felt Alexander's erection harden even more as he moaned and nipped on her neck with more ferocity. He grabbed her hair and, wrapping it around his hand, pulled her head back. She let out a small cry as he positioned himself at her apex, pushing gently over her folds, teasing her.

"Do you like that, Olivia?"

"Yes," she whispered, feeling like she was going to explode the second he entered her.

"Yes, what?" he growled.

"Yes, Mr. Burnham."

Alexander plunged into her from behind, filling her quickly. He pulled out and Olivia panted at the loss of contact.

"I need you," she breathed as he teased her highly sensitized clit.

"Say it again," he exhaled, rubbing himself up and down against her.

"I need you, Alexander."

He moaned as he slammed into her again, causing them both to scream out in pleasure. He pulled out one more time, slamming back into her before reaching his hand around, toying with her swollen nub. Olivia closed her eyes, relishing the pleasure.

"Open your eyes. I want you to watch me fucking you," he growled. Olivia opened her eyes and watched Alexander maintain a relentless rhythm. "Do you like watching me take you, Olivia?" he asked, his breathing ragged as he continued thrusting into her, each motion filling her even more than the time before. "Say it, Olivia. Say it turns you on."

"Fuck…" She closed her eyes, lowering her head. Alexander grabbed her hair, pulling her head back so she had no choice but to stare at him in the mirror as he continued driving into her.

"Goddamnit, Olivia. Fucking say it!" Alexander pummeled into her, desperately needing to hear those words.

"Yes, Alexander! I love watching you fuck me!" She was so turned on. She was a bundle of sensation.

He picked up the pace to a torturous speed and felt Olivia tense around him, knowing she was on the brink of release.

"Come with me, love." He felt her shudder around him as he slammed once more, finding his own release. He leaned over her back, helping to steady her legs. She was grateful for the extra support as she tried to catch her breath. "Come. Let's get you in the bath."

~~~~~~~~~~~

"Sir?" A blonde woman opened the door to Donovan's office. "Paul Flinnigan is here."

217

"Okay. Send him in."

He entered the room, closing the door behind him.

"So, how did it go? I could really use some good news today, Paul. Burnham is fucking up my plans in a big way."

"It went well. Simon's behavior while in prison has been exemplary. He's been considered a model inmate. The staff had nothing but great things to say about him at the hearing."

"Get to the fucking point," Donovan growled, perusing photos on his laptop. He was trying to place the face of the man he saw in the snow earlier that day. He looked so familiar. None of it made any sense.

"He'll be released one week from Friday so you better get the rest of that money together."

"No problem. Make sure you meet him upon his release and bring him to me immediately. We need to start planning for the next phase. This is good news, Paul. Very good news."

"Yes, sir. See you next Friday." He stood up and left.

Donovan breathed a sigh of relief, thankful that his plans were finally coming together, before picking up his phone. "Cheryl, it's me. We ran into a bit of a problem."

"Again?"

"Don't fuck with me today, okay? You've been by her side nearly every day for the past month and nothing's happened."

"I know, but that's because Burnham usually has more than one agent watching her. He's smarter than we give him credit for. But I think I may have a solution to our little problem about him always being around Olivia. Maybe we can use one of his exes to drive a wedge between them?"

Donovan thought for a moment before responding. "Do you think that's a possibility?"

"I think so. He leaves quite a trail of women scorned, particularly one."

"Who? The girl he was supposed to marry? I thought she left town."

"No. Not her. Someone else. This woman was banned from his building a few months ago and we've all been given strict instructions to make sure she cannot contact Olivia in any way. So I think we could use her as an asset."

"Is she the type to agree?"

"From what I know, she'll do anything for a buck."

Donovan laughed. "That's my type of girl. Can you secure her cooperation?"

"Yes. Adele Peters will be attending the same charity event as Burnham this weekend. I am scheduled to be on his security detail that evening. I'll make the approach then. And listen to this…"

"Yes?"

"She grew up in Mystic with Burnham and…"

"And Olivia."

"Exactly."

"Holy shit. That's perfect. Great work, Cheryl."

"Thank you."

Donovan hung up and started to think that everything would soon fall into place. He could use Adele Peters to drive a wedge between Alexander and Olivia, giving her information that would tear Olivia's perfectly structured world apart. He would work with Simon to help him become more sympathetic, hoping Olivia would see that. Simon would win Olivia's trust, then he would find those documents. Finally.

CHAPTER THIRTY-THREE

LIKE A PRINCESS

AFTER MUCH NAGGING BY Kiera all day on Thursday, Olivia decided to accompany Alexander to the charity auction. What was there to be afraid of? Except possibly running into numerous women that Alexander had slept with, including the woman he left standing on the altar. Olivia came from a different world than that which Alexander lived in. Yes, she had money, but she didn't flaunt it. Not like that.

Since she had nothing to wear, she forced Kiera to take a personal day on Friday to help her shop. In exchange, Olivia promised her a day of pampering on Saturday... Massages, manicures, pedicures, and hair styling. How could Kiera say no to that?

"Okay, bitch. Ready to get this show on the road?" Kiera shouted across the coffee shop when she entered.

Olivia rolled her eyes as Kiera made her way over to the table she was sitting at, Carter standing stoically near the entrance. "You sure do know how to make an entrance, don't you?" Several businessmen in nicely tailored suits watched with lust in their eyes as Kiera sat down across from Olivia.

She shrugged, grabbing the coffee Olivia held out for her, bringing her lips to the cup, savoring the warm liquid. "Ready for your day of shopping?" Kiera asked excitedly once the caffeine entered her system.

"I think so. I'm still a little nervous about this, though," Olivia said.

"Why? I don't get it."

220

"I don't know. This whole world Alexander lives in is so far from anything I've ever dealt with. There's crazy money, and I'm just worried I won't be accepted, ya' know?" Olivia looked down, nervously tapping her nails against the small black bistro table as people flooded into the shop, desperate to get their morning caffeine fix. The sun had finally come out to play, melting some of the snow from the day before, and spring was in the air.

"Pssh, whatever. You just show them you've got more money than all of them put together. Because you totally do."

Olivia exhaled, pushing her empty coffee cup to the edge of the table. "I know, but you know me. I don't care about showing off how much money I have. I'm just worried I won't fit in."

"Don't try to fit in. You've never done that before, and that's why Alexander loves you so much."

Olivia stilled in her chair. "No. He's not in love with me, Kiera. No way. We barely know each other. I mean..."

"What? Spit it out, Libby."

"It's just that we were only together for like two months before I..."

"Before you ran like the fucking coward you are," Kiera spat playfully at her friend, winking at a tall guy walking past their table on the way to order his coffee. Olivia sighed, wishing she could be as bold as her friend.

"Yes. Before I ran. So we've only been back together for a month. And I guess I just don't think you could really fall in love with someone that quickly."

"So let me get this straight. All that agony you felt when he turned you away, that was all because you just *liked* him?" Kiera raised her eyebrows, glaring at Olivia with her arms crossed.

"Well..." She leaned back in her chair, not comfortable with the direction their conversation had taken.

"Well, what? What the fuck are you so scared of?"

Olivia lowered her voice. "You know what."

"He calls you 'love' all the time. You seem to be okay with that."

She sighed. "That's different. That's like calling me 'babe' or 'sweetheart' or something like that. It doesn't mean he loves me."

Kiera got up from the table, grabbing her friend's hand and pulling her out of the coffee shop, Carter following closely behind as they walked up the street toward a dress boutique. "You're crazy. He loves you. You love him. And if you're too scared to put a label on it, whatever." She opened the door to the swanky shop, and they were soon immersed in trying to find the perfect dress, Olivia thankful that Kiera hadn't continued their conversation about her and Alexander and that horrible word that scared her to her core.

After shopping for several hours and trying on dress after dress, Olivia was ready to give up and call Alexander to tell him that she was not going with him.

"Come on. Last one, I promise," Kiera begged, thrusting a dress into her arms and shooing her back into the dressing room.

"Fine," Olivia replied unenthusiastically. Nothing had been working out for her that day. They had spent hours going from boutique to boutique, searching for the perfect dress, but nothing made Olivia feel good. Not one dress was even close to what she needed to have on her body to feel confident enough to get through the charity auction. Maybe she was fooling herself thinking that she could really live in Alexander's perfect little world. He had everything...good looks, charm, money, a killer smile, a beautiful body that sent electricity through her entire being every time he was close. And the way he used that body... Olivia started panting as she stood in the dressing room just thinking about that body moving on top of her and beneath her and everything in between.

"You okay in there?" Kiera shouted, bringing Olivia back from her thoughts.

"Yeah," she replied weakly. "Just a second." She looked at the dress that Kiera had chosen. It appeared simple enough and that was what Olivia wanted. Something simple, yet elegant. And the dress fit the bill. Sliding the silk over her head and pulling up the zipper, her jaw dropped. The deep champagne shade accented her olive tone, making her skin seem to glow. The gown drew attention to her best features, with a deep V in the front and an even deeper V in the back, showing off her rather sculpted back. It clung loosely to her hips before falling to the floor, a slit running up almost the entire length of her right leg.

"Holy shit!" Kiera exclaimed when Olivia walked out of the dressing room. "You look fucking smoking! You need that dress, even if you don't wear it Saturday night. Damn. I wish I had long legs like yours." She looked Olivia up and down, taking in her tall, lean frame.

"Oh, stop it, Kiera. You know you're hot." Olivia turned to look at herself in the large one-hundred-eighty degree mirror.

"Oh, I know that, but I wish I was taller. That's all." She grabbed a few pieces of jewelry off a nearby case and helped Olivia accent the dress. When she was done, Olivia stood draped in simple red jeweled accessories, contrasting perfectly with the deep champagne hue in the long elegant dress. Carefully stepping into a pair of champagne-colored heels, Olivia knew she had found the perfect dress.

"What do you think?" Kiera asked quietly as Olivia stared at her reflection.

"I feel like a princess."

Kiera smiled, squeezing her friend's arms. "Good. Let's buy that dress and go have a drink."

Olivia nodded.

CHAPTER THIRTY-FOUR

MINE

AFTER THEIR DAY OF shopping, Olivia returned to Alexander's place, quickly running downstairs to one of the guest rooms and hiding her purchases in the massive closet. Runner followed, wondering what she was doing down there. "Come on, boy," Olivia said, heading back upstairs. "Let's start dinner while we wait for Daddy."

Walking back into the kitchen, staring out through the large windows overlooking the waterfront, boats bobbing up and down in the distance, a strange feeling rushed over her. Everything seemed so perfect. She was happy. Smiling, she thought how far she had come since Alexander allowed her back into his life. As they slept together each night, Alexander wrapping his arms around her as she drifted off, she felt like she had finally found a home. Home was anywhere that Alexander was, and the thought both excited and frightened her.

She made her way to the large temperature controlled wine cave just off the kitchen to pick out a bottle for dinner. Looking at the clock, she wondered what was keeping Alexander in his office after six on a Friday night. Her mind started to race, thinking about all the possible reasons why he could be detained. After finding a nice pinot noir, she quickly retreated back to the kitchen to find her new cell phone.

Olivia: *Hey. Everything okay?*

Several long moments passed with no response. What if something happened to him? Should she go to Martin's condo on the lower floor to see if he knew anything? But if Martin was home, then Alexander would be home. He never went anywhere without Martin. Or, at least, she didn't think he did. She really didn't know. Making quick work of the cork, she poured herself a large glass of wine, needing the alcohol to calm her nerves.

Pacing back and forth, Runner close behind her every step of the way, Olivia quickly finished her first glass of wine. She looked at the clock...six-thirty. With shaking hands, she poured another large glass and walked to the windows, looking out over the city, her heart racing as she mentally ran through every possible scenario about why he wasn't home yet. Finally, she heard her phone ding. Leaping over the couch, she grabbed it.

Alexander: *Sorry, love. Meeting ran late. Just need to finish a few things and then I'll be home. I miss you terribly.*

Olivia breathed a sigh of relief as she typed a response.

Olivia: *Miss you, too. I was really worried something bad happened to you.*

Her hands still shook uncontrollably as she raised her wine glass to her lips, hoping to calm her nerves. The thought of losing Alexander caused Olivia to panic. She couldn't imagine life without him. Kiera's words from earlier in the day replayed in her mind. Did she love him? Is that why she couldn't control her rapid heartbeat at the thought of Alexander being ripped from her like everyone else in her life?

He's okay. Olivia had to keep repeating that phrase over and over again as she made her way back to the kitchen, grabbing what she needed to make her seafood risotto. As her heart began to slow, she decided that music would help cheer her mood a bit. She grabbed her iPad and started to stream music to Alexander's surround sound system.

She put on one of her playlists as she busied herself preparing their meal for the evening. Runner sat by the kitchen island, patiently waiting for any crumbs that may come his way, watching as Olivia chopped onions and garlic before throwing it into the sauté pan. Cooking helped take her mind off her fear of losing Alexander. She thought she was over that, but now she wasn't too sure.

~~~~~~~~~~

After receiving Olivia's text that she was worried about him, Alexander bolted out of his office, feeling guilty for not having his phone with him during his meeting.

"Martin! Let's go," he shouted, walking briskly down the long corridor toward the elevator bank.

"Have a nice weekend, Mr. Burnham!" his receptionist called out as he scurried into an elevator with Martin.

The ride from his office building to the waterfront seemed unbelievably long. All he wanted to do was wrap his arms around Olivia and tell her that she didn't need to worry about him. He wasn't going anywhere. Ever.

A few excruciatingly long minutes later, Alexander stepped into the foyer and punched in the door code. When he entered his penthouse, the sight that greeted him very nearly stopped his heart.

A smile spread across his face as he watched Olivia dance along to music blaring throughout his entire home. Runner greeted him at the door, but Olivia continued to remain blissfully ignorant of his presence. Alexander stood a few feet from her, staring, hoping she wouldn't notice him just yet while he enjoyed the view of her perfect body moving to a driving beat, wearing a pair of yoga pants and a tight pink tank top.

Alexander listened to the song. It was clearly about sex. When Olivia sang about only getting off when in a certain position, he couldn't help himself.

"I hope that's not the case, love."

"AAAAAGGGGGGHHHH!" Olivia screamed, jumping at the sound of a voice, ramming her back against a large pantry door. She clutched her chest, willing her heart to stop beating so fast. After several intense moments, she calmed down enough to see that it was Alexander. He leaned against the kitchen island, apparently enjoying the show, smiling, his dimples popping.

"Holy shit. You scared me," she exhaled.

Alexander laughed as he stalked across the kitchen toward her, leaning his hand on the wall and placing a gentle kiss on her neck. She punched him in the arm. "Don't ever creep up on me like that again. Jackass."

He smiled, looking down at her, before his eyes grew intense. "But, seriously, you don't only come when you're on top, do you, Olivia?"

She stood on her toes, her mouth a mere breath away from his ear, sending shivers throughout his entire body. "You know that's not the case," she whispered before playfully smacking his ass and walking back to the stove to continue with the risotto.

Alexander walked up behind her and turned off the heat on the burner. "Humor me, love. I want to make sure," he said, his voice deep with desire. He placed his hand possessively on her stomach and trailed kisses down the side of her neck. She moaned in response and felt him harden behind her. He lowered his hand under her yoga pants, finding that sweet spot, slipping two fingers inside of her. She thrust with his motion.

"This is mine," he growled.

Olivia moaned.

"Do you understand, Olivia?" he asked as he continued to torture her, pushing in and out, his thumb brushing her clit.

She moaned again, unable to form any response. Heat coursed through her body as she melted with Alexander's words. It was true. She was his in every way possible. Her heart, body, and soul belonged to him. No one ever came close to making her feel as whole and complete as Alexander did.

He swiftly lowered her pants and threw her over his shoulder, slapping her ass. She yelped in surprise, and he walked over to the couch, dropping her on her back. After ridding himself of his pants, he crawled on top of her, savagely entering her.

"I said. Do. You. Un. Der. Stand?" Each syllable was met with another thrust.

Olivia moaned out in pleasure when Alexander placed his thumb back on her overly sensitized clit.

"Yes!" she screamed loudly as Alexander pushed into her even harder and faster. "It's yours."

"What's mine, Olivia?" he growled, continuing his torturous rhythm.

"My pussy!" she yelled, shuddering around him as he thrusted into her.

"That's not all that's mine." He pulled out of her and quickly flipped her onto her stomach.

"Get on your hands and knees, Olivia."

She quickly obeyed.

Alexander reached between her legs and wet his fingers with her juices. "Mmmm," he said. "Always so wet."

She leaned in to his fingers, desperate for his touch. "And greedy." He pulled out, trailing his fingers up to her ass. He slowly pushed one finger inside of her.

Alexander leaned down, nipping her shoulders. "This is mine, too," he whispered.

Olivia moaned, meeting his finger as it explored unchartered territory.

"Say it, Olivia."

"It's yours, Alexander."

He gently pushed his erection inside of her sex, still keeping his finger inside of her ass. "What was that?" He moved slowly inside her, the sensation an overwhelming feeling of fullness.

"It's all yours, Mr. Burnham," Olivia whimpered. "My entire body."

Alexander growled, picking up his pace and pumping into Olivia even harder. "I want you to come again."

Her breathing increased. "I don't know if I can."

Alexander reached around her with his other hand, pinching her nipple. "Oh, really?"

"Fuck," Olivia screamed out, her orgasm catching her by surprise.

"That's it, love. Give it to me," Alexander growled and Olivia fell apart, the orgasm never seeming to end. He continued his relentless rhythm and, within moments, pushed into Olivia one last time, shouting her name in total ecstasy.

It took several moments for their breathing to return to normal, Alexander clutching onto Olivia's hips as he slowly came down from his orgasm. He gradually pulled out of her and helped her put her pants back on before attending to himself.

Picking her up, he walked over to the kitchen as she wrapped her legs around his waist. He set her down on the kitchen island and kissed her, invading her mouth with his tongue. "Well, I'm glad we've settled that," he said, pulling away and heading in the direction of the staircase.

"What's that?!" she shouted back.

"You definitely don't only come when you're on top." He winked as he disappeared up the stairs to shower before dinner.

After running down the hall to the bathroom to clean up, Olivia returned to put the finishing touches on their risotto, an infectious grin on her face as she thought about the feel of Alexander's body as it moved on top of and behind her. Would she ever get tired of that man? She highly doubted it.

Lost in her thoughts, she didn't realize when Alexander approached behind her as she stood stirring the risotto, making sure the texture was perfect.

"I'm sorry I worried you before. The last thing I ever want to do is give you a reason to worry about me." He turned her around and stared into her big brown eyes. "From now on, I'll make sure I always have my cell on me, just in case. I'm so sorry, Olivia."

He pulled her into a tight embrace. She inhaled deeply, loving the smell of his aftershave and body wash. Running her hands up and down his muscled back, she felt a familiar throbbing sensation between her legs. Just one touch made her body come alive.

Wanting to forget about how wrecked her nerves were for that half-hour, she simply nodded. "It's okay. I know it's stupid."

Pulling out of the embrace, Alexander looked at her face, her features so soft. There was such a strong resemblance to her mother. He wanted to say something, but stopped himself. "No, Olivia. It's not okay. I gave you a reason to doubt me. I made you panic and I hate that."

Olivia cocked her eyebrows, looking at him with a questioning look on her face. *How did he know?*

"The bottle of pinot on the counter is half gone. And the corkscrew still out with the cork on it indicates you just opened it. Anyway, it's not important." He placed a kiss on her forehead. "Now, feed me dinner, wench." He slapped her ass playfully. She loved that side of him. It wasn't often that the playful side emerged, but when it did, she couldn't help but feel a warmth oozing through her entire body.

CHAPTER THIRTY-FIVE

CLARITY

THAT EVENING, OLIVIA STAYED in, deciding to forego playing with the band, trying to rest up for the following day. After dinner, she relaxed on the couch with Alexander. As she lay on her back, propping her feet up on his lap, she did some reading. Occasionally, she would gaze at him as he reviewed case files, wondering how she got so lucky to have him in her life.

As he turned a page in the document that he was reviewing, his muscles flexed, bulging the arms of his tight gray shirt. She couldn't help but smile and stare at him over her e-reader, blushing when she remembered what they had done on that very couch earlier, her eyes now shifting down to the jeans that fell so nicely from his hips.

"Can I help you with something, Miss Adler?" he asked, lowering his dark-framed reading glasses.

Fuck... Those are hot!

"No. Just enjoying the view," she smirked, licking her lips.

"Really? And how is the view?" His voice was sweet with a hint of humor.

"Slightly obstructed," she giggled, the effects of the wine coming through.

Alexander put the file he was reviewing on the coffee table. "How is that? Anything we can do to fix that?" His voice changed from playful to serious and sensual.

She gazed into his eyes and simply nodded.

"What do you want, Olivia?"

"You. Naked." She secretly loved it when he asked her what she wanted. It almost gave her a feeling of control but, deep down, she was well aware that when it came to Alexander, she had no control over what that man did to her.

Alexander stood up, taking off his glasses.

"No. Leave the glasses on," Olivia said, her breathing growing heavy.

He smiled. "Anything I can do to make you happy." Placing the glasses back on his face, he stripped off his shirt and jeans, standing inches in front of where Olivia sat on the couch, his erection in front of her face.

"Is this less obstructed, darling?" He looked down at her, her eyes wide.

She nodded, speechless. After nearly eight months, he could still take away her ability to form thoughts.

"Suck, Olivia." It wasn't a request. It was an order. She willingly obeyed.

Wetting her lips, she opened her mouth and took him in, licking as she went. He thrust into her mouth, placing his hands on top of her head, guiding her. She picked up the pace, desperately wanting to taste him. Alexander moaned in pleasure when she gently bared her teeth every so often.

"God, I love it when you suck my cock, Olivia," he said, his breathing becoming labored as he drove faster and faster. "Do you like my cock in your mouth?"

She moaned, her tongue tracing his length as he pushed further and further into her mouth.

He looked down at her as she continued to keep rhythm with him. "Look at me, Olivia." He grabbed her hair, pulling her head back, her eyes wide, unable to avoid his own blazing stare. "Why are you always so difficult? Just tell me you love sucking my cock."

Her heart raced at his words. Something about the dominant side of Alexander turned her on more than anything, but she liked making him work for it a little. It made her body flame even more because, when she didn't immediately obey, he became rough, and she liked it that way.

Pulling back, she stared into his eyes. "Yes, Mr. Burnham. I

232

love sucking your cock," she said sweetly, her soft voice making Alexander twitch with longing.

"Good. Now suck, Olivia. I want to come in your mouth."

She smiled before wrapping her lips around him. He moaned out as she picked up the pace, taking his large erection in her mouth. She grabbed him underneath and started to caress him, sending him over the edge. He emptied into her mouth, breathing her name as he finished. Olivia reveled in the taste of him as he ejaculated, smiling that she could do that for him.

Stepping back, Alexander stared at the woman in front of him for several moments, making Olivia feel slightly self-conscious.

"What are you thinking about?" she asked, breaking the growing silence.

"Just wondering how I got so lucky." He grabbed her hands in his, pulling her off the couch. "Let me help you with these." He quickly took off her yoga pants and tank top. She looked down to see that he was already erect again.

"You're an animal," she joked.

"Oh, Olivia. You have no idea. You do this to me." He pulled her toward him, kissing her deeply.

"Get on the couch, but kneel. Lean back so your back is on the sofa, and hold on to your ankles."

She gave him a questioning look.

"Just trust me," he whispered against her neck, sending shivers through her core.

She did as he asked.

"We're going to have to invest in some handcuffs, I think." He took a step back, admiring the view. "Damn, baby. You look hot right now. I knew all that yoga would come in useful one day."

Olivia stared at the ceiling, waiting for him. She was starting to become unhinged in anticipation. Several more moments passed and Alexander had yet to move toward her.

"WILL YOU JUST FUCK ME ALREADY?!" she shouted.

Alexander growled and rushed to the couch, positioning himself over her, and roughly entered her.

She knew why he wanted her in that position. Her pelvis was lifted to him and it made the sensation so much deeper. He continued to slam into her in a punishing rhythm and then slowed down, barely moving as he filled her.

"Alex, please," Olivia begged. "You're driving me crazy over here."

A smile spread across his face as he pulled out, teasing her clit with his erection. "Oh, really? Why's that? Do you want to come again? You've already had two orgasms today, Miss Adler. And now I have, as well. I'm not so sure I can come again after that fantastic blow job so I'd say we're even."

Olivia's mind raced. She needed some form of release. She was still wound tight, regardless of the two mind-blowing orgasms she had experienced earlier that evening. She needed to get off again, and soon.

"Don't you agree?"

Olivia shook her head, her chest rising and falling with heavy breaths. "No. You're being a tease, Alexander. Just let me come."

He leaned down, feathering kisses across her chest. "Always so greedy, aren't you? It can't always be about you." He took her nipple in his mouth, biting, causing Olivia to scream out in pleasure. She felt like she was going to come just from the feeling of Alexander's teeth on her nipple, gently pulling.

"Please, Mr. Burnham," she begged sweetly, hoping that giving him what he wanted would help. "Please let me come."

He traced circles around her nipple, his tongue roaming up to her neck. He gently tugged on her earlobe with his teeth. "Well, since you asked so nicely, Olivia, I'll give you what you want."

He gently thrust back into her, his motions slow and sensual.

"Wrap your legs around me," he said breathlessly. "I don't want any space between us right now."

Olivia obeyed, releasing her ankles from the grasp of her hands, and wrapped her legs around his waist.

"Fuck," he exhaled as she met his motion thrust for thrust. "I just can't get as deep as I want to," he said. Olivia's mind reeled from the thought of Alexander being any deeper inside her. She didn't think she could take anymore of him. She was already filled to the brim and ready to explode after only a few gentle thrusts.

He felt her body tighten beneath him and a smile crept across his face. "Let go, Olivia. I want to hear you scream my name, knowing I'm the only one who can make you come like this."

He pumped harder and it was all too much for her to handle. "ALEX!" she shouted as she came undone around him, her body shaking as she spiraled further and further down from her orgasm. After a few more pumps, Alexander found his release again, leaning down and biting Olivia's neck as waves of pleasure overtook his entire body, his orgasm taking him completely by surprise.

As his breathing began to slow, Olivia caressing his sweat-drenched hair, his cell phone started buzzing. He groaned, glancing at the coffee table to see who was calling.

"Damn it! I'm sorry. I have to take this." Olivia cringed as he quickly withdrew from her, grabbing the phone and running into the study.

"Martin. What is it?" he barked into the phone.

"Sorry, sir. I hope I'm not interrupting."

"Go ahead. Any news?" Alexander asked, still trying to catch his breath.

"Miss Adler's cell phone was never recovered, I'm afraid. It was nowhere to be found. Hopefully someone just saw it and grabbed it. However..." Martin hesitated on the other end.

"Yes. What is it?"

"There is the possibility that the suspect retrieved it. We were able to lock it remotely, but we haven't been able to track it so it must have been turned off. We will continue to monitor it. Once it's turned back on, we'll know immediately."

"Is that all?"

"No, sir. There's more. We ran facial recognition of some of the security cams. I just got the report back. And, well..."

"Yes. What is it?"

"It matched a Mark Kiddish." There was a pause before Martin continued. "I'm sorry, sir."

"That's okay. I need to call my sister."

"There's just one more thing. We saw one other person on the street the day of the incident. He was sitting on the bench across the street from your building. When we ran facial recognition on him to see if he's also involved, we got a hit."

"Who is it?"

"Well, that's the thing. According to the file, this person died over twenty years ago. Last name is DeLuca. Giacomo Deluca."

Alexander's heart stopped. It couldn't be. His mind raced with the possibility that Olivia's father was still alive.

"I'm going to keep running facial recognition to see if it could be a mistake."

"Okay. Thanks. I'll be in touch, Martin. And from now on, Miss Adler goes nowhere unaccompanied. Double up her agents, if you must. Triple them. Do whatever the fuck it takes. Do you understand?"

"Yes, sir. And I'm sorry."

Alexander hung up and immediately dialed his sister's number.

"Hey, Alex. What's up?"

"Carol, we have a bit of a problem."

"What's that? Is something wrong?"

Alexander proceeded to tell his sister what had happened the day before. How Olivia lost her protection detail. How she walked from her appointment in the Prudential Center to her house. How she kept walking and was followed. How she tried to lose the tail, but it didn't work. And how she ended up running, scared.

"Martin was able to pull up some of the street camera feeds. He found a guy matching the description that Olivia had given us. The timing was right." He stood up and walked over to the large windows in his study, leaning his head on the chilly glass pane. "Oh, sis," he moaned.

"Let me guess. It was Kiddish."

"Yeah, it was."

"Listen, Alex. I don't want to alarm you, but if Kiddish is doing his own dirty work now, shit must be bad."

"I know. I just…" He paced around his office, staring at all his old family photos. Photos of Olivia as a little girl. Photos of them in the sand. Then he stopped on a photo at the house in Newport when he and his parents went to visit one Christmas. That was their last Christmas together. Olivia wanted to play house, but before she would allow Alexander to play house with her, he had to marry her. So they had a play wedding ceremony. Her mother had snapped a photo of him wearing a top hat, Olivia wearing a long veil and a white dress. His heart dropped when he saw that. He knew his answer.

"What is it Alex? Are you okay?"

All of a sudden, everything became clear. "I just can't lose her. That's the girl I'm going to marry."

"Alex, I know you don't want to hear this from me again, but I think it's time you tell her. And it's time you finally opened that letter. There may be some answers there because, right now, I'm coming up empty. I can't find anything on this guy. But I do know that his father never did any of his own dirty work. He would hire other people to do the real work. That's how he and everyone who's hired him have gotten away with it. This could be bad."

"I know," he sighed, resigning himself to do the one thing he was scared of most. "Just… Give me a few more days. I'm taking her to the charity auction tomorrow night. I'll tell her after that. I promise."

"Okay. You'd better or, at some point, *I* will tell her. You can't keep this from her forever. She's bound to figure it all out eventually."

"I know," he said quietly.

"Okay. See you tomorrow."

"Carol?" Alexander said, grabbing his sister's attention, debating whether to tell her that facial recognition returned a hit on Jack DeLuca, even though he had supposedly been dead for over twenty years.

"Yeah?"

"Nothing," he exhaled. "Love you, sis."

"Love you, too."

Alexander hung up, thinking about how he could possibly

tell Olivia the words she should never have to hear. Retreating back to the living room, his entire body warmed as he admired her curled up next to Runner, fast asleep. She looked so peaceful. He wanted to keep her there with him forever.

He gingerly picked her up, trying not to wake her. As he carried her upstairs, his heart sank. He prayed that this wouldn't be one of the last nights he would ever hold her. He hoped she would forgive him for not telling her the truth when he was simply trying to protect her. That's what he swore that he would do all those years ago.

CHAPTER THIRTY-SIX

NOT GONE

A LITTLE GIRL LAY in a hospital bed. Tubes were attached to her and a machine measuring her heartbeat maintained a steady rhythm. That's all Olivia heard for days, the constant beep...beep...beep... Voices sounded around her. She recognized some of them and desperately willed her eyes to open, but she couldn't muster the strength. She felt something against her arm. Mr. Bear. Pulling the bear closer, she cried, wondering if anyone could even see the tears that fell from her eyes.

Hours passed. Maybe days. Olivia had no idea. She felt a small hand, not much bigger than her own, take hers. It had to belong to a child. "Olibia. You need to wake up now. Please," the voice begged. Olivia tried and tried to open her eyes, but she couldn't.

Then nothing. Again. She pulled Mr. Bear into her arms once more, knowing that she needed to keep him close for some reason. More time passed before she heard two voices speaking low. They didn't belong to a child, though. They belonged to two older men.

"Thomas, I understand what you're saying, but this is my decision," one of the voices said forcefully.

"Is this really necessary?" another voice asked.

"Of course it is! It's the only way. They knew, Thomas. They knew." A small cry erupted from the voice. "I need to protect everyone. She's dead, Thomas. She's fucking dead and this is the only way I know. They've threatened to hurt everyone close to me. They've already killed my wife! Who's next? My daughter? Me?" he said, the fear in his voice evident. "You need to do this. Pay off whoever you have to, but make sure it happens."

"If you're sure," the voice called Thomas said.

239

"*I am.*" *There was a brief pause.* "*Just one request, though. I know there will be new identities, but…please, still call her Olivia. If not her first name, at least her middle name. When Marilyn found out she was pregnant, she was so excited. She just knew she was having a little girl. She called her Olivia since day one. Please, whatever you do, just keep that name. For Mary.*"

"*You're sure about this? You won't be able to see her. She will grow up without a father.*"

"*She's already lost her mother.*"

"*But Jack… There's got to be another way.*"

"*There's no other way! They want me dead! They want everyone dead! They need to think that we perished in that crash. If they don't believe that, they'll keep coming after everyone I hold dear, including you and your family. I cannot have that on my conscience.*"

"*You're not thinking clearly. You were just in a nasty accident.*"

"*I've never had as clear of a head as I do now, Thomas.*"

There was a loud sigh. "*Okay. Fine. I'll get it done. We'll assign a protection detail for you once you are relocated. I won't be able to tell you where Olivia will go.*"

A small cry sounded in the room. "*I know, but it needs to be done. Her mother will be looking down on her, making sure she's safe. It's all I can hope for.*"

~~~~~~~~~~

"Olivia. Wake up, please." Her body shook violently, sweating and crying as Alexander tried to bring her back from whatever she was dreaming about. It scared him to his core to see her like that. He had witnessed Olivia's recurring nightmares many times in the past, but never had he seen something so frightening.

Her eyes flung open as she inhaled deeply, taking in her surroundings and trying to remember where she was. She was lying in an oversized bed with a cherry wood frame. The fireplace across from the bed flickered a soft glow, and a dog kicked in his sleep up on a bed next to the hearth, apparently chasing squirrels in his dreams. *Runner.* Runner was there. She looked at the person next to her on the bed. *Alexander.* It was only a dream. She breathed a sigh of relief.

Alexander leaned over to his nightstand and flicked on the light. He looked at Olivia as she sat up, covering her naked body with the light sheet. Her entire face was void of any emotion as she watched his every move.

Olivia gazed into those same green eyes she dreamt of nearly every night. She was starting to lose her mind. What was happening to her? This dream was something new. Did someone fake her death to protect her? It sounded so absurd.

"Olivia, please. Talk to me. I need to know that you're okay."

It wasn't real. It couldn't have been. It was only a dream, but her father's voice was so clear. It was as if no time had passed since the last time she heard him.

"Yes. I'm fine," she said quietly, her hands still shaking. "I just had that dream again. I'm sorry for scaring you." She turned away from him, pulling the duvet over her, and tried to go back to sleep. Alexander eventually turned off the light, certain that she was keeping something from him. He wrapped his arms around her, pulling her close and trying to comfort her.

"Do you think my father might still be alive?" she asked quietly just as Alexander was about to fall asleep.

He stilled, turning Olivia to face him, desperately searching her face, hoping she would tell him why she asked him that question. After his conversation with Martin earlier, and now Olivia's question, he wondered if maybe her father *was* still alive. "What makes you ask that?" He planted a kiss on her forehead.

"I've been seeing him and hearing his voice in my dreams lately. A few months ago, I dreamt that he made it out of the car and shot the man who hurt the little boy. And then tonight, I dreamt that I was in a hospital bed. All I could hear were voices, but I heard my father's voice, as well as my uncle's voice. But they were calling him Thomas and not Charles. They were talking about some sort of relocation. When my uncle told my father that he would never see me again, he just agreed. They said something about needing certain people to believe that we were all dead, or else they would never stop." A tear fell down Olivia's cheek.

"Shhhh. It's okay, darling. Like you said, it was just a dream." He pulled her into his arms, soothing her quiet cries. What if her father really *was* still alive? His father told him that they never made it out of the hospital, dying from complications of the crash. He clearly lied about Olivia. Did he do the same about her father?

"The boy was there, too," she said softly.

"When?" Alexander asked nervously.

"In my dream. Before I overheard the two men. I heard the little boy speak, begging me to wake up. I tried so hard to open my eyes, but I just couldn't."

A tear escaped Alexander's eye. He knew the exact moment she was referring to. The last time that he saw her. The day after the accident. He remembered his father allowing him to go see Olivia in her hospital room, and he begged and begged her to wake up. But she didn't. And that was the last time he ever saw her. A few hours later, his father told him that she didn't make it. That was the day his life changed, too.

Chapter Thirty-Seven

Strawberries and Champagne

"LOVE, I'M SENDING FOUR agents to the spa with you today," Alexander said the following morning as they sat eating breakfast. "Marshall is the only female. She is *not* to leave your side, do you understand?"

Alexander looked serious. It wasn't worth arguing with him that day, not after her restless night. She had trouble falling back to sleep after her dream. She couldn't shake the feeling that had started to form in the pit of her stomach.

At ten o'clock, Marshall appeared in the foyer. Olivia watched as Alexander greeted her, her tall, fit frame slightly intimidating, even standing next to someone like Alexander. She was clearly in shape and Olivia had no desire to mess with her. "Pleasure to see you again, Miss Adler."

"Agent Marshall, I've told you to call me Olivia or Libby." She had grown tired of all of Alexander's employees using her last name. Her name was Olivia. She didn't want to only be known as Miss Adler. That wasn't who she was.

Marshall looked at Alexander with a questioning look.

This man is ridiculous, Olivia thought. "Fine. Call me Miss Adler." Was she starting to lose her entire identity to the man standing next to her?

"Just give us a moment, please, Marshall."

"Yes, sir." She stepped into the foyer, giving Alexander and Olivia some privacy.

"Olivia, love," he said, brushing a lock of her hair behind her ear. "I'm sorry about the extra security but, after the other day…well, it's just necessary until I can get some answers."

"Fine," Olivia exhaled, reluctantly agreeing to his demands. He was all business that morning. She wanted the playful Alexander back from the night before.

He pulled her into a tight embrace, stroking her back as he planted gentle kisses on her forehead, her nose, her cheek, her other cheek. He gently brushed his lips against hers. Sparks flew through Olivia's body at the innocent contact of his lips on hers. She immediately forgot that she was irritated with him and his absurd protection details.

Alexander pulled back, his eyes aflame, before leaning in for a more passionate kiss. Their tongues intertwined as Olivia ran her hands through his hair, pulling his head closer to hers, not wanting to break the contact. She needed him desperately after the previous night. Alexander had become the one thing in life that she needed in order to get past the nightmares. He had become her own personal nepenthe. She smiled at the thought.

"Have a good day, gorgeous," Alexander murmured softly into her ear, trailing kisses across her face and down her neck.

Olivia moaned in response.

She felt him smile against her body. "Keep making those sounds and I'll make you late for your first spa treatment."

Her breathing increased. "Good. I want you to make me late."

Groaning, he lifted her up and she wrapped her legs around his waist. "Okay. We'll make it quick then." He carried her up the stairs to the bedroom, quickly ridding her of her clothes and sliding into her.

~~~~~~~~~~

Several hours later, Olivia returned to the penthouse from her spa outing with Kiera, feeling fully refreshed after a massage, manicure, and pedicure, as well as having her hair styled and make-up professionally applied. She was nervous enough about that evening as it was. She wasn't going to leave anything to chance, and that included making sure she looked perfect.

Alexander heard the door open as he sat at the kitchen

island, enjoying a glass of scotch before changing into his tuxedo for the evening. He turned, his jaw dropping. Olivia stood in front of him, her hair and makeup done for the evening. She looked amazing even in her jeans and cardigan. She never wore a lot of makeup so this was an entirely different look altogether.

He stared into her deep, dark eyes that had taken on a smoky quality, making them look even bigger than they normally were. She smiled, causing her cheekbones to look more pronounced and Alexander noticed a hint of blush, helping to define her high cheeks. His eyes stopped when he saw her lips. They were deep, vibrant red. The combination of her olive skin, dark hair expertly curled and pinned loosely to the side of her nape, and dark eyes made those red lips stand out even more.

"Olivia," he said breathlessly. "You look amazing." Alexander blinked repeatedly, trying to calm his growing erection.

"Just wait until you see me in my dress, darling." Olivia winked. "I'll be back soon." She made her way into one of the large guest bedrooms where she had hidden her dress the day before. She walked into the closet and reached for the Victoria's Secret bag, thankful that Kiera had convinced her that some new lingerie was in order for the special occasion. The dress was cut in such a way that she couldn't wear a bra, but she didn't think Alexander would mind.

She pulled on a red lacy thong and matching garter belt before sitting on a dressing chair to put on her thigh-high stockings, clipping them to the belt. She grew excited thinking about Alexander's expression when he took her dress off her later that evening. And he most certainly would be doing that. Olivia was sure of it.

She unzipped her garment bag and stepped into the gown. Standing back, she looked into the mirror on the wall, hardly recognizing the woman that stood in front of her. She never had a reason to buy a formal dress before. In high school, her uncle forbid her from going to the prom. In fact, she was surprised her uncle let her participate in *any* extracurricular activities. Anything one-on-one seemed to be rather off-limits. Group activities were generally okay. Prom was a big fat no. She thought about all the normal high school milestones she missed out on because her uncle thought he needed to protect her.

Olivia wished she had known him better, but she didn't. He was more an authority figure that she had to deal with when she needed something. There was no closeness with him. Still, he was her world. After her parents died, he was the only family she had.

Snapping out of her thoughts, she finished getting ready by putting on a pair of ruby drop earrings that matched perfectly with her multi-strand necklace of gold with ruby accents. She stepped into her champagne stilettos and gingerly walked up the stairs, holding her clutch and wrap, both the same shade of red.

Alexander was standing at the kitchen island dressed in his tuxedo when he heard Olivia walk up the steps. His heart beat madly, anxious to see how she looked. Turning in the direction of the stairs, he beheld the vision standing in front of him. His mouth dropped, unable to form any words.

Olivia smiled as she sauntered up to him. "The great Alexander Burnham, speechless? I'm shocked." Olivia leaned in, breathing those words on his collar. She could tell he was incredibly aroused at that moment. His tuxedo pants did not do a good job at hiding it. He grabbed her hand and held her at arm's length, admiring her dress before spinning her and pulling her back into his chest, holding her in an intimate embrace.

"You look amazing, love."

"As do you, *love*," Olivia smirked, gazing at him in his tuxedo. He always looked great in a suit, but his tuxedo took it to a whole new level. Whomever said a suit is like lingerie for men was absolutely right. Something about Alexander all dressed up turned Olivia on more than she could remember.

"Champagne?" Alexander asked, grabbing a bottle from the wine chiller.

"Yes, please."

He expertly popped the cork, the vapor flowing out of the bottle.

"I love that sound," Olivia said, watching as he poured her a glass, handing it to her.

"It's a close second for me," Alexander said, a smile on his face.

"To what?"

He wrapped his arm around her waist, bringing her body flush with his once more. "The sound of your laughter, of course. When we were apart, I missed that beautiful melody more than life itself." He leaned down, kissing her neck, inhaling her scent.

His words made Olivia's heart race. She loved how sweet he could be at times.

"Come." He grabbed her hand and led her past the couch to the windows in the living room. Smiling, he opened a glass door that Olivia had never noticed before. Stepping out onto the large expansive balcony, she gasped at the amazing view. Despite it being a chilly March evening, the fire pit and heating lanterns kept them warm as they stood admiring the city down below, drinking their champagne.

"What a view," Olivia muttered, looking over the waterfront, the sun setting behind the building painting the sky in a pink hue as a gentle breeze blew through the air.

"Yeah, isn't it? I remember growing up, coming to visit my older sister. She would always take me to Kelly's on Revere Beach where we would watch the planes landing at Logan," Alexander said quietly, his eyes trained on the runway in the distance. "I always thought about how nice it would be to be able to fly away just like those airplanes. After that, I always loved being near airports, watching people coming and going. Whenever I was sad or upset, I always reminded myself that it was possible to get away. So when I found this place and I was able to watch the lights of the airport in the distance, I had to have it."

"When did you move to Boston?"

"I went to Harvard for a semester before dropping out and joining the Navy. I didn't come home for about two years. At that time, my dad had moved the company's headquarters here. Originally, they were based out of Providence, which was less than an hour from my family's house in Mystic. We had a branch of the company located here already. We have offices all over the country. As we grew bigger and bigger, he felt Boston should be the headquarters. There's more international flights going and coming than in Providence, which is important for clients and it's not New York. Plus, Carol was working as a cop, and it's always good to have someone on the police force helping you out." He looked down at the girl in front of him, knowing that the main reason his father moved to Boston was to keep an eye on Olivia while she attended Boston College. He was still floored at the thought that she was in Boston all those years and his father knew about it, but never said a word. He didn't think he would ever forgive him for that. Not when he watched Alexander struggle nearly his entire life with losing her.

"Your sister…she's much older than you, isn't she?" Olivia asked, bringing him back from his thoughts.

"Yeah. Well, Carol was a mistake," he smiled. "She's forty-six. I'm thirty and Tyler is twenty-one. Mom was eighteen when she found out that she was pregnant with Carol. Dad was going to marry her anyway, but that made them marry a little earlier. Then Dad was sent overseas right after she was born. Vietnam and all that. He was lucky to make it out alive. He went to Harvard after that and, eventually, got in with the CIA." He paused briefly, wondering what Olivia knew about the man she referred to as her uncle. He couldn't remember the last time he spoke to someone about his father, apart from his siblings. It actually felt good. Maybe he needed to talk about him so that he could begin to overcome his anger toward his father for abandoning and lying to him all those years. But forgiveness wasn't in the cards.

"He worked clandestine services," Alexander continued. "He spoke a bunch of different languages. As you can imagine, he was never around. It wasn't until my mom threatened to walk out on him when my sis was a teenager that he decided to leave the CIA and start his own private security firm. He surrounded himself with the best and the brightest, and built the company up. His thought was that if you paid people enough, they couldn't be bought, making us one of the most successful security firms. And we still adhere to the same principle."

Alexander stared out in the distance while he continued talking, Olivia listening intently. For someone she felt so comfortable with, she was surprised at how little she really knew about him and his past. He never opened up to her about his father before so now that he was talking, she didn't want to interrupt. She wanted to learn more.

"It wasn't until after the company was started that I was born. I remember hanging out with Dad when I was little. I think I was the only one who was ever close to him. He was gone when Carol was growing up. He didn't start the security company until she was almost out of high school. And by the time my little brother was born, he was gone again. He was only truly around the first nine years of my life."

Alexander looked down. He had never realized that he was the only one who really spent any time with his dad. All the memories of their summers on the beach flooded back to him. He remembered holding baby Olivia for the first time. He was only two and she was not yet a week old when his parents took him down the street to the Deluca's house.

"*She looks funny,*" Alexander remembered saying to his parents.

"*It's because she's brand new, Alex. All babies look funny when they first arrive.*" His mother gingerly placed the little bundle into his small arms, helping him hold her. Olivia started to cry. Alexander remembered looking at his mother, wondering what to do with a crying baby.

"*Alex, darling, just tell her everything's going to be okay, that you're going to be friends. Go on...*"

Alexander returned his eyes to the swaddled baby and began to rock her. "*Don't cry, Olibia,*" he said, unable to pronounce her name correctly. "*We're going to be best friends.*"

A tear slid down his cheek at the memory.

Olivia reached for his face, catching his tear. "I'm sorry. I know it's tough." She slid into his shoulder and he put his arm around her, pulling her close. He thought how well she fit in his embrace. Just like two pieces of a tragic puzzle.

"Excuse me, sir, ma'am," Martin interrupted. They turned in unison to see Martin standing in the doorway.

Alexander nodded. "Yes, Martin?"

"The car is ready out front for you."

"Thank you," he replied.

Martin quickly exited, leaving them alone.

"Miss Adler, are you ready?" Alexander held his arm out for Olivia.

"Yes, I am, Mr. Burnham." She slid her arm through his and he led her down to their waiting limousine.

CHAPTER THIRTY-EIGHT

COME CLEAN

ALEXANDER ESCORTED OLIVIA THROUGH the lobby of the Four Seasons by Boston Common, avoiding photographers as much as possible. He steered her toward one of the large banquet rooms at the hotel, flanked by both Carter and Marshall. Upon entering, servers greeted them, carrying champagne. Alexander grabbed two glasses, giving one to Olivia.

She looked around the room, estimating that there had to be several hundred people there. Everyone milled about, socializing. They all seemed to know each other, except Olivia. Nerves coursed through her body as she tightened up, wondering why she had agreed to accompany him. She knew she was out of her element as she watched him shake hands and pose for photos, leading Olivia across the room to their assigned table.

"Alex, darling." Olivia watched a woman in her mid-sixties get out of her chair and move toward Alexander, pulling him into an embrace.

"Hello, Ma." He placed a kiss on her cheek. Olivia hated meeting the parents. She didn't know how to act. It wasn't something she had ever had to deal with before. Why did she agree to come? Her heart started to beat rapidly and her hands became clammy.

"Don't worry. They'll love you," Alexander whispered, leaning down and brushing his lips against her neck, having noticed her apprehension.

"Ma, this is Miss Sarah Olivia Adler," he said, turning toward Olivia. "She prefers to go by Olivia."

"Olivia, dear. Oh, it is such a pleasure to finally meet you." She pulled Olivia into a tight embrace, squeezing her affectionately. "I've heard so much about you!"

Olivia was surprised at the warm greeting. "Mrs. Burnham," she said pulling out of the hug. "It's wonderful to meet you."

"Please. Call me Colleen, dear," she replied before turning to her son and giving him a searching look. Alexander shook his head, as if saying 'not now'. Olivia watched the exchange, not knowing what to make of it.

"Olivia, you remember my sister, Carol," Alexander said as Carol pushed out of her chair, standing up to greet her.

Olivia hardly recognized Alexander's sister in the elegant long black gown and diamond jewelry that she wore. "Yes. Detective Wilder, it's wonderful to see you again," she said as they shook hands.

"Please, it's Carol."

"Okay." Olivia smiled nervously.

"Olivia," Carol said. "This is my husband, David."

Olivia surveyed Carol's husband, seeing the cop in him. His strong, muscular body filled out his tuxedo quite nicely.

"Nice to meet you, David."

"Likewise, Olivia." They shook hands.

"And you remember Tyler," Alexander said, motioning toward his brother.

Olivia remembered seeing Alexander's brother very briefly that night outside of Johnny D's, but she was never really introduced to him. Now, as she stared at him, a dumbfounded look crossed her face. He looked like an exact replica of Alexander, even if he was several years younger. Same green eyes. Same dark hair. He was slightly less muscular and a little shorter, but the facial features were alarmingly similar. There was no mistaking that they were brothers.

"Great to see you again, Olivia," Tyler said, wrapping his arms around her. *This family likes to hug,* she thought.

"You as well, Tyler. Please call me Libby." She noticed the two brothers exchange a look.

"Alex, darling!" a voice shouted through the large banquet room.

Alexander rolled his eyes. "What is *she* doing here?" he said under his breath.

"Come now, dear," Colleen said. "She's an old family friend. Her parents have always been very involved with this charity. We had to extend them an invitation so play nice."

"Money grabber," Tyler said under his breath.

Alexander laughed, straightening up when he saw Adele approach.

"There you are, Alex. I've been looking all over for you!" Adele wrapped her arms around him, his face remaining flat.

"Adele, you remember Miss Olivia Adler, don't you?" He smirked as he motioned toward Olivia.

"How could I forget? The woman you left poor Chelsea on the altar for," she sneered, looking at Olivia with disgust. "Anyway, can I steal you for a minute, love?"

Olivia shuddered at the term of endearment that Adele used for him. That was hers, and hers alone.

He glanced at Olivia, her stony eyes trained on Adele. "Olivia, *love*," he said, emphasizing the term of endearment. "Will you be okay for a minute?"

She smiled. "Of course, Alexander, *love*."

He laughed as he led Adele away from his family, spinning around to face her when they were alone, his eyes wide with fury. "What is it, Adele? What could possibly be so important that you had to drag me away from my *girlfriend* and my family?"

"Whoa! Easy there, bad boy," Adele said, crossing her arms. "I just wanted to see who you would choose. Obviously, you value *my* companionship more than that trash you brought with you tonight."

Alexander exhaled. If she knew how wealthy Olivia really was, she would definitely be singing a different tune. She would probably try to be best friends with Olivia, just to be around someone with a large bank account.

"Adele, Olivia is not trash. She's very special to me." He glared at her, watching her lips turn up into a mischievous grin.

"So sorry to hear about you and Chelsea," she said, placing her hand on his bicep. "It's such a pity, isn't it? She would have been good for you. I half expected that you'd finally smarten up after her, though, and realize that you need to date someone with social standing and not just that girl you keep attaching yourself to."

"Enough, Adele!" Alexander said forcefully, stepping away from her. "Now, if that's all, I'll be rejoining my family, and that family includes Olivia." He turned to leave.

"Wait, Alex. Come sit with me," she pleaded with him, all bitchiness gone from her tone. "My father would love to see you. He always had a soft spot for you. I know I disappointed him with the way I turned out."

"Adele, stop," he said softly. "Don't say things like that. He loves you. Maybe a little too much."

"I don't care about that, Alex," she replied, her voice sweet. "I just wish *you* would love me. All those years we spent hooking up with each other. Can you really say it all meant nothing?" She looked up at him, her eyes pleading.

"Adele, I never said that. It's just…" He trailed off.

"What? It's just that I wasn't Olivia? Well, I'll tell you what, Mr. Burnham…" she hissed, her voice full of venom.

Alexander's eyes flung wide open.

"Oh, that's right. I remember what you like." She winked. "That bitch sitting with your family is not her, either." She stormed off.

Alexander exhaled loudly. "If only you knew, Adele," he said to no one as he turned to head back to his family and his Olivia.

Throughout their five-course meal, the family engaged in relative small talk, asking Olivia about herself. Alexander had warned them ahead of time to steer away from questions about her family. They followed his demands.

"So, Olivia, Alexander says you're a musician." Colleen turned to face her, dabbing her mouth with a napkin after finishing the delicious grand marnier soufflé that they served for dessert.

"Yes, I guess you could say that. I've been playing piano as long as I can remember."

Alexander and his sister shared a meaningful look.

"And I used to sing in a band in college. I just recently started performing again. We usually play at MacFadden's in the Financial District on Friday nights."

"I've been there," Tyler said to everyone at the table. "They're really good. You guys should check them out."

"Thank you," Olivia said, blushing.

"Well, our Alex here is quite the musician, as well," Colleen interjected. "He was so insistent on learning to play when he was a little boy."

Alexander glared at his mother, regretting all the wine he had poured for her throughout the evening.

"He was in love with this girl. Her parents were close family friends so they practically grew up together. Anyway, her mother was an accomplished musician and taught her to sing and play all these musical instruments at such a young age. And poor Alexander over here had such a crush on the girl, but he thought that the only way she would love him was if he learned to play and sing. So he secretly had her mother teach him. It was so cute."

"Mom, stop," Alexander interrupted.

"Oh, Alex. Hush. It's not a big deal."

"So you learned to play to romance a girl?" Olivia smirked. "Whatever happened to the girl?"

Alexander stared into Olivia's eyes, a solemn look on his face. "She was taken from me."

Olivia looked around the table, tears starting to form in his mother's and sister's eyes.

"Oh, I'm sorry, Alexander. I didn't realize you were talking about you-know-who." The table grew silent. "Excuse me. I'm going to go freshen up." Olivia stood up, as did Tyler, David, and Alexander, who motioned to Marshall to accompany her.

When she was out of earshot, Colleen immediately spoke. "Darling, you need to tell her."

Alexander stared at his mother, dumbfounded. "How do you know? Did Carol say something?"

255

"Oh, Alex. I had a feeling something was going on. Women are much more perceptive than men are. After the DeLucas were involved in that horrific car accident, your father became so distant. He let slip that someone was after them. He said that Olivia died in that crash, that they all did, but I didn't believe him. We had gone to their funerals and, at the viewing the night before, all the caskets were closed. You couldn't even open them if you wanted to.

"Then all the summers he left to go to Charleston, I had a feeling that he knew more than he let on. I just had a feeling he was protecting that little angel from whatever killed her parents." His mother looked into his eyes with a look of remorse.

"So you knew all this time that she was alive and you watched me struggle with it?" he said in disbelief. "I've made myself go mad at times, debating whether I lost my mind. I would see her everywhere I went. And when I finally gave up hope and had moved on, I met this girl. Why didn't you say something sooner?"

"I don't know. I guess I was hoping that I was wrong because if I was right, I knew that someone else could figure it all out. If that's the case, she could be in a world of danger. I'm scared for her. Your father wouldn't fake medical records if it wasn't necessary. You know that."

Alexander looked around the table at the faces of his family and knew that his mother was right.

"Open the letter, dear. Stop trying to blame your father for everything. I know you like to retain control over everything and you think ignoring that letter is your last big act of defiance, but is it worth it? If I know your father, that letter won't just contain apologies because that wasn't his style. I can assure you that it contains information. You need to know. *She* needs to know. You need to come clean." Colleen reached over the table, placing her hand on top of his. "For her."

"Yes, Ma. For her."

Chapter Thirty-Nine

An Agreement

OLIVIA WAS REALLY STARTING to hate the constant security escort. Marshall wasn't too bad, but at least with a male agent, she had some semblance of privacy when she went to the restroom.

"I'll be fine in there, Agent Marshall," Olivia said, pushing open the door to the ladies' room.

Marshall held the door for Olivia and followed closely behind. "I'm sorry, ma'am. I have my orders. I could lose my job if I don't follow them."

Olivia exhaled loudly. "Controlling bastard."

Agent Marshall laughed. "Yes, ma'am. He certainly can be."

Olivia smiled at her, surprised at her response.

"I'll just wait right here, Miss Adler," Marshall said, pointing to a vanity sitting area in the posh bathroom.

"Okay. Thank you."

Olivia went about her business. When she exited the stall, she was met with a tall blonde woman, Marshall close behind her.

"I'm sorry, Miss Adler. I tried to stop her. I'm under strict orders that she is not to come near you."

Olivia looked at Marshall. "It's okay." She turned back to the blonde. "What do you want, Adele?"

"Just to have a little talk about my Alexander."

She exhaled loudly. "Are you really this delusional, Adele? And, seriously, what is it about bathrooms that scream confrontation?" She was feeling rather snarky.

"Just take this as a warning from someone who has been in the same position as you. He *will* leave you. It may not be for me, although that would be great. I could really put his bank account to good use. But, regardless, he'll toss you aside, just like everyone else. I'm sure he told you when you first met him that he doesn't date. He only fucks. I mean, look at what happened to poor Chelsea. He left her at the fucking altar."

"It's different with us, Adele. We actually care about each other, not just the size of the other person's bank account. We have something real."

"I'm sure you do," Adele said, raising her eyebrows. "It feels that way when he's fucking you, telling you that your pussy and ass are his, right?"

Olivia looked at her, wide-eyed.

"And then all you can do is whimper out, 'Yes, Mr. Burnham, all yours', as he's pounding into you." Adele batted her eyes. "It certainly does feel real, doesn't it?" She turned, leaving Olivia completely speechless.

She looked at Marshall through her water-filled eyes, unsure of what to say. "Excuse me, Miss Adler. I'll deal with her."

"Thank you," she said, finally finding her voice, her chin quivering slightly. "I'll just be another minute."

Marshall followed Adele out of the ladies' room, walking through the hotel lobby and catching up to her in the corridor leading to the banquet hall.

"Miss Peters," she called out.

Adele spun around. "I know, I know. Alex doesn't want me talking to his precious little Olivia," she spat out vindictively.

Marshall took a few steps toward her. "You have no idea, do you? Do you know how precious she really is?" she asked, raising her eyebrows.

Adele exhaled loudly. "I don't care about that."

"What if I said I know someone who could make it worth your while *to* care?"

Adele lowered her voice. "I'm listening."

"My boss will offer you ten million to do something for him."

Adele looked at Marshall, questioning her. "Alex wants me to do something for him?"

"No, not Alex. Someone else entirely."

"Agent Marshall..."

"So, can you help us or not? Ten million could certainly go a long way, Miss Peters."

Adele stood there and thought about that. She could stop chasing rich guys and finally provide for herself. "What do I have to do?"

"When the time comes, you'll receive a piece of very important information." She handed Adele a burner phone. "And your only job is to use that information to drive a wedge between Alexander and his little Olivia. Follow?"

"Well, how do I do that?"

"Oh, Miss Peters. You're smart enough to figure it out, I'm sure," she said before narrowing her gaze at her, her voice stern. "You mention a word of this to anyone, and I don't think I need to spell out what the consequences will be."

"Agent Marshall..."

"Please. Call me Cheryl. Do we have an agreement?"

Adele paused briefly before sighing. "Yes, Cheryl."

"Good." Marshall turned and walked back toward the ladies' room. "And feel free to get a jump start. I'll try to give you a wide berth."

Adele stood there, holding onto the cell phone, thinking about what she just agreed to do. She knew that Alexander was happy with Olivia, and she did care about him. Could she live with herself if she caused their break-up? Well, if it led him back to her, maybe she could.

~~~~~~~~~

Olivia needed some air after her confrontation with Adele. Quietly opening the door to the ladies' room and scanning the lobby, she breathed a sigh of relief when she found it to be relatively clear, at least of her security team. She discreetly left the restroom, walking through the large lobby, her heels clicking loudly on the marble floor as she slid out the front door of the hotel.

She leaned against the brick building, thinking about what Adele had said. She knew so much about what Alexander liked intimately. Olivia knew that she wasn't the only one, either. But then she thought about all the times that Alexander was so gentle with her, almost as if he was telling her something with the way he moved inside her body. Almost as if he…

No, Olivia thought. She pushed that thought far away, scared to even think about it.

CHAPTER FORTY

Too Soon

IT WAS A CHILLY March night, but Nathan Roberts didn't care as he sat on a bench on the outskirts of Boston Common Park, his eyes set on the Four Seasons. He was desperate to keep his eyes on Olivia. He knew Alexander was protecting her, but he couldn't help himself. Nathan needed to keep her alive.

About three hours after he saw her enter the hotel with Alexander, he was shocked to see her walk through the front doors alone. His mind started to race. He kept his eyes trained on her, looking for anything suspicious as she leaned against the large building.

He watched her stand in the cold for several long minutes, shivering. He contemplated going up to her to give her his jacket, but he couldn't approach her. He would risk her remembering, and he didn't know what she knew already.

Nearly ten minutes after she exited the hotel, Nathan saw a frenzied motion from within the lobby. Turning his head in that direction, he saw Alexander and one other agent running.

~~~~~~~~~~~

Fear covered Alexander's face as he searched the lobby, frantically shouting something. He headed toward the front doors, yelling orders at his other agent.

"Olivia!" he bellowed, running outside, searching up and down Boylston Street, desperately looking for her. He breathed a sigh of relief when he saw her standing against the building, her teeth chattering.

"Jesus Christ, Olivia," he said, running to her and wrapping his arms around her trembling body.

"What is it, Alex? What's going on?" she asked, staring at him with a confused look on her face.

"I didn't know where you were, love," he said softly. "We were all so worried." He embraced her tighter, pulling her to his body, planting kisses on her head. "You're shivering."

She looked up at him, her lips turning blue. "It's freezing out here."

Alexander peeled off his tuxedo jacket and draped it around her shoulders, covering her arms and back. As she gazed into his brilliant green eyes, she was immediately reminded of the night that they first met, amazed at how far they had come since then.

He tilted her chin back. "I was so worried that I lost you. Agent Marshall told me that Adele accosted you in the ladies' room. I want you to understand that you mean so much more to me than she knows, Olivia. I hope you know that."

She exhaled. "I know, Alexander. I know Adele's just trying to get me angry with you. We both have a past, but all I care about is the present. You're my present, Alexander, and I know I'm yours. It's going to take a lot more than some vindictive words to make me run. I told you. I'm done running."

He pressed his lips to hers, kissing her with such passion, telling her with his mouth how important she was to him. She reached up and clutched his face in her hands, pressing her body against his as he ran his hands over her.

Pulling out of the kiss, he stared down at her. "I need to stop kissing you or I'm going to take you up to a suite and fuck you until you can't walk anymore," he explained, his breathing labored as his eyes burned into her. "Okay?"

She stood on her toes and kissed his neck. "I think I'd enjoy that, Mr. Burnham."

He moaned, pulling her head to his chest, warming her in the frigid March air. As he stood on the city streets holding her, Alexander scanned the area, an occupational hazard. His eyes landed on someone across the street on the edge of Boston Common Park. He squinted, wondering if his eyes were deceiving him.

"Let's get you inside," Alexander said, returning his gaze to Olivia when he felt her shivering in his arms.

She nodded, dropping her arms and walking back toward the entrance of the hotel. Alexander took one more quick glance across the street before entering the front doors. The park bench was empty.

When Olivia and Alexander made their way back to the banquet hall, the servers had come around and cleared the tables. A twenty-piece big band had replaced the four-piece string quartet that had been playing during dinner and many guests had started to dance.

"May I have this dance?" Alexander looked at Olivia, reaching his hand out to her. She grabbed it and he led her onto the dance floor. The opening notes of *Let's Fall In Love* sounded through the elegant room. As he took her in his arms, he placed one hand on the small of her exposed back, exhaling as his did so. The feel of her skin still made it difficult for Alexander to maintain his composure.

She gazed up at him, savoring the feel of his hand on her body as he led the dance. Olivia was surprised how well he glided across the dance floor. "You're quite a good dancer, Mr. Burnham. Still surprising me after all these months." Olivia winked at him.

"You're not so bad yourself, Miss Adler." He beamed down at the woman in his arms.

"Where did you learn to dance?"

"Do you remember the girl my mom was talking about during dinner? The one I was madly in love with when I was a little boy?"

She nodded her head. "Your other Olivia?"

"Yes. Well, she would always say that she would only marry me if I could dance. She would say that she couldn't possibly be seen at a ball with a man who had two left feet. According to her, princesses needed a prince who could show off on the dance floor." Olivia looked at him, the memory clearly painful for him, his words stirring a memory deep within her own brain.

"I'm sorry, darling," she said, leaning her head against his chest as they continued to dance, Olivia wondering why the story about his childhood friend sounded so familiar.

"So am I," Alexander whispered so she couldn't hear him.

Over the next several hours, Alexander led Olivia around the dance floor, not wanting to miss any opportunity to dance with her.

"May I cut in?" Tyler said to Alexander toward the end of the night.

"Sure, but keep your hands above the waist, little bro." Alexander smirked.

"Tyler," Olivia said, putting one arm around his neck and clutching his hand with her free one.

"Hi, Libby," he replied, grabbing onto her waist, heeding his brother's warning to keep his hands on an appropriate part of her body.

"Enjoying yourself?" Olivia asked, noting that Tyler danced just as well as Alexander. Maybe it was genetic.

"I am, but if I had to dance once more with Ma, I was going to lose it." He laughed, nodding toward his mother, now dancing with Alexander. Olivia followed his gaze, her eyes settling on the beautiful man that she knew so intimately.

"You make him very happy, you know," Tyler said, bringing Olivia's gaze back to his.

"Oh, yeah?"

"Yeah. I don't think I've ever seen him so happy. I mean, and this was before I was born and all, when he lost his friend, it took him years to get over it. According to Ma, they were inseparable growing up, and he took it hard. And don't even try to talk to him around his birthday. He's such a brood."

Olivia looked confused. "What do you mean?"

"That's when she died. August twenty-fourth. Same day as his birthday. That's why he never celebrates it. He usually goes down to Connecticut and sits at her grave. Fun way to spend your birthday, huh?"

Olivia was shocked. She didn't realize that was his birthday.

"Well, it must have been hard," she said, snapping back. "I know how difficult it was for me when I lost my parents at such a young age." Olivia couldn't believe that she was openly talking about her parents. She reflected briefly about how far she had come in the several months she had known Alexander and how she could barely recognize the woman she was before. "I used to have trouble talking about them, and I don't think I ever really got over their deaths. Sometimes it's doing the little things in order to keep them alive in your heart. That way, they're never really gone," she said, recalling Alexander's words to her that day months ago when they were at Beer Works.

Olivia looked up to see Alexander standing over his brother's shoulder. "I'll take over from here, Tyler," Alexander said sternly.

"Okay. It was a pleasure, Libby." Tyler bowed and left them.

"I'm sorry about that," Alexander said, bringing Olivia's body close to his once more, leading them across the dance floor with ease. "I don't want you to get the wrong idea and think I'm still hung up on a girl I knew when I was a little boy. I'm not."

"Alexander," Olivia interrupted. "It's okay. I get it. You suffered a loss at such a young age. I know what that feels like. And everyone has different ways of coping with loss. Music was, and still is, mine. If you need to sit by her grave every year, I understand."

Alexander smiled, planting a gentle kiss on her forehead, relishing the feeling of her in his arms as the song finished.

Polite applause sounded from the guests in attendance before the pianist started playing the opening notes of *A Kiss To Build A Dream On.*

"Dance with me, love." Alexander pulled Olivia back into his embrace, and they began to move around the dance floor to the melody. Alexander gazed down at her, his adoration for her swelling in his chest. How could he possibly explain to her how important she had become to him? She had always been important to him, but now that he knew it really was her, how

265

could he put that into words?

He pulled her into his chest and leaned down as they swayed to the music. Alexander began to sing along with the band. Olivia sighed at the sound of his voice crooning those words to her, knowing that he sang them only for her, just as she sang each night for him.

As the song ended, Alexander dipped Olivia back, leaning over her, and kissed her passionately in the middle of the dance floor. Reaching up, she ran her fingers through his hair, loving the feeling of his silky locks as she communicated with her mouth how much she needed him. She couldn't imagine life without Alexander in it, but she still wasn't able to admit that she loved him. It was too soon.

~~~~~~~~~~

"We can wait in here," Alexander said, motioning to the hotel lobby after they made their way out of the banquet hall. "That way you don't freeze while we wait for Martin."

Olivia thought about it. "No. That's fine. I could use some fresh air. Plus, I've got a hot guy to keep me warm." She winked as she walked in the direction of the front doors leading out onto Boylston Street.

Once outside, she took a deep breath, inhaling the chilly Boston air. Alexander looked around nervously. He relaxed once he realized that the only people on the street were fellow party-goers, as well as other tourists and bar hoppers out for a good time on a Saturday night in Boston.

He looked down at Olivia and couldn't hold back anymore. "Here. Come with me." He reached for her hand and pulled her around the corner of the hotel into a side alley.

Pinning her back against the building with his hips, he devoured her mouth, letting his hands explore her body. It was a body that he had become so well acquainted with those past several months, a body that he was scared to lose.

His hands rested on her ass. Olivia wrapped her arms around his neck and her legs around his waist as he lifted her up.

"Do you feel what you do to me?" Alexander asked breathlessly, pulling his mouth from hers for a brief moment before diving back in. Olivia moaned. She didn't care that they were out in public. She wanted him right there. Alexander planted needy kisses down her neck, her shoulders, her chest. He pulled back once more and stared into Olivia's eyes, slowing his breathing down and dropping her legs.

"Do you have any idea how important you are to me?" Alexander asked sweetly, staring into those beautiful brown eyes.

Olivia shook her head, glancing down at her feet.

"Hey. Look at me."

She snapped her eyes back to his, their eyes meeting.

"You. Are. So. Important. To. Me." He emphasized each word. "Olivia, I…" He hesitated telling her what he really wanted to say to her, fearful that she would run, even after all the assurances she had given over the past several weeks that she was done running.

"What?" she asked, her heart racing.

A smile crept across his face. "I had a wonderful time with you tonight." They would get there, Alexander thought.

"As did I," Olivia replied, planting one more kiss on his lips.

"Well, the night is still young, Miss Adler." He glanced at his watch noting that it was only eleven. "Where to now?"

"Well, Kiera said she was going to MacFadden's with Bridget and Melanie. Apparently, the DJ cancelled so Mo's band is filling in. Want to go?"

"Sure. Should we go home and change first?"

"Um, that's probably not a good idea. Once we're home, I think we'll find other ways to occupy our time rather than go to a bar. Don't you agree, Mr. Burnham?"

"Ah. Of course. You're right about that." Alexander grinned. "To MacFadden's then." He grabbed Olivia's hand and led her out of the alley just as Martin pulled up in their limo.

CHAPTER FORTY-ONE

OH SO HOT

OLIVIA MANEUVERED THROUGH THE crowd of people on the second floor of MacFadden's, spotting Kiera down front and center, staring up at Mo, Melanie and Bridget dancing behind her. The guys were performing a new song that evening. It was a great tune for Mo's incredible vocal ability. He had such an amazing voice and Olivia couldn't believe that he still played in bars. She thought he would have had a record deal by now.

When Mo finished the song, he looked down, saw Kiera there, jumped off the stage and gave her a kiss. And not just a friendly kiss, either. Olivia couldn't believe her eyes. Up until that point, they had kept their "relationship" quiet, not really wanting to label it.

"So, Mo and Kiera?!" Alexander looked at Olivia, questioning.

"It's been going on for a bit, but I guess they just kind of made it official!" Olivia shouted.

"Drink?!" Alexander asked with a raised voice, trying to be heard over the noise.

"Yeah! Sapphire tonic, please!"

Alexander went over to the bar to get their drink order just as the band took a break before their next set.

Kiera saw Olivia and ran over to her, brimming with enthusiasm. "You made it! Oh, my god!" she shouted, taking in Olivia's appearance. "You look amazing! Holy shit! If I was a lesbian, I'd take you out back and do you right now." Kiera laughed as Melanie and Bridget walked up behind her, waving at Olivia.

"But, apparently, you're not, are you, Care Bear?" Olivia commented, smiling.

"So you saw that, huh?" Kiera asked, referring to the kiss.

Olivia gave her a hug. "I'm so happy for you. He's a good guy, and you're great. You deserve each other."

"Is Tyler with you?" Melanie asked before taking a sip from her drink.

Olivia raised her eyebrows. "What's going on with you two?"

Bridget laughed. "Oh, she's in it."

"What do you mean?"

"He's all she's been talking about since she met him last month, but the two of them are too shy and stupid to do anything about it."

"Come on, Bridge!" Melanie protested. "He's just so fucking hot!"

"He's probably saying the same thing about you, ya' know?" Olivia said. "If you dig him, make your move. Want me to give him your number?"

"HELL NO!" Melanie shouted. "That would make me look desperate."

Olivia rolled her eyes. "Whatever. You let me know when you do." She turned to look for Alexander, finally spotting him at the bar talking to Mo. Her heart warmed when she saw how well they got along.

A half-hour later, the band went back on stage and started their second set. A lot of people in the crowd noticed that Olivia was in the audience and kept coming up to her asking if she was performing that night. She hadn't thought about it.

Alexander excused himself briefly when it got close to midnight. "Sorry, love. Nature calls."

"Okay. I'll be fine with the girls here," she said as they stood off to the side by the bar, giggling about setting Melanie up with Tyler. "Oh, and the bathroom downstairs will probably have shorter lines. If you need any help in there, let me know."

His heart skipped a beat when she winked at him as he turned to leave, giving some serious thought to grabbing her, dragging her to the bathroom, and burying himself deep inside of her.

The boys finished their next song to resounding cheers. Then, out of nowhere, a bunch of guys began chanting, "We want Libby! We want Libby!"

Mo stepped up to the microphone. "I guess some of the male population in attendance have noticed that Miss Olivia Adler is here." Cheers and catcalls were heard throughout the bar. "And, boy, does she look good tonight." Mo looked at her, searching for an answer of whether she wanted to get on stage. She nodded, smiling. "Okay, Livvy. Get your butt up here."

Alexander heard Mo announce Olivia and immediately returned to the second floor just as someone shouted his name. "Alex, darling!" the voice called as he listened to Mo sing the opening bars of the Kid Rock and Sheryl Crow song, *Picture*. It was a slower song and the audience was grooving along.

Alexander hesitated, not wanting to see the source of that voice, knowing all too well who it belonged to. He slowly turned around and watched as Adele made her way up the stairs.

"What are you doing here, Adele? How did you know I would be here?" His brow furrowed, watching Olivia walk up to the microphone, the audience cheering wildly for her as she sang the second verse.

"I saw you leave the charity auction so I had my driver follow you." She climbed the remaining steps and grabbed Alexander's arm, pulling him with her toward the bar. "Buy me a drink, will you?"

Alexander rolled his eyes. "What do you want, Adele?"

She just smiled. "You, Alex. I want you."

Olivia looked out over the audience during the instrumental break and couldn't believe her eyes. 'Plastic Surgery Barbie' was dragging Alexander toward the bar, no doubt trying to convince him to buy her a drink. Olivia was not normally the jealous type, but why was she there? She ignored it as she walked back up to the microphone to finish the song, Mo and her trading lines, the audience singing along with lit smart phone screens waving in the air.

The song ended and Alexander met Olivia's eyes. He sent her a pleading look. Adele wouldn't leave his side.

"She is quite talented, isn't she? I can see why you like her," Adele said. "But it won't last. You'll come crawling back to me one of these days. I just know it." She smiled at Alexander, kissing his neck before he took a step away.

Olivia saw the entire exchange and turned to Mo, smiling. "Let's do one more." She laughed to herself as she began to introduce the next song.

"Thanks, everyone. One more song and then I'm out of here for the evening to spend some time with my hot boyfriend." The crowd cheered and Olivia met Alexander's eyes, a wide smile across his gorgeous face. As it quieted down again, she grabbed the microphone off the stand and walked toward the front of the stage. "Ever date someone who had a psycho bitch ex?" she blurted into the microphone, glaring at Adele. The audience erupted in applause, laughing. Adele's eyes grew wide.

"Yeah. Well, sometimes, they need to take the fucking hint and move on, don't they? This is *Put the Gun Down* by Z.Z. Ward. Enjoy y'all!"

"Y'all?" Adele sneered at Alexander.

"Shut it, Adele."

"Trash, Alex. She's fucking trash."

Olivia counted off and began singing, the percussionist keeping a simple beat behind her vocals. She slinked around the front of the stage with the microphone in her hand, glaring at Adele as if sending her a message to back off from her man. Alexander was hers and she was not about to lose him.

She hit the first chorus and Alexander busted out laughing. He didn't think it was possible, but he fell even more in love with the girl on the stage.

"What are you laughing at?" Adele growled, her face bright red.

"This," Alexander smiled. "Olivia's giving you the big 'fuck you' and it's awesome." He simply laughed as Adele continued to stand there, pouting.

The audience grooved along to the driving beat of the song,

Olivia belting out the lyrics. It was unlike anything Alexander had ever heard her sing before. It was upbeat and rocking, her voice strong, almost demanding. She was staking her claim. Her claim to him, and it turned him on.

Men in the audience whistled as Olivia moved across the stage, singing the second verse, touching her body through her silk dress in such a way to cause anyone to want to leave with her. She stopped when she reached a group of drunk guys, throwing her right leg out slightly, locking eyes with Alexander as she inched the slit of her dress up, showing the lacy stockings attached to her garter belt.

"Fuck," Alexander breathed softly as he felt his erection twitching. The whistles coming from the males in attendance were deafening.

"You think that's cute, do you?" Adele asked. "She's trashy, Alex. What self-respecting woman would get up on stage for everyone to gawk at? I'm surprised they're not throwing dollar bills her way, for crying out loud!"

Alexander laughed again. "Adele, you're just jealous that she gets all this attention from having a raw talent that she didn't have to pay thousands of dollars to some plastic surgeon for."

Adele faced forward, her blood rising as she continued to watch Olivia move around the stage.

Olivia began the final chorus, the crowd singing and dancing along with her. She jumped off the stage, not really knowing what had possessed her to do that. She made her way through the audience, her eyes trained on one person alone, singing and dancing with a few people before reaching Adele standing next to her man. She grinded up against Alexander, her back to his front, his erection growing from the contact, as she glared at Adele.

Alexander placed his hand possessively over Olivia's stomach, kissing her neck, and she kept singing. Adele's mouth went wide with shock and the audience lost it, cheering for Olivia.

Once the driving beat picked up again, Olivia immediately turned and made her way back to the stage, finishing the song to a raucous applause. She noticed that Adele no longer stood next to her man.

Alexander was so incredibly turned on by Olivia's performance that he needed to feel her right then and there. As the audience cheered for the song, for his Olivia, he jumped up on the stage and, taking deliberate steps, embraced her, dipping her low, kissing her fully and passionately, running his hands up and down the side of her dress. Olivia had never been kissed with such vigor and intensity in all her twenty-eight years. She melted into his arms, never wanting the kiss to end, not caring that there were hundreds of witnesses to their passion.

The audience erupted in whistles. Cell phone cameras flashed as Alexander continued his exploration of Olivia's mouth, sending electric shocks throughout her core.

He pulled away and smiled at her, her face red and her breathing heavy. "I think that was the hottest thing I've ever fucking seen in my entire life," Alexander growled in her ear before lifting her to her feet and jumping off the stage, allowing her to have the spotlight she so rightly deserved.

Olivia turned around to see her band mates give her a big thumbs up.

"That was hot, Livvy," Mo whispered.

She fanned herself, thinking that it was oh so hot.

~~~~~~~~~~~

Olivia and Alexander returned home after last call, squeezing as much fun out of their evening as they possibly could. Stumbling into the bedroom, it was apparent that they had both consumed a fair bit of liquor throughout the night.

"Let me help you out of your penguin suit there, Mr. Burnham," Olivia giggled.

"What's so funny, Olivia?" Alexander asked, looking into her large eyes.

"I want you naked," she slurred into his ear, her breath hot on his neck, making his entire body tingle with anticipation. He had been thinking about that very moment all night long, particularly once he caught a glimpse of her garter belt at the bar.

"Your wish is my command."

Olivia sat on the bed, wanting a front row seat for the show, and watched him step out of his shoes. He slowly started to unbutton his shirt, torturing Olivia, who tried to remain patient. "Do you need a hand, Alex?" she asked, getting off the bed and walking the few short steps to where he stood. She was just a breath away as she bore her eyes into his, searing his body.

"I could always use a hand," Alexander replied, stepping out of his pants and standing in just his boxer briefs. He grabbed Olivia's hand and thrust it down his shorts.

"Fuck," she exclaimed, grabbing onto his large erection. "You are always ready, aren't you?" She stroked him, although he didn't need any help getting ready for what she was planning.

"This is what you do to me, Olivia. I just can't get enough of you." He glared at her, his eyes burning with desire, as she continued torturing him with her hand.

"Dress. Off. Now," he growled.

Olivia took a step back, removing her hand, and slid her arms out of the dress, allowing it to pool at her feet.

Alexander gawked at her, his mouth wide open. He stepped toward her. "This is staying on," he said, brushing the garter belt that she was wearing. "So are the stockings and shoes."

He dropped to his knees and dotted her stomach with kisses, savoring the taste of her delicious body. Gingerly sliding her thong to one side, he pushed a finger inside, circling her. She let out a moan of pleasure as he continued teasing her, already feeling a build-up of pressure around his finger. "Do you like that, Olivia?" he asked between kisses.

"Yes," she exhaled.

"Sorry to cut to the chase, darling, but I can't wait any longer," Alexander said, sliding her thong down her legs. "Get on the bed, on your hands and knees."

Olivia did as she was told, walking over to the bed and positioning herself as Alexander asked, looking over her shoulder at him.

"Face front."

Olivia obeyed, not making a sound. She heard his briefs fall to the ground and felt him climb up on the bed behind her.

He caressed her ass with one hand as he inserted a finger into her with another. She moaned, moving with him against his finger.

Out of nowhere, he slapped her right check, causing her to scream out in pleasure. *Why did that feel so good?* He caressed her left cheek and then slapped it. Olivia moaned, her body on fire from the anticipation. He went back to her right cheek, caressing and smacking. He removed his fingers from inside her, getting ready to enter her. He caressed her left cheek, smacked it, then immediately slammed into her.

"FUCK!" Olivia screamed.

"You like that, baby?" Alexander said, pulling Olivia's hair back. He pounded into her, his pace relentless. She couldn't respond, her mind racing from the incredible sensation of Alexander filling her from behind.

"Tell me you like it hard. Say it," Alexander growled.

"I LIKE IT HARD!" she screamed.

"Of course you do," he said, thrusting into her in an even more punishing rhythm.

He released Olivia's hair, reaching around in front of her, finding her swollen clit, toying with her as she began clenching around him, her orgasm imminent.

Suddenly, he pulled out and removed his finger.

"NOOOOO!" Olivia shouted.

"What do you want, Olivia?" Alexander asked.

She turned to look at him over her shoulder, still on her hands and knees.

"Face forward, Olivia," he demanded.

Her head snapped back front. "I want you," she panted.

"You want me? Where do you want me?" he asked, rubbing his erection against her wet clit.

"Inside of me."

"What do you want inside of you? My fingers?" Alexander inserted a finger inside of her, making her whimper in pleasure. She rocked back and forth, wanting her release. He quickly withdrew.

"Is that all you want inside of you?"

She remained quiet, unable to handle all the feelings going on in her body.

"Answer me, Olivia," he ordered.

"No. I want more."

"What do you want?"

"You. Now." She could barely put a sentence together. Her thoughts were all over the place. All she knew was that she was close to becoming unhinged and she needed Alexander desperately.

"We already went over that. What part of me do you need, Olivia?"

"I WANT YOUR FUCKING COCK!" she screamed.

"Now, now, Olivia. No need to shout," he said coyly before bending down. Leaning over her, he whispered in her ear, "Where do you want it?" He rubbed his arousal against her apex.

"Inside me." *This man is torturing me!* Olivia thought.

"Where? In your mouth? Where do you want it?" He started to rub her clit again, causing her to squirm.

"In my pussy. Now."

Alexander slowly slid into her again, growling. She moaned out as he placed his hands on either side of her hips, guiding her back and forth, over and over again.

"God, you feel so good, Olivia. I'm not going to last much longer."

Olivia moaned again, that clenching feeling starting to overwhelm her.

"Do you like it when I take you from behind?" he asked quietly, his breathing erratic. "I love this view of you. God. Your ass is amazing."

"Yes, Alexander. Fuck, yes!" she screamed out, waves of pleasure coursing through her body as her orgasm overtook her entire being.

He watched her shake beneath him, loving that he could make her fall apart that quickly. "That was fucking hot," he said, pumping into her one last time before finding his own release, grunting her name while he helped to steady her legs. She collapsed on her stomach, her legs shaking from the orgasm still ravaging through her body. Alexander fell down next to her, pulling her body against his, wrapping his arms around her, and biting her shoulder as she drifted off to sleep from pure exhaustion and ecstasy.

CHAPTER FORTY-TWO
THE "L" WORD

THE FOLLOWING MORNING, OLIVIA awoke after a fitful night of sleep, waking up several times in the middle of the night, screaming. She glanced beside her in the bed to see Alexander still fast asleep. She was completely restless so she slipped on a pair of yoga pants, a t-shirt, and her sneakers before going downstairs to check on Runner to see if he needed to go out.

Olivia walked over to her purse and checked her cell phone, surprised to see several text messages from Kiera.

Kiera: *Oh my god, Libby! You're famous! Cell phone photos of that kiss last night are ALL over the internet. They want to know who Alexander Burnham's mystery woman is! EEK!*

Olivia's heart dropped into her stomach. She had forgotten that he was a bit of a local celebrity. He was wealthy, but so was she. They had been dating on and off for several months, and only a few photos had turned up on the internet. Most of them were fairly blurry. She knew that Alexander had been trying to keep her out of the spotlight as much as possible and she appreciated that.

Grabbing her laptop out of her bag, she waited for it to boot up as she walked over to the large couch in the living room, noticing how dreary it looked outside. *It looks like a cold day to be outside watching the St. Patty's day parade*, she thought to herself.

Once her MacBook had finally started up, she immediately went to the Google image search page and typed in

Alexander's name. She was not too surprised when she was immediately inundated with various photos of the man with green eyes. Some were from different charity events. Some from various sporting events. They were mostly photos she had seen months ago during her darkest time. She noticed one, in particular, that she had missed before. It was from the Red Sox game the weekend they had met. There she was, sitting next to Alexander, watching the game rather enthusiastically through her sunglasses. Then she noticed Alexander. He wasn't looking at the game. He looked at her as if she was the only person in the world. As if the game wasn't going on at all. Her heart fluttered from the obvious affection that he had for her early on in their relationship.

Olivia clicked on the photo and a gossip website popped up. The caption read, *"Wealthy Bachelor spotted at ball game with mystery woman"*. She scrolled down, reading the article speculating on whom Alexander was with. The comments were all over the place. Some saying she was a prostitute. Some saying she was a family friend. She couldn't believe that people would actually waste their time caring about who dated whom. Olivia wondered how many other stories were out there and why she never bothered to look at any of them before.

Then she found a newer story, time-stamped just a few hours earlier. The article contained a relatively clear cell phone picture, taken the previous night when Alexander jumped up on stage and dipped Olivia back, kissing her passionately. She stared at the photo, her face flushing from the memory.

"Good morning, beautiful," Alexander said, walking over to her and planting an affectionate kiss on her neck.

"We've been outed, darling," Olivia laughed, showing him the gossip website.

"Oh, do tell. What have they been saying about us?" He joked, trying to hide his true feelings. He was worried. He was scared. He was concerned for Olivia's safety.

She started to read the article to him: "'Sad day for the ladies of New England and possibly the entire country. It seems that Alexander Burnham is officially off the market. Again. For those of you who don't remember, it has only been a month since he so unceremoniously left Miss Chelsea Wellington at the altar. Rumor had it that it was for another woman. Finally, a month later, we know who the mystery woman is. Our sources say that he has been seen around the greater Boston metropolitan area these past several months in the company of one Sarah Olivia Adler. They have been rumored to have dated last fall and have recently re-kindled their relationship, but we didn't have confirmation until late last night.

"'Miss Adler is a wealthy heiress who runs Downtown Wellness, located in the Financial District of Boston. She is a Boston College graduate who is apparently not only 'smoking hot', according to one of our interns, but also a talented musician. At least we know she's not a gold digger.

"'Suffice it to say, we are all heartbroken over here at *Blush Magazine*. But did you see that kiss? I'm all hot and bothered just thinking about it. I don't ever remember seeing him kiss Miss Wellington that way. Sorry, Chelsea. You clearly didn't stack up close to Miss Adler'."

Olivia glanced at Alexander. "Did you hear that? I'm smoking hot!" She laughed. Normally, she would be worried about being outed in a gossip magazine, but she didn't care. She wanted the world to know that Alexander was hers and that she was his.

"I'm sorry, darling," he said, a nervous look on his face. "I was rather careless. I didn't mean to bring attention to you. I shouldn't have done that. I'll have my publicist do some damage control."

"It's okay, Alexander." Olivia nuzzled into his arm as he draped it around her, holding her close. "It was bound to come out eventually." She looked up into his eyes. He still looked unsettled at the news. Why was he so upset? Surely he had dealt with this type of publicity before, unless…

Olivia shot out of his embrace. "You're ashamed of me, aren't you?" she asked, staring at him. Everything finally made sense. Throughout the previous evening, every time a photographer came by, Alexander made sure that Olivia wasn't in the photo with him. Why? "It's because I'm not part of your perfect little social circle, isn't it?"

"No, love. How could you say such a thing? I'm not ashamed of you. I want the world to know you're mine and only mine." He smiled, trying to put Olivia at ease. "But I'm concerned for your safety now that this news has gotten out. You're going to be inundated with phone calls. They'll be camping outside of your house. I just need to know that you won't get hurt."

"I'll be fine, Alexander," she said, her irritation showing. "It's news now, but I'm sure it will all settle down after a few days. They'll move on to bigger and better things."

"Maybe you're right, but we'll up your protection detail anyway. If I am not with you, you are not to go anywhere without both Carter and Marshall. I'll add a few more agents, as well. Do you understand?"

Olivia glared at him. Why did he think that she couldn't take care of herself? "I'm not a child, Alexander," she spat out. "I have been doing just fine. You don't need to worry about me. What's the worst that could happen? That someone takes a picture of me?" Her heart dropped into her stomach. Of course! Everything immediately became clear. She stood up and marched over to her purse, collecting her things, ready to bolt. It was all she knew.

"Olivia, be rational. What are you doing?" Alexander said, trying to calm her down.

She spun around, her eyes blazing with fury. "You're seeing someone else, aren't you? That's why you're so worried about these photos getting out." It all made sense. "Is that where you were earlier this week? There probably was no training exercise was there? Is that why Adele was at the bar last night, too? You're still fucking her! Are you still fucking Chelsea, too?" She should have known he couldn't just change his ways overnight. For years, he was known to have slept with woman after woman, never settling down until he met her.

"No, angel, no!" He rushed to her.

Tears threatened to escape from Olivia's eyes. How could she be so stupid? Of course he would have women fawning all over him. Why would he possibly want her? She wondered how long he had been sleeping with other people.

"I'm so stupid. I should have known. I'm sorry for wasting your time, Alexander." She grabbed her purse and her laptop bag, walking into the foyer toward the elevator. She pushed the call button repeatedly, willing the car to arrive faster.

"Olivia, please," Alexander said, running to catch up to her. "You're overreacting. Chelsea doesn't compare to you."

Her jaw dropped, unable to form any response, furious with him. *This is why I never get close*, Olivia thought. The pain is too much.

"That didn't come out right. I didn't mean it like that," he said, reaching out and touching her arm.

"Don't touch me." Olivia felt sick to her stomach. She let her guard down and allowed herself to open her heart to someone, only to have that person rip it painfully from her chest.

Or maybe she was frightened of her feelings and was using this as an excuse to leave him. Again.

The elevator car arrived and Olivia entered, deciding to not think about that anymore.

"Olivia, please. Don't go." He placed his hands on the door, preventing it from closing, trapping her there.

"Why? Just call one of your other girls. I'm sure they'll gladly come over, and you can tell them over and over again how their pussy is yours. How many other pussies are yours, Alex?"

He ran his hands through his hair, exasperated that the morning had taken such a turn.

"I LOVE YOU!" Alexander cried out. "All right? There's nobody else. There's never been anyone else, Olivia. I've been waiting for you my entire fucking life."

Olivia pushed the stop button on the elevator. "What did you say?" she asked quietly, taking a step toward Alexander, her eyes narrowed. She could feel the heat coming off his naked chest.

"I said, I love you, Sarah Olivia Adler," he replied quietly, brushing the hair off her face. "And I know you love me. You're just scared. That's why you're doing this. Because you're scared of your true feelings. I beg you. Just let me love

282

you. Please."

He caressed her cheek and she shuddered. She couldn't love him. It was too soon. It was too scary. "Don't say that. You don't love me." She placed her hands on his chest and gazed into his eyes. "And I don't love you." She pushed him out of the elevator car before releasing the stop button, leaving him standing in the foyer.

"OLIVIA!" he shouted, banging on the elevator doors.

Chapter Forty-Three

Self-Destruction

ALEXANDER REPEATEDLY PRESSED THE call button, willing another elevator to come quickly. After a few brief moments that felt like an eternity and still no elevator, he punched a code into the door leading to the stairwell and ran down twenty-five flights as fast as he could.

At that moment, Olivia emerged onto the street, tears streaming down her face. How could she have been so stupid? She fell for his charm and alarmingly good looks. Why did he get so upset when the gossip magazines had picked up a story about their relationship? He didn't appear to be upset when he posed for all those photos with Chelsea. There could only be one answer.

Olivia didn't know what she should do so she ran down the busy Boston streets, thankful that she had put on her sneakers when she got up that morning. She was rather chilly with just a t-shirt and jeans on, but she relished in the brisk March air, welcoming the coldness to dull the pain. Bolting down Atlantic Avenue, she quickly hailed a cab and gave the driver Kiera's address. She couldn't face going home. Not yet, anyway. As the cab pulled away, she almost thought she heard someone faintly yelling her name.

~~~~~~~~~~~

"OLIVIA!" Alexander screamed again as he reached the street. He frantically searched for her, unable to locate her among the masses of people heading to watch the parade that morning. "What have I done?" he asked to no one in particular. He sobbed openly on the street, burying his face in his hands. He knew confessing his love would scare her, but she was about to walk out on him. Again. He thought that maybe, if she knew what she meant to him, she would come to her senses and see how irrational she was being.

After several moments passed and Olivia did not return, he went back to his penthouse and immediately entered his study. He sat down at his desk, picking up the photo of the two of them on the day of their play wedding. He resolved right then and there that Olivia was a girl worth fighting for, and that was exactly what he planned on doing. He picked up the phone.

"Carter," he growled into it. "Find her."

~~~~~~~~~~

"Olivia? What's wrong?" Kiera asked, answering her door. She looked at Olivia standing on her doorstep, shivering, tears flowing down her face.

"Oh, Care Bear," she sobbed as her friend pulled her into her arms, hugging and comforting her.

"Come on. Let's get you warmed up."

Olivia started sobbing harder, thinking about just a few days previously when she had been followed after her therapy session and Alexander had run down to the street after he received her message. He had said the same thing. *Let's get you warmed up.* Olivia was fairly certain that she could find pieces of Alexander dotted throughout her entire existence.

She walked into Kiera's living room, sitting down on her couch and pulling a blanket around her shoulders. "Do you want some coffee, Libs?" Kiera asked, going into her kitchen and grabbing a mug from the cabinet.

"Yes, please. Might as well make it an Irish coffee, though. I need the alcohol this morning."

Kiera grabbed a pod from a basket and put it in her one-cup brewer, adding some whiskey. She quickly returned with two steaming cups, sitting on her reading chair opposite the couch.

A movement in the hallway caught Olivia's eye. "Oh, Kiera. I'm sorry. I shouldn't have come over. I didn't realize you had company." Olivia got up, ready to leave, when Mo appeared in the living room with just his t-shirt and boxers on.

He walked over to where Kiera sat and planted an affectionate kiss on her forehead. "Morning." Mo smiled.

"Morning." Kiera gazed into his dark eyes. Olivia stared, feeling slightly jealous of her two best friends.

Mo tore his eyes away from Kiera, eyeing Olivia. "What's wrong, Livvy? You don't look too hot."

"Great. Thanks, Mo. You really know how to make a girl feel good about herself," she sobbed out, heading toward the door.

Kiera grabbed a box of tissues and extended her arm. "Libs, sit your ass back down. You're not going anywhere."

"Fine," she said, stomping back to the couch, grabbing a tissue and blowing her nose.

"Now, tell me what happened."

"Do you want me to leave, Livvy?" Mo asked, a look of concern on his face.

"No. You can stay."

He sat down next to Olivia, placing his hand on her leg as a sign of comfort.

"Okay, Libs. Spill it," Kiera said, taking a sip of her coffee.

"Alexander freaked out when I said that the gossip mags had gotten wind that he was involved with me. He said it was some bullshit reason of trying to protect me because everyone would be calling me and staking out my house now. But then it came to me. The reason he was freaking out is because he's ashamed of me. He's trying to hide me from all the other girls he's obviously banging. So I went to leave, and he told me he loved me, that I'm the only girl for him, and that he's been searching for me his whole life." Olivia sobbed.

"What did you say to that?" Kiera asked, knowing only too well what the answer probably was.

"I told him there's no way he could love me. It's just too soon," she responded quietly, visibly cringing in anticipation of her friends' reactions.

"Livvy," Mo said. "You've been seeing each other since August. It's almost April, for crying out loud. I'm not counting those few months that you pushed him away because that was just fucking stupid."

Olivia glared at him.

Mo's voice softened as he looked at his friend. "Love doesn't have a start date. It doesn't have a 'use by' date. It doesn't have an expiration date." He turned to look at Kiera, his affection for her obvious. "I should have told you years ago that I loved you, but I was too scared of your reaction."

Kiera blushed. "I love you, too, Jack."

Olivia had forgotten for a minute that everyone called him Jack. She stared at the two most important people in her life, wishing she could have what they had. She had that for a brief moment, but she couldn't possibly love Alexander.

"He's definitely sleeping with other people. I just know it. Why would he be so worried about our relationship being public knowledge? It's the only explanation that makes sense."

"Sarah Olivia Adler!" Mo shouted. "Do you have any idea how unreasonable you sound right now?!"

She shook her head and looked over at Kiera, hoping she would understand where Olivia was coming from. Kiera nodded her head, indicating that she agreed with Mo. Olivia mouthed *traitor* to her friend. Kiera shrugged.

"He loves you and you're finding any reason you possibly can to push him away. Come here." Mo grabbed her arm and sat her down at the kitchen table in front of Kiera's laptop. He punched Alexander's name into the Google images search and clicked on a photo that Olivia hadn't seen yet. It was taken the night before, but it wasn't of the kiss. It was taken before the kiss. Olivia was up on stage singing. It looked like it was taken from the side of the stage. Alexander's face was in focus and he simply gazed at Olivia as if she was the only thing in life worth living for, a sparkle in his eyes.

"Look at that, Livvy," he said, gesturing to the screen. "Can you honestly tell me that man does anything other than worship the ground you walk on? I see the way he looks at you. I've seen it the past several months. He would do anything for you, and you just walked out on the best fucking thing that has ever happened to you. AGAIN!" Mo's voice was rising, his anger showing. He took several deep breaths as Olivia stared at him, wide-eyed. He had never raised his voice like that to her before. "I thought you got over all your self-destructive bullshit," he said quietly.

Olivia continued to stare at him, unsure of how to respond. "I'm sorry," she apologized weakly.

"It's not me you should be apologizing to." Mo stormed out of the kitchen, leaving Olivia shocked.

She looked to Kiera sitting silently in the living room. "What if I don't love him?" she asked quietly.

Kiera shrugged, not knowing how to respond to Mo's outburst, either.

Olivia grabbed her bags and walked out the front door, wanting to be alone for a minute to think. She didn't get her wish. As she opened the door to hop in a cab, photographers were set up, snapping photos.

"Shit. How the fuck did they find me here?" she mumbled. Immediately, a black SUV pulled up in front of Kiera's house. "Of course." Carter and Marshall both exited the vehicle, Carter getting rid of the photographers as Marshall tried to get Olivia into the car.

"No, thank you. I don't need a ride. I can walk, thank you very much."

"Ma'am, please. It's for your safety," Marshall pleaded.

Olivia looked back at Carter who had successfully gotten rid of the photographers. "I'd rather walk."

"Well, we'll still be escorting you home, whether you're in the car or not." Marshall went to speak with Carter as Olivia stood there, glaring at both of them. After a few moments, Marshall returned. "I'll walk with you, but Carter wants you to take his jacket. He says he'll lose his job if anything happens to you, including getting sick because you're too fucking stubborn to get in the car." Olivia looked at Marshall, shocked. "His words, not mine, ma'am."

Olivia turned her head toward Carter, her mouth wide open. He handed Olivia his jacket and shrugged. *If one more person shrugs at me today, I'm going to scream*, she thought, stalking off onto Clarendon Street, Marshall close behind. Carter followed slowly behind them in the car. *This is ridiculous.* "I'm not a fucking child," Olivia muttered under her breath.

"Well, you certainly seem to be acting like one, ma'am," Marshall said.

Olivia stopped in her tracks and looked at her, her mouth wide open again.

"With all due respect."

Olivia turned and continued to walk faster.

Marshall's cell phone rang loudly and Olivia groaned, knowing all too well who was on the other end. "Marshall," she answered curtly. "Yes, sir... I understand sir... I'm sorry, sir, but we had to compromise... Yes, sir... One moment, sir..." She turned to Olivia. "It's Mr. Burnham." She held the phone out. "He would like to speak with you."

"I don't want to talk to him right now," Olivia spat out loudly so he could hear her.

"DAMN IT, OLIVIA! START ACTING YOUR FUCKING AGE!" Alexander shouted through the phone. Olivia could picture him, sitting in his penthouse, pulling his hair with that exasperated look on his face. She wondered if he still had his shirt off, his chest heaving with deep breaths as he shouted. His delectable body... *No, Libby. Focus*, she reminded herself.

She grabbed the phone. "I *am* acting my fucking age. How did you find me anyway, Alex?"

"I tracked your cell phone, Olivia. You ran out with no security. Not very smart after what happened earlier this week," he growled.

"Stop following me! Or sending your minions to follow me!" She took a deep breath before lowering her voice. "I don't need you to always try to fix things, Alex. Some things are just too broken." He was silent on the other end, as was Olivia.

He exhaled. "Olivia, love," he sobbed quietly, breaking the awkward silence. His voice pained her heart. He was clearly upset. That was not the voice of a man who would hurt her.

"Alex, please. I just need some space. Some time. I just...I just need to think."

"What is there to think about? This isn't that complicated."

"Maybe not for you, but it is for me."

"Olivia, answer me this. And don't think. Don't let that brain of yours get in the way. Do. You. Love. Me?"

She stood silent on the sidewalk, staring at cars crawling down the Boston Streets. Did she love him?

"I can't do this right now, Alex. Time. Please. Just give me time."

"I'll wait the rest of my life for you, Olivia Adler. You're the love of my fucking life. This doesn't happen every day. I'll give you the space you need. Just know that I will always wait for you."

Alexander heard a quiet sob on the other end of the phone. "Always, love," he whispered before hanging up.

Taking a deep breath, he opened his top desk drawer, finding the envelope that had plagued his conscience the past several years. He stared at the letter, unsure whether he really wanted to know what information it contained. Why should a simple piece of paper petrify him so much? But it did. Then again, if he wanted Olivia to get over her fear of love, he would have to face his own demons.

He slid a finger underneath the seal and pulled out the faded piece of paper. As he read, his heart sank. It was so much worse than he ever imagined. Olivia's dreams were right.

CHAPTER FORTY-FOUR

ANSWERS AND QUESTIONS

DEAR ALEX,

IF YOU'RE reading this letter, it means I'm dead. I knew this day would come eventually, but I'm just glad that it took over fifteen years to happen.

First, I want to apologize to you for never being there when you were growing up. I know it wasn't easy on you, and I'd like to say that I regret my actions, but there were circumstances involved that were out of my control.

You see, son, Olivia never died in that crash. I've been keeping her hidden since she woke up in the hospital all those years ago. She didn't remember anything so it was quite easy to manipulate her brain into believing whatever I told her. I couldn't let anyone know she was still alive. I was the only one who knew who she really was.

The reason I'm telling you this now is that someone, somehow, has found out that she never died in the crash and that I've been protecting her all these years. I don't know how, but they know.

Her life is in danger.

Your Uncle Jack worked for the CIA as an analyst. About a month before the accident, your Aunt Marilyn came to me for help. Jack had uncovered some pretty heavy shit, pardon my French. He didn't know who he could turn to for help. A lot of the key players were higher-ups in various government agencies, offices, and what have you.

He discovered a ring of politicians that was accepting large kickbacks from shell corporations in exchange for distribution of U.S. military equipment and classified information. These shell corporations were, in fact, various terrorist organizations. Back then, we weren't as organized as we try to be now when it comes to terrorist activity.

Regardless, he had amassed a great deal of evidence and had begun to approach some of these traitors, asking them to come forward and turn themselves in. Well, instead of coming forward, they hired Jacob Kiddish, a well-known "cleaner". Unfortunately, Kiddish had never gotten caught. Although he was suspected to be involved in disposing of threats to various politicians on more than one occasion, that was just speculation and nothing ever stuck. He ran a legitimate consulting business and no one ever connected the dots to him.

Kiddish followed the DeLucas on that day in August all those years ago. It was him who ran their car off the road and into a tree. Olivia's mother died on impact. When I ran to the car, she was already dead. You know now that Olivia survived, but so did her father. He is alive. He shot Jacob Kiddish that day. We put his body in the DeLuca's car, knowing that it would blow up at any minute from the gas leak.

The only reason I'm giving you this information is so that you continue to monitor both of these cases. Kiddish's son is back at it. After his father "disappeared", Mark Kiddish took over the consulting business, including the "cleaning" part of it. He had been working with his dad for years, so we knew that would happen.

Someone out there knows that Olivia is still alive, but it does not appear that Jack's identity has been compromised. These people have hired Mark to clean up the loose ends that his father left behind. My guess is it's the same people who hired his father all those years ago. Part of me thinks they were never off this case.

They think that Olivia knows where the incriminating documents are that Jack left behind, hidden. This information could implicate hundreds of powerful people. Help her. Please. That way, my death wasn't in vain. I beg you. Do the right thing.

I'm proud of you, son. Carry on the business as I would have.

Love,
Dad

Alexander looked at the letter. He had so many questions, but there was nobody to answer them. Then, something caught his eye. He grabbed the envelope and was able to make out script on the flap that was written in almost white ink. If the envelope wasn't so faded, he never would have noticed it.

There is a safe room installed in my office. You may have found that already. If not, go there. It will give you the rest of the information you're looking for.

His heart raced. *Safe room?* he thought to himself. "Fuck!" he shouted, knowing exactly what his father was referring to. Alexander always thought that the room contained company files from before its move to a paperless system. "Martin," he spat into the phone. "Bring the car around. I need to go to the office immediately."

Within ten minutes, Alexander ascended the twenty-nine stories to his office. It was a Sunday so his non-essential office staff was not working, giving him plenty of privacy. He dashed down the hall, frantically punching the code into his office door. After swinging the door open, he ran to the bathroom, opening a small door on the far side of the tiled room.

He looked down at the stairs, knowing that all the answers lay just below him. Taking a deep breath, he descended the flight of stairs. He ran into a large metal door and quickly punched in his code, worried that it wouldn't work. He breathed a sigh of relief when the door beeped, allowing him access. The sight before his eyes was overwhelming.

He entered the large reinforced steel room that seemed to take up the entire floor between the twenty-eighth and twenty-ninth story of the building. All along the walls, banker's boxes were stacked high.

Upon closer inspection, he realized that the boxes contained items from Olivia's past. His father had erased her life, but kept everything in those boxes.

Alexander grabbed a box and lifted the lid. He gasped. "Mr. Bear."

CHAPTER FORTY-FIVE

SCARED

"NOW, OLIVIA, WHAT IS it about Alexander's declaration of love that scares you?" Dr. Greenstein asked.

"What makes you think I'm scared?" she responded as she glanced out the window. It was a dismal Tuesday in March. There was a mixed precipitation falling. Olivia hated that type of weather. It made her angry. Either snow or rain, but don't do this in the middle bullshit. It seemed that everything irritated her lately. Well, at least since she ran from Alexander Sunday morning after he said the three words that scared her most.

"Well, it's fairly obvious, isn't it? You're trying to find some excuse to not have to say those words back. Olivia, do you remember the last person you said 'I love you' to?"

Olivia searched her brain for a memory of saying those words. She was coming up short. She couldn't remember. It wasn't the day of the crash. When her father had told her that he and her mother loved her, instead of responding in kind, she simply said, "I know".

"I can't remember," she said quietly.

"Olivia, I want to try something." Dr. Greenstein got up and pushed a button, causing the blinds to drop on the windows, shielding all the light from the room except for a dim lamp on the desk. "I want you to lie down and close your eyes."

Olivia looked at the doctor like she was crazy.

"Please, Olivia. Humor me."

"Fine," she exhaled as she lay down.

"Now, I want you to just breathe for a little bit. Inhale and exhale." Dr. Greenstein's voice had changed to a soft singing-type sound.

"Just keep breathing and focus on that alone. Shut the rest of the world out. Forget about everything. It's just you and me, okay? Inhale. Exhale." Olivia relaxed, listening to the doctor's gentle voice.

"Now, let's go back for a minute. What do you remember about growing up? Before the crash, what memory stands out?"

"I remember playing the piano with my mom. I remember singing with her."

"And what songs did you sing?"

"A lot of Beatles songs. My mother loved the Beatles."

"Do you remember any of the songs you would sing with your mom?"

"I'm trying."

"Picture yourself sitting at the piano with your mother."

"I am."

"Look at the piano keys. What notes is she playing? Can you visualize it?"

Olivia held her hands up as if she was playing the piano, tracing where her mother's hands would have been, humming along to a slow, haunting version of *If I Fell*, the memory of singing the song while her mother played the piano making her smile. She was singing that song to someone...someone other than her mother.

"Good, Olivia. Good. So you can remember. Now, even if you don't remember telling your mother that you loved her, do you remember feeling the love you had for her at that moment?"

"I remember singing that song for someone else... There was someone else in the room...a boy with green eyes. I loved him... I know I did, but I just can't say those words."

"Do you think the reason you're so scared of telling Alexander you love him is because you regret not telling your parents, and this green-eyed boy that you've been dreaming of, that you loved them?"

"But that was just in a dream. The only memories I have of my life before the crash come from my dreams."

"Are they just dreams, though? Okay, sit up, dear."

She sat up and the doctor opened the shades, the grayish light filtering into the room once more. "Olivia, when we go through a traumatic event, our bodies try to protect themselves. That includes the brain. You experienced a traumatic event when your parents died. Your brain tried to protect you by shutting out certain memories. Now your brain is showing you more about what happened that day and before, telling you it's okay for you to face these fears of yours. I need you to start doing that."

"But I've been dreaming about other things, too. Stuff that definitely could not have happened. My father is dead so why are my dreams telling me he's not?" Olivia questioned, staring at the doctor.

"I don't know, Olivia. Our brains sometimes take our deepest wishes and try to turn them into reality."

She sat and thought about everything that the doctor had been saying to her. "I don't know if I can. I don't think I can tell Alexander that I love him."

"But you *do* love him, don't you?"

Olivia shrugged her shoulders, hoping to avoid answering that question, desperately trying to convince herself that she didn't love him.

"Think about that feeling of total contentment you had when you would play music with your mother. Do you remember what that felt like? The love you felt for her?"

"Yeah. So what?" Olivia rolled her eyes.

"Have you ever felt something similar when you were with Alexander? And don't focus on when you've been intimate together."

Olivia sat there and thought about it. She remembered how she felt when she abandoned Alexander all those months ago. How she felt when he found her in Florida and she lied to his face, saying she didn't care about him. How, when she found out he was engaged, she didn't think she would survive. How, when she came back and poured her heart out to him, he turned her away. It was painful, but was it love? Why did he have to say those three little words? Of all the words in the English language, the word "love" scared her the most.

"Olivia, I know you. I know that you have trouble expressing your feelings normally. I know this is scary for you. Love is scary, but it's part of the human experience."

Olivia remained silent, thinking about what the doctor was saying. She wasn't just scared of her feelings for Alexander. She was petrified, worried that something would happen to him. She cared deeply for him, but would it always be enough? Olivia knew that she was an extremely frustrating woman. Would Alexander always stand by her side?

"I'm sorry, dear," Dr. Greenstein said, interrupting Olivia's thoughts. "We're out of time for today, but I want to pick this up on Thursday. In the meantime, remember that pain you felt when you walked out on Alexander back in October. And the pain you felt when you thought he was about to marry another woman. Relive that pain somehow. Remember the heartache. Think about whether that pain was from loving him, and express those feelings to him."

Olivia left the office, thinking about what the doctor said as Carter drove her home. She cared for Alexander, but it couldn't be love. She made it her mission to take the next few days and really convince herself of that.

CHAPTER FORTY-SIX

SLIPPING AWAY

IT WAS DAY TWO of no contact from Olivia, and Alexander thought he was going to lose his mind. He tried to respect her wishes and give her time to think about things, but it was driving him crazy.

He had spent the last few days going through all the stuff that his father had boxed up in the safe room...photos, trinkets, and tons of paperwork. There were deeds to property owned by a corporation set up by his father years ago...the beach house on Cape Cod, the house in Mystic, a house in Charleston, a house on Folly Beach. Alexander soon found the corporate paperwork. Sarah Adler was named sole shareholder.

He scoffed. *She doesn't even look like a Sarah!*

As he rummaged through box after box, his thoughts were consumed by Olivia and the past that she knew nothing about. He couldn't stand the thought of another second without her. She had asked for time and Alexander wanted to give it to her, but there were more pressing issues now. He felt like she was slipping through his fingers yet again. He swore to protect her and, with the new information he had learned, that was becoming more and more difficult, particularly considering that her true identity was known by people who could do serious harm to her. He had two of his best people on her protection detail, but he felt lost, not being able to see her himself.

So many times he had dialed the first nine numbers of her

phone number, stopping before dialing the last. How much longer could he possibly go on feeling like this and how could he possibly tell her everything now? That they were kids together? That he swore he would always protect her? That he cried at her funeral? That he never gave up hope she was alive? That his father kept her protected all those years and gave his life for hers? That her own father had found patterns in various kickbacks and government contracts? That some of these politicians were found to be in bed with known foreign terrorists? That her father had tried to force those responsible to come clean or he would expose them? That they were killed by a "cleaner" in order to silence him? That someone knew the evidence Olivia's father had collected was never destroyed? That they seem to believe Olivia has the answer to the location of the evidence? That they would stop at nothing to destroy that evidence, including destroying anyone who got in the way?

His cell phone rang, waking him from his thoughts. "Hey, Carol. What's going on?"

"Alex, thank God. I've been trying to get in touch with Olivia and she's not calling me back," she said frantically.

Alexander stood up and walked over to his office window. "Slow down. What's going on? Is something wrong?"

"Simon is being released this Friday. And his lawyer was good. He got the protective order thrown out. The board agreed that he had been punished enough, and all evidence indicated that he had turned things around and that his attack on Olivia was just an isolated event. He'll be free to contact her with no repercussions."

"That protective order was just a piece of paper anyway. Don't worry. Marshall and Carter have been keeping an eye on her," he responded dryly.

There was a long pause. "Is everything okay, Alex? I heard about what happened. Granted, I never know if anything on those gossip websites is true."

Alexander slumped into his chair. "I guess it's true. I freaked when I saw pictures of us together. There had always been some out there, but now they know her name. And, with everything going on, I was just worried for her safety. I'm pretty sure Kiddish knows who she is."

"You're right about that," Carol said.

"Yeah. So I may have overreacted a bit, knowing that it would be even harder to protect her with her name being associated with mine. She thinks it's because I'm ashamed of her and still sleeping with Adele and Chelsea. Which I'm not, but I know it didn't look good."

"You suck with women, Alex!" Carol exclaimed.

"Hey. Watch it!" he replied jokingly before lowering his voice. "I told her I love her, Carol."

The line went quiet as she processed that information. "How did that go?" she asked, finally breaking the silence.

"She told me that I couldn't possibly love her."

"*Do* you love her?"

"Of course I do!" Alexander shouted. "I've loved that girl ever since I can remember!"

"Calm down, Alex. Are you sure your love is for her, or for the girl you knew all those years ago?"

"It's the same fucking person, Carol!" Alexander slammed his fist down on his desk.

"I know that," she replied calmly.

"Carol, I can't lose her again." He exhaled loudly. "I opened the letter, and it's so much worse than I thought. Than we *both* thought."

Alexander told her all the information he had learned, leaving out the part about Olivia's father still being alive. Carol told him that she would look into Kiddish and see if she could come up with anything on him or his alias, Donovan O'Laughlin. Nothing had turned up in the last eight months and she wasn't sure she would learn anything new. Their father did not know many of the details of Olivia's father's investigation into corruption, how high it went or who was involved, apart from basic speculation so that was a dead end.

After a long conversation, he hung up, promising to get together with her sometime during the weekend. He flipped open his laptop and sat staring at one of the pictures that had circulated the internet over the weekend. The now infamous kiss. The photo that started everything…and ruined everything.

Then a light went off in his head. Olivia was scared of being left alone, of being abandoned. She had admitted this many times, saying that she was trying to work through those issues, so her defense mechanism kicked in to push him away. It all became clear why she acted the way she did. She was scared to give her heart to someone only to be left alone again.

She loved him and he knew it.

He picked up his phone. "Mo? It's Alex. I need a favor."

Chapter Forty-Seven

Ball of Fire

"Why, hello sunshine," Mo said when Olivia barged into his house around five Wednesday evening. He scowled when he saw Olivia's face. She hadn't been herself since Sunday. She was moody and irritable.

"Jesus. Who lit the fuse on your tampon?" Kiera joked.

"Yeah, whatever." Olivia glared at Kiera standing by Mo's side. At first, she was happy when Mo and Kiera got together but, now, she was over it. If she couldn't be happy, then no one could. And she had spent the last twenty-four hours trying to convince herself that Alexander did not make her happy and was bad for her. It wasn't going very well.

"Let's get this rehearsal started," she said before heading upstairs to Mo's music room.

Mo looked at Kiera for an answer as to why Olivia was so moody. "Don't look at me," she responded.

"Stop talking about me behind my back!" Olivia shouted down the stairs. "And stop thinking I'm fucking crazy! I'm sick of it!"

Photos had surfaced mid-day Sunday of Olivia storming out of Alexander's apartment building; of him running outside minutes after she left; of him shouting on the street, shirtless; and of him sobbing outside his building. And then of Olivia getting into a cab, hence how the photographers found her at Kiera's. The magazines took the photos and concocted some story about how Olivia couldn't deal with the pressures of a public relationship and she cracked. She was tired of all the

302

internet sites simply publishing one unfavorable story after another.

Olivia set up her guitar and amp as the guys shuffled into the music room. They ran through the songs that Mo had chosen for their sets, doing Olivia's songs first so that she could get out of there. When they finished running through the last song Olivia would perform with them, she turned to Mo. "Let's add one more, if that's okay." She had calmed down significantly since first arriving at Mo's. Music had that effect on her.

"Sure, Livvy. Which one?"

"That Delta Rae song we rehearsed a few weeks back. Let's do that one."

Mo glared at her. "Are you sure?"

"Yes, Giacomo. Damn fucking sure." The two friends glared at each other, Olivia willing Mo to try something stupid. The other band members stared at their stand-off, wondering what was going on. With a sigh, Mo started strumming his guitar and Olivia sang.

As she left Mo's that evening, she noticed two black SUVs parked down the street. "Fucking stalker," she muttered before cranking the engine to her Audi.

~~~~~~~~~~

Nathan Roberts had been sitting in his rental sedan outside of a house in Arlington where Olivia went every Wednesday evening for band rehearsal. He continued keeping an eye on her and was aware of her and Alexander's rather public break-up, even though the news of their relationship had only hit the gossip magazines hours beforehand.

Just an hour after Olivia arrived at the house in Arlington, he saw her storm out, jumping in her car and speeding down the street, heading back toward the city. He was about to follow her when a black SUV peeled out, tailing her. He maintained his position, not wanting anyone to become suspicious.

At that moment, Nathan saw a man get out of another black

SUV and walk up the front steps of the house that Olivia had just left. It was Alexander. He felt bad for him. He looked rather sad, his shoulders slumped forward as he waited for someone to answer the door.

~~~~~~~~~~~

"Hey, Alex," Mo said, welcoming him into the house. Alexander turned to look at the street, noticing a gray sedan, the driver's eyes trained on him. "The guys are upstairs. Are you sure about this?"

He turned his head back to Mo. "Yes. I've never been so sure about anything in my entire life." He grinned, following Mo up the stairs of his house.

"What if she doesn't go for it? I mean, she's been a ball of fucking fire lately. Get too close and she'll burn you, man."

"Mo," Alexander turned to him, stopping at the top of the stairs. "This is true love, and it's worth fighting for. If I don't do this, if I don't at least try, I will regret every second of every minute of every day for the rest of my life."

Kiera came out of the upstairs study, running toward Alexander. "Ooh!! Let me see! Let me see! Let me see!" she said excitedly, jumping up and down.

Alexander reached into his pocket.

"Oh, Alex," she exhaled.

Chapter Forty-Eight

As Good As Dead

AFTER RETURNING HOME FROM rehearsal and making a quick dinner, Olivia walked over to her large bay window and sat down, staring at the SUV that Carter sat in, his eyes trained on the house. She was reminded of all those months ago when Alexander turned her away after she came groveling back. She remembered sitting in that exact spot, staring into Alexander's eyes as he sat in his SUV. She recalled the pain she felt after she returned, begging him to take her back. And then the incredible hurt when he turned her away, ready to marry Chelsea. But the pain she was feeling that night was far worse. Deep down, she knew that she did love Alexander. She was just too scared to admit it. Why couldn't she just admit that she loved him? Why was she so frightened of saying those three little words to him?

Olivia's breath caught when she saw a second SUV pull up in back of the one that Carter sat in, Martin sitting behind the wheel. She raised her hand to the glass, desperate to close the gap between her and Alexander, knowing he would be in the car with Martin.

Olivia closed her eyes, picturing him and his smile. His eyes. His arms around her. She thought about how much she loved waking up next to him. How much being in his presence calmed her and made her heart swell. How perfect it felt when she fell asleep in his embrace each night. She slowly opened her eyes.

Alexander stared through the rear windows of the SUV at his Olivia, a sad look on her face as she sat in the bay window of her house.

"Sir, do you think she's going to say yes?" Martin asked, turning to look at his boss.

Alexander saw tears falling down Olivia's cheeks as she mouthed three words to him, the darkened glass of the car windows acting as a barrier, shielding her from getting hurt after muttering those words.

"Martin, I'd bet my fortune on it. Let's get back home," he said after debating whether to go to her, deciding to give her the space she requested. At least for the time being.

A block from Olivia's house, Alexander noticed the same sedan that had been parked out front of Mo's house. "Martin, stop here for a minute, please."

"Is everything okay, sir?"

Alexander wasn't sure what to think of it, but he could no longer take any chances when it came to Olivia's safety. There was a very real threat against her life.

"I'm sure it's nothing. Just give me a minute," Alexander said, getting out of the SUV and removing the safety on his gun as he crossed the street, looking at the man behind the wheel. He knocked on the window, signaling the occupant to get out of the car.

The man slowly exhaled and opened the door, standing up.

Alexander remained silent for a moment, wishing his eyes were betraying him. He knew that wasn't the case. "So it's true then," he said to the man. "My dad not only faked her death, but yours, as well. Isn't that right, Jack?"

Nathan Roberts didn't know what to say. He should have driven away when he saw Alexander approaching, but what good would that do?

He took a deep breath. "What does she know, son?"

"Nothing, Mr. DeLuca," he replied, placing the safety back on his gun and sliding it into his holster. "She has no idea. I didn't believe it myself at first."

"How long have you known it was her?"

Alexander didn't know whether he should say anything. He had known almost immediately. There were too many coincidences. That was probably why his father hid Olivia away for so many years. Anyone would have eventually been able to put all the pieces together if they were familiar enough with the story.

"Since August."

"Fuck," Nathan replied under his breath. "And she has no idea?"

"She's starting to remember." Alexander looked at the man standing next to him, remembering all those years ago. He looked the same, albeit with more gray hair. He was tall, almost the same height as Alexander. He had an athletic build and Alexander could see from where Olivia got her smile and skin tone. Olivia's face, though, she got from her mother.

"Nathan. Call me Nathan. Please." He looked over his shoulder, fearful someone on the street could have overheard their conversation.

"Sorry." Alexander looked at Olivia's father. "Nathan."

There was a long pause before Alexander spoke again. "She's been having these dreams, you know. Nightmares, really. She wakes up covered in sweat, screaming. She had a dream the other night about a conversation you and Dad might have had. About faking your deaths?"

Nathan bowed his head. He felt guilty for involving Olivia in the mess that he had created. It wasn't supposed to be like that, but he felt as if there were no alternatives. Thomas had to fake his death and, in turn, hers. "It had to be done."

"Why?" Alexander asked, pacing the street. He was losing his grasp on the entire situation. Almost overnight, Olivia's father had miraculously appeared. Things were spinning out of control, and he couldn't deal with that. He couldn't risk losing her. Again.

"I was stupid, Alex. I tried to do the right thing, or what I thought was the right thing. I had a ton of evidence about corruption and ties to terrorist organizations. Some serious shit. I saw all these patterns when I was working at the CIA. I don't want to get into it now. The less you know, the better. I tried to convince these people to come forward and turn themselves in. These were some very important people, higher-ups in various organizations. I couldn't tell anyone what I had found. I didn't know how deep it ran."

"So why did you have to fake both your deaths?"

"They wanted me dead! And they weren't going to stop until it happened. I knew something was wrong about a month before that accident. Marilyn got worried and asked for your father's help. He suggested I turn over the evidence, but I didn't know who to trust."

He gazed off into the distance, the memory of that summer difficult to talk about. "A few months before, I placed a bunch of documents in a small locked chest to keep them safe, at least until things died down and I could turn it over to someone that I could trust. Someone I knew would do the right thing. And then the accident happened and I saw an opportunity to save both of our lives so we paid off a doctor and there you go."

"But why did you have to do that to Olivia?"

"Those documents were still out there, Alex. Those were the days before the internet. You had one copy and that was it. I had the only proof of what was going on, and they weren't going to stop until my entire family was dead. If I destroyed it myself, these people would never be brought to justice. Then, just before the accident, we picked up chatter to the effect that they would kidnap Livvy and make her lead them to the documents. They knew so much, right down to the fact that everything was locked in a box somewhere." He let out a quiet sob.

"How could she lead them to something that she didn't know the location of?" Alexander looked at him suspiciously.

Nathan stayed silent, his eyes meeting Alexander's, a guilty look spreading across his face.

"She knows?!" Alexander exclaimed. "Were you fucking crazy?!" His eyes grew wide with fury. He was most certainly losing control of the situation. This was so much worse than his father's letter let on.

"Olivia was so smart for her age, and we were playing our treasure map game. She wanted to create the map for once. She grabbed the box from me and said that once she buried it, she would draw me a map. I agreed before I realized that the chest contained all those documents. By the time it occurred to me, it was too late. She's the only one who has any idea where it's buried. And, believe me, I've looked everywhere. Our beach house. Our house in Mystic. Her grandparent's house. The few weeks before the accident, I searched high and low for it. It could be anywhere. I'm a complete fool. You'd think with all my intelligence training that I wouldn't make such a stupid mistake. But you know how it is when Livvy looks at you with her big brown eyes, so full of hope...you just melt. I've regretted that lapse of judgment every day since then. It's tearing me apart."

Alexander leaned in to Nathan. "You know they're after her again! You know that, right?! They found out that Dad was protecting her all those years. They must have tortured him to death. You should have seen his fucking body. But he refused to give out her location so they killed him."

His voice softened as he thought about Olivia and the difficult life she'd led. "She's lived most of her life jumping from one city to another and that's probably the only thing that's kept her alive since Dad died. But now, *Jack*," he hissed. "Now that she's back, someone figured it out. It didn't take *me* long. They want her and I don't think they'll stop until they have her." Alexander felt guilty speaking to Olivia's father that way, but he couldn't help himself. He was having trouble understanding why his father and the man standing next to him did what they did. And he didn't know if he could ever forgive either of them for ruining a young girl's life under the guise of protection. But wasn't he doing the same thing? Wasn't keeping the truth from her for all those months just as bad?

"I know, Alex," Jack said, bringing Alexander back from his thoughts. "I understand all of that."

"I don't think you do! This is your fucking daughter we're talking about here. You need to come clean. Find that box and turn it over. Save her life!"

Nathan exhaled loudly. "It's not that simple. Jacob Kiddish never left any loose ends, and I'm sure he's taught his son that same lesson. Olivia and me, well…we're both loose ends."

"We can protect you both," he said quietly, his mind racing from what Olivia's father was saying. "My firm…"

"Alex, it won't ever end. Not until the people responsible are behind bars. Until then, my life, *her* life, will always be in danger." Nathan looked up the street. "I know you love her. You always have. Please. Protect her. Save her from all this. She can't know about her past or that I'm alive. She can't know anything about what these people are after. If she knows, she may remember something, and if she remembers and gives these people what they want, she's as good as dead." Nathan opened the door to his car. "She may be as good as dead anyway, but at least this way there's still a chance." He closed the door and sped off, leaving Alexander standing in the street.

CHAPTER FORTY-NINE

AGAIN

IT WAS THE SAME dream. The crash. The boy with the green eyes pulling Olivia out of the car. The boy getting hit over the head. Olivia's father shooting the man, then darkness. She heard the voices again. Her uncle and her father arguing. Then nothing. Then brightness. People shining lights in her eyes.

"Hi, princess. It's me." *She looked to the source of the voice, desperately trying to recognize it, but she couldn't place it. She didn't know where she was. She didn't know who he was. What was going on?*

"Where am I?" *Olivia squeaked out.*

"Oh, dear. You were in a car accident." *The man rushed to her side.*

"Where's Mommy and Daddy?"

"I'm sorry. I'm so, so sorry." *She looked at the man. He started crying, tears streaming down his face.* "I didn't get there soon enough."

"Are they okay? Or did they go to heaven?"

"They're in heaven, angel."

Olivia's lip trembled. She knew that if they were in heaven, she wouldn't be able to see them for a long time.

"Do you remember anything, princess?"

"I don't."

"What's your name?"

"I can't remember. I think it started with...I can't remember," *she said, crying.*

"Where do you live?"

Olivia started to get nervous. She couldn't remember. "I don't know," *she sobbed.*

"It's okay, dear. Your name is Sarah Olivia Adler. You're six years old.

311

You live in Charleston, South Carolina, and nothing bad will ever happen to you again."

"How do you know? Who are you?"

"I'm your Uncle Charles. And I'm going to protect you, always."

Olivia shot up, breathing heavy, clutching her chest. She scanned her room, looking for some sort of comfort. And then she remembered. Her one source of comfort was gone. She ran out on him after he declared his love for her.

Falling back on her bed, she brought a pillow to her chest. "It's for the best, right, Nepenthe?" she said to the cat. "I know I love him, but I shouldn't. And he shouldn't love me, either." Nepenthe jumped off the bed, giving Olivia an irritated look. "Oh, don't you start with me, too. Traitor." She turned over, her mind racing.

~~~~~~~~~~~

"Okay, Livvy, are you ready?" Mo asked toward the end of their second set that Friday night.

Olivia scanned the audience, her gaze meeting those green eyes she saw in her dreams. "Yeah. Let's do it." She knew Alexander wouldn't stay away from MacFadden's.

"Are you sure, Olivia? I mean, really sure?"

She turned to look at Mo. She hesitated for a second, and he looked at her with a hopeful expression on his face. She recalled the doctor recommending that she express her feelings to Alexander. Olivia was taking her advice and using the best form of expression she knew…music.

"Yes," she hissed, glaring at him.

Mo's face dropped before walking back to the microphone to introduce their next number. "Alright, guys. We've got another new song for you. Miss Olivia Adler, ladies and gentlemen!"

The crowd cheered as Olivia looked out over the audience. Kiera stood down front and off to the side next to Alexander. *Co-conspirators*, she thought to herself. *Fuck 'em all.* She smiled a little when she saw Melanie and Tyler standing together, his arm draped around her. But then she realized that she wasn't supposed to be happy. She was supposed to be angry. At what, she couldn't remember anymore. Angry that Alexander said he loved her? But that didn't make any sense. None of it did.

"Thanks everyone. This is by a new band that I discovered a few months back called Delta Rae. You should all really check out their new album. It's fantastic. Anyway, this is *If I Loved You*." Olivia looked down at Alexander, his eyes hopeful.

Mo started strumming his guitar. Olivia grabbed the microphone out of the stand and stood center stage, staring into Alexander's eyes.

He returned her gaze, searching those brown eyes that he had loved his entire life. Her voice was soft and smooth. He listened to the lyrics as she sang about how perfect her life would be if she loved him.

Then the drums kicked in and Olivia began to belt the first chorus, walking over and standing directly in front of Alexander, their eyes never breaking. The words pained Olivia to say, but she had to tell him that she didn't love him. She couldn't. Love was too painful. She needed to protect herself so she had to push him away. Again.

Alexander's heart sank. *This song? Why this song? It couldn't be true.* He saw the love in her eyes. She was just scared. It was entirely reasonable to be frightened. She'd loved and lost so early in life.

Olivia sang the second verse, her voice back to being soft and sweet, thinking about all the nights Alexander held her and soothed her tears when she woke up screaming. She felt the love in those moments. Even in that first week together, it was as clear as day. He had loved her since the very beginning.

As she continued singing, trying to convince herself that she didn't love him, the pain she was in from pulling away from Alexander was etched on her face.

Alexander was certain that she was singing that song to protect herself. It was all she knew. She was scared, but she just didn't realize how perfect her love, whatever form it came in, was for him.

Olivia's gaze intensified as she sang the bridge. Her chin

quivered, thinking about whether Alexander really was the one for her. Was she making a mistake pushing him away again? She remembered the heartache she felt all those months when he was gone. It was an unbearable pain, and it had retuned over the past few days.

She sang the last verse softly, tears starting to flow down her cheeks. Gazing into Alexander's green eyes, she saw the hurt spreading across his face. As her voice carried through the bar, she realized the words she sang weren't true, no matter how much she wanted them to be. She *did* love him. She knew she did. He made her happy, and she was an idiot for wanting to push him away. Again. Why did she overreact when he told her he loved her? He had sworn time and time again that he would never leave her, and that's what scared her. She wasn't scared to love him. She was scared to love and *lose* him. Olivia didn't want to lose Alexander again. She loved him more than she had loved anything or anyone.

Her lip trembled and she began sobbing. The room grew silent as she finished the last verse, the band patiently waiting for her vocal cue to start the final chorus.

It never came.

Olivia stormed off the stage, crying uncontrollably as she tore down the stairs. She could hear the audience cheering, not knowing that they hadn't finished the full song. Pushing people out of the way, she made a bee-line outside for some fresh air.

Alexander stood in shock as he watched Olivia storm out of the bar. He turned to Kiera. "What just happened?"

"Looks like she couldn't finish the song, Alex. Go get her." She winked.

He quickly turned and ran through the crowded bar, taking the steps two at a time. He saw Olivia run through the front doors and out onto the Boston streets.

"OLIVIA! WAIT!!" Alexander shouted after her as she stomped down the street. The air was cold, chilling her to the bone.

She stopped on the sidewalk at the sound of his voice, refusing to turn around. "Please, love. Please," he begged.

"What, Alex? What do you want?" Olivia asked, choking

the words out through her tears. She crossed her arms over her stomach, trying to keep herself warm. She felt Alexander approach behind her, the familiar electricity present.

"What do I want?!" He grabbed her shoulders, turning her around to face him. "Haven't I made myself perfectly clear over the past several months?!" He ran his fingers through his hair.

Olivia stared at him, tears streaming down her face as she leaned against the brick building.

He slowly walked up to her and placed his hands on either side of her head, leaning over her. "You, Olivia! I want you!" he exclaimed passionately. "I want you every second of every day. I want the good. I want the bad. I want the sweet. I want the ill-tempered. I want the hot. I want the cold. I want the crazy, irrational, exasperating pain-in-the-ass girl that I love with my entire fucking heart." He took a deep breath before lowering his voice, the look on his face sincere. "I want the sexy, beautiful woman that makes me whole, Olivia. And I am not going to stop until you admit that you love me. I know you do so stop running from it. You've been running from love all your life. It's standing right here in front of you, embracing you. What are you so scared of?" He stared into her eyes as they searched his, looking for an answer. "What are you scared of, love?" he whispered in her ear.

"What do you want me to say, Alex?" she asked quietly.

"I just want you to tell me how you feel, Olivia. The truth."

Several intense seconds passed as Alexander stared down at her, bracing for her answer. Her eyes traced over his face. His green eyes were so full of sadness. She could see the hurt all over his body. He looked good, but there was something missing from his usual spark.

"Okay!" Olivia shouted. "I love you, Alexander! Okay?! Is that what you want to hear?! You want to hear how I want to get married and have beautiful babies?! Because I do! I love you so fucking much that it hurts!" Tears continued to fall down Olivia's face as Alexander pulled her close, stroking her hair and kissing her head, trying to calm her down.

"I've loved you since I saw you running that day back in

August at Boston Common. And then I started to love you even more when you came and adopted Runner. I loved you so much that I ran from you. I fell in love with you even more when you came after me and found me, begging me to come home with you. And then it broke my fucking heart when I saw you with another woman because I loved you then, too.

"And every day I spend with you, I fall even more in love. And the days we're apart, I feel like I could die from the fucking heartache because I'm missing such an important part of me. It feels like I can't go on breathing or surviving when you're not with me, and that's what I'm fucking scared of. I'm scared that you'll leave me, just like everyone else in my life that I've ever loved, and I'll never survive."

She cried into Alexander's chest, soaking his suit jacket. "I'm scared to death to love you, but I'm more scared to walk away from you," she sobbed out. "There. I've admitted it. Are you satisfied now?"

"Sshhh… It's okay. I'm not going anywhere. I promise."

She took several deep breaths, reveling in the feeling of being back in Alexander's arms. It had not even been a week, but it felt like an eternity since those arms had held her.

"Olivia, look at me," Alexander said, coaxing her head up. A brilliant smile spread across his face. "There's the girl I love." He wiped the tears from her eyes with his finger. Olivia let out a small laugh as she tried to compose herself, shivering from the chilly March air.

"You must be freezing out here, wearing just that," Alexander said, eying Olivia's black open-back halter top.

"You do a pretty good job at making me all hot and bothered, Mr. Burnham," Olivia said sweetly.

Alexander laughed. "Come, love. Let's get you warmed up." He pulled her close to him and led her back toward the noisy bar.

He stopped right before the front door. "Hey, Olivia?"

"Yes?"

"I love you."

Her heart swelled. Standing on her tip-toes, she planted a gentle kiss on his lips. "I love you, too, Alexander Burnham," she murmured.

"That's my girl."

CHAPTER FIFTY

I WILL

ALEXANDER AND OLIVIA MADE their way back upstairs just as the band finished their song. Alexander met Mo's eyes, nodding. "Alright, ladies and gentlemen. It's a special night. We've got a local celebrity in our presence. Let's get him up here. Alexander Burnham. Come on, bud!"

Olivia looked at Alexander and then back at Mo. "What's going on?" she asked.

"Hell if I know." He smirked. "Come on." He pulled Olivia through the crowd of people, and she noticed that the stage was set up slightly differently. A chair sat slightly off center, positioned in such a way so the person sitting could see the audience as well as the performance on stage.

Alexander hopped up on stage, shaking hands with Mo and the guys. Olivia stood in front of the stage with Kiera, who winked at her, squeezing her arm, as if saying she was glad they worked things out. Melanie and Tyler smiled at Olivia. "Glad you're giving my brother another shot," Tyler joked. "He's been impossible to deal with this week."

"So has Libby," Melanie joked.

Olivia rolled her eyes before returning her gaze to the stage and Alexander, watching as he grabbed the microphone out of its stand and walked over to where Olivia stood. "Oh no, love. You're not getting out of this." He held his hand out to her. She looked at him, questioning. "You can trust me," he whispered in her ear, helping her back onto the stage and leading her over to the chair. "Have a seat, gorgeous."

"What's going on, Alexander?" she asked nervously. She always loved being up on stage, but she had no idea what was going on. And that scared her more than anything.

"You'll find out," he winked. Olivia sat down, her heart thumping in her chest.

Alexander put the microphone back in its stand and walked over to his Martin guitar, picking it up to check the tuning. He played a quick chord, getting the note he needed to start the song.

"Set?" Mo asked him.

"Set," he replied.

Mo counted the band in and Alexander immediately began singing The Beatles *I Will*, looking at Olivia sitting in the chair.

Olivia gasped. He was singing a song to her, a song that she had heard many times in her dreams. It all seemed so familiar.

Tears streamed down her face as she watched Alexander sing the chorus, staring into her eyes, declaring his love for her, letting everyone know that she possessed his heart. But that song. There was something about that song. She tried to remember, but the memory wouldn't come. Olivia tried and tried. There was just something so familiar about that exact moment.

Alexander began the last verse, staring intently at Olivia, singing the words to her. She wiped her eyes, trying to hide her tears. She felt so much love for the man singing to her. Her heart felt like it was going to explode.

Alexander and the band finished the song and the audience cheered. He took off his guitar, placing it back on the stand before grabbing the microphone and walking toward Olivia as he motioned for the audience to quiet down.

Olivia's heart began to race. Alexander brought the microphone back to his mouth. "Olivia, love, to answer your question from before...I'm not satisfied." His voice rang through the bar, no one making a sound, the crowd glued to the drama unfolding in front of them.

She looked at him, a confused look on her face.

"You asked me if I was satisfied. Well, to tell you the truth, I won't be satisfied until I can wake up next to you every day for the rest of my life."

Olivia stared into his eyes as her entire body trembled.

After a few excruciatingly quiet moments, Alexander took a deep breath and swiftly lowered himself to one knee.

Olivia, and half the audience, gasped.

"Alex. What are you doing?" Her eyes scanned the crowd, cell phone cameras flashing away. Olivia knew that photo would soon be all over the internet.

"Sarah Olivia Adler, I fell head over heels in love with you the minute I laid eyes on you, and my love for you has only grown over the past eight months. Even when you left me, and I almost married someone else, I never stopped thinking about you."

The audience chuckled.

Olivia could barely see anything, her eyes turning into kaleidoscopes because of all the tears she shed.

"I can't stand the thought of not spending the rest of my life with you." He set the microphone on the floor and reached into his pocket. He produced a small black velvet box. "Will you please do me the honor of being my wife?"

He flipped open the box. Olivia's eyes went wide when she saw the beautiful ring. It was a three-karat round cut diamond with small stones circling the larger one and inlaid into a platinum band.

"Oh, Alex. It's gorgeous."

Alexander took the ring out of the box and held it up to the tip of her ring finger.

"Marry me, Olivia. Make me the happiest man on the planet."

All of a sudden, she knew why she remembered that song and that moment. Her dream. The green-eyed boy singing that song for her, then morphing into Alexander. And then him getting down on one knee with a ring box in his hand. Maybe her parents had been watching out for her. Maybe her mama had been sending her a message with the dreams. She immediately knew her answer.

Olivia smiled and nodded fervently. "Yes."

"Yes?" Alexander asked excitedly, sliding the ring on her

finger.

"Of course, Alexander." She pulled his face toward hers, crushing her lips against his as they both stood up. "A thousand times yes," she breathed into his mouth.

He pressed his body against hers, kissing her sweetly, his tongue gently caressing hers. She ran her fingers through his hair, relishing the taste of him, never wanting that feeling to go away.

"Come on, you two. Get a room," Mo interrupted. Alexander pulled away slowly, planting gentle kisses on her nose and cheeks.

"So, Livvy. What's your answer?" Mo asked.

Olivia held up her left hand, grinning.

CHAPTER FIFTY-ONE

COMPLETE

ALEXANDER OPENED THE DOOR to the SUV, helping Olivia into the waiting car.

"Miss Adler. Wonderful to see you again," Martin said, winking.

"You won't have to call me Miss Adler for much longer," Olivia replied, smiling wide.

Alexander got in the car opposite Olivia. "Where to, love?" He grabbed her left hand, sending shivers down her spine as he planted gentle kisses on her knuckles and ring, rubbing his lips against her soft skin.

Olivia felt her stomach clench, her body heating up just from the simple gesture. Alexander looked into her eyes, waiting for an answer. "Your place, Mr. Burnham," she said in a quiet, sultry voice.

"Your wish is my command, the future Mrs. Burnham."

Olivia giggled. She loved the sound of that.

Within a few minutes, Martin dropped Alexander and Olivia off in front of his building. "Thank you, Martin. I'll call you if I need anything else."

He ran around and opened Olivia's door for her, leading her through the lobby of his building and into a waiting elevator. "Let's go home." The elevator door opened to the penthouse. Alexander picked Olivia up, cradling her in his arms.

"Put me down, Alex," she laughed.

"No way. I need to carry you over the threshold, darling."

Olivia playfully smacked him. "That's on our wedding night, jackass."

He leaned down, pressing his lips gently to hers as he stood in the foyer. She reached up and ran her hands through his dark hair. "I'm just practicing, love," he whispered against her lips, punching the code into the wall. The door opened and he walked in, his lips never leaving hers.

"Maybe we can try practicing a few other things for our wedding night, too," she whispered, her eyes wide with yearning.

Alexander slowly put her down, making sure she had her footing, his eyes intense. He peered down at her, his gaze burning a hole through her body. She backed up against the wall, unable to take her eyes off of him.

He pressed his body against hers, leaning down to whisper in her ear. "What kind of things did you have in mind, Olivia?"

She swallowed hard. Her body was on fire, her heart racing in her chest. "You know... Things..." She raised her eyebrows.

Alexander trailed kisses along her jaw. Olivia moaned, feeling that familiar tingling sensation overtake her being. He tugged on her earlobe, pulling it between his lips. "You're going to have to be a little more specific." His breath was hot on her skin. "What kinds of things do you want to practice?"

He wrapped his hands around her body, lifting her up, forcing her legs around his waist, using the wall to support her. He gently thrust against her and she threw her head back, moaning out when she felt his erection between her thighs.

"Olivia, look at me," Alexander growled. Olivia's eyes met his. "What do you want to do?"

She pulled Alexander's head toward hers, crushing her lips to his, telling him with her mouth what she wanted. Her tongue invaded his mouth, exploring him in a way that she never had before. She ran her fingers through his hair, pulling it. The kiss was so much more meaningful than any other kiss they've ever had.

Alexander groaned and Olivia could feel him get even

harder. He pulled his mouth from hers, breathless. "Please, love. Tell me what you want to do. You're driving me crazy here." He grabbed her hair, pulling her head to one side. He kissed her neck, sending volts of electricity through her body.

"I want you to take me to your bed," she whispered.

Alexander continued kissing her neck, sucking and biting. "What do you want to do there?"

Olivia knew what she wanted to do. She just had trouble saying the words, and Alexander knew that. She didn't just want to fuck like they usually did. She wanted so much more than that.

"Please, Olivia. Say it," he begged her softly, the dominating lover nowhere to be found.

She looked into his green eyes, the love he had for her evident. "I want you to make love to me, Alexander."

He growled, pressing his lips to hers. "I've been waiting eight months for you to say that to me."

He put his hands back around her ass. "Hold on tight, love," he said before making his way up the flight of stairs, her legs still wrapped around his waist.

He kicked open the door to the master bedroom, carrying Olivia over to the bed, gently lowering her down before crawling on top of her.

She grabbed the back of Alexander's neck, forcing his mouth to meet hers as his hands explored her body. He ran his fingers across her stomach. She savored the feeling of the silk top pressed against her body as he teased her nipple through her shirt. "No bra, Miss Adler?" he asked. "I could get used to that."

Olivia leaned her head back, her body overwhelmed with the sensation of his fingertips tweaking her nipples through the soft fabric. He slowly lowered his body, planting kisses on her stomach, lifting her shirt up slightly.

She squirmed, her breathing heavy, becoming slightly unhinged when she felt Alexander's tongue trace circles around her belly button. "Oh, god," she exhaled.

Alexander's hands glided up the side of Olivia's stomach, gently lifting her top over her head. He explored her body with his tongue, slowly inching his way up to her chest. "You are so beautiful, Olivia. I can't get over how fucking amazing you are." His tongue circled her nipple, taking it between his teeth.

"Alexander, please," she breathed out. "I can't take it much longer."

"Patience, beautiful. Let me love you," he said, torturing her other nipple with his mouth. She moaned, running her fingers up and down Alexander's back, pulling his shirt off.

He threw his shirt on the ground before unbuttoning Olivia's jeans, quickly ridding her of the rest of her clothes before stripping out of his.

Olivia pulled him back down to her, invading his mouth with hers as she wrapped her legs around him, circling him around his erection.

Alexander groaned, pulling on her bottom lip with his teeth, placing kisses down her neck, her chest, her stomach, her hipbones. Olivia glanced down, meeting his eyes as he positioned his mouth between her thighs.

He flicked her sex with his tongue, making her moan out. "Do you like that?" he breathed, the vibrations of his voice on the most sensitive part of her body turning her on even more.

"Yes, Alexander," she moaned.

He continued his exploration of her with his tongue, taking his time. She was in the moment of complete and utter rapture. Her heart swelled as she thought of the love she had for him, and the love he had for her. At that moment in time, everything was perfect. She was finally getting beyond her past. She finally opened her heart up to love, and received love in return. For the first time that she could remember, she felt that she had finally found her place in the world. With Alexander.

Olivia cried out when Alexander sucked on her clit, inserting two fingers, circling her, massaging that sweet spot inside her. She was climbing higher and higher, and she knew it wouldn't be long before she fell over the edge again. Alexander felt it, too.

"Come for me, love," he said. "I want to feel you shake."

"Alex!" she shouted out as tremors ran through her. He continued massaging her, milking her orgasm. Her mind was a blank slate as her orgasm coursed through her body, the spasms never seeming to end while Alexander watched her body tremble beneath him.

When the aftershocks finally subsided, Olivia pulled Alexander's head toward hers, kissing him full on the mouth, tasting her on his lips and tongue.

"I taste good," Olivia said.

Alexander moaned, incredibly turned on. He positioned himself between her legs and, very slowly, entered her. He wrapped his arm around her back, raising her closer to him, not wanting any space between them.

Slowly, he moved in and out, kissing her body all over.

"God, Olivia, you feel so good. I love you so much."

A tear ran down her cheek, the love she saw in Alexander's eyes overwhelming. She was so deliriously happy at that moment. She always enjoyed sex, and sex with Alexander was always incredible, but there was something about that moment, with him moving inside of her, that was so much bigger than anything she had ever experienced. She felt full and complete.

Alexander continued his slow movement, wanting to savor every feeling that he had. He brought his mouth back to Olivia's, brushing her lips with his tongue. She threw her head back, moaning, as she felt the familiar clenching sensation in her stomach. Alexander felt her tighten around him as he began to move quicker.

"Are you going to come again?" he asked, his eyebrows raised. He was still surprised that he could make Olivia feel that good.

"Yes, Alexander," she exhaled, closing her eyes.

He picked up the pace, maintaining a gentle but fast rhythm, his breathing becoming labored. "I want you to say it, Olivia. Say what I want to hear when you come."

Olivia opened her eyes, staring at him, her orgasm imminent.

Leaning down, Alexander brushed his lips against her neck. "Please, Olivia. I need to hear it."

He moved inside her and almost immediately Alexander felt

her tense up around him.

"I love you, Alex!" Olivia shouted as she came undone again, her eyes wide as she stared into Alexander's eyes, her declaration of love sending him over the edge.

"I love you, too, Olivia!" he exclaimed, nuzzling her neck, nipping gently as he emptied inside her.

"Holy crap," she said as Alexander lay on top of her, their breathing ragged.

"You can say that again, love," he smirked.

"That was amazing."

"I'm glad you enjoyed yourself, Miss Adler."

Olivia looked at Alexander, their eyes meeting. "I'm pretty sure you enjoyed yourself there, too, dear."

"You have no idea," he growled, kissing her neck, rolling her onto her side. They lay in bed, staring into each other's eyes.

"I love you, Olivia."

Her heart swelled. "I love you, Alexander."

He pulled her closer, her head nestled in his chest as she toyed with the little bit of chest hair that he had.

"You make me so happy," she exhaled, enjoying the feeling of being in Alexander's arms again.

She shot up. "Holy crap! I have to plan a wedding!"

Alexander pulled her back down. "That can wait. We don't have to do anything big. Whatever you want." He held her in his arms, listening to her breathing normalize as she drifted off to sleep.

He knew he was in deep now. She agreed to marry him. Would she ever forgive him if she found out who he really was? Could he really keep that from her? He wasn't sure.

"I love you, Olibia," he said, kissing her forehead.

~~~~~~~~~~

Late Friday night, Simon walked into Donovan's office after his attorney indicated that it was okay to go in.

"Donovan, hi. Good to see you again," he said awkwardly, extending his hand to the intimidating man in front of him.

327

Donovan looked up from an article he was reading on his laptop, ignoring Simon's hand.

He nervously placed it in his pocket.

"Have a seat, Simon."

He quickly sat down.

"I'm going to cut to the chase. I was hesitant to agree to your demands, but then I got to thinking that you could be rather useful. You see, Olivia knows you. You attacked her, which wasn't the smartest thing you could ever have done."

Simon looked down, embarrassed that he fucked up so bad with one simple job.

"But then you went to prison. We're going to present you as a reformed prisoner. Someone who has gone through anger management and is now sober. Someone seeking forgiveness."

Simon looked at Donovan. "I don't follow."

"You will be compassionate, begging for Olivia's forgiveness. Tell her it's part of your therapy. At a point in the near future, we'll be driving a wedge between her and Burnham. You see, he was a childhood friend of Olivia's. He knows who she is and has kept that from her these past eight months. That little piece of information will tear her fucking world apart, allowing you to come back in and help her pick up the pieces of her shattered world. Earn her trust, Simon. Refrain from any sort of sexual relationship. Get the information and then…" He held his hand up imitating a gun. "Bang bang."

To Be Continued…

A TRAGIC WRECK PLAYLIST

Payphone - Maroon 5
Sad - Maroon 5
Boston - Kenny Chesney
Agape - Bear's Den
Accidental Babies - Damien Rice
When I Was Your Man - Bruno Mars
All We Ever Do is Say Good-Bye - John Mayer
Say Something - A Great Big World & Christina Aguilera
Gravity - Sara Bareilles
Eve, the Apple of My Eye - BellX1
No Other Plans - Jillian Edwards
What Did I Ever Come Here For - Brandi Carlile
You To Thank - Ben Folds Five
Ashes and Wine - A Fine Frenzy
Laid - James
A Kiss to Build a Dream On - Louis Armstrong
Picture - Kid Rock and Sheryl Crow
Put the Gun Down - Z.Z. Ward
If I Fell - The Beatles
Love Somebody - Maroon 5
If I Loved You - Delta Rae
I Will - The Beatles

ACKNOWLEDGEMENTS

WHERE DO I EVEN begin with my acknowledgements this time around? It's amazing how much everything has changed since I hit that little publish button on a sunny, hot day back in August. It was a Tuesday. I remember. Because it was half-price wine day at one of our local bars here in SoCal where the hubs and I call home. I just finished my last review of *A Beautiful Mess* and we decided to go out for lunch and some vino to celebrate. I had already uploaded my manuscript to kindle direct and was really just waiting until the time was right to hit "publish". After we returned home, I put on my playlist and what song comes on? None other than *A Beautiful Mess* by Jason Mraz. It was a sign. So I hit publish. And nothing has been the same since. People started to overwhelm me with their positive responses. I had people telling me how much they wished they could be Olivia, despite the fact that she's cray-cray, just so they could date Mr. Burnham (or as we now call him Mr. B.)

And there are so many people I need to thank now. I know I'm going to forget some people and I apologize. First off, my wonderful P.A., Jessica Green from A Girl Amongst Books Blog. She makes my life easier so I can focus more on writing and less on more mundane tasks. And she's an amazing person and friend. And I'm so happy she stumbled on my page and my book.

I also need to give a big thanks to book bloggers everywhere. Thank you for supporting independent authors. Posting and pimping our books on your Facebook, Twitter, and Blogs is what helps us spread word about what we've done. Without the help of these people, who don't make a dime off what they do, those of us who prefer to remain independent would have a hell of a time with marketing. There's so many bloggers I want to thank, but first is Terrie Honeyball over at Obsession is a Book Blog. She was one of my very, very first early supporters. She came on board pretty much the same day I put my first book up on Goodreads back in July. And she's supported me ever since.

Then there's Stefani Tabakovska from I Read Books. I sent her an ARC of *A Beautiful Mess* and just a few short days later, she contacted me and asked to be on my street team. I had no idea what she was even talking about. I did a little research and figured I'd give a shot. So I decided to form a team of girls to help me promote my book, thinking that maybe ten people would like my book enough to want to join. Little did I know that I'd now be overseeing a team of over fifty amazing women, and there are even more people who contact me on a regular basis asking to join.

This amazing group of women promote my books in their home town and on different social media sites and I would never have experienced the success I have without them. So they get a huge, huge thank you. I don't know how I can ever repay them, but I hope granting them access to read this book back in September helped. So thanks to all you amazing women! Alexis Brodie, Anna Kesy, Brenda Mcleod, Cecilia Ugas, Cheryl Tuggle, Christine Davison, Chrissy Fletcher, Cindy Gibson, Claire Pengelly, Crystal Casquero, Crystal Swarmer, Danielle Estes, Eann Goodwin-Giddings, Ebony McMillan, Erin Thompson, Estella Robinson, Jamie Kimok, Janie Beaton, Jennifer Goncalves, Jessica Green, Johnnie-Marie Howard, Kathryn Adair, Kathy Arguelles, Kathy Coopmans, Kayla Hines, Karrie Puskas, Keesha Murray, Kimberly Kazawic, Lea James, Lindsey Armstrong, Lori Garside, Lori Moore, Marianna Nichols, Meg Faulkner, Megan Galt, Natasha Rochon, Nicola Horner, Nicole Chronister, Pamela McGuire, Rachel Hill, Shane Zajac, Shannon Baker-Ferguson, Shannon Palmer, Suzie Cairney,

Tabitha Strokes, Tiffany Craig, Tracey Williams, Yamara Martinez. Much Love and TEAM CAM! :-)

Also big thanks to my amazing Beta readers who devoured the entire three book series in about a week or two. Lynne Ayling, Karen Emery, Natalie Naranjo, Stacy Stoops thank you so much for reading for me, not knowing what you were getting yourselves into. And thank you for supporting and helping to spread the word about my books. If it wasn't for your positive words of encouragement, I never would have published at all.

None of this would have been possible without the love and support of my friends and family. My parents, Don and Linda Martin raised me to love to read and express myself creatively. They, alongside my two eccentric sisters, Melissa Morgera and Amy Perras, and my best friend, Kerri Deschaine, gave me inspiration to do whatever I wanted to, whether that was arguing in a court room or writing a romance novel.

Another big thanks to my incredible editor, Kim Young. She was absolutely amazing when going through my manuscript. It was as if she knew exactly what I was trying to say, but couldn't because of the millions of different thoughts filtering through my brain at that moment. So thank you, Kim, for being able to read my mind.

And of course, I need to thank the most important person in my life. My husband, Stan. Without his support I wouldn't be able to have this phony-balogna job of being a writer. He's the only one I'll ever want to throw oysters off the side of the deck with. Always.

Last, but certainly not least, I want to thank you…the readers. My fans. For loving what I do. For loving my characters. And for constantly supporting me. I would be nowhere without all of you. So, from the bottom of my heart, thank you for being the best fans a girl could ask for.

About the Author

T.K. Leigh, otherwise known as Tracy Leigh Kellam, is a producer / attorney by trade. Originally from New England, she now resides in sunny Southern California with her husband, dog and three cats, all of which she has rescued (including the husband). She always had a knack for writing, but mostly in the legal field. It wasn't until recently that she decided to try her hand at creative writing and is now addicted to creating different characters and new and unique story lines in the Contemporary Romantic Suspense genre.

Her debut novel "A Beautiful Mess" has garnered relative praise, having been an Amazon Best Seller, an Amazon Top-Rated book. Recently, the book was named by *The Guardian* as a top reader-recommended self-published book of 2013 as well as a 2013 Reader's Favorite in *Publisher's Weekly* in addition to being named an Amazon Romance Editor's Fan Favorite for Top Debut Author and Best Page Turner.

When she's not planted in front of her computer, writing away, she can be found running and training for her next marathon (of which she has run over fifteen fulls and far too many halfs to recall). Unlike Olivia, the main character in her *Beautiful Mess* series, she has yet to qualify for the Boston Marathon.

Made in the USA
Lexington, KY
27 March 2015